THE LYRABIRD'S SONG

The Lyrabird's Song

PRERNA ASHOK

For anyone whose life didn't go to plan.

CONTENT WARNING

This story explores life and love as well as loss and grief. There are discussions of death in different forms. This book contains potentially triggering subject matter, including past trauma, death of a parent, and mental health issues. It also contains explicit sexual content and depictions of violence. Please read with care.

LENEIRA

Gothborg
Portal
SKANDOR
Bluestone
Quarry
Portal
Portal
SAILON
TERRALEA
LaHong
Erindell
Delphos
ISLES OF
MINOS

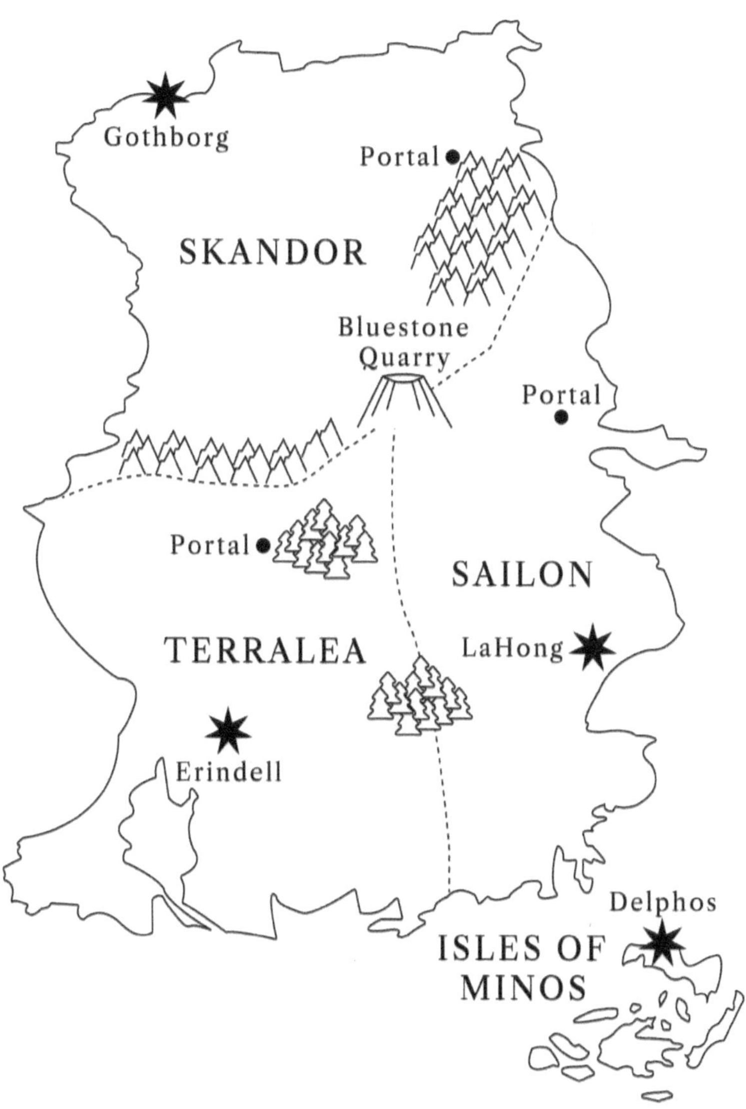

PROLOGUE

I f ever there was a place to go about unnoticed and unmarked, it was Istanbul. Ever since the war in the human realm and rebel uprising in Leneira one hundred years before, travel between realms was strictly controlled. Only a privileged few could use the portal on rare occasions. Raz, an assassin, was one of only three Leneirans in Istanbul that evening after a carefully timed maneuver between a rotation of guards. He had only a minute before the new roster of guards took up their positions, but Raz slipped through the Leneiran gateway and entered one of the busiest cities in the world undetected.

The moon shone brightly, a pearly orb hanging serenely in the black velvet sky. It was almost midnight, and people still littered the streets, but the loud chatter that mingled with the honking and screeching of cars during the day had simmered down to a gentle hum. He made his way through the heaving crowds cramped in the bazaars and narrow cobbled streets with a long, thin bag slung over one shoulder, which he held onto tightly. Impatient old women laden with large shopping bags chivvied dawdlers and tourists pausing every few feet to snap photos of the exotic sights. Those new to the city often tripped over the thousands of cats that seemed to rule Istanbul.

Despite having visited the human realm only a handful of times, Raz navigated through the old town with the ease of a local. It was no different to the corridors and alleyways of Erindell. Restaurants and cafés were filled with patrons who lingered over cups of tea and the last glasses of wine.

The sounds of the thriving metropolis had dissipated earlier, and only the odd cyclist rang their bell as they turned corners and whizzed through the streets. The faint sounds of music from bands and singers crooning old folk songs from centuries gone by floated on the wind down the twisting alleyways and cobbled side streets.

The scents of grilled meats and sweet, fruity smoke from *shisha* pipes filled the air as locals relaxed into the comfortable divans and lounges at the open-air coffee shops and stalls. Raz didn't pause to enjoy the sights and sounds of Istanbul's old town that warm spring night. He focused on his destination: Sultanahmet Park.

Traffic, especially in Istanbul, was still something he hadn't grown accustomed to—it had been easier before automobiles and motorcycles. He eyed the trams and cars warily before crossing the road, head swiveling left and right the entire time to avoid a collision with a reckless driver.

Raz kept to the shadows of the trees that marked the edges of the floodlit square, remaining unnoticed by the handful of devout locals preparing for the next prayer session at the Blue Mosque opposite the Hagia Sophia. Checking his watch, he increased his pace.

Corruption was rife in the country, and Raz used it to his advantage. It didn't take more than a few whispered words and an envelope stuffed with wads of *lira* notes to persuade a Hagia Sophia guard to take an early break. After glancing around furtively to make sure no one was watching, he opened the door at the base of a minaret and ascended the rickety, spiraling iron staircase to the balcony, where he crossed the threshold and made his way to a hidden niche.

What made Raz a valuable asset to his clients was the fact that he was forgettable. Those who came across him could not recall details of his appearance when he disappeared from sight. Even with modern technology and advanced cameras, he never showed up on CCTV footage. At best, the people he came across could recall vague features, but nothing that would immediately identify him to authority figures.

Raz glanced down at the square where a handful of people were leaving the place of worship—locals who preferred the quiet of the late hour to soak up the spiritual atmosphere and tourists who had stumbled into the mosque by accident. Very few visitors realized it was open all night. Those who did their research took advantage, taking photos and admiring the interior architecture without being jostled by tour guides and crowds.

Food cart vendors had packed up for the day, and police officers with cigarettes pushed between their lips huddled in a group near the main road. The guard from the Hagia Sophia had joined them, careful not to draw attention to the envelope stuffed with *liras* tucked away in his uniform pocket. The group grumbled about having to work the night shift and paid no attention to the happenings in Sultanahmet Park. Nothing ever happened there after the tourists left.

So far, everything had gone according to plan. Raz unpacked his equipment and started setting up the tripod. He pulled out a vial of dark liquid hidden in his coat, feeling the weight of the contents inside. Raz knew better than to question the idiosyncrasies and theatrics of his long-standing client. They had worked together enough that they understood not to ask too many questions about the assignments or personal lives. Both recognized enough of the other to threaten blackmail, but an unspoken trust balanced delicately between them.

He had been given specific instructions. Crouching down on the dusty floor, he unstoppered the vial and poured out the dark liquid. A bullet fell out with a soft *thump* and Raz picked it up carefully. Holding the item between his thumb and index finger, he examined it. Satisfied the bullet had not been compromised by the liquid, he loaded it into the weapon.

When Raz finished setting up the tripod and added the rifle, he adjusted and tweaked the positioning of both, keeping an eye on the square below. A lone woman had exited the Hagia Sophia via the main entrance and was slowly making her way toward a bench in the middle of the park. Even from a distance, Raz's keen eyes noted the branded sneakers that only travelers wore and the haphazard way the woman covered her hair with a scarf. She wore jeans, a T-shirt, and a leather jacket despite spending the better part of an hour in the stuffy atmosphere of the Byzantine building. She sat down on the bench and pulled out her phone, paying no attention to her surroundings.

A breeze rustled through the square as Raz peered through the scope of his rifle and assessed the woman whose head was bent over the screen. A lock of dark wavy hair fell across her face from under the headscarf that had slipped past her hairline and was slowly making its way down the back of her head. A frown marred her attractive features as she scrolled. In her other hand, she held some sort of talisman or piece of jewelry, her thumb idly tracing over the pattern. She appeared to be in her mid-thirties—a mere child compared to Raz's four hundred-odd years.

Two men approached the bench from the back of the park. Their bearing and clothing indicated they came from a wealthy background; Raz caught sight of elegant bespoke suits under their dark coats and polished leather shoes shining in the moonlight. They spoke in low voices to each other and barely paid attention to the woman when they sat on the same bench.

Raz frowned as he took in the three people. Once he pulled the trigger, he would have to make a swift disappearance before anyone realized what happened. The chances of the police near the main road being alerted and investigating were slim. In any case, Raz would be long gone. He was the best assassin in Leneira for many reasons.

A quick glance at his watch indicated there was still a little time for him to adjust his setup. As he assessed the angles and monitored the wind, Raz recalled his daring escape from Terralea Palace prison and how he'd met his client. Despite the fact that he lacked the ability to manipulate the elements as many Leneirans could, he had mastered the art of breaking in and out of the most secure locations in both realms. It was a testament to his skill, and he had spent over three hundred years disappearing from crime scenes without a trace.

Raz glanced down at his watch again—the unintended witness could still walk away. He pressed his eye to the scope of the rifle once more. The older of the two men had been aware of the woman's presence and left a polite gap between the two of them. His fair head was turned toward his companion, and Raz could make out the man's clear-cut profile—straight nose, scrubby blond mustache and beard flecked with streaks of gray, prominent cheekbones, and wavy blond hair, also dusted with gray swept back from his face.

His companion was younger, with dark hair and thick brows drawn together in a frown as he listened to the older man. Raz was unable to make out his features other than the straight nose and high cheekbones. He was thrown into relief by the faint light of a nearby lamppost that suggested both men were related.

After yet another glance at his watch, he decided to proceed as planned. After all, he was paid to do the job, not offer personal opinions or act on his own feelings. He adjusted the tripod slightly, checking his target was still in place. When he was satisfied, Raz took a step back and waited patiently for the signal from the Blue Mosque directly opposite the Hagia Sophia.

$$\sim 1 \sim$$

Elena sat on a bench in Sultanahmet Park directly in front of the Hagia Sophia. It was close to midnight. She scowled at the memories that cropped up on her phone of the last time she and her parents had been together. Lake Michigan at the Fourth of July fireworks display, celebrating her mom's birthday—their last breakfast of the trip. She scrolled through the family photos on her phone, growing angrier at her parents. Especially her mother.

When she and her mom booked their vacation to Türkiye the year after Elena's dad died, it was meant to be a bonding trip to help them heal. They had gone through the usual stages of grief until they finally accepted their circumstances and vowed that they would spend more time together. Elena remembered her mom pulling out a travel brochure, closing her eyes, and letting the pages fall open, landing on a two-week tour of Türkiye.

Elena immediately went online to book flights, accommodation, and the tour, her mom's excitement contagious and bringing Elena happiness for the first time since her dad's death. Barely six months later, she was back at the same funeral home making arrangements once more. That time, instead of sadness at the loss of her only parent, Elena was angry beyond belief at her mother's thoughtless and reckless actions that resulted in her death. The trip had been forgotten until barely a month before.

Her computer made a pinging sound, and a small window popped up on the screen. Elena stared at the note, frozen—it was a reminder to apply for her visa.

Her computer pinged again, and a new calendar entry flashed up on the screen. Elena leaned forward and read the details of both reminders carefully before frowning. She stood abruptly, her head popping above the cubicle. Without a second thought, she stalked toward her boss's office.

"Ellie!" Elena cringed at the nickname. Harold's smile revealed his yellow teeth as he took her in. Harold Schwartz was a balding, middle-aged man at Klein and Co. Pharmaceuticals, where Elena worked as a Marketing Assistant.

"Harold, I can't present at next month's conference," Elena told him without preamble or niceties. "I'm going on vacation."

"You're still going?" He gaped at her.

"Why wouldn't I?" Elena asked, irritated. She folded her arms across her chest and glared at the man. "It's been in your diary for a year. I gave you plenty of notice."

When the plane to Istanbul had taken off smoothly from O'Hare International Airport, Elena had a brief moment of panic, wondering if she had done the right thing. The seatbelt sign switched off, and the plane leveled in the air as Elena brooded over the fact that she had worked at the same company for seven years without taking more than a few days off at a time.

"Well, you told us that you were going with your mom, and since she's no longer..." he trailed off awkwardly, breaking eye contact.

Elena raised a brow. "So you thought I wouldn't go by myself?"

"Well, uh. Ah." He rubbed a hand over his chin, the skin rasping against his stubble. "It's the Middle East," Harold blustered. "It's dangerous for women..." he faltered under her livid expression.

"I'm going," Elena said flatly. "And I'm leaving my phone behind."

"You can't!" Harold exclaimed. "What if we need to contact you?"

Seven years! How had the time gone by so quickly? And she had never been promoted in all that time. She was good at her job—and several others, inevitably picking up the slack for those who didn't share the same work ethic she did. For the past few years, Harold had treated her like his PA because his own assistant was the most incompetent woman Elena had ever met.

"Last time I took my phone with me, you called me in the middle of my mother's funeral because you couldn't locate a file," Elena said between gritted teeth.

"You didn't have to answer," the man mumbled, beads of perspiration appearing on his forehead.

By the time the flight crew served packets of stale pretzels and drinks, Elena had counted on both hands the number of work emergencies she had fixed in the last year. The sleepless nights of the past few months finally caught up with her, and she slept soundly the entire flight. Her apprehension about whether going on the vacation was a good idea was forgotten somewhere over the Atlantic Ocean, and her worries melted away.

Elena shook her head and turned on her heel. "I'll email you my notes with all file locations and information for the conference," she called over her shoulder as she left his office.

Elena's thumb swiped over her phone screen, and she opened the photo gallery to look at the pictures she had taken on her first day in Istanbul. It had been a whirlwind, leaving her senses tingling with new experiences. She had arrived in the afternoon, and after checking into her hotel, she forced herself to leave her room as soon as she unpacked and freshened up to avoid the trap of succumbing to jetlag.

She had gathered a small purse with only her phone loaded with a map app, wallet, key card, and hotel business card, wrapped a light scarf around her neck, and pulled on a jacket. It was still cool, and the light breeze from the Bosphorus Strait carried a hint of the smell of fish. Elena walked the short distance to the Spice Bazaar, relieved that her hotel was in the heart of the old town. It meant that she didn't have to navigate the city by taxi and haggle over fares. The heaving crowd was mostly made up of tourists like herself who took in the sights of the old buildings and stopped to take pictures of cats on the streets—they were everywhere, even lounging on countertops in shops, staring haughtily at the people who stopped to exclaim and laugh at the sight.

After wandering around all day, Elena returned to her hotel for dinner, where the waiter did an excellent job of persuading her to try a cup of the famous thick, rich, sweet coffee after her meal. He delighted in watching her nearly gag on the finely ground sediment that had settled at the bottom of the cup. Turkish coffee was meant to be sipped leisurely until only the dregs remained undisturbed, not gulped down like an espresso. But no one thought to tell her that.

Elena forced herself to swallow the gritty coffee grounds, feeling that spitting them out would be a bigger faux pas, and drank all the water that had been served with the coffee to wash it down. Knowing that sleep would evade her after that, she headed to the Hagia Sophia to walk off the meal and visit the mosque.

The warm, stuffy atmosphere and silent chamber agitated her. With nothing to distract her, Elena drifted to the dark corners of her mind she had been fighting for the past few weeks. She was alone in the world, having lost the only two people she loved and who mattered to her.

Her mind spiraled, unable to be tamed by the mindfulness and breathing exercises her therapist recommended. Her thoughts weighed too heavily, and she finally decided to leave the mosque, opting to sit on a bench in Sultanahmet Park to take in deep lungfuls of fresh air—well, as fresh as it could be on a muggy night in one of the largest, busiest metropolises in the world.

Elena pulled out her mom's old police badge and rubbed it, the way she did when she was upset. Both her parents had been police officers with the Chicago PD and lived by the force's motto: *We Serve and Protect.* They had been allowed to keep their badges when they retired, having served in the force for their entire working lives, liked and respected by everyone.

It humbled Elena when she remembered how passionate her parents had been about serving the community and upholding peace and safety. She knew very few people who were as selfless as they had been. Even then, Elena couldn't fathom the way they willingly risked their lives every single day. They had both gone to work knowing the dangers of the world. The irony was that both her mom and dad had lived to enjoy a few years of retirement before her dad died of a heart attack, and her mom...

Elena was yet to process the anger and resentment building within her.

She forced herself to think of something other than her mom's death and warily glanced at the two well-dressed men sitting beside her. Despite having been in Istanbul for only a few hours, Elena didn't think they looked like the casually dressed, relaxed locals she had encountered. They also carried themselves with an alertness and stiffness that came with the discomfort of being in a new country. It was something Elena immediately recognized, having adopted that demeanor herself when she stepped out of the hotel.

Tourists, she decided. They didn't look or sound local. The older of the two had light blond hair and a short, scrubby beard streaked with gray, whilst the younger was dark and clean-shaven. She wondered what two distinguished men were doing sitting on a bench at midnight in the middle of Istanbul. Eavesdropping casually on their conversation, she made out a few stray words.

"Your mother and father..." the older man muttered in a slightly accented, deep voice.

Elena blanched and tuned them out. She didn't want to hear about families. It was still too raw. She focused on the mosque and noticed a shadow moving on one of the minarets of the Hagia Sophia. It was definitely bigger than the hundreds of cats that roamed the streets. *Is that the man who made the call to prayer?*

She squinted up at the balcony but couldn't see that far. Angling her phone upward slightly, Elena pretended to take a photo of the Byzantine building in front of them. She zoomed in on the camera; the grainy screen showed a figure dressed in dark clothes. They were fiddling with something in front of them. The long pole could be a tripod or stand if Elena squinted.

She continued watching their movements through her camera phone, tilting it and pretending to adjust the framing. The men sitting next to her were still too deep in their conversation to notice her own actions. No one else seemed to have seen the mysterious person setting up a tripod and adjusting various tools and devices.

Her frown deepened at the peculiar happenings when a movement from the person made her heart stop. A rifle was perched upon the tripod and aimed her way.

She didn't know what to do besides continue watching them through her camera phone. *Is this a terrorist attack? Who are they planning to kill at this hour in an empty square?*

Elena panicked and looked around to see if she could alert anyone, but the area was otherwise empty. The last group of worshippers had left the Hagia Sophia some time ago, and those praying at the Blue Mosque were already inside.

Elena held her breath, and her hands began to shake as she watched the assassin aim the weapon directly at the bench on which she sat. In hindsight, she should have pressed the record button, but in the moment, disbelief overwhelmed any rational thinking she might have possessed.

The crackling of a microphone behind her indicated the *muezzin* was about to begin the call to prayer at the Blue Mosque. In the next second, time slowed down; the *muezzin* started the call to prayer, and some instinct had Elena leaping in front of the men beside her, startling both of them. Her grip tightened on the badge as she flew through the air, the edges digging into her palms and leaving indents in the skin.

A stinging in her chest grew into a burn that spread from where the bullet had lodged itself in Elena's sternum. She jolted back slightly before crashing to the ground, landing heavily on her arm and banging her head against the cold, hard concrete. Her mother's police badge was still firmly in her grasp. The sounds of the call to prayer grew faint and distant, punctuated by a soft, splintering sound. Elena succumbed to a moment of numbness, but then the pain overtook her other senses. Spots of bright light clouded her vision, and ringing bellowed in her ears, but the ghost of a smile played on her lips.

The men sitting beside her leaped up, one of them bending over her and rolling her onto her back. The other whipped his head around frantically, muttering under his breath. The last thing Elena remembered before passing out was an intoxicatingly heady scent of cedar and sandalwood that enveloped her before she succumbed to the darkness.

~ 2 ~

"Uncle Zanthus, are you okay?" the younger man asked anxiously, leaping to his feet and looking over his companion. When he established his uncle was fine, aside from looking slightly shaken, he kneeled down and pulled out a handkerchief from his pocket. He placed it over the bullet wound in the woman's chest to stem the blood flow. Her chest was moving ever so slightly—still alive.

"Tarrick, we need to leave," Zanthus ordered as his eyes darted between the woman's small body, curled up on the dusty ground, and Sultanahmet Park. His gold-flecked, vivid blue eyes blazed with anger and fear. "We need to get back to Terralea at once."

Tarrick looked up in disbelief. "And leave this woman here?"

"We don't know her," Zanthus growled.

The *muezzin* finished the call to prayer. His magnified voice had masked the sounds of the bullet being fired and their initial shouts and exclamations. But suddenly, the silence in Sultanahmet Park was deafening.

Tarrick followed his uncle's gaze, which lingered on the Hagia Sophia as he assessed the area. The building was devoid of people at that late hour. Tarrick's dark brows dipped over his amber eyes as he took in the scene. Faint voices carried on the wind from the main road. No one seemed to have heard any of the chaos during the call to prayer.

"Tarrick, let's go," Zanthus said roughly. "It's too dangerous. We cannot linger."

Tarrick glanced down at the woman's face, and his expression softened as he took in the slightly upturned lips and peaceful expression. He frowned again when he noticed the red stain blooming across her chest. The base of the bullet lodged in her sternum was visible amidst the blood slowly bubbling out of the wound. Her breathing had slowed down, and she took in shallow breaths as she held onto the last thread of life.

"We can't leave this woman," Tarrick said, scooping her up. The woman hardly weighed anything. "She saved our lives. We need to take her with us."

Zanthus's jaw dropped. "Divine Beings! Have you lost your mind?" he asked in a strangled voice. "She could be a rebel!"

"A rebel who took a bullet for us?" Tarrick raised a brow.

Zanthus shook his head in disbelief. His eyes darted around the square once more. "We need to go now!"

"Agreed." Tarrick nodded and stood.

"Not with her." Zanthus groaned at the sight of his nephew holding onto the woman.

"Get her bag," Tarrick ordered, jerking his head toward the fallen purse on the ground. "And her phone. Adina can heal her before we question her and find out whose side she's on."

Tarrick ignored his uncle grumbling under his breath as the older man collected the items scattered on the floor. Zanthus tucked the woman's personal items into a deep pocket of his coat, and the two men swiftly made their way across the square. They picked their way carefully along a dark path that led to Gülhane Park, Istanbul's oldest public park that skirted the edges of the Topkapi Palace. When they reached a large oak tree nestled along the edges of the area, Zanthus glanced around furtively to make sure they weren't being watched, but at that hour, it was deserted. A light breeze blew through, carrying the scents of freshly dug earth and cut grass.

Zanthus pressed his hand against the tree and held it there until the wood shook and splintered beneath his palms. Both men took a step back as a gaping hole appeared in the middle of the trunk.

A soft moan drew Tarrick's attention to the woman in his arms, and he instinctively tightened his hold on her. Her eyes remained closed, but the expression on her face indicated she felt the pain radiating through her body in her semi-conscious state.

"Nearly there," he murmured. His voice was calm, but he shifted impatiently, knowing they had only minutes to get the woman proper medical attention at the portal outpost before they returned to Terralea Palace.

Tarrick and Zanthus stepped into the gap in the tree trunk that was large enough to fit them comfortably. The familiar pressure closed in on them as the portal entrance shrank behind them, and they were enveloped in darkness.

Home, Tarrick thought to himself.

He hoped the woman was unconscious so she couldn't feel the pain from the bullet wound. Even though travel between the realms was quick and barely noticeable, this time, Tarrick noticed every change in air pressure and the walls of the portal pressing against them. The entrance to Leneira grew before them, and the air vibrated with a restless energy. Or perhaps that was the adrenaline coursing through his veins.

He stepped out of the tree trunk and took in deep lungfuls of cleaner, lighter air. The moon hung low and bright in the Leneiran sky, just as it had in Istanbul. But the stars were more luminescent, glittering in the clear velvet sky.

They had arrived on the outskirts of a forest. The trees and lush grass met the dry, dusty desert where Terralea's furthest outpost was located. It was easy to control and record Leneirans traveling between realms—not that any traveled anymore, choosing to stay in the relative safety and comfort of their realm. Tarrick cursed the distance between the portal and Terralea Palace.

"Your Highness," a male voice called out from nearby. "We weren't expecting you back so soon."

"Is the physician awake?" Tarrick squinted in the darkness as a guard approached them. He was a recent transfer from the Royal Quarter and keen to prove himself as a worthy portal guard. The guard held up a ball of flames in his bare hand, illuminating his youthful face, and nodded.

"We're wasting time," Zanthus growled.

The guard led the two men into the forest to a camp where a dozen large tents were set up in a small clearing. The men and women sitting around the campfire stood to attention when Tarrick approached and bowed their heads, murmuring respectful greetings.

The guard who had met them at the portal led the way to a tent. Bright torches impaled into the ground at all four corners illuminated the inside. An older man was hastily scrambling out of his bed and pulling on a tunic to cover his paunchy torso.

"Your Highness, Lord Zanthus," he greeted the men breathlessly once his head poked through the collar. He smoothed down his gray hair. "How can I be of assistance?"

"This woman took a bullet to the chest," Tarrick said, carefully placing said woman down on a narrow cot to the side of the tent. "Can you stop the bleeding and keep her stable for now? My sister can heal her properly when we take her to Erindell."

"I'll do what I can," the physician replied, hurrying over to examine the patient. He rattled off a number of items to the young guard, who stood quietly behind Tarrick and Zanthus. The guard leaped to attention and nodded at the physician's requests for supplies.

"We will also need horses," Tarrick said. He glanced down at the physician carefully cutting through the neckline of the woman's shirt with a pair of scissors to examine the wound. "Fast ones."

"How about a *pihasi*," a teasing voice said from the entrance.

Tarrick whipped his head around. "Leon?"

"What are you doing here?" Zanthus frowned.

"Hello, brother, Uncle Z," Leon greeted them with a grin on his handsome face. His smile faltered and the bright blue, gold-flecked eyes widened as Leon took in the sight of them.

"Who is that?" he asked in a hushed voice, focused on the body in the cot.

"We were attacked in Istanbul, and this woman saved us," Tarrick bit out. "What did you mean by *pihasi*? Is Lin here?"

"You were attacked?" Leon's eyes darted to Tarrick, who made an impatient noise and turned to the cot pointedly.

"Right," Leon said hastily. "Lin sent a couple of Empath guards to verify security for the Peace Summit."

"Why is she sending *her* guards to *our* portal?" Zanthus rounded on Leon.

Leon shrugged. "They're about to leave if you want to speak with them."

Tarrick addressed Zanthus. "Make arrangements to borrow the *pihasi*." His gaze swung to Leon. "Find out everything there is to know about this woman. Use the portal if you have to, but when you come back, seal it. No one enters or leaves Leneira without my permission or knowledge."

The young guard returned with the items the physician requested and placed them on a low table beside the cot.

Zanthus thrust the purse at Leon and crooked his finger at the young guard to accompany him. He continued muttering under his breath as they left the tent.

"But who is she?" Leon sputtered, looking at the purse in confusion.

"We don't know," Tarrick replied, turning around to watch the physician's progress.

Leon frowned.

"We don't know *yet*," Tarrick amended, glancing back at Leon. "She would have been carrying some ID." He jerked his head toward the purse that Leon was clutching to his chest.

Leon unzipped the purse. "She's American," he said, pulling out a passport and flipping it open to the photo ID page. "Elena Marie Russo. Thirty-five years old, from Chicago. First time using this passport. Arrived in Istanbul today," he added, flipping through the pages.

Tarrick nodded. "Use the usual channels and connections to find out what you can about her."

"She should return to Istanbul when the physician is done with her," Leon advised. "One of the guards can take her back to her hotel."

Tarrick raised a brow at him. "Don't you want to know why she jumped in front of that bullet? And if she's a rebel?"

"She's clearly not," Leon scoffed, gesturing to the passport. "And why would a rebel take a bullet for you?"

"Us," Tarrick corrected him. "Uncle Zanthus could have easily been the target too."

"Right." Leon rolled his eyes. "Between the royal advisor and the future king of Terralea, the rebels chose to shoot *Uncle Z*?"

The physician looked up nervously. "Your Highness?"

"Prince Leon is being asinine." Tarrick glared at Leon.

The prince rubbed his chin thoughtfully. "I guess Uncle Z keeps an awful lot of secrets."

Tarrick's glare intensified.

"Did you consider the possibility that this Elena Russo could have been the target?" Leon gestured with the hand that held the passport.

Both the physician and Tarrick stared at him with incredulous looks on their faces.

"She could be in the mafia." Leon waved the passport at them. "A rival family might have taken a hit out on her."

The physician opened his mouth to make a remark but shook his head and returned to cleaning Elena's wound. Tarrick looked at Leon in irritation, but his brother stared back, wide-eyed. "Why don't you go help Uncle Zanthus?"

Leon departed hastily, sensing his brother's growing ire.

The physician stood up with a troubled look on his face.

"What's wrong? Is she alive?" Tarrick demanded at the man's expression.

"There's something strange, Your Highness," he said hesitantly.

Tarrick moved closer to the cot and inspected Elena. Most of the blood had been cleaned up, but there was still a pool of red liquid around the wound.

"Something in the wound is hindering my ability to treat the injury," the physician explained, kneeling down again.

Tarrick crouched down and watched carefully as the man conjured a small sphere of water that swirled at the tips of his fingers. The physician slowly lowered the water to Elena's chest, and it streamed down his fingers.

"You see?"

Tarrick gaped at the sight. The water *should* have been flowing into the bullet hole to clean the blood and gore, but the small streams merely bypassed the area and trickled down to her collarbones. He noticed the damp patches beneath Elena's neck.

"I've tried several times," the physician said, sounding frustrated.

Tarrick didn't utter a word as he moved his hand over Elena's body and called forth a pool of water between his fingers. He let the droplets fall onto her chest, but the same happened again. It was as though an invisible force field around the wound prevented the water from touching the area.

"I shall have to clean it and extract the bullet manually," the camp physician sighed. "It will take longer, but I've already administered a sleeping draught and a tonic to numb any pain."

Tarrick nodded, looking relieved.

"I hope the princess and the royal physician will be able to heal her."

Tarrick caught the note of worry in his voice.

"Let's keep this between us for now," he said in a low voice.

The physician nodded. He furrowed his brow and turned his head toward the table, where his surgical instruments lay. A scalpel rose in the air and gently floated in their direction. A look of relief washed over the physician's face as he snatched the tool from the air and immediately set to work easing the bullet out of Elena's chest.

Tarrick moved around the tent collecting a bowl and clean cloths, discreetly testing his elemental abilities. The bowl filled with water at the blink of an eye. The torches spiked into the ground flickered brightly at his glance. The dust and dirt that coated his shoes from Gülhane Park and the desert sands fell away the moment he cast his gaze on them and silently willed the earth to retreat. His shoulders sagged in relief, knowing his abilities remained intact, but that raised a host of other questions and worries.

When the physician tied off the bandage around Elena's chest, Tarrick moved silently to his side.

"Check for any amulets or talismans that could be warding her," he instructed the physician, who nodded.

The man held out a bowl in which he had placed the bullet he had extracted. Tarrick took it to the table and examined it closely.

"What's going on?" Zanthus demanded.

Tarrick snapped his head up and saw his uncle standing at the entrance, looking at the physician, aghast. Leon's handsome face was mingled with horror and disgust. Tarrick glanced over to the cot at the physician pulling up the hem of Elena's shirt.

The poor man froze at the sound of Zanthus's voice and blushed a deep red.

"It's not what it looks like, my Lord," he stammered.

"There's something repelling our abilities," Tarrick said calmly. "The physician is checking to see if this woman is wearing something that's warding her."

Zanthus and Leon's jaws dropped.

"I can't see any bluestone, Your Highness," the physician reported in a strangled voice, pulling down Elena's shirt and moving away from her as quickly as possible.

"You think she's carrying bluestone?" Leon gasped.

"It's the only known substance that can nullify our abilities." Tarrick shrugged. "But the bullet seems to be an ordinary one."

The tent fell silent.

"So not a mafia war," Leon said with a nervous chuckle.

Tarrick rolled his eyes and stood.

"Maybe you should take her back, Tarrick," Leon said in a low voice, sounding worried for the first time. "It'll look bad. A human woman in our realm. Bluestone. People will talk. It's like history repeating itself."

"Think of the Peace Summit," Zanthus added with a frown on his face. "There's too much at risk."

Tarrick turned to look at Elena, sleeping peacefully. Her chest moved up and down, indicating her steady breathing. She was still pale and had a slightly pinched look on her face. He noted the purple shadows under her eyes and the downward curve to her lips, undoubtedly from the pain when she had regained momentary consciousness.

"No," he said decisively. "We keep her here."

"Why?" Leon demanded.

"Don't be absurd!" Zanthus exclaimed at the same time.

"We need to find out how she was able to resist our abilities. Besides, she's in as much danger as you and me, Uncle," Tarrick glanced up at Zanthus. "Whoever fired that bullet would have seen us take her. They might attack her again so she doesn't talk. We keep her with us until we know what's going on, and we keep everything that has happened tonight between ourselves and the royal council." Tarrick glared at everyone in the tent. The physician gulped and nodded immediately. Leon nodded but was less afraid of his brother.

"We can say she got drunk and blacked out," Zanthus argued. "She's an American tourist. No one would believe her."

The frown on Tarrick's face deepened. "This. Woman. Saved. Our. Lives," he said through gritted teeth.

Zanthus merely glared back.

Leon cleared his throat. "Okay, so I'll find out what I can about Elena Marie Russo," he said. "If I don't return by morning, better check in with the mafia."

~ 3 ~

Elena was floating on a cloud. She couldn't remember the last time she felt so languid and relaxed. Birds twittered and the wind rustled through the trees, adding to the tranquility. A soft breeze blew strands of hair across her face, and she lifted a hand to brush them away. Her eyelids fluttered open, and it took her a moment to realize she was not in her own bed. She wasn't even in her hotel room in Istanbul.

Confused and disoriented, Elena shot up and scanned the sumptuous room, taking in the decorative candle sconces on the walls with white pillar candles that had burned down to different heights. Her gaze traveled around the room, pausing on the intricately carved wardrobe before landing on the balcony framed by sheer white curtains dancing in the breeze. It jutted out past the room walls, and Elena drank in the sight of the cloudless blue skies outside.

A dark timber door to the side led to a bathroom. Next to it was a large fireplace with colorful patterned tiles on the surround and colored glass studs that protruded from the mantel shelf. In front of it was a small dining table with detailed engravings along the legs and two accompanying chairs.

Throwing back the covers, she wondered how she had accidentally wound up in what seemed to be a very opulent Turkish hotel. When researching Türkiye, Elena had found a number of luxury hotel websites with pictures of similar rooms to the one she was nestled in. The brightly colored and patterned cushions, throws, bed runners, rugs, and finishing touches added warmth to the room and made it feel cozy and welcoming. Exotic. Romantic, even.

Her gaze landed on a strange-looking bird that was perched on the back of an ivory-colored wingback armchair in the corner of the strange room. Elena and the creature stared at each other. The bird cocked its bright pink head to the side, observing her with beady black eyes. It had the body of a sparrow but long, wispy feathers that changed color from bright pink to purple, blue, green, and yellow.

Elena had never seen or heard of a bird like that. It was like a creature from a fantasy novel. It both stood out and belonged in her room, surrounded by the colorful accents reflected in its feathers. She slipped out of bed cautiously, her feet sinking into the plush rug underfoot, too entranced by the creature to appreciate the softness or note the colorful pattern woven into it.

She moved slowly so as not to frighten the bird, and it eyed her curiously as she approached. She assumed it was tame when she managed to reach the chair without so much as a wing flap. It continued staring at her as she stretched out a hand for it to perch on.

"That's a *lyrabird*," an unfamiliar female voice said from the doorway. "They are only native to Terralea, so you won't find them anywhere else."

Elena jumped at the sound, and the creature took off out the balcony doors, startled by her sudden movement.

She spun around to find a beautiful, petite woman with sparkling brown eyes and a mischievous smile entering the room. The woman had a few freckles dotted over her delicate nose and high cheekbones. Her heart-shaped face was surrounded by a mass of light brown waves and curls that fell to her shoulders. She wore a loose-fitting, long-sleeve, sky-blue tunic embroidered at the neckline and hem with a leather braided belt around her waist. Underneath, she had on dark leggings and brown boots. She carried a tray laden with food and small pitchers of water and juice.

Elena struggled for words at the sight of the woman.

"Good morning," she greeted Elena in a musical voice.

"Where am I?" she asked, not returning the greeting.

"Leneira," the woman replied, putting the tray down carefully on the table. "I wasn't sure if you'd like a sweet or savory breakfast, so I brought you a little of everything."

"Leneira?" Elena asked nervously, glancing out the window. "Is that near Istanbul?"

The woman bit her lip as she rearranged the items on the tray. "I'm not sure I'm the best person to explain," she said, looking Elena up and down. "I'm sorry," she apologized. "I know it's not what you wanted to hear."

Elena's mind finally caught up as she remembered the assassin, the call to prayer, her ridiculous leap, and the pain. Her hand flew to where she remembered feeling the bullet pierce her skin.

"What happened?" she gasped as her breathing became panicked.

The strange woman poured a cup of tea, oblivious to Elena's growing alarm. "You almost died." The woman held out the cup and saucer to Elena. "You lost a lot of blood, but I was able to heal you. It's a good thing my brother brought you to me when he did."

Elena looked down at her chest. A small, pale pink circle where the bullet had entered was the only sign she had been injured. She ran a tentative finger over the area but didn't feel a thing, noticing for the first time that she was wearing a lacy white nightdress that didn't belong to her.

"The scar will fade," the woman told her, placing the cup and saucer on the table when it was clear Elena wasn't moving any time soon. "It's the best I could do."

"You healed me?" Elena asked slowly, trying to work out how long she must have been unconscious if a significant wound had turned into a scar with no signs of surgery or stitches.

"I'm the only Terralean who can heal others instantly," the woman said proudly. "We have physicians, of course," she added. "The portal physician had to heal you without using his elemental abilities for some reason. Even my magic took longer than usual. The royal physician and I think bluestone fragments in your wound blocked it." She frowned. "But once we cleaned your wound again and checked for infection, it healed right up."

Elena stared at the woman in disbelief. She might as well have been speaking another language. "What?" Elena finally asked.

The woman seemed momentarily confused at the question.

"I suppose my abilities work a bit differently than most." She frowned. "I need to set the intention to heal as I hold my hands over the wound or injury." The woman demonstrated by holding out her hands, palms facing the floor as though hovering over an invisible body. "I focus on what needs healing, and it does."

There was silence as Elena tried to absorb what she was hearing. The idea that she was still lying on the ground bleeding out in Sultanahmet Park crossed her mind. Maybe it was all just a bizarre fantasy playing out in her last moments.

The woman continued studying Elena, and realization dawned on her face. "Oh, right! You don't have our kinds of abilities in the human realm, do you?"

"What do you mean *abilities*?" Elena frowned. "Who are you? Where the hell am I?"

"Oh, sorry!" the woman laughed. "I forgot to introduce myself! I'm Adina—Princess Adina, at your service," she curtsied.

"Princess?" Elena repeated weakly, wondering if she would get any answers or just more questions.

"Princess Adina of Terralea," she confirmed.

"Terralea." Elena desperately searched her memory for any mention of the name, somehow knowing none would be found.

"You're in the realm of Leneira." Adina took a seat and motioned for Elena to join her. She picked up a pastry off the tray and nibbled on the corner, watching Elena slowly cross the room and sink into the other chair.

"Here, why don't you eat something? You must be starving." Adina nudged the tray of food toward Elena. Her stomach rumbled, but she still had many questions.

"How long have I been asleep?" Elena frowned, still rubbing the scar that, by all rights, should still be bandaged and scabbing over.

"A few days." Adina shrugged. "The portal is a few days' travel, but Tarrick and Uncle Zanthus used *pihasi* and brought you back quite quickly."

"Portal," Elena said blankly. "*Pishasi?*"

"The portal to the human realm," Adina explained gently. "Once you were all healed, Tarrick and Father ordered everyone to let you sleep as long as you needed to recover."

Elena picked up a pastry absent-mindedly, still trying to process all the new words and names being thrown at her.

"And it's *pi-ha-si*." Adina grinned. "They're winged horses. I've always wanted to ride one."

"I've been here a few days?" Elena exclaimed in panic, not registering the mention of winged horses.

"Yes," Adina replied, looking slightly alarmed at the expression on Elena's face.

"I'm supposed to be on the tour," Elena said frantically, trying to remember the itinerary. *Am I meant to be in Cappadocia? Or Antalya?*

A knock on the door interrupted the erratic thoughts going through Elena's mind. She had booked a group tour so she and her mother had a guide with them at all times so they didn't get lost and didn't have to navigate an unfamiliar country where they didn't speak the language. It would appear that she *had* gotten lost—in a magical realm where nothing made sense. It was a bigger adventure than she had anticipated and one that started to scare her.

"Come in," Adina called out cheerfully, popping the rest of the pastry in her mouth.

A tall man entered and closed the door carefully behind him. Elena's heart stopped when she took him in. He was the most handsome man she'd ever seen. Wavy dark hair swept across the brown skin of his forehead. He had a chiseled jaw, high cheek-bones, and warm amber eyes that took in the scene. Elena could make out muscular arms and torso under the long-sleeve fitted navy tunic he wore. He wore dark pants and polished boots. Despite the simplicity of his attire, he had an air of authority.

"Brother!" Adina exclaimed. "Come to thank your savior properly?"

The man stepped closer to the table, and the scent of sandalwood and cedar washed over Elena. Her eyes widened. *This is the man I took a bullet for last night?* Heat rose to her cheeks at the sight of him. *Perhaps a few days in this strange place wouldn't be too bad.*

~ 4 ~

Tarrick frowned at his sister's casual demeanor. "Thank you, Elena," he said stiffly before turning to their guest.

Before he could stop himself, Tarrick's eyes trailed over the thin nightdress that hugged Elena's curves. She blushed and tried to cover herself by folding her arms across her chest. Tarrick remembered himself, and his gaze snapped up.

"Elena, this is my brother, Tarrick." Adina waved her hand toward him. "His Royal Highness, *Prince* Tarrick," she corrected herself, standing and grinning widely at her brother.

"Prince?" Elena stammered, her cheeks reddening further.

"No need for formalities," he brushed away Adina's comment, trying to dispel the awkward moment. "These are ... unusual circumstances." He turned to his sister. "Your manners, Adina," he reproached her.

"Oh." Adina had the grace to look embarrassed. "I'm sorry, Elena. I should have let you get dressed first." She turned away.

"I still have questions," Elena objected as the two of them stepped toward the door.

"We will answer all of your questions," Tarrick promised, glancing her way. "In due course." He stared at her, his expression softening slightly, and Elena rubbed her crossed arms awkwardly.

A loud knock at the door made them all jump.

A male voice called out from the other side, "Tarrick! Adina! Are you in there? The council is ready."

Tarrick's eyes snapped to the door, and he muttered a curse under his breath.

"Coming!" Adina sang out. She turned back to Elena and explained, "Our other brother, Leon."

"Please eat," Tarrick gestured to the breakfast tray. "And make yourself at home. We will come back and collect you shortly."

He gently shoved Adina toward the exit. She gave Elena a friendly wave before she and Tarrick stepped out. Tarrick closed the door quickly behind them.

"Was that necessary, Leon?" He glared at his younger brother. Wavy flaxen hair was swept back from his handsome face, which bore a mischievous grin.

"Did you wake up on the wrong side of the bed, brother?" Leon laughed.

Adina giggled. "Tarrick's smitten."

Leon's brows shot up his forehead, and he eyed his brother with glee.

Tarrick rolled his eyes before glaring at Adina.

"I'm not," he bit out. "I'm *not!*" he repeated loudly when his siblings exchanged evil grins.

"Methinks you do protest a little too hard." Leon winked at him. "You forget I saw her too. Although, she was a little pale and covered in dust last time."

"She's nice," Adina jumped in. "A bit shy. But I guess that's to be expected." She turned to Tarrick with a pleading look on her face. "Can she stay for a while? Please?"

Tarrick stared at his siblings in disbelief. "Have you two been smoking water pipes again? She could be a rebel."

"No, she's not," Leon scoffed. "We've done the checks and read her file. Mother and Father agree she's an ordinary woman who just happened to come between you and a bullet."

"Then why the royal council meeting?" Tarrick argued.

"Formalities." Leon waved an impatient hand. "Procedure. You know how Uncle Zanthus likes things done properly. Mother has already asked the staff to make sure she's comfortable and has everything she'll need while she's here."

"Don't you want her to stay, Tarrick?" Adina turned to her brother.

"I don't think *she* wants to stay, Adina," he pointed out. "Besides, she's a *human*. And the Peace Summit starts in a few days."

"Once she realizes where she is and I show her around, she'll love it here," Adina pouted. "Besides, I'll be bored by myself while you two are discussing important matters and negotiating deals with King Halder and Queen Lin."

"Trust me, those meetings are no picnic," Leon muttered, earning himself a glare from Tarrick.

"She's a *human*," Tarrick emphasized again, feeling irritated. "That won't help us if Halder and Lin find out. And Lin will know instantly."

While Leon and Adina bickered about ways to hide Elena's presence during the Peace Summit, Tarrick pinched the bridge of his nose and prayed for strength. Adina was far too perceptive and had noticed him gaping at Elena earlier despite his best efforts to maintain a calm demeanor. The truth was, he was intrigued by the woman and wanted to know the reasons behind her actions. Those dark eyes and lush curves had caught him off guard too.

He had to be careful. Zanthus and his father had already had words with him about bringing Elena to Terralea, although his father had been more understanding once Tarrick had explained the predicament he'd been in. He could not allow himself to fall for another human woman and put his family in danger yet again.

He interrupted his siblings. "Leon, go tell the council I'll be there shortly," he instructed.

His brother nodded, and after poking his tongue out at Adina, who in turn made a face back at him, he spun on his heel and walked down the corridor.

Tarrick turned to Adina. "Don't you have lessons to go to?"

She crossed her arms and glared at him. "I'm 103 years old. I was done with *lessons* fifty years ago."

"Is that all?" Tarrick wrinkled his forehead, feigning surprise.

Adina broke into a grin, and she punched his arm. Hard. "Ass."

Tarrick grinned back. He tamped down the guilt that rose every time he thought about how it was his fault that Adina had led such a sheltered life within the palace walls.

"Listen," he lowered his voice and dared a glance at Elena's door. Despite his best efforts to distance himself from the woman on the other side, he found himself saying, "I can't promise anything, but if the council agree she's innocent—"

"Which she is," Adina said firmly. "I've read her file."

"How did you—" Tarrick closed his eyes and shook his head. "Never mind. *If* they all agree and we can come up with a plan to hide her from Halder and Lin, I'll ask her if she'd like to stay for a bit."

Adina's face brightened, and she threw her arms around Tarrick, squeezing tightly.

"Thank you," she said, her voice muffled by his tunic.

"It's a big if, Adina," Tarrick warned, trying to extract himself from his sister's vice-like grip. "Elena has to agree to it too."

She grinned at him. "I knew you liked her."

"I don't," Tarrick said half-heartedly, but Adina had already released him and turned to flit away. "No spying!" he called out after her, knowing his instructions would be ignored.

He groaned inwardly once his sister disappeared from sight, wondering if and how he would be able to make it through the next few days with a clear head.

***

Tarrick knocked on Elena's door when Kyra—the servant his mother had sent to help Elena bathe and get dressed for the day—left the room.

The door opened, and all thoughts of maintaining his composure fled his mind as his gaze lingered on the pale blue, sleeveless dress that clung to her curves for longer than strictly necessary. The delicate, gold-embellished thin straps dipped into a shapely V across the bodice, the plunging neckline revealing the pink scar on Elena's chest. The bottom half of the dress was loose and flowy with slits down the sides, and she wore gold sandals, laced around slim ankles.

An attractive pink tinge bloomed on Elena's cheeks and over the bridge of her pert nose as Tarrick's eyes swept up to her face. The return of color was indication enough that she had been healed. Damp brown hair framed her oval face and streamed down her back.

Tarrick didn't trust himself to look below her neck again, knowing the sight of the bullet wound and the dress she wore might cloud his judgment. He needed a clear head; he had just as many questions for her as she did for him. Probably more.

"Didn't Kyra help you wash and dress?" he asked, grateful Leon wasn't around to hear his winning opening line and tease him about it later.

Elena looked blank for a moment before replying, "She did."

She was short, like Adina, only coming up to his chest. She also lied like his sister.

Tarrick raised an eyebrow and stared skeptically.

Elena tilted her chin up defiantly.

"She should have dried your hair," he finally said.

"The room didn't come with a hair dryer. Or electrical outlets," Elena frowned, tucking a damp strand behind her ear. "It's fine. I prefer to let it air dry."

They stared at each other until Elena's cheeks colored under his scrutiny. He blinked and watched her hair dry instantly. Relief washed over him as he noted there was no resistance to his elemental abilities. Elena continued to stare at him, not showing signs of acknowledging what had happened. Tarrick realized she truly was innocent and had no idea of where she was.

"Look," she said, finally breaking the silence. "You've been really generous with letting me stay here while I recover, but I need to go back to Istanbul and catch up with my tour."

"You're not going anywhere," Tarrick told her.

"Excuse me?"

"You'll be staying here for now." His eyes pierced her. "Security in Terralea has been tightened. The portal was sealed after we brought your belongings and secured the entrance to the human realm. No one can enter or leave. Including you."

Elena gaped at him. "You can't keep me here against my will," she sputtered. "That's abduction."

"You're safe here," he replied impassively.

"I don't even know where *here* is!" Elena all but shouted in her frustration.

"I'm taking you to the royal council now, where they want to question you about what happened in Istanbul. I'll answer any questions you have after," he said, unfazed by Elena's tone.

The air grew tense, and she looked ready to launch herself at him.

Tarrick shifted slightly on his feet, forcing himself to stay calm. "It's just a formality. Uncle Zanthus and I already told them what happened, and my guards have confirmed you're not a threat."

"How reassuring," Elena said drily, trying and failing to check her temper.

Tarrick wordlessly opened the door and stepped to the side to allow her to leave first.

Elena narrowed her eyes, willing him to back down and do as she asked. He didn't budge, merely waiting for her to leave the room.

Elena sighed. "Fine."

The corner of Tarrick's lip quirked up ever so slightly.

She stepped out into the hall, and Tarrick followed, feeling her shy away as he brushed past her to lead the way. He glanced back and slowed down his pace when he caught her taking in the surroundings. Elena examined the patterned plush runners over the dark wooden floors before looking up at the crystal chandeliers with white candles in holders, hanging from the ceilings. In the bright sunlight, they threw spots of rainbow color on the walls. Decorative vases stood on plinths, and tapestries hung from the ceiling all the way down to the floor, adding color and warmth. The woven scenes depicted animals in forests, *lyrabirds* in trees, temples, ornate buildings, and seascapes.

Elena's eyes swept the corridor as though looking for signs of something familiar. Palace staff scurried around corners, and Tarrick walked on, not offering any explanation.

He said casually, "Terralea Palace is one of the most secure buildings in the country. Our guards are trained in manipulating the elements as well as hand-to-hand combat."

"Do their abilities include being invisible?" Elena asked, injecting as much snark as she could.

Tarrick smirked but didn't answer.

"Your belongings are being searched," he continued. "And we will have a guard assigned to you at all times while you're here."

"Why do I need a guard?"

Tarrick stopped so abruptly Elena almost walked right into his back. He whirled around with a frown.

"There's still an assassin at large," he told her in a low voice. "Until we find them and get to the bottom of what they were planning, you're at risk."

As she put together the pieces of what had happened in Istanbul and the conversation they'd had in her bedroom, the enormity of the situation dawned on her. She looked up at him in dismay.

"My guards are working overtime to find this person," he said gently.

Elena cast her eyes downward, and her voice wobbled. "I didn't know."

Tarrick rubbed his chin, feeling slightly regretful at his forthright manner.

She peeked up at him. "Wait! You're going through my stuff?" Elena asked, horrified. "How did you even know where I was staying?"

"You carried a card with your hotel's name on it," Tarrick said stiffly, turning on his heel and continuing down the corridor. He increased his pace as they neared the council chambers.

They stopped at a large wooden door that had a lone guard standing outside, who bowed when the prince approached. The guard wore a red tunic with a gold emblem embroidered over the heart, dark pants, and polished boots. Tucked into the leather belts around his waist was a sheathed dagger, the only weapon. Elena eyed the blade apprehensively and moved closer to Tarrick.

"I apologize for my anger," Tarrick said to her, his gaze dropping to the scar on her chest before quickly meeting her eyes again. He reached out for the handle and paused. "This is all happening at an inconvenient time, but I want you to know that your safety is my priority, and I won't let anything happen to you while you're here."

Elena was taken aback by the apology and didn't reply.

"I know you're upset and confused, but try to stay calm during this meeting," Tarrick murmured before opening the door. "Don't let them intimidate you."

~ 5 ~

Elena swallowed hard and took a deep breath before stepping into the council chamber. Her heart was racing as she was greeted by the sight of six people sitting along one side of a long wooden table in the middle. They eyed her with varying expressions of interest, curiosity, and disdain.

To hide her growing trepidation, she took in the bright, airy room and the ornate gold cornices and pilasters. A grand chandelier hung from the decorative medallion in the center of the ceiling. Various moldings and friezes highlighted the height of the room, making it feel spacious. Floor-to-ceiling windows lined one side of the space, looking out into the palace gardens.

The bookworm in Elena was itching to browse the titles that sat in the tall bookshelves opposite the windows and run her fingers over the leatherbound, embossed spines lined up neatly along the shelves. A large, decorative fireplace was set into the wall behind the table.

Once again, there was no sign of modern equipment or electronics. Elena was starting to believe she really was in another realm. It was impossible to function without basic technology, even in the most remote parts of her world.

Tarrick guided Elena to a wooden chair in front of the table. A shiver ran down her spine when he placed a gentle hand on her back and nudged her forward. It was the second time he had touched her directly. Not that she was counting or anything.

He stood beside the chair until she settled herself, then walked over to the empty seat at the end of the long table next to a beautiful woman. She seemed to be in her late fifties with blonde hair pulled back in a bun at the nape of her neck. Her fair skin was luminescent, and she had the brightest blue eyes Elena had ever seen. Even from where she sat, Elena could see flecks of gold in the woman's irises. She had a kind face and was the only one smiling at her.

Elena glanced around at the other people. Her palms grew sweaty, and she tried not to fidget with everyone focused on her.

The eldest man at the far end of the table cleared his throat and shuffled the papers in front of him. "Elena Marie Russo." She was startled at the use of her full name. How could those people know who she was? "Welcome to the meeting of the Royal Council of Terralea."

The man was wizened, with bushy gray eyebrows and thinning gray hair. Despite his evident age, he assessed Elena with alert, dark eyes. "We have present today His Majesty, King Arran."

The king sat in the middle of the table, directly in front of Elena, and inclined his head in acknowledgment. The resemblance to Tarrick was striking, but there were deliberate differences, like the salt and pepper hair swept back from his bearded face. Laugh lines radiated out from his twinkling amber eyes, and Elena noticed his hand covered that of the blonde woman next to him. *She must be the queen—Tarrick, Leon, and Adina's mother.*

"Her Majesty, Queen Amaya."

The blonde woman smiled warmly at Elena, inclining her head at the introduction.

"His Highness, Prince Tarrick."

Tarrick continued to watch Elena with an unreadable expression on his face.

"His Highness, Prince Leon."

A young man with golden hair who had been taking notes when the meeting started paused his scribbling to look up at Elena and wink at her. Tarrick narrowed his eyes at Leon's casual manner.

"Royal Advisor and Head of the Royal Guard, Lord Zanthus."

The older blond man sitting on the king's other side gave her a curt nod. He had the same piercing blue eyes and fair hair as the queen and Leon. Elena wondered if they were related. He surveyed her suspiciously, his expression devoid of the warmth and friendliness that the queen radiated. There was something vaguely familiar about the way he sat back in his seat, at ease with the proceedings, that Elena couldn't place.

"Lady Netta, Governor of Erindell."

The woman with rich brown skin and curly black hair pulled back high on her head bowed her head without smiling. She appraised Elena with shrewd, dark, upturned, feline-like eyes. Like Tarrick, her neutral expression gave nothing away.

"And myself, Lord Rokeby of Fayne province, representing the Council of Nobles," he concluded the introductions with an inclination of his head. Rokeby slid a sheet of paper under the pile and reached for a small item in front of him. "Is this your passport?" He held up the small booklet.

Elena nodded, relieved to see it safe but also kicking herself for thinking she had been smart to slip the hotel's business card into her purse in case she got lost. No wonder those people knew so much about her; she had basically advertised her identity and the location of her belongings. She spotted the small crossbody bag she had been carrying with her in Istanbul, packed with all the items she had thought essential, sitting in front of Rokeby.

Tarrick may have told her that the meeting was just a conversation to confirm what had happened, but Elena's parents gave the same spiel to criminals and suspects before an interrogation. A wave of emotion took over as she remembered the summers she had spent at the station when her parents had been unable to find a sitter. She had watched them in action from the safety of the room on the other side of a two-way mirror. A lump formed in her throat when she realized she didn't have anyone back home waiting for her calls or messages to know if she was safe. Her colleagues assumed she was on vacation. Without her phone, they wouldn't know if she was in danger. She fought the urge to snatch her bag from Rokeby and run out of the room as fast as possible.

"Please tell us in your own words what happened in Sultanahmet Park."

Elena hesitated. She opened her mouth, but the words froze on her tongue.

"You're not in trouble, Elena," Tarrick said gently. "We just want to know what you saw and heard."

She glanced at him. His expression hadn't changed, but the tone of his voice diffused some of the tension she was feeling. Her eyes flicked along the table. At the sight of Zanthus scowling at Tarrick—he clearly disagreed with the prince's assessment of Elena's innocence—she clutched the fabric of her dress and tried to discreetly wipe her sweaty palms.

"Tell us about what happened when you left the Hagia Sophia," Tarrick prompted, ignoring the looks Zanthus and Rokeby were shooting him. "That is where you came from, isn't it?"

Elena nodded. She took a deep breath and spoke. "I was sitting on a bench when I saw a shadow moving on the balcony of the minaret at the mosque," she started to recount to the council.

"What were you doing there at midnight?" Zanthus interjected. Elena immediately bristled at the accusatory note in his voice, but she bit down her anger and took a few deep breaths to calm herself.

"Zanthus." The king frowned. "Let the young woman speak."

"Apologies, Majesty," Zanthus bowed.

"I was jet-lagged," Elena explained in a steady voice. "I had visited the Hagia Sophia and wasn't ready to go back to my hotel, so I sat on a bench for a while. Two men sat on the same bench" —she gestured toward Tarrick— "but they didn't bother me. When I saw the shadow moving, I thought it was strange, so I used the zoom feature on my camera to try and see what was happening. I thought it was the call to prayer—"

"Is this the camera you used?" Rokeby held up her smartphone. Elena nodded, cringing at the sight of the shattered screen and cracks all over the device.

"Yes."

"You didn't record this?" Netta asked in a deep, throaty voice.

"No," Elena admitted. "I wasn't thinking clearly and didn't know anyone was in danger. I only realized it was a gunman when they set up a rifle on the tripod."

"You could see that on the camera?" Amaya asked.

"Yes, the zoom tool is pretty powerful," Elena told her. "That was when I looked around for police, but there were none at the time."

"Did you see the assassin's face or any distinguishing features?" Rokeby leaned forward.

"No," Elena shook her head. "They wore dark clothes and moved too quickly for me to see their face. I heard the crackling of the microphone from the minaret of the Blue Mosque behind. That's when I jumped in front of Tarr—Prince Tarrick and the other man," Elena finished.

"Why?" Zanthus's blue eyes pierced her own as if trying to read her mind.

"I-I'm sorry?" Elena stuttered.

"Why did you jump in front of the prince?"

"I-I don't know," Elena mumbled, rubbing her arm unconsciously. She remembered in vivid detail ruminating on the circumstances surrounding her mother's death before she took that fateful leap. But that was something deeply personal she wasn't about to share with strangers who seemed to think she was a threat when she had, in fact, saved the lives of two of their people. "I just did."

She glanced up at the small bag sitting in front of Rokeby and, for the first time since waking up, missed having her mother's police badge to hold on to. Tarrick frowned at his father, trying to catch his attention, but Arran was watching Elena intently. The king's handsome face gave nothing away. Amaya tilted her head to the side and watched Elena shift uncomfortably in the silence.

Rokeby tapped his pen thoughtfully on the table. "It is odd that a young woman would take a bullet for two strange men," he finally said.

"Is it?" Elena asked nervously. Her eyes darted around the room. Sweat trickled down her back despite the cool breeze drifting in through the open windows. "I thought it would be a good deed."

"A good deed?" Zanthus raised an eyebrow.

"Yes," she replied. "It's what my parents..." she trailed off and dropped her gaze, unable to meet their hard stares any longer. She glanced up at Tarrick through her lashes, but he kept his face blank.

"Does this have anything to do with you risking your life for our prince?" Zanthus held up a small, shiny object.

Without thinking, Elena shot to her feet. "That's mine," she said abruptly, holding out her hand. Her fear gave way to rage at the thought of that man holding onto her mother's badge that entire time. The blood was pounding in her ears so loudly she didn't hear Netta's soft gasp and Rokeby's exclamation at her visceral reaction. She studied Zanthus, who wore an expression of triumph. His relaxed demeanor didn't change as he held up Elena's most treasured possession.

A wave of recognition hit her as she stared at the man. "I jumped in front of you too," she said quietly. Anger simmered at being interrogated so aggressively by a man whose life she had saved.

Zanthus's lips curled into a snarl. "Pardon?"

"I didn't jump in front of Prince Tarrick specifically," Elena explained, clenching her fists by her sides. "I jumped in front of both of you. I didn't know who the shooter was aiming for."

Another long minute of silence followed as the council assessed her. Elena realized she was still standing, fingernails piercing the skin of her palms. She forced herself to sit back down and rearrange her face into a polite mask. Tarrick knit his brows together, and Zanthus began to turn purple in the face.

"Do you know what bluestone is?" Zanthus snapped at her.

"Some kind of building material?" Elena shrugged.

A tense silence followed her response. Leon smirked as he continued scribbling. Netta glanced at the queen, and the expressions on both their faces softened slightly. The crease between Rokeby's brows smoothed out, and he tilted his head to the side.

"Have you been approached by anyone offering you a large sum of money or the promise of magical ability?" Zanthus continued his line of questioning.

"I don't take bribes." She frowned at the strange question. "And I don't know what you mean by magical ability."

"Just answer the question."

"No, I haven't." Elena shook her head again. "And I don't appreciate your tone," she added, feeling her temper rise again.

The tension in the room was palpable, and Leon didn't bother hiding his grin as he continued scribbling notes.

Tarrick broke the silence. "We're done here." He didn't raise his voice, but everyone straightened in their seats and turned toward him.

"She could be fooling us, Tarrick," Zanthus said unconvincingly. "Remember what happened the last time a human—"

"It's not the same." Tarrick narrowed his eyes until they were slits in his tanned face.

"A woman we knew and trusted for four years turned on us and nearly brought this realm to its knees," Zanthus snarled, banging his hand on the table, making everyone jump. He stood abruptly, nearly sending his chair flying back. "I'll be damned if I let that happen again."

Tarrick stood as well, glaring at the older man.

Everyone gaped at the two men, who looked ready to rip each other apart.

"It's not the same, Uncle Zanthus," Leon said in a placating tone. "Not all humans are like that. We have access to her therapist's notes. Our profilers have done a thorough background check and have told us she's not a criminal psycho—"

"You have access to *what*?" Elena snapped at the young prince.

"Oh, shit," Leon mumbled, turning bright red and ducking his head. Tarrick whipped his head toward his younger brother.

Before he could launch himself at Leon, Amaya spoke up for the first time, her voice tinged with anger. "Leon, that was out of line."

"I'm sorry," the prince peeked at Elena apologetically. "That wasn't meant to come out—"

"Here's an idea," Elena said loudly. All eyes swiveled back to her. "My presence seems to be a big problem for you all, and I don't want to stay here any longer than I have to. So why don't you give me back my stuff and take me back to the human world, or realm, or whatever through this ... portal ... and we can all pretend this never happened."

"I'm afraid you will have to stay here for a while." The queen glanced between Tarrick and Zanthus, and dipped her head. The anger faded from Tarrick's face as they both sat back down slowly, but the resentment lingered on Zanthus's face. He turned back to Elena with a cold, calculating expression.

"The portal to the human realm has been sealed, and no one can leave or enter," Amaya continued.

"What do you mean?" Elena demanded. "I'm an American citizen, and I've done nothing wrong. You can't keep me here."

"It's not that simple." The queen shook her head sadly. "There's a lot we don't know, and we have to protect our people until we know for certain the reason behind the attack and find the culprits. We are yet to determine if this was the action of one disgruntled person or if there is a much larger threat to our people. We also care about *your* safety, my dear."

"Please," Elena begged, starting to panic at being trapped in a strange, dangerous world. "I'm just a tourist on vacation. I'll sign an NDA and won't say a word to anyone about any of this. Please let me go back home. I won't even go on the tour. I'll book the first flight out of Istanbul."

The king sighed heavily. "My children will explain everything, but for now, you must know that we are very grateful for what you did, and you are our most welcome guest," he said gently.

"Your Majesty, I must protest," Zanthus argued, and Elena narrowed her eyes at the man. She didn't understand why he was so against her and convinced she was a criminal. "We can't have this woman wandering about unchecked until we know for certain she is not a threat or part of the growing rebellion."

Elena opened her mouth to snap at him again. She couldn't believe he had the nerve to talk about her like that as though she wasn't there.

"What growing rebellion, Lord Zanthus?" Netta swooped in, sounding concerned. "My sources have not reported anything."

"I have access to classified information, Lady Netta," he said dismissively. The governor pressed her lips together at his condescending remark but remained quiet. "I was going to bring this up in, ah ... private." He gave Elena a disdainful look.

"I'm not a rebel," she protested, her voice cracking slightly.

"That's enough," Arran spoke, authority underpinning his words. He gave Zanthus a stern look. "This was meant to be a conversation to confirm that Elena witnessed the assassin aiming for you and Tarrick. Not an interrogation or accusation of her involvement with the rebels. Leon is right; our team has done a thorough background check on the young lady. I've read the reports myself, and she has done our realm a service. She deserves to be treated with the same courtesy and respect we give all our guests."

Tarrick stood and walked to Elena's side. Everyone tracked his movements.

"Please, let me go," she whispered, meeting his gaze. "I don't know anything. I'm no threat to you."

A shadow of emotion passed across Tarrick's face, and he glanced up at the council members watching them.

"I have a good deal to explain to Elena," he said firmly.

Nobody argued or protested this time, but the tension in the room was still thick. Amaya and Leon were the only people who didn't stare at Elena warily.

Arran cleared his throat. "Very well, son. Perhaps you can show our *guest*" —he emphasized the word as he glanced up and down the table— "the grounds and answer any questions she may have."

Only Netta and Rokeby dipped their heads in acknowledgment of the king's statement. Tarrick gave his father a sharp nod before looking down at Elena and tilting his head toward the door.

"Can I have my stuff?" she asked timidly. She was stuck there for the foreseeable future, and until she learned more about where she was, she couldn't make plans to escape. The only way she would learn anything would be to play by those people's rules and abide by what they said.

"Certainly," Leon replied, plucking the bag from Rokeby's pile of papers and her mother's badge from Zanthus and holding the items out to her.

She took the articles without a word and turned back to Tarrick.

"Let's go," he said, leading her to the door without waiting for anyone's permission to leave the room.

Elena glanced back at the council members talking quietly amongst themselves before following Tarrick.

~ 6 ~

Elena shoved the badge inside her small shoulder bag and tucked it in the drawer of the nightstand in her room. She barely glanced at the suitcases that had been brought up and left at the foot of the bed while they had been in the council chambers. Tarrick said he wanted to explain everything to her in the garden away from prying eyes and ears.

They walked in silence through the palace hallways and down the stairs to the sweeping entrance. The guards on either side of the heavy wooden doors stood to attention when Tarrick approached, and at his nod, they opened the doors.

Tarrick was acutely aware that the tone of the meeting contradicted what he had promised Elena. It was clear from her answers that she had nothing to do with the rebels or any conspiracies to take down the Terralean royal family. But the prince was at a loss. He had no idea of how to reassure Elena and convince Zanthus and the others that she was not a threat without them dragging up his past and using it against him. As future king of Terralea, there was no room for error, especially after what happened during the uprising a hundred years before.

Elena blinked in the bright sunlight and peered up at the blue sky. Tarrick led her through the gardens, passing flowers and low-hanging fruit on trees. She eyed the bright berries nestled among spiky, dark leaves and paused by bushes with pink and blue leaves.

When Tarrick was certain no one was around to hear them, he asked in a curious voice, "To whom did that badge belong?"

Elena glanced up at him, the slight crease on her forehead indicating she was still tense. "My mom. We buried Dad with his, but it's the only thing I have left of Mom that means something to me."

"You were holding onto it pretty tightly when you jumped in front of us," Tarrick commented lightly. When Elena didn't respond, he pressed on, "Most people would have held onto their phones or bags when faced with a threatening situation."

"Do I need to be worried about these rebels?" Elena asked. "Who are they anyway?"

"No," Tarrick replied quickly. At her look, he offered a small smile and said, "Uncle Zanthus's position means he's overly cautious about security. You're safe here. If the rebels move to attack, we'll know straight away."

"He seemed adamant that danger was close by." Elena frowned. "Why would he lie about that?"

Tarrick didn't reply. He didn't reveal that it was the first time he, too, was hearing about rebels stirring up again. They had been quiet for decades, with only a few skirmishes in some of the regional towns.

The gardens were vast. A few *lyrabirds* flew overhead. The sound of running water from a nearby stream mingled with voices murmuring quietly behind hedges and hidden groves. Paths and trails between flower beds led to different areas of the garden. Tarrick continued on his chosen path without looking at either side.

"Listen, Tarrick," Elena said hesitantly. Tarrick slowed his walk and turned to her pleading brown eyes. It took every ounce of effort not to pull her into his arms and soothe her fears, not knowing what else he could say to comfort her. "I'm obviously getting in your way, and the council seems to think I'm a danger to you all. Why don't you just take me to the portal and let me go back?"

"Aside from the logistical nightmare that is riding with you across half the country to the portal and overriding all the extra security measures we've put in place since sealing it?" He raised a brow.

Elena scoffed at his explanation and crossed her arms.

He sighed. "The Peace Summit starts tomorrow with delegates from all around the realm arriving for talks and negotiations. We've already allocated our guards and resources to making sure this summit goes smoothly. There is a lot at stake, and having you here ... complicates things," he rubbed his chin awkwardly.

"I'm sorry someone tried to take you out at such an inconvenient time," Elena said sarcastically. "And sorry for complicating your life by saving it."

Tarrick's mouth twitched at the mullish expression on her face.

"Apology accepted," he said with twinkling eyes. "And thank you, again, for saving my life."

He continued walking with Elena on his heels, bristling at his manner. They approached a small clearing where stone benches circled a fountain. The area was surrounded by a wall of trees except for the entrance.

Tarrick recognized Adina's distinctive tinkling laughter carrying in the wind. They entered the clearing to see her sitting on a bench with a guard, who looked at her with longing as she threw her head back and laughed loudly. She replied to whatever he had said as she twirled a bright pink flower in her hand, smiling coyly, oblivious to their audience.

Tarrick paused at the entrance. "Let's make a deal," he said, looking back at Elena. "You stay here during the Peace Summit, where I know you'll be safe. Once it's over, I'll take you back myself. It will be my way of repaying you for my life."

Elena's brows shot up. "Even if you don't find the assassin?"

Tarrick studied her. "Even if we don't find the assassin," he confirmed.

"Deal." Elena stuck her hand out to shake on it.

Tarrick slowly took her hand in his and squeezed lightly, holding her gaze. She blushed and dropped her eyes to his callused hands, where faint scars shone against his tanned skin. They both let go quickly. Tarrick flexed his hand by his side and cleared his throat while Elena let her hand drop by her side, turning toward Adina.

The guard immediately stood to attention, wiping the smile off his handsome face, bowing as the prince strode closer. Tarrick nodded at the guard and stopped in front of Adina, who peered at him with a slightly irritated expression.

"I trust my sister has been behaving herself, Erik," he addressed the guard, unable to resist taking revenge on Adina for claiming he was infatuated with Elena. His words were formal, but his tone was laced with a hint of laughter.

"She has, Your Highness," Erik replied without turning his head. His ebony skin was smooth and flawless. The red tunic stretched over his broad chest and clung to his muscular arms. He, too, carried a sheathed dagger at his waist, the standard uniform of all royal guards.

"I'm not a child, Tarrick," Adina huffed out. "How badly did they interrogate you, Elena?"

"Uncle Zanthus is being difficult," Tarrick replied on Elena's behalf. "Lord Rokeby and Lady Netta will come around. They didn't really buy that she was conspiring with the rebels to take us down" —he flashed Elena an apologetic look— "but you know how they don't like speaking up when Uncle Zanthus has the floor."

Adina's eyes widened.

"Mother and Father convinced him to let her stay," he sighed, holding an arm out to the bench, indicating for Elena to take a seat—she didn't move.

"But Elena hasn't *done* anything," Adina protested. "Uncle Zanthus is so paranoid."

"I know." Tarrick rubbed a hand over his weary face.

"What did Leon say?"

"Nothing helpful," Tarrick muttered. "Put his foot in it a few times, as always."

"I can't believe he's allowed to be on the council, and I'm not." Adina rolled her eyes.

"Can someone please explain what's going on?" Elena asked.

Tarrick glanced at her. She was still angry, but out in the garden away from the council chambers, her shoulders had relaxed. It was clear from the way she glanced around the space that she was torn between wanting answers and itching to explore. "Perhaps Adina should explain," he said finally. "I should talk to Father about a plan."

He nodded at Erik, who inclined his head again. The prince turned on his heel and walked off without saying goodbye.

*****

Elena cursed at the sight of Tarrick walking away. After promising to explain everything, he had palmed off the task to his sister. Her hand tingled at the memory of their handshake, and she tried not to think about what his hands would feel like on other parts of her body. She turned to Adina with an expectant expression on her face.

"I promise he's more charming than this," Adina sighed. "They're already on edge with the Peace Summit coming up, and now with an attempt on his and Uncle Zanthus's lives, everyone is so jumpy."

Elena didn't respond and stared glumly at the ground instead.

"It's not all bad." Adina nudged her. "He'll come around once it all dies down."

"I should have just stayed at the hotel that night," Elena muttered.

"I know it's not the holiday you planned," Adina said gently. "But we can still have fun together. There will be feasts and parties during the Peace Summit this week."

Elena looked at her inquiringly.

"I should probably tell you where you are first." Adina tapped her chin with a finger.

"That would be a good start," Erik said drily, relaxing his stance now that the prince had left. He continued glancing at the entrance to the clearing in case anyone else should come by unexpectedly.

"Elena, meet Erik, my *personal* guard." She winked at the attractive man. He bowed his head at Elena, fighting back a grin at Adina's frivolous manner. "Erik, this is Elena."

"So I gathered," he laughed, white teeth flashing against his dark skin.

"Nice to meet you," Elena said. "Perhaps *you* could tell me where I am and what's going on? I've been promised an explanation, but no one has told me anything yet."

"You're in the country Terralea, in the enchanting realm of Leneira," Adina told her with a dramatic flourish. "Home to their Majesties, King Arran, Queen Amaya, and their Royal Highnesses Prince Tarrick, Prince Leon, and Princess Adina." She pointed to her own chest, grinning.

Elena blinked slowly, trying to process.

"Enchanting?"

Adina's eyes twinkled mischievously as she extended her hand. A flickering ball of fire formed in her palm, and Elena's jaw dropped in amazement. Just as she was about to say something, Adina closed her hand, then reopened it to reveal a cluster of shimmering water droplets glistening in the sunlight like tiny diamonds.

"Here, hold this." Adina thrust the flower she had been holding at Elena, who took the flower and watched as the crinkled pink petals closed and opened as though an invisible hand was pinching the petals together.

"She's manipulating the wind," Erik told her.

"We're Elementals," Adina explained. "We can control and influence the elements. The people who live in Skandor are Shifters—they have the ability to change into wolves—and the Sailonese are Empaths—they can read minds and emotions."

"You're joking!" Elena exclaimed.

Adina shook her head, grinning.

"An Empath would have been useful in that meeting," Elena said.

"You sound like Leon," Adina laughed sympathetically. "He keeps pushing to have ambassadors from every country. But he seems to be fixated on the Empaths for some reason," she mused more to herself. "Don't worry. Our council members know you're not a rebel or a threat to us, but they have to keep up appearances and go through the process."

"Who are these rebels? Everyone keeps talking about them."

The smile faded from Adina's face. "They are Leneirans who don't have any special abilities. There have always been conflicts between those who have abilities and those who don't. The last rebel uprising was horrific. It happened a hundred years ago, and thousands of people died from both sides."

"Was this when the human woman was here?" Elena asked, remembering the uproar it had caused at the meeting.

"What woman?" Adina asked curiously.

Elena shrugged, surprised the princess didn't know. "Lord Zanthus said she almost brought the realm to its knees."

Adina studied Elena for a moment. "I don't know anything about this. But I'll find out." She glanced up at Erik, who wore a blank expression. He lifted a shoulder in response to her silent question and shook his head. Evidently, he didn't know about the woman either.

"So, if you can manipulate the elements, how did so many people die?" Elena asked.

"Our powers aren't infinite," Adina explained. "It takes a toll on us when we use them, and depending on the strength and level of training an Elemental has, recovery times can be long. It's the same for Empaths and Shifters. Even the most powerful of them need time to restore their abilities"

"I see. So if Leneirans can manipulate the elements, shift into wolves, and read minds, how did so many people die?" Elena furrowed her brow, still unable to comprehend the devastation when those without power had gone up against Elementals, Shifters, and Empaths.

"Our abilities give us an edge, but when faced against hundreds of people using weapons made of bluestone, it's pretty much an even playing field," Erik spoke up.

"They mentioned bluestone too," Elena said.

Erik nodded. "The only substance known to nullify our abilities."

"We think the assassin used a bluestone bullet," Adina said somberly. "I had to wait for the royal physician to remove all of the shards where you were hit before I could heal you."

Elena rubbed the scar, feeling queasy.

"Don't worry," Adina assured her. "We made sure every little bit was removed. You shouldn't feel any effects."

"It doesn't affect those without elemental powers," Erik said in response to Elena's concerned look.

"That's why they keep trying to overthrow the rulers and take out Elementals, Shifters, and Empaths—so they can take control of the land," Adina continued. "There are rebel factions along the borders of Terralea and Skandor."

"Are all powerless Leneirans rebels?"

Adina shook her head. "We used to have ordinary Leneirans living in Terralea," she said sadly. "They were born here, but it was difficult for them to find work. Those of us who can use our powers work faster and more efficiently. Now, most of them live in Sailon under Queen Lin's protection."

"The Empaths know when someone is lying to them," Erik said. "So it's pointless for rebels to infiltrate her country. There are Leneirans on the Isles of Minos, too, where there are only a handful of Seers with the ability of foresight."

"What about Sk-Sk—" Elena asked, fascinated.

"Skandor," Adina supplied.

"It's mostly barren, icy lands," Erik told her. "The people there are just as cold and unfriendly as the land. The Shifters are able to survive in their wolf forms. I can't imagine anyone without at least the power to control fire living there by choice."

Elena mulled over the information.

"You can also heal?" she asked Adina.

"I can." The princess nodded. "Some Leneirans are blessed with extra abilities. I can heal, our father can wield lightning, and Tarrick can shift into a jaguar with impenetrable skin and metal claws."

Elena's eyes widened as she tried to imagine such a beast. As Adina listed off the royals from the other Leneiran countries, Elena pinched herself several times to make sure she wasn't dreaming. She was starting to feel like the assassin at large was the least of her worries.

~ 7 ~

"A dina!" a male voice rang out in the garden. "Are you out here?"

"Over here," Adina called back. "It's Leon," she told Elena.

The prince appeared in the clearing and broke into a smile.

"Our esteemed guest." He threw out his arms and glided over to where they were seated. "A pleasure to formally make your acquaintance. And a thousand apologies for my earlier thoughtless comments," he ended with a flourish of a bow.

Elena held out her hand to shake his, but instead, he dragged it up to his lips and brushed a light kiss over her knuckles.

"Dramatic," Adina muttered, rolling her eyes. Erik's mouth twitched, but he bowed respectfully to the prince.

"I must congratulate you," Leon told Elena, ignoring his sister. "I haven't seen our brother and uncle this rattled in years. You must teach me your ways."

"I apologize if I've offended them." Elena bit her lip. Perhaps she should have toned down her sarcasm and checked her anger earlier.

"Not at all!" Leon laughed. "It's quite entertaining."

"Leon," Adina warned. "Don't upset Elena. She's been through enough."

"My apologies again," he said, blue eyes twinkling. "It seems to be a habit around you. But I must admit, I can't think clearly around a woman who carries a police badge and throws herself in front of my brother to save his life."

Elena cringed at his words, but Adina stared at her in awe.

"You're a police officer?" she asked, sounding impressed.

"My parents were. I was carrying my mother's badge," Elena said shortly.

Adina looked at Elena shrewdly but didn't probe.

"So are you gossiping about the feasts and balls coming up?" Leon asked, going red and changing the subject quickly.

"Hardly," his sister snorted. "We've been teaching her about Leneira."

"It's a fascinating place," Elena said.

"Not as fascinating as the human realm," Leon sighed. "All that progress and innovation."

Elena shrugged. "I guess. The magic here seems more exciting."

"Leon and Tarrick have both spent time in the human realm," Adina said. Elena noted the jealousy in her voice. "But that was before the uprising. Since then, the Royal Council said it was too dangerous for me to study there as they did."

"You studied in the human realm?" Elena asked curiously. "Why?"

"Tradition," Leon explained. "All members of the royal family and some nobles spend time in the human realm to learn from your world. We like to scope out any technology or advancements we can bring back to Leneira. Our grandfather installed Terralea's plumbing system, and Father brought back fountain pens." He grinned. Adina snorted, and Erik let out a bark of laughter.

"Electricity would have been useful," Elena mumbled, thinking of her phone. Not that charging the broken device would have helped.

"My brother wanted to go as far as establishing human-Leneiran relations. It was a nice dream at the time, and might have worked if the rebels hadn't tried to wipe us all out," Leon shrugged. Despite his blasé attitude, he shuddered at the memories.

Elena sat up in amazement. "Hang on! You mean the uprising from a hundred years ago? How old are you?" she exclaimed.

"Leon's *old*," Adina drew out the word while Leon nudged her.

"You don't look older than thirty." Elena squinted at his face.

"I knew I liked you from the start," he beamed.

Adina shook her head. "You spend enough time and money at the apothecary in Erindell on all those lotions and potions."

"And it's clearly paying off," Leon shot back at her. "Take note, little sister. One day, you'll be begging for my secrets."

"I have plenty of time before I need to worry about looking like an old shoe," Adina sniffed.

Erik's shoulders shook with silent laughter. "Leneirans can live hundreds of years," he explained to Elena over the bickering siblings. "The oldest recorded Leneiran was almost 800 years old before they passed on."

Elena's head spun at the thought of living for 800 years, but she saw her chance. "Who was the human woman your uncle mentioned?"

All traces of good humor and playfulness left Leon's face.

"Yes, Leon, do tell us about this woman," Adina leveled a stare at her brother.

"What woman?" Leon asked innocently.

"You tell us," Adina persisted.

"The one Lord Zanthus said almost brought the realm to its knees," Elena supplied, leaning forward to watch the prince's reaction.

"He was being dramatic, as usual," Leon said lightly, but his jaw tightened and expression turned wary. "She must have been visiting the realm at the time. I was at the portal outpost and didn't get to meet her. Adina, you were a baby and didn't know anything beyond your next feed and diaper change."

Adina stuck her tongue out at him. "Like you knew any better when *you* were a baby."

"Anyway," Leon said loudly. "It's been a long time since humans were here and everyone is on edge. Which is why we need to keep the fact that you're a stranger to the realm a secret, Elena."

She stared at him in disbelief. "This is ridiculous," she finally huffed. "I can't go back, and I'm in danger if I stay. What am I supposed to do? Hide in my room for the entire summit?"

"That was Uncle Zanthus's suggestion." Leon gave a nervous laugh. "But Tarrick and Father talked him out of it."

Elena scowled and noted the way Leon rubbed his chin awkwardly—the same way Tarrick had earlier. She shook her head to clear away thoughts of the enigmatic prince and focused on what Leon was saying.

"We'll tell everyone you're a friend of Adina's visiting for the week," he explained. "The council decided it was the best way to protect you."

"What if someone asks me to light a candle?" Elena asked sarcastically. "They'll realize I have no magic when I ask for a box of matchsticks."

"You'll always have Adina, Tarrick, or myself with you," he promised. "We'll deter people asking you to light candles or refill water glasses," he added, trying to lighten the mood again.

Elena chewed her bottom lip, thinking over the plan.

"I'm so glad you'll be here for the celebrations, Elena!" Adina said excitedly. "My vision for one of the feasts is a gold theme."

"Classy," Leon snorted, then yelped when the princess poked him in the ribs.

"We'll need to mark her," Adina said, picking up Elena's slim wrist and turning it over to examine the inside.

"Excuse me?"

Adina, Erik, and Leon held up their left hands to show her the mark on their inner wrists. It appeared to be a compass with detailed images in each quadrant; the crest of Terralea that was embroidered on the guards' tunics.

"All Leneirans are born with the mark of the country and lineage they're born into, regardless of whether they have powers or not," Adina explained.

"You are not tattooing me!" Elena exclaimed, yanking her hand out of the princess's hold.

"It won't be permanent. We'll just use black ink and reapply it as it fades," Adina told her.

"You're now Lady Elena, daughter of Lord Taib from Selindor province," Leon declared, smiling at her. "You went to school with Adina here in the Royal Quarter while your father was on the Council of Nobles and serving at the palace. You're visiting your dear friend after many decades apart."

"So after being accused of conspiring with rebels to kill your brother and uncle, I'm now a hundred-year-old tattooed aristocrat" —Elena lifted a brow— "who has to blend in with the rest of the Elementals and constantly be on my guard in the presence of other royal visitors."

"I thought it was a good cover," Leon mumbled.

"This was *your* idea?"

"It was better than keeping you locked up in your room for a week," he said defensively.

Elena stared at the prince. "Are all of you this dramatic?" But a shiver ran down her spine as she recalled Adina's descriptions of the Shifter beasts and other powers that Leneiran royalty could wield.

"We definitely would have been friends if you had been at school with me." Adina laughed.

"Am I the only one who can see the many ways this plan can go horribly wrong?" Elena shook her head in frustration.

"Don't worry," Leon said soothingly. "It took some convincing, but the royal council agreed to the plan and are all on board. Only they and a few trusted guards" —his eyes flicked to Erik, who nodded— "and palace staff know about your real identity."

"Nice to know they agree on something," Elena muttered.

"They're all under strict orders to go along with the plan while King Halder and Queen Lin are here," he continued.

"Won't Queen Lin know it's a lie?" Elena pointed out. "She's an Empath, right? She'll know straight away that we're all lying to her."

Leon shook his head. "Empaths need to make physical contact with the person they're reading. Well, we can shield our minds from her, but it takes decades to master that skill," Leon rambled. "Maybe just don't dance with any Empaths or shake their hands. Just to be on the safe side." He gave her a wry smile.

"How will I know who's an Empath?" Elena asked, anxiety spiking through her once more. "And what will happen if someone finds out?"

"Leon, stop scaring Elena," Adina scolded. "Lin is amazing. She has strong morals." The princess turned to Elena. "Don't worry, as long as you're not a threat to us, she won't reveal your secret."

But Elena was far from reassured.

"She's a good queen," Leon agreed. "You'll like her. But we need to protect you from Halder, his entourage, and all the other Terraleans who will be staying here this week."

"I don't get a say in this, do I?" Elena sighed.

"I'm afraid not."

"Would've been nice to be consulted on this plan before roping me into it," she grumbled.

"We've had to move quickly," Leon explained. "Word of the attack on Tarrick and Uncle Zanthus has already spread, but no one knows the details, and we want to keep it that way. It's for everyone's safety."

Leon might have put forward a convincing argument, but Elena had an uneasy feeling the danger was within the palace walls. Unfortunately, she still didn't know enough about the realm and its people to voice her concerns. She reminded herself about the deal she struck with Tarrick, and that she would only have to go along with the charade for a few days.

"Alright." She sighed again, addressing Adina. "Tell me everything I need to know about Lady Elena."

~ 8 ~

"**J**ust tell me about my life and what I would have learned in the last hundred years," Elena said wearily.

"You should know Terralea's royal history," Leon mused out loud, rubbing his chin again. "As much of it as possible."

"Be realistic, Leon," Adina huffed. "No one is going to ask her about the last dynasty or Grandfather's preferred water pipe flavor. She's a lord's daughter, not a princess-in-training."

"Someone might," Leon muttered. "I wouldn't put it past Halder's people."

"One of us will be with her to deflect or answer any of those questions," the princess pointed out.

"Your father is Lord Taib," Leon told her. "He oversees all agricultural production in Terralea."

"He has the largest wheat and grain farm in Terralea," Adina added. "And travels around the country to check in on other farmers and suppliers. He reports to the palace once a month to inform Father of how the harvest is faring and if anyone needs additional resources or has a surplus of produce that can be traded with Sailon and Skandor."

"Why isn't he here now?" Elena wondered.

"The Council of Nobles don't stay at the palace during Peace Summits, except for one representative, which is Lord Rokeby this year," Leon explained. "They essentially run the country and tend to their own responsibilities. With the upcoming harvest season, Lord Taib needs to be on the ground, so to speak, looking after

Selindor while the royal council deals with King Halder and Queen Lin."

Elena nodded, relieved at Leon's simplified explanation of Terralea's political structure. "And what do I do when I'm on the farm?"

Leon opened his mouth to answer, then closed it, frowning. "Cut wheat?" he suggested.

Adina rolled her eyes at the brother.

"Trust *you* not to know what a lady does," she said, ignoring the middle finger Leon displayed in response.

"Ladies outside Erindell visit members of their community, host events, manage their households, receive other lords and ladies, keep up with their correspondence..." She listed everything, counting with her fingers.

"It sounds very different to what I used to do," Elena muttered, rubbing her arm, feeling as though she had traveled back in time.

Erik gave her a sympathetic smile.

"*That's* what ladies do?" Leon asked in horror. "That sounds awful."

"If you spent less time preening in the mirror and more time amongst our people, you would know it's not all bathhouses and coffee shops," Adina said loftily, flicking an insect off her pants.

"I don't preen," Leon shot back.

"Beauty fades, but dumb is forever," she said smugly.

Leon opened his mouth to fire back a retort, but Erik cleared his throat to keep the siblings on track. They continued to pile Elena with information and quiz her on everything she had learned so she was word-perfect on the details of her life as "Lady Elena."

Elena's head spun with information that Leon and Adina had thrown at her, along with the odd interjection and additional detail from Erik. She was taught how to address the royal families, titles, and the proper way to curtsy—her knees protested at having to bend awkwardly over and over again until Adina declared it was perfect.

The sun had made its way across the sky. The shadows were longer, and the sky boasted vivid streaks of neon pinks, oranges, and yellows fading into the dark purple night. A cool breeze swept through the garden—a brief reprieve from the heat of the day. Torches dotted around the gardens came to life with dancing flames that Elena suddenly realized were lit with Elemental magic.

The flames adjusted so every leaf and blade was illuminated in the area, a few patrolling guards altering the brightness as they passed. She thought back to all the breezes and changes in the air, wondering how many had been natural and how many had been Elementally controlled.

"It's dinnertime," Leon announced, standing up and rubbing his stomach. He offered an arm to Elena.

She walked back to the palace with the trio for the evening meal, which Leon informed her would be held in the family's private dining area. Elena tried to protest, insisting she was perfectly happy eating in her room. Leon and Adina ignored her, and she found herself being frogmarched to a brightly lit dining room where the king, queen, Tarrick, and Zanthus were already seated around a large round table. The dining room was simply furnished and decorated with accents of color in the embellishments to add warmth.

Leon and Adina slid into their seats, leaving Elena the empty chair next to Tarrick, who stood up and pulled out the chair for her to take a seat. Zanthus narrowed his eyes and pressed his lips into a thin line but said nothing.

"Thank you," she murmured as she lowered herself into the cushioned chair.

"How was your afternoon, my dear?" Amaya asked kindly. She and Arran looked at Elena almost fondly, and she gave them a slight smile in return. It was a completely different atmosphere than the council chamber earlier.

"It was good, Your Majesty," she replied, glancing at Leon, who nodded approvingly at her correct use of the title. "Prince Leon and Princess Adina filled me in on everything I need to know."

"There's no need for formalities with us," Leon said, winking at Elena. "You can just call us Leon and Adina."

Zanthus gave Leon a disapproving look that the prince pointedly ignored.

"You're related to the royal family, Lord Zanthus?" Elena asked politely.

"Was it his charm and wit that gave it away?" Leon smirked.

"He's my brother." The queen was amused. "We come from a nomadic tribe in the north known for our distinctive eyes."

"They're beautiful," Elena said, gazing into the blue depths of the queen's kind orbs. It wasn't just the color; her gentle, motherly nature comforted Elena.

"Why, thank you," Leon quipped, earning himself an eye roll from Adina.

"Here." Tarrick placed a glass of wine in front of her, and Elena accepted it gratefully. Forgetting herself for a moment, she took a large gulp to soothe her nerves, earning a giggle from Adina. Realizing too late what she had done, Elena tried to plaster a dainty smile on her face to cover up her embarrassment.

Tarrick looked at her in amusement. Without taking his eyes off her reddening face, he reached out for a carafe of wine that floated over to his outstretched hand. He refilled her glass as Leon took a large gulp of his own wine, smacking his lips enthusiastically, drawing the entire table's attention to himself.

Zanthus cleared his throat and addressed Arran, moving swiftly over the awkward moment.

"I have prepared the contracts for Halder and Lin," he said. "I can bring them to your office tonight to review before they arrive tomorrow."

Amaya frowned at the turn in conversation.

"We can review them in the morning," Arran told Zanthus as he sipped his own wine. "They don't arrive until the evening. We have plenty of time."

"But we will also need to go over the contingencies and strategies—" Zanthus started to argue, but the king cut him off.

"Zanthus, we have a guest, and it's already been a long day." Arran gestured toward Elena. "I will look over everything tomorrow morning."

"Very well," Zanthus acceded, lowering his head and glaring at his glass of wine as if it had personally offended him.

The door opened, and palace staff dressed in embroidered cream tunics carried in platters of food, which they laid in the middle of the table.

"Please help yourself, Elena." Amaya offered her a smile, waving a hand elegantly over the spread.

"Try this stew," Adina said eagerly, passing over a large bowl filled with a wonderfully spiced casserole that made Elena's mouth water. "It's my favorite."

Elena helped herself to a little bit of everything that Leon and Adina sent her way. They explained the flavors that she could expect so the spices and heat weren't a surprise. She was so enthralled by the explosions in her mouth that she didn't notice Tarrick refilling her wine glass and smiling slightly at her reaction every time she tried a new dish. Arran nudged Leon and passed down a few platters, indicating he should send them Elena's way.

"Well, I'm glad to see you have enjoyed the food." The king chuckled at the sight of her empty plate. "Tell us more about yourself, Elena?"

She swallowed a mouthful of food and looked at him thoughtfully.

"I'm afraid I live a very solitary, uninteresting life, Your Majesty," she finally said.

"I'm sure that's not true." The king studied her with twinkling eyes. "A beautiful, vibrant young woman like yourself must be living a full life."

Elena blushed at the compliment before looking back at Arran with a wrinkled forehead. She tilted her head to the side. "You must have confused me with someone else, Your Majesty," she said, a shy smile playing on her lips.

Leon snorted into his bowl of stew, and Adina giggled. Arran's smile widened, and Elena's shoulders dropped further as she relaxed into the meal and company.

"I work sixty-hour weeks, and on the weekends, I go for long walks and read books." She shook her head ruefully at how pathetic she had let her life become in the past few years. "I used to go out to jazz clubs. I love music."

"Why did you stop?"

"I didn't have anyone to go with," she said after a pause, unsure if it was appropriate to bring up her ex-boyfriend to the king. He had hated jazz, and dragged Elena to baseball games instead, insisting she would come to enjoy the sport in time. She hadn't. "I also run. I enjoy running marathons."

"Mar-a-thons," Adina said slowly. She looked at Elena inquiringly.

"They're long running sessions," Elena explained. "I usually run about thirteen miles. It takes me two hours."

"You do that *willingly*?" Adina exclaimed, looking equal parts revolted and horrified.

Elena laughed hard and scanned the table to take in everyone else's reactions. Her eyes locked with Tarrick, who was staring at her intently. Elena's cheeks heated under his gaze.

"Perhaps you should try it, Adina," Leon chuckled.

"I can think of much better ways to spend two hours," Adina shuddered.

"Like spending your afternoons at the coffee shops in Erindell, gossiping with the locals?" Leon rolled his eyes.

"Running helps me think." Elena reluctantly turned back to Adina.

"What could you possibly think about for two hours?"

Elena dipped her head and mumbled, "stuff."

"What st—"

"Adina, you're prying," Tarrick interrupted, cutting off his sister's line of questioning.

Elena shot him a grateful look, and he nodded his head a fraction, a soft, understanding expression on his face.

"Good to know fifty years in school and university has done wonders for your intellect," Leon said drily to Adina. The princess gave him a disdainful look and turned her head to the side, pretending to scratch her cheek with her middle finger in Leon's direction. Arran chuckled softly as Amaya closed her eyes and shook her head in despair.

"Do you do manual labor?" Adina asked Elena.

"No," she told her. "I sit at my desk all day and work at a computer. Running also helps me stretch out my legs and forces me to move."

"Computer?" Adina wrinkled her forehead at the unfamiliar word.

"Those machines I told you about," Leon explained. "The ones where you can write correspondence and work on calculations."

Elena smiled at the overly simplistic explanation.

"Interesting." Adina turned to Elena in wonder. "Perhaps I could accompany you back to the human realm and spend some time learning about your world. But don't put me down for running."

Elena opened her mouth to tell Adina that she would gladly show the princess where she lived, but Tarrick cut in.

"Adina, the human realm is too dangerous for you."

"Elena seems to manage just fine," his sister argued.

"She did get shot," Leon muttered.

"Not. Helping. Leon." Adina narrowed her eyes at her brother.

"We'll discuss it another time," Arran said firmly, putting an end to any further argument on the subject.

The staff returned to clear the empty dishes when everyone had eaten their fill. A tray of colored glasses filled with steaming mint tea was placed in front of Elena, along with sugared jellies and sweets in crystal bowls. Everyone helped themselves to tea and sweets, including Elena, despite her full stomach.

When she sat back in her chair, a smile playing about her lips, Tarrick murmured to her in a low, teasing voice, "Who knew all it took to simmer down all that anger was a proper meal."

Elena gave him a lazy smile, too happy and relaxed after the most delicious meal of her life to snap back a retort. In a food-filled daze, she took in the handsome features of his face—the chiseled jaw, high cheekbones, straight nose, thick, arched brows, and glowing amber eyes. He wasn't smiling, but the tension that previously lined his face had disappeared. His expression softened as he tilted his head slightly, watching her.

"Mom always used to carry snacks with her when I was a kid." Elena laughed despite herself. "She said that whenever I got cranky, all I needed was food or a nap."

Leon opened his mouth to comment, but Adina nudged him to be quiet. The king watched the exchange with an indulgent smile.

The beginnings of a smile on Tarrick's face took shape when a small coughing fit from the other side of the table interrupted their conversation. His head snapped toward his uncle. Zanthus beat his chest with a fist and took a large gulp of tea to clear whatever was lodged in his throat, muttering under his breath.

"This was all delicious." Elena turned to Arran and Amaya, smiling. "Thank you so much for your hospitality," she directed her gratitude toward Zanthus in an effort to make amends for their earlier hostilities, but the royal advisor ignored her as he sipped his tea.

"I'm so glad you enjoyed it, my dear," the king said delightedly. "I'm sure my children have told you to expect official events and parties over the next few days. They will be feasts for all your senses."

"I'm looking forward to it," she said, genuinely interested in seeing the Peace Summit unfold after hearing so much about it. "Will I be required to attend all of the events?"

"Not the meetings that take place during the day," Zanthus answered. "The evening meals, yes. Tomorrow night's welcome feast will be just a small taste of what to expect, as our guests will have traveled a long way to be here, but the following nights will showcase the best of Terralea. There will be food, music, and dancing unlike anything you would have seen," he said smugly.

Elena nodded and smiled politely at the presumptuous statement. She had already encountered men like Zanthus—entitled with an overinflated sense of self-importance. They never paid attention to the people they deemed lesser. Instead, they pandered to those in power in the hopes of getting a slice of the spotlight and taking credit for work they never did themselves.

"So I'm free to do whatever I want during the day?" Elena asked, hoping she wouldn't be told to stay in her room the whole time.

"Yes," Tarrick spoke to her directly. "I'll assign a guard to stay with you. You're free to explore the palace and the Royal Quarter, but for your own safety, Erindell is off-limits."

"On that note, we should all stay within the safety of the Royal Quarter during the Peace Summit," Zanthus added, his eyes darting between Leon and Adina. They stared back at their uncle with unreadable expressions on their faces.

Elena remembered the younger siblings telling her about Terralea's capital city. It sounded exciting, with innumerable alleys and corridors lined with artist studios, galleries, tea and coffee shops, eateries, bathhouses, and historical places of interest that led to the central open-air market square. According to Adina and Leon, the market served a dual purpose; it was filled with local vendors selling fresh food and daily items during the day, and by night, it was the heart of the town's entertainment, with live performances and events taking place.

"The palace library has plenty of reading material to occupy your time," Zanthus said, seeing the disappointment on Elena's face. "The archivists and scribes would be happy to help you find something suitable."

"Thank you," Elena said, deciding to omit asking if Zanthus considered the spicy romance novels she indulged in "suitable."

"We should retire for the evening, my dear," Arran said to his wife.

"Yes," the queen agreed, standing up and placing her napkin on the table. "But I shall walk Elena to her room first."

Everyone trooped out of the room behind Elena and the queen, who soon parted from the others. They walked toward the guest wing of the palace, and Amaya glanced behind to make sure they were out of earshot.

"I wanted to thank you personally for what you did for my son and my brother," she told Elena. "With the summit coming up, I wasn't sure we would get the chance to speak privately.

"You see, I may be queen, but I am a mother first and foremost, and my family is my world. I wanted to let you know that if you feel lonely or wish to speak to someone about anything." She stopped and stared at Elena with her brilliant blue eyes. "*Anything at all, my dear, I will gladly listen.*"

"That's very kind of you, Your Majesty," Elena murmured, breaking eye contact and staring at the ground. Her chest tightened. The maternal warmth and comfort in Amaya's words was something Elena had missed deeply. She was suddenly fearful that her darkest thoughts and feelings weren't as well hidden as she'd thought.

As though reading her mind, the queen explained gently, "I'm over 500 hundred years old. I have seen everything—more than you can imagine, including the untimely loss of loved ones."

Amaya hesitated before reaching out a hand to take Elena's and squeeze it gently. "I know you felt it was a violation of privacy when Leon mentioned we had access to your therapy records."

Elena grimaced at the memory of the council chambers, the accusations, the uncertainty, and having to defend herself.

"I won't apologize for the steps we took to keep our people safe." Amaya shook her head slightly. "But I can assure you that only those of us with the highest clearance and discretion read those, myself included. When I read about your mother and father..." Her voice caught as she trailed off sadly. "Only those of us who have been through the same things recognize the signs in others."

Elena nodded, touched by the queen's kindness and understanding.

"I know the last few months have been difficult, but I can see you are strong and will get through this," Amaya told her. "You may feel like a shadow of yourself right now, like there's no hope, but remember, even in the darkest night, a star can shine brightly if it so chooses to."

Elena squeezed Amaya's hand, feeling a lump in her throat. They walked in silence the rest of the way to her room.

"How did you know? How did you get through it?" Elena asked hesitantly. "How did you move past the anger?"

"In these situations, we are rarely angry at the people who left us," Amaya replied softly. "We find it more difficult to be kind and forgiving in order to move on, so we direct our anger at those who are no longer with us, thinking it will make us feel better."

Elena opened her mouth to speak, but closed it again, shaking her head.

"It's so easy to blame ourselves for so much that goes wrong," Amaya said gently. "But you should know there was nothing you could have done to change things. What other people choose to do is beyond our control."

"I thought Mom didn't love me enough to keep herself safe, throwing herself in front of a stranger to save their life." Elena said in a low voice, sadness sweeping over her. "Just before the bullet hit me, I think I had some clarity that she was just doing her job as a good person in this world. But it hasn't stopped me from feeling angry at what she did and blaming her for my unhappiness since she died."

"During one of the worst wars in our history, I blamed myself for the deaths of my loved ones who went into battle until I realized that nothing I did changed the fact that people were dying around me every day." Amaya sighed. "I had to change *my* thinking, otherwise, I would fall into that dark pit of despair where I would be even less helpful to my family. To my people.

So, every night, I reminded myself that I had made it through another day when so many others hadn't. Every day I lived was a gift. It gave me strength knowing my loved ones were watching over me, seeing me *live* and doing what I could to serve others and fulfill my duty. And then I met Arran, and when I trusted him enough to talk about it, I realized I was stronger than I'd let myself believe. I began to find the joy in living again."

"I just feel so alone," Elena whispered, blinking back the tears that had gathered while Amaya had been speaking.

"My darling, you are never alone," the queen said, taking her chin and lifting it. A tear spilled onto Elena's cheek that Amaya gently brushed away with her thumb. "We carry our loved ones in our hearts. I feel as though I have met your mother through you. She would be so proud of you for living up to her legacy. That talisman you carry with you may be a physical reminder of her, but your actions are your mother's spirit guiding you."

Hope swelled in Elena's chest. Hope she had not felt for a long time.

"Thank you, Your Majesty." She gave the queen a crooked smile. "I needed to hear that."

"You *are* stronger than you believe right now. I hope you realize that and choose to shine brightly again," Amaya told her. She bade Elena goodnight at her door and embraced her before turning and making her way to her private quarters.

Elena's room was bathed in a soft glow from candles dotted on the bedside tables and in the bathing chamber. She washed her face and brushed out her hair before opening her suitcase and pulling out her own pajamas, glad for something familiar and comforting to wear after a whirlwind day.

She blew out the candles and lay in bed staring at the ceiling in the dark, wondering if it had all been a dream and reflecting on Amaya's words. The events of the long day and barrage of information caught up with her, and her breathing slowed down along with her thoughts. Before she had a chance to drift to sleep, a sound at her balcony had her jolting up in bed and clutching the blanket to her chest. With her heart in her mouth, she watched a shadowy figure silhouetted by moonlight creep through the parted curtains at the balcony into her room.

~ 9 ~

Elena sat up in bed and squinted in the dark, her heart pounding. Before she could call out, the candle on her bedside table flickered to life, a low flame illuminating Adina's face. The princess held a finger to her lips in warning.

"Hurry up and get dressed," she urged Elena, throwing a bundle at her.

"Why?" she hissed.

"We're going out!"

"Out where?"

"To the Full Moon Festival in Erindell. Hurry up! I also need to apply the mark," Adina told her, eyes darting to the door.

"Will we get into trouble if Tarrick and Lord Zanthus find out?" Elena asked, scrambling out of bed.

"They told us not to go during the Peace Summit." Adina grinned at her. "The summit doesn't start until tomorrow."

Elena shook out the outfit Adina had brought her. It was a simple dark dress with an embroidered, fitted bodice.

"Are you sure about this?" she asked the princess. "If Lord Zanthus finds out—"

"He won't!" Adina said impatiently. "Come on! You're on holiday!"

"But the rebels—" Elena started to argue

"Don't worry. I sneak out all the time and have never been caught," Adina whispered. "And there are no rebels in the city. *Trust* me, I'd know."

"How—" Elena started to ask, but Adina gave her a little shove in the direction of the washroom.

Elena's curiosity won over—especially after hearing Leon and Adina talk about the capital city—and she slipped into the washroom and changed quickly. When she returned to the bedroom, Adina was sitting at the table, focused on tracing something on a piece of paper with a stylus by candlelight. Her tongue stuck out of the corner of her mouth as she dipped the stylus into the ink pot on the table.

"Take a seat," she said in a low voice, nodding at the empty chair across. Her voice didn't leave room for argument, so Elena did as she was told. Adina instructed her to hold out her wrist.

Elena rested her arm face up on the table, and the princess bent over her wrist, meticulously drawing on the Terralean crest.

"We'll need to wear these too," Adina whispered, inclining her head toward two masks on the table that would sit across the top halves of their faces, hiding their identities. They were both pearly white with silver whorls and curling lines in intricate patterns that covered the surface. Sequins, beads, and chains embellished the edges. The masks had silver ribbons attached to the corners that could be tied at the back of their heads to hold the masks in place. "Everyone wears them at the festival."

Elena was relieved at the masks; if they were able to slip in and out of the palace without getting caught, maybe she could have a little fun with Adina. She felt a burst of excitement at the thought of experiencing Erindell's nightlife and seeing elemental powers.

Elena leaned in closer and examined the mark Adina was meticulously inking. She noticed that each quadrant of the design symbolized a different element; a delicate leaf unfurled for earth, a single water droplet captured the grace of water, vibrant flames radiated the energy of fire, and the final quadrant evoked the force of wind with swirling lines, curves, and spirals.

"It won't pass under close scrutiny," Adina said softly. "But it will do at a distance."

"It's gorgeous." Elena admired the princess's skilful design.

When the ink dried, they put on the masks, and Adina blinked to snuff out the candles. She grabbed Elena's hand and led her out to the balcony. The princess perched herself on the sill and tugged her to do the same.

"I can't jump that far," Elena said in a horrified voice.

"We're not jumping." The princess dragged a protesting Elena up onto the sill beside her. Elena shivered, but not from the cold. She glanced down at the grounds that seemed far away when she was balanced precariously on the railings of the balcony. "We're gliding."

"Wha—"

Adina clamped a hand over Elena's mouth to muffle her scream as they both leaped off. Elena let out a few colorful curses, and thoughts of death crossed her mind before a pocket of wind under her slowed their plummet to the ground below. She gasped when she landed on the gravel footpath, stumbling slightly, but Adina held her up so she didn't face-plant the ground.

"We need to be careful with the extra guards around," Adina advised. Elena didn't point out that she could count on one hand the number of guards she had seen the whole day. She trusted Adina knew if there were hidden patrols sweeping the grounds.

They crept through the gardens, keeping to the shadows and avoiding the patrols until they reached the ivy-covered stone wall surrounding the palace. Adina scanned the area, and Elena held her breath as she watched the princess scale the wall using the ivy as hand and footholds. She copied Adina's movements, feeling for secure knots and branches in the wall of leaves, and tried to land softly when they dropped over the other side.

"Almost there," Adina murmured, moving swiftly down the sloping flagstones. "This is the Royal Quarter. There are still guards."

They ran across the grounds, making it to the bottom of the hill, where they nearly collided with a patrol group when they turned around a corner. Adina tugged them to an empty coffee cart, which they ducked behind just in time as they waited for the group to move on. They made it to the outer wall marking the border of the Royal Quarter and Erindell, and were about to climb over just as someone cleared their throat behind them.

"Going somewhere, Princess?"

"Erik!" Adina exclaimed, hopping down from the ivy and turning to face her guard with an innocent smile.

The guard eyed his charge sternly. His arms were folded across his chest, and he stared down Adina, waiting for an explanation.

"I wanted to show Elena the Full Moon Festival," Adina explained, unperturbed by the guard's unsmiling expression.

"Despite Lord Zanthus's explicit instructions to stay in the Royal Quarter?"

"The Peace Summit hasn't started yet," Adina argued.

"There's an assassin still at large with intentions of hurting your family." Erik frowned. "And a growing number of rebels in Terralea, according to Lord Zanthus's reports."

"Hence the plain clothes and disguises," Adina pointed out.

"You're a member of the royal family deliberately disobeying instructions and taking a guest unprotected into Erindell," he reproached her. "Everyone is already on high alert with the Peace Summit and the attempt on your brother and uncle's lives, Adina. You should know better."

Adina bit her lip and lowered her eyes.

Elena felt guilty for wanting to see Erindell despite the dangers Erik had pointed out, but she hated feeling caged and told what to do. She wanted to rebel against Lord Zanthus and do something for herself, especially after the egotistic lord hadn't thanked her for saving his life and dismissed her at dinner.

"Come with us, Erik," she whispered to the guard.

Adina's face brightened. "Yes, come with us," she urged.

He shook his head. "I'd get into a lot of trouble with Lord Zanthus and Prince Tarrick, not to mention the king and queen."

"We won't get caught," Adina promised. "We'll get you a mask and borrow a tunic on our way."

"I took an oath to protect you, Princess," Erik said, his expression softening slightly. "I can't let you go, knowing the risks out there."

"This way, you can be with us and make sure we don't get into trouble," Adina reached out and pulled his hand. "If we get caught, I'll take full responsibility."

Erik studied Adina and sighed. "You'd sneak out even if I sent you back, wouldn't you?"

She beamed. "You know me so well."

"I've only known you your entire life," Erik muttered, glancing around to make sure there were no guards in the area to catch them. He watched as Adina scaled the ivy and jumped over to the other side. Elena grinned at him and did the same. A minute later, Erik dropped down beside her and straightened, dusting himself off.

"This is exciting," Adina breathed, her eyes sparkling and a wide smile back on her face.

"Are you sure you want to do this, Adina?" Erik asked. "It's not too late to go back."

"Yes," she exclaimed. "Elena *has* to see the Full Moon Festival."

They made their way through the winding alleyways and narrow streets of Erindell. Tall buildings rose on either side, their facades painted in bright colors that stood out even in the torchlight.

Balconies draped with flowers and trailing vines hung overhead, adding to the charm of the place. Elena tried to take in the riot of colors and the unique architecture around her. The streets were so tight it was a squeeze for the three of them to walk side by side. She couldn't imagine how crowds could move through such tiny, maze-like paths.

Drums, music, and the buzz of laughter and chatter greeted the group when they entered the market square. Elena blinked several times as she took in the large bonfire that crackled in the middle of the square, flames dancing high into the night sky, almost touching the full moon that hung low and bright.

Tents and marquees lined the edges of the square, where vendors sold food and drinks. There were colorful rugs and low tables in each tent around which poufs and stools were arranged for patrons to sit and talk. White masks covered everyone's faces as they milled about the square, holding plates and bowls of food or carrying trays of a variety of drinks.

In one corner, a man was entertaining a group of children by throwing pieces of paper folded into the shapes of birds and making them fly overhead; he held his hands up and moved them slowly to guide the paper birds.

Elena was so mesmerized she didn't notice Erik bending down to murmur something in Adina's ear. The princess nodded, and he ducked behind a tent, disappearing from sight.

In another corner, a crowd watched a young woman work over a small flame to create colored glass ornaments. Elena paused, fascinated as the woman flicked her wrist to increase the size of the flame as she worked quickly with various tools to pull and stretch the malleable glass. Her eyes flicked over to the bowl of water beside the flame, and a small stream flew out of the bowl onto the tools she was handling and slowly trickled down to cool the glass as she continued to twist and turn the piece. The crowd clapped when she held up the finished ornament—an abstract piece with coloured stripes winding around the shape, specks of metallic hues adding playfulness and charm.

"That was incredible," Elena breathed. "She made that so quickly."

"It would have taken her centuries to master her craft," Erik said, sidling back to the women. He had found a plain dark tunic and was tying a mask at the back of his head. "Those of us born with elemental powers spend decades learning to control it and use it for everyday needs."

"Come on, let's get a drink." Adina pulled them toward a tent where a heavily mustached man stood behind a table laden with small glasses on saucers. Behind him hung a small shelf lined with bottles of varying shapes and sizes, all filled with different colored liquids.

"We'll get a table," Erik said, nodding to an empty one in the tent with two small poufs. He and Elena sat down and continued people-watching while musicians played a lively tune around the bonfire. Elena turned her attention to a woman suspended in the sky, twirling and dancing with a serene smile on her face.

"She must have been a Royal Guard to be able to do that," Erik admired. "It takes a lot of energy to harness the wind and use our powers for that long. We're the only ones in the country who are trained to such a high level."

"Here we are." Adina walked over to the table, balancing a small tray holding three glasses filled with a milky liquid. She placed it down in the middle, and Erik raised an eyebrow.

"Strong start," he commented, helping himself to a glass.

"What is this?" Elena asked, taking a glass and sniffing the liquid cautiously.

"It's *araki*," Erik said.

"Terrelea's finest," Adina said proudly, taking a seat and picking up a glass. "Cheers!"

Elena tapped her glass against Erik's and Adina's and took a sip.

"It's delicious," she hummed happily as the cool, licorice-flavored drink slid down her throat. It was refreshing, with a sweet aftertaste at the back of her tongue.

"Careful, it's strong," Erik murmured.

A warm, happy feeling spread through Elena as she continued sipping. She drummed her fingers on the table in time to the beat of the music. A group of men next to them shared a water pipe that emitted a sweet, fruity cloud of perfume. The aroma lulled her into a relaxed state as she enjoyed soaking in the festive atmosphere. The noise grew louder around them as more people entered the tent for refreshments.

She barely heard Adina and Erik's explanations of what was happening as she continued taking in the sights and sounds of Erindell. The dancer in the air flew gracefully back to the ground and bowed to applause. The music morphed to an energetic, tribal drumming. Erindellians began to dance around the large bonfire, now emitting sparks and flames that portrayed the shapes of animals against the velvet night—horses, lions, jaguars, and wolves all danced hypnotically. It was an intoxicating mix of color and sound as everyone swayed and moved to the beat of the drums.

Around the fire, a man and woman held hands with a small child, all three dancing in a circle, their shapes dark silhouettes against the bright flames. The woman lifted the child into her arms, and the man stepped forward to close the gap and hold them both to him, running his hands up and down the woman's back.

Elena's gaze lingered on the couple, intrigued by the man moving gracefully despite his large frame. The swept-back hair and the way he held himself were inexplicably familiar. The intimate way the couple danced was at odds with the way the rest of the Erindellians danced in large groups. The man leaned down to murmur something in his companion's ear, and she shook her head, continuing to sway with the child in her arms. They continued to take turns to lean in and talk to each other, nodding and shaking their heads in response to what the other had said. Elena wondered how they could hold a serious conversation over the intense drumming and energetic movements of the dancers around them.

She scanned the crowd dancing around the bonfire. Adults clapped their hands and danced to the beat while children jumped excitedly, twirling and spinning out of time. Their laughter and squeals of joy mingled with the sounds of the drums.

Out of the corner of her eye, she saw a young man come over to their table and hold a hand out to Adina, requesting a dance. She followed him willingly to the edge of the crowd. They danced energetically, both their faces glowing from sheer ecstasy.

Elena noticed Erik's fierce gaze on the pair. "You should cut in," she told him.

The princess continued to dance exuberantly with the stranger, marking him every time he spun her to keep her balance. The skirt of her dress billowed out and twirled with the movement as she effortlessly followed his lead.

"I can't," he muttered. "I'm just a guard. She's a princess."

"So?"

"She will probably marry a noble, as all Terralean princes and princesses have done."

"Perhaps the two of you could change that," Elena suggested, sipping more *araki*.

"It's not done." Erik shook his head firmly.

"Change has to start somewhere."

The guard didn't reply. He continued staring morosely at the princess as she swayed her hips and threw her head back in laughter. The man clapped his hands in time to the drum beat and danced around her.

"800 years is a long time to live, wishing and regretting," Elena said.

That seemed to snap Erik out of his brooding, and he threw back the rest of his *araki*. To Elena's surprise, he stole her *araki* too and stood up.

"Attaboy!" Elena grinned.

Erik approached the couple and held a hand out to Adina, bowing at the waist. Elena couldn't see their expressions, but the man Adina had been dancing with moved toward a group of women who welcomed him into the fold. Their dresses were covered in silver coins and beads that caught the light of the flames as they shimmied and spun.

Erik pulled Adina close to him and placed his hands on her waist. She wound her arms around his neck, and they swayed slowly, ignoring the heady drumming and fast pace of the music, dancing to a tune only they could hear.

The movements and sounds around Elena were contagious, and when she could no longer resist the call of the music, she downed her drink and made her way to the bonfire. Soon, she was dancing and twirling and shaking her hips with strangers, a big grin on her face and the feeling that she was capable of anything.

She let the natural ebb and flow of the crowd move her around the fire until she bumped into someone and turned around with a laugh and apology on the tip of her tongue. Strong hands caught her shoulders to steady her. The familiar scent of cedar, sandalwood, and something masculine filled her nose and sent a jolt through her core. She looked up with her heart in her mouth to see blazing amber eyes behind a white mask staring back at her.

~ 10 ~

"**F**uck," Elena muttered.

"What the hell are you doing here?" Tarrick growled, dragging her away from the bonfire to the edges of the square. It was still crowded enough that no one paid them any attention; everyone was engrossed by the dancing and the musicians.

He pulled her behind an empty stall where they wouldn't be seen. "Well?" he demanded, standing in front of her with folded arms across his muscular chest. His glare softened as he took in the sight of her in the slightly damp black dress that clung to her curves after dancing and sweating by the bonfire.

Elena's eyes widened at the sight behind him.

A raven-haired buxom woman with red lips holding a small girl on her hips had followed them. It was the woman he had been dancing with earlier. The girl had fallen asleep and burrowed her face in the woman's hair. Chubby arms clung around her neck, and Tarrick inwardly groaned as he tracked Elena's gaze.

Elena turned back to him, but before she could say anything, the woman spoke in a husky, low voice, "We're going home now. I'll let you know if I hear anything."

Tarrick merely nodded and watched as they disappeared down the nearest alleyway.

"Is that your chi—" Elena began to ask, but Tarrick cut her off.

"You're not supposed to be here, Elena," he said, sounding angry and afraid. "Did we not make it clear that you are in danger?"

"Elena!"

They whipped around. Adina and Erik pushed through the crowd at the edge of the square to reach them. Tarrick glared at his sister when she stood in front of him.

"Tarrick, I can explain," Adina said in a rush.

"You better," he rumbled. "Do you have any idea how much trouble you're in? *All* of you."

Erik dropped his eyes to the ground, embarrassed and ashamed.

"It's my fault," Elena said, stepping in front of Adina. She craned her neck to look up at Tarrick. He raised an eyebrow above the mask. "I really wanted to see the Full Moon Festival after Adina told me all about it. *I* made them bring me into town."

Tarrick continued to stare at her without saying a word.

"I promise this will never happen again," Elena said. "I'll stay in the palace for the rest of the week."

"A pretty speech." Tarrick rolled his eyes. "But I've known my sister and all her tricks for a long time."

"Don't patronize me," Adina snapped. "If you treated me like an adult, I wouldn't have to sneak out. *You're* not supposed to be here either!"

"You need to act like an adult in order to be treated as one." Tarrick looked over Elena's shoulder at his sister.

"Fuck you, Tarrick." She glared at him. "I'm sick of everyone telling me what to do and talking to me as though I don't know what's going on."

Tarrick sighed and dropped his hands. They were starting to draw attention, and it was not the time or place to be berating his little sister.

"Erik, take them back to the palace straight away. No detours."

The guard nodded and glanced at the angry princess beside him. "Let's go," he said.

Tarrick stepped aside, and Erik led the way to a narrow, winding street off the market square. Adina stalked past her brother, fuming, and Elena followed without a word. She glanced over her shoulder to find Tarrick watching them leave. When he dragged the mask off, worry lined his face.

***

Adina grumbled under her breath the entire way back to the stone wall that marked the edge of the Royal Quarter.

"What was he even doing with that woman?" the princess asked aloud to no one in particular.

"That's Madame Zorra," Erik told her. "She owns a pleasure house in Erindell," he explained.

Adina gave him a sidelong stare. "And how do you know that?" she asked in a frosty voice.

"I've had to go there on the odd occasion to remove ... patrons ... who weren't observing the rules," he replied, sounding embarrassed.

The women stopped and stared at the guard.

"So what was Tarrick doing with *her*?" Adina asked in amazement. "And was that *his* child?"

Erik shrugged and seemed as uncomfortable as Elena felt over the night's revelations.

"He's got some nerve, telling me off for bending the rules while he's fornicating with women who own pleasure houses." Adina shook her head before continuing to make her way up the small hill.

"That's a bit harsh." Erik frowned. "Madame Zorra is a formidable woman who runs a lucrative business. And you don't know for sure that it was Tarrick's child."

Elena mentally facepalmed herself. The guard was not winning any points with the princess.

Adina snorted. "Of course you're defending that woman and the future king of Terralea."

"I didn't mean it like that." Erik shook his head and paused before softly adding, "Princess."

"How old do you think that girl was?" Elena intervened.

"Only eight years old, I should think," Erik speculated.

Adina wrinkled her forehead and mused aloud as she tried to work out what Tarrick was doing eight years before. Elena furrowed her brow. Even though she had known the prince for less than a day, he didn't seem to be the kind of man who would frequent pleasure houses, much less have secret children with one of the owners.

Elena kept quiet, determined to fight her attraction to the prince. *It's purely physical,* she told herself. It had nothing to do with the way his presence and attentiveness calmed her at dinner, or how he almost smiled at her during a civil conversation, or the way he seemed to care for Madame Zorra and the little girl.

It's none of my business, Elena told herself firmly. Besides, she was only there for a few days and had a role to play to get herself out of that mess. Getting entangled in the personal life of Tarrick would only complicate things and possibly delay her return to the human realm.

They reached the wall that lacked any ivy or climbing aids on that side. Elena watched as Erik lowered himself and locked his hands together, fingers intertwining to give Adina a leg up. She placed a foot in his hands and nimbly leaped into the air, flying over to the other side, where she landed with a soft thump.

"Your turn," Erik whispered. Elena copied Adina's movements, allowing the wind to carry her over while gravity did the rest of the work. She stumbled slightly when she landed in a crouch next to the princess, who was brushing dirt off her dress. A moment later, Erik landed next to the women, manipulating and shifting the wind to carry him over the wall, and they all silently climbed up the hill back to the palace, keeping to the shadows and hiding behind trees and bushes as guards patrolled the Royal Quarter.

They eventually reached the second wall unnoticed, and Erik gave them a boost as he had before. It wasn't long until they were under Elena's balcony.

"Now what?" she asked, realizing they hadn't told her the plan to get back into her room.

Erik and Adina exchanged a glance.

"Together?" he asked the princess, and she nodded.

"Together."

"What are you doing?" Elena hissed as she levitated off the ground.

"Getting you back up," Adina whispered back, frowning in concentration as she slowly raised her arms. Erik did the same, and the familiar pocket of wind gently lifted Elena higher and higher until she was level with the balcony. She reached out to the sill and scrambled over, glad to feel the solid surface beneath her feet. Elena decided the idea of being able to fly was more appealing than the act itself.

She peered back down into the garden and gave the couple a small wave. They waved back and slipped into the shadows hand in hand. Despite the unexpected and abrupt end to the night, Elena had enjoyed every minute of it, and she fell asleep smiling at the memories of dancing by the bonfire, carefree and surrendering to the music.

That night, she dreamed of Tarrick. Of the almost-smile he had given her at dinner and of the way he danced by the bonfire. She dreamed of the woman who spun with him, his hand on the crook of her back until Elena herself spun, the warmth of the fire flickering beside her. Until she was the woman who danced with Tarrick in the firelight.

Their eyes met, the amber in his blazing with flames when his large hand ran down her back and pulled her close, his voice whispering soft words into her ear.

~ 11 ~

Despite the late night, Elena woke just after the sun rose. She stretched out, luxuriating in the warm morning breeze that wafted through her window. It was a novelty, waking in her own time to birds chirping and the rustling of leaves instead of the blaring tones of her alarm.

A pile of neatly folded clothes was placed at the end of her bed, likely left by a maid before she woke up. Elena slipped out from beneath the sheets and quickly washed and dressed for the day. The navy dress with simple embroidery along the hem was similar to the one she had worn the day before. She tried to wrangle her hair into an elegant updo since her default ponytail seemed far too simple for *Lady Elena of Selindor*. Unfortunately, pieces of hair kept falling out of the knots and buns she attempted, so she settled for a thick braid instead. Just as she tied off the ends, there was a knock at the door.

"Hurry up, I'm starving," Leon greeted her. "We've been waiting for you and Adina."

"Good morning, Your Highness." Elena rolled her eyes but grinned at the prince, who was tapping his foot impatiently.

He grinned back and held out his arm to her. She closed the door and smiled briefly at the guard on duty, who didn't acknowledge either of them.

"They really don't like me here, huh?" she murmured, tucking her hand into the crook of Leon's arm.

"Don't be ridiculous," he said dismissively. "That's just how he is."

"You know him?" Elena asked as they walked down the hall.

Leon nodded. "That's Serkin, one of Uncle Z's guards. He's on door duty today and probably not happy about it." Leon took in Elena's clothes and hair. He wrinkled his nose. "What's with the braid? Kyra normally does elaborate updos that take *at least* an hour."

"Who?"

"Kyra," Leon repeated the name. "Mother's handmaid. She's meant to help you wash and dress while you're here."

"I don't need help," Elena replied, confused. "I'm capable of washing and dressing myself. Besides, if she's your mother's maid, I'm sure she has better things to do than style *my* hair."

Leon simply knitted his brows.

Elena scowled at him and reached behind to pat the braid, making sure all her hair was still in place. "It was nice of her to leave me the clothes so I knew what to wear," she offered.

"She brought you clothes but left without helping you dress?" Leon asked.

Elena shook her head. "She must have left them when I was sleeping. They were on my bed when I woke up."

Realization dawned on Leon's face, but he shook his head and increased his pace, practically dragging Elena along. When he didn't provide any explanations about Kyra's mysterious behavior, she asked, "Where's Adina?"

"I thought she might have been with you." Leon raised a brow. "She didn't answer when I knocked on her door."

They entered the family dining room, where the king and queen were already seated, sipping cups of tea.

"How did you sleep, my dear?" the king asked jovially.

"Very well, thank you, Your Majesty," Elena smiled, sliding into her seat.

A plate of food was placed before her, and she thanked the server, who bowed and took his place by the door. Her mouth watered at the pile of fluffy scrambled eggs dotted with specks of red pepper flakes, served on a large piece of toasted bread. The aromatic, melted spiced butter that garnished the eggs dripped down the edges. Slices of cheese, cucumber, and slivers of cured meat were placed on the side. Elena had never seen such an appetizing breakfast before.

"Please, go ahead and eat." Arran waved his hand. "We won't stay long."

The door opened and Tarrick entered, looking alert and devastatingly handsome in a formal, full-sleeved embroidered tunic. He took the seat next to Elena without looking at her, his cedar and sandalwood scent invading her senses. Again, that inexplicable pang of jealousy hit Elena when she recalled the way he and Madame Zorra had danced at the festival the previous night. She shifted slightly away from him in her seat and focused on cutting the cheese on her plate.

"How are you this morning, darling?" Amaya asked.

"I'm well, Mother," he replied, spearing a slice of cucumber from his own plate.

Adina walked in, yawning and squinting around the bright room. She wore a floaty, pale green, full-length dress with a gold embroidered belt at her waist.

"Morning," she mumbled, dropping into a chair and reaching for the glass of water in front of her.

"Are you alright, Adina?" Amaya asked.

"Just a bit tired," she replied. "Been up reading all night."

"Reading?" Leon grinned, shoveling spiced eggs into his mouth.

"I can read," Adina said defensively.

"I'm not questioning your ability." Leon rolled his eyes. "Since when are you interested in reading?"

"Keep rolling your eyes, Leon," Adina shot back. "Maybe you'll find a brain cell back there."

"Adina," Amaya reproached her daughter, but Elena caught sight of the queen's lips twitching. "It costs nothing to be nice."

"Some days, it costs me my sanity," the princess muttered before shoving a forkful of cured meat into her mouth.

"I remember how nice it was being an only child," Tarrick mused aloud. Elena choked on her tea. She had witnessed Leon and Adina arguing and jibing at each other the previous day, but it hadn't occurred to her that Tarrick might have the same sense of humor or playful streak. Every time she was with him, he was broody and serious.

"Was your household this chaotic, Elena?" Arran asked, lips twitching.

"Only during football season, Your Majesty," Elena chuckled. "My dad was very, um, passionate and very, ah, vocal when he defended his team. Even if they lost."

"Our children are not usually this uncouth." Amaya gave her an apologetic smile amidst the protests and sounds of indignation from Leon and Adina.

"I've heard worse," Elena assured the queen. "Trust me, this is a *civilized* conversation."

Amaya raised an amused brow and went back to sipping her tea with quiet dignity.

"I didn't expect a royal family to be so casual." Elena grinned at Adina.

"We don't get a lot of time to be together." Arran beamed at his family. "These are precious moments and rare occasions where we can relax and shed the formalities of royal life."

"I'm honored you feel comfortable around me." Elena's eyes twinkled at the king.

"It's best my siblings get their asinine comments out of their systems now before the Skandorians and Sailonese arrive." Tarrick grinned at Leon, who returned the smile and added his middle finger for good measure. "King Halder and Queen Lin would be scandalized by the lack of decorum and sophistication."

"Tarrick, you have another 600 years to be an ass," Leon sighed. "Why don't you take a day off?"

"Case in point." Tarrick inclined his head. "Leon, you are living proof that the Divine Beings have a sense of humor."

Adina squealed with laughter as Arran snorted into his cup of tea. Elena giggled at Tarrick's rare display of banter with his siblings and relaxed demeanor.

The queen gave Arran a look, and the king cleared his throat to put an end to the bickering. But before he could attempt to bring his offspring in line, Zanthus strode into the dining room with a large sheaf of documents that he placed in front of Leon.

The grin slid off the prince's face, and his jaw dropped at the sight. Adina craned her neck to peer at the handwritten notes, frowning as she tried to read the scribbled words.

"Your Majesties," he greeted the king and queen, ignoring the others. He was dressed formally in a dark tunic embroidered with gold thread, shiny black belt at his waist, and pressed dark pants and polished boots. The easygoing, casual atmosphere shifted, replaced by a more somber one. Adina's smile disappeared, and she turned back to her plate of food. Even Tarrick sat a little straighter, all signs of earlier playfulness having evaporated.

"I need three copies of these documents, Leon," he told his nephew. "My scribe is busy this morning."

"I was going to show Elena around the palace," Leon objected. Adina snorted.

"I'm sure Adina will be more than up to the task," Zanthus said drily, his eyes flicking between the two women.

"Tarrick, you should read the contracts Zanthus sent over this morning too," Arran told his eldest son. "They're in my office."

"I already looked over them and made my notes last night," he said.

Arran was impressed, but Amaya frowned.

"I hope you haven't been working too late," she reprimanded him.

"This is an important summit," Tarrick said. "Everything needs to go to plan."

"Already taking the reins, brother?" Leon joked.

"There are a few levies and agreements Halder will not agree to," Tarrick ignored Leon and addressed his parents. "I've suggested some compromises that might sway him."

"Very well, I'll take a look," Arran nodded.

"Will you show Elena around the palace today, Adina?" Amaya asked her daughter, who was picking at her food.

The princess nodded. "I thought I'd show her the library and training grounds."

"The training grounds?" Leon gave his sister a sidelong glance. "What for?"

"Might be interesting for Elena to see Terralea's elite in action." Adina shrugged.

"I'm happy to see everything Adina shows me," Elena said. "I'd like to understand elemental powers."

Zanthus's eyes narrowed at her, and he darted a glance at Tarrick, who wore a neutral expression.

"Halder and Lin are on track to arrive this evening," Arran told everyone. "Make sure you're at the entrance ready to greet them."

There were nods all around the table.

"Let's get out of here," Adina muttered to Elena.

Elena stood and bowed to Arran and Amaya, wishing them a good day as she followed the princess out into the hall.

"Leon is going to be cranky this afternoon," Adina predicted. "Those documents are tedious. Making copies of them is his idea of hell."

"Why did Zanthus give him the job?" Elena asked curiously. Only Tarrick's role and future were clear; he would be King of Terralea one day—and probably a good one, from what Elena had seen so far, barring his fraternization with women from pleasure houses.

"I suppose he sees Leon becoming Tarrick's advisor one day," Adina said. "But I don't think Uncle Zanthus will retire even when Tarrick becomes king. He really likes knowing the ins and outs of the country and getting involved in running Terralea."

"What will you do when Tarrick is king?"

"Marry strategically." Adina rolled her eyes.

"Really?"

"Probably," she shrugged. "That's what Uncle Zanthus and Father have hinted at."

"Do you want to marry strategically?"

"Erik and I spoke last night." Adina blushed and glanced over her shoulder to make sure they were alone.

"And?" Elena prompted, grinning from ear to ear.

"I didn't realize he had feelings for me," she said with a shy smile. "I always thought he was handsome and charming, and I feel so comfortable around him. But he's been my guard since I was a child. I didn't know if he felt the same way about me." She bit her lip.

"I take it he does?" Elena smirked.

Adina nodded, unable to hold back her smile. "He told me that he's had feelings for me for a long time but had to stay professional because he loves his job. A princess and a guard have never had relations in Terralea's history."

"I saw the way he looked at you last night when you were dancing with that stranger," Elena said happily. "I told him that maybe the two of you could change that. It's happened in my world—where royalty marry commoners—and it's worked."

"Maybe." Adina sighed. "We'd have to convince a lot of people."

"I don't see the problem." Elena shrugged. "It's not as if you're going to be queen. Wait." She stopped walking and she turned to her friend with wide eyes. "Can you become queen?"

"I've never really thought about it." Adina wrinkled her nose. "I always assumed after Tarrick, his son or daughter would rule."

They continued walking down the long corridor. Adina paused in front of a set of double doors and smiled at her friend. "Brace yourself."

She opened them slowly, and Elena gasped at the library before her. It was a large room with wall-to-wall, floor-to-ceiling shelves filled with books. Rolling ladders leaned against the shelves at every interval. Wrought iron spiral staircases in the corners at the far end of the room led up to the second and third levels. The domed ceiling was dark blue with ornate geometric patterns painted in gold and a large chandelier hanging from the middle. Dark wooden tables and chairs were tucked into the recesses of the room. Those sitting at the tables wore loose-fitting cream pants and dark green tunics. They wrote intently, consulting piles of books as they worked. Elena squinted at the tunics and the Terrelean crest embroidered in gold thread on the left sides, just like the royal guard.

"Your Highness," a soft female voice came from Adina's other side. Elena stepped around to see a gracious, red-haired curvy woman with bright green eyes. Unlike the others in the library, she wore a long, flowing dark green gown with a gold belt at the waist. "A pleasure to see you. How can I help?"

"Celine, this is Lady Elena," Adina introduced. "She's a friend visiting for the week, and I'm showing her around the palace. She loves to read and wanted to see the library."

"Welcome, Lady Elena," Celine smiled at Elena, who smiled back shyly. "I'm the head archivist of the Royal Library. You are welcome any time."

"Thank you," Elena said. "This is a beautiful space."

"That's very kind of you to say," she replied, dipping her chin. "If you need any help finding books, please don't hesitate to ask. My archivists are available to assist." She gestured to the uniformed staff, who moved slowly amongst the shelves.

"Thank you, Celine. I'm sure Lady Elena will visit very soon." Adina grinned at her friend, who was still gaping at the room.

"There are books about the human realm here, too, if you get homesick," Adina murmured when Celine glided back to her duties.

Elena pictured herself spending the week getting lost amongst the books in the library, but Adina pulled her to the main entrance, eager to get into the sunshine. She reluctantly followed the princess through the gardens to another part of the palace grounds she hadn't seen before. There were more guards in the area, clustered in groups discussing defense strategies.

"I noticed there aren't many guards inside the palace," Elena remarked.

"We lost a lot of people during the uprising." Adina nodded. "It's been difficult to recruit and replace the numbers over the years. We've had to spread out the guards who remained and were willing to join. Our people aren't trained to defend themselves, so the guards are stationed around the country. We have elite guardians at the palace. A palace guard could fight off three or four people on his own, so we have fewer here."

"Do you mean rebels or Elementals?" Elena asked, impressed.

"Both," Adina replied. "You'll see what I mean soon. We've also brought in a few more guards from the provinces just for the Peace Summit."

They came to a large clearing that had a number of training rings cordoned off with rope. A guard stood on his own, facing four others who held out their hands, preparing to launch an attack.

Training uniforms consisted of tight pants and boots for the men and ... nothing else. Elena had never seen so many bare chests in one place and had to make sure she wasn't drooling at the display of chiseled abs and hard pecs.

The women wore the same pants and boots, but had black tank tops that already clung to their bodies under the heat of the sun.

"These are the training grounds," Adina explained unnecessarily.

"Are you sure it's okay for me to be here?" Elena asked nervously. "What if Lord Zanthus doesn't want me watching the guards train?"

Adina snorted disdainfully.

"He suspects the kitchen staff of conspiring against our family even though they served my grandfather."

"Still..."

"You're not the enemy, Elena." Adina shook her head. "We have enough of those to recognize the people who are really against us."

Raised voices alerted them to an argument taking place in the middle of a smaller, dusty training ring. Zanthus, Tarrick, and a group of guards stood in the middle. The royal advisor was livid, while the guards wore expressions of frustration.

"What do you mean you've lost your abilities?" Zanthus exploded.

"We cannot manipulate the elements, my Lord," one of the guards replied, looking at the ground in embarrassment. "Our powers seem to have stopped working this morning."

~ 12 ~

"How did you find out?" Tarrick asked in a calm voice, the least ruffled of everyone gathered.

Adina moved closer, chewing her lip anxiously. Elena followed her gaze to a guard in the group—Erik.

"We were going through the drills, and six of us were unable to conjure a wall of fire the way we normally do," the guards' spokesperson explained. "We went through all the other exercises, but water, air, and earth didn't respond to our commands either."

Erik caught Adina's eye and shook his head a fraction in warning. She ignored him and walked up to her brother, Elena trailing behind.

"What's going on?" the princess demanded.

"Adina!" Zanthus exclaimed. "You shouldn't be here." He frowned at the sight of Elena.

"I want to know what's happening." Adina ignored Zanthus and stared at her brother.

To his credit, Tarrick didn't send them away. "These guards appear to have lost their elemental abilities," he explained, gesturing to the group. "As far as we know, they've all kept to their routine and stayed in the barracks." He scanned the guards assembled and paused on Erik. "Except those who were on duty last night."

Elena was close enough to see a muscle tic along Erik's jaw, but the guard said nothing as he stood to attention and stared straight ahead.

"Just six guards?" Adina raised an eyebrow at the group standing before them. A few shifted in embarrassment.

Adina scowled and raised a hand. Erik was the only guard who didn't flinch. He stood tall with a rueful smile and raised a hand half-heartedly. In the next moment, a loud smack echoed around the ring, and he reached up to wipe away water droplets dribbling down his face. His companions looked disappointed, as though hoping for a sign that the lapse in their abilities was only temporary. However, Erik was unable to manifest any Elemental defense against the globule of water that Adina had pelted at him.

"Adina!" Tarrick waved his hand toward Erik with an irritated look at his sister.

The water on Erik's face instantly disappeared, and he smoothed his features back to a stoic expression. But Elena could see the hurt and anger in his eyes.

"I'm sorry, Erik," Adina mumbled, rubbing her arm awkwardly.

"That's okay, Pri—Your Highness," Erik murmured, shoulders drooping slightly.

"Right before Halder and Lin arrive," Zanthus muttered angrily. "We cannot be seen to be weak. Our unique powers are the leverage we use to negotiate with both our allies. How can we fulfill our promises to defend Leneira if our most elite guards cannot manipulate the elements?"

"We don't know what's caused this anomaly, my Lord," the head guard spoke apologetically. Tarrick frowned at Zanthus, who continued glaring at the group in front of him that didn't react to his disparaging statements. They continued to stand tall and maintained straight faces.

"We'll send the royal physician to examine everyone. If anyone else discovers they have lost their elemental abilities, and if any of you can think of anything out of the ordinary that has happened in the past twenty-four hours, please come directly to myself or Lord Zanthus," Tarrick addressed the group. "For now, focus on the physical training exercises. We still need guards who are capable of hand-to-hand combat and using weapons. Our elemental powers are only a part of who we are."

At that, Zanthus threw Tarrick a nasty look that the prince ignored as he continued speaking to the guards. "I expect to see all of you performing your usual duties and keeping to the roster," he said firmly, indicating there would be no room for argument or exceptions.

"Yes, Your Highness," the guards all murmured and bowed. An expression of relief crossed more than a few faces, as though they expected to be punished or suspended for being unable to use their powers. They split off and chose weapons that were lined up in racks along a brick wall—swords, wooden poles, archery equipment, and a host of other lethal daggers, scimitars, and throwing knives.

"*I* can think of an anomaly that has occurred in the last twenty-four hours," Zanthus said, looking directly at Elena. He didn't bother to keep his voice down, and a few guards looked around curiously. She narrowed her eyes. The royal advisor really despised her for some reason, and the feeling was mutual.

"Uncle," Tarrick said warningly. He threw Elena an apologetic look.

"If you think Elena had anything to do with this—" Adina started to speak heatedly.

"I'm not ruling anything out," Zanthus snapped back. He turned to Tarrick. "I will not have history repeat itself and everything we have fought for destroyed by this ... human!"

The guards in their vicinity didn't bother hiding their surprise. They stopped what they were doing and stared at the argument unfolding before them. Elena's cheeks heated with embarrassment as all eyes were pinned on her.

"Enough!" Tarrick thundered. "What happened last time has no bearing on what's going on now."

"You've always had a soft spot for *human* women," Zanthus sneered. "It will be your downfall, nephew. Mark my words. She's already disrupting the guards' roster, and her presence is making the staff nervous. They remember what happened the last time a human woman entered this realm."

"This is completely different, and you know it, *Uncle*," Tarrick said in a low voice. His eyes swept the area, and he glared at the guards who had paused their training to watch Zanthus's outburst. They leaped into action when Tarrick eyed them threateningly and continued their drills. "We should report to my father and check if any other palace staff have been affected," he said stiffly before turning on his heel and walking purposefully back toward the palace without a backward glance.

Zanthus huffed angrily and swept away.

"Ass," Adina muttered, looking at their retreating backs. "He's become worse these last few weeks. He really believes *he* rules the country and not my father."

"I've had to deal with his kind before," Elena said, slipping her arm through Adina's and guiding her to a stone bench in the shade. "There's nothing you can say or do to stop a man like that."

"I wonder what that was all about." Adina tapped her chin thoughtfully. "The thing with the human woman."

"You haven't managed to find out yet?" Elena asked, disappointed.

Adina shook her head. "There's nothing in the history books about humans in Leneira since before the non-magical people came to be." At Elena's inquiring look, she added, "When a Leneiran and a human mate, their child inherits the lifespan of a Leneiran, but not the powers."

"Riiiight," Elena drew out the word, finally making sense of the division between people in the realm. "That's unfortunate."

"I know." Adina nodded sadly. "But by the time the people worked out what had happened, it was too late. An entire generation of Leneirans without special abilities were born, and they continued to populate the realm. Right before the uprising, the Leneirans were split evenly between those with special abilities and those without."

"There's really nothing recorded about what happened with this woman a hundred years ago?" Elena sighed in frustration.

"I'm sorry," Adina offered. "I'm still trying to find out what I can, but it must have happened just after I was born or when I was a baby. Leon and Tarrick are so secretive about the events leading up to the uprising whenever I ask them. With the Peace Summit coming up, everyone is on edge, and I don't want us banned from the feasts if I ask too many questions. Maybe there's another way to find out what happened."

Elena huffed in reply, kicking a pebble on the ground. She couldn't shake the nagging feeling there was more to the story.

"I hope Erik will be okay." Adina turned her head back to the ring with worry in her eyes. "He didn't mention anything about losing his powers this morning before he left for training."

"Do you know what might have caused them to stop working?" Elena asked.

"Only bluestone is known to stop our abilities," Adina replied. "And he hasn't come into contact with any. I can't imagine how any of the guards would come into contact with it. Leneirans are strictly forbidden from harvesting the stone. All three countries have guards stationed around the only known bluestone quarry to protect it as part of the agreement between Terralea, Skandor, and Sailon."

"And if it had been something he ate or drank, it would have affected all of the guards?"

"That's right," Adina nodded. "All guards eat in the barracks. The palace cooks make food for everyone, so if it had been the food or drink, we would have all been affected."

They sat in silence pondering the guards' predicament. Elena watched in fascination as the unaffected guardians threw up walls of water against flames, used the wind to help them levitate and launch aerial attacks, and stirred up the earth under their opponents' feet. Orders were barked to avoid stumbling and falling into craters. One guard found himself caught in a patch of quicksand. Another overseeing the drills called out formations and positions while those performing the exercises moved seamlessly with controlled, practiced movements to execute defensive and offensive tactics against their opponents.

Compared to the Erindellians from the previous night, whose wrinkled foreheads and looks of concentration had shown the energy and focus the manipulation demanded, the guards made it look effortless as they worked through each exercise without breaking a sweat.

"If only Father would let me be more involved with the royal council and ruling of the country," Adina said gloomily, watching the guards in the smaller training rings pick up swords and start dueling. They went through the motions as instructed, the initial deflation of having lost their powers shaken off the minute they started warming up and pairing off with each other. The sounds of blows and heavy breathing filled the air from the smaller rings as the guards sparred with each other.

"Half of Zanthus's policies go against the best interests of the Terraleans. He doesn't realize the people don't care for trade deals with Skandor. The taxes he keeps inflicting to fund our defenses are hurting their livelihoods." Adina watched Erik size up a larger guard.

They circled each other, and even from that distance, Elena caught a flash of Erik's white smile and his opponent's answering smirk. They attacked, and she gasped at the display of speed and strength when they tackled each other. Erik grunted when his opponent landed a blow to his abdomen, but he retaliated with a well-placed fist to the guard's jaw. They bounced back on their heels, arms raised and eyes locked on each other before attacking again.

"Have you told your father you want to be part of the council?" Elena asked. "It sounds like you know what your people want. It could help them more than Zanthus's assumptions about what's best for Terralea."

"I've tried." Adina chewed her bottom lip. "But he doesn't think I'm being serious. Leon and Tarrick tell me a little bit about their meetings and listen to my ideas, but even they get voted against because they're young and inexperienced."

"No one likes change." Elena frowned.

"I know!" Adina exclaimed. "But if we don't change, nothing will."

"Not going to lie, I fear change too," Elena admitted sheepishly.

Adina raised an eyebrow. "You've adapted to the change in your holiday plans quite well," she pointed out.

"I guess I have." Elena gave a small laugh. "If the royal council weren't so suspicious of me, you could have used me as an example to make your case." She chuckled. "But since I'm public enemy number one, according to Lord Zanthus, I'd probably do you a disservice by advocating for you to be on the council."

"Perhaps you could talk to my brother about it," Adina suggested.

"Leon?"

"Tarrick," Adina said with a sly smile. "I think he would listen to you."

Elena snorted. She watched a female guard with dark skin and hundreds of tiny braids pulled back in a thick ponytail step into the training ring and interrupt Erik, who had managed to wrangle his opponent into a headlock. He released the guard, who jerked up, gasping and massaging his throat. The three of them had a quick conversation before Erik nodded and stepped back.

"No, really," Adina protested. "He seems to be taken by you. I bet you could convince him to do anything."

"We've had a handful of interactions. Every time he looks at me, I think I'm in trouble." Elena folded her arms across her chest, drew her brows together, narrowed her eyes, and flattened her lips, making Adina squeal with laughter at her imitation of Tarrick. "And after last night, I'm pretty sure he's convinced I'm a bad influence."

"I guess you don't see the expression on his face when you're not looking at him." Adina's lips quirked upward.

Elena dropped her arms and looked at the princess quizzically. "What do you mean?"

"I've never seen him so torn." Adina sounded suspiciously like she was holding back laughter. "Leon was right. It is entertaining to see Tarrick rattled like this."

Elena was speechless. She turned back to the ring and watched the female guard standing in the middle. Blindfolded.

As she waited for Erik and the other guard to attack, her hold on the long wooden pole in her hands tightened. She stood with her legs slightly apart and bent at the knees, anticipating their moves.

"Although, I suppose if what Uncle Zanthus said about him and human women is true..." Adina broke off, frowning.

"Was Tarrick involved with this human woman?" Elena asked, trying to put the pieces of the puzzle into place.

"Maybe?" Adina wrinkled her forehead. "It would explain why he doesn't care for Terralean women. The lords on the Council of Nobles keep shoving their daughters his way and hinting heavily about what good matches they would make, but he always manages to give them the slip at feasts or negotiate deals without agreeing to marriage."

"He looked like he cared for Madame Zorra last night," Elena said lightly, looking away and hoping her reddened cheeks didn't betray the jealousy she felt thinking about them.

"Jealous?" Adina smirked, eyeing the blushing woman.

"No," Elena mumbled.

The female guard moved gracefully on light feet, sweeping the pole at the sound of attacks coming from the front, back, and the sides. Neither of the men got close enough to lay a hand on her, though she managed to land a few whacks across their torsos and backs when they got too close. Their grunts and cries told her she had hit her mark.

"I don't think that's a serious relationship." Adina frowned. "Or a relationship at all. There's no way my brother would be courting the owner of a pleasure house. There must have been another reason they danced together last night. And I'd *know* if he had a child in secret with her—or any woman."

They watched Erik and his opponent hold up their hands in surrender and back away from the female guard. She tore off the blindfold and smirked at the men, who were panting and doubled over in front of her. After clapping them both on the back—harder than they were expecting, judging by the way they collapsed onto the dusty ground—she sauntered out of the ring. The guard replaced the wooden pole in the rack before heading to the barracks.

"Let's go to the library and lose ourselves in some books," Adina said, standing up and sounding more like her usual cheerful self. "I'll show you where the romances are shelved."

"How do you know I read romances?" Elena demanded.

"I might have gone through your stuff," Adina admitted sheepishly. "When my brother was checking up on you while you were asleep. I saw the books you brought on your holiday."

Elena shook her head, smiling. "We need to talk about boundaries..."

~ 13 ~

Elena and Adina spent the rest of the day in the quiet library, flipping through books and browsing the shelves. No one disturbed them, and Elena lost herself in a romance novel by a Leneiran author that her friend told her lived in Erindell. Adina pored over tomes detailing the technical aspects of Leneiran powers, hoping to find a way to use her healing abilities on the guards who lost their magic. Unfortunately, none of the reference books she read had any useful information, and she despondently threw each one on the growing pile in front of them.

Elena had to be dragged out when the sun began to set, only agreeing to leave when Celine told her she could take the book with her.

"You're a strange woman." Adina shook her head with a smile.

Elena continued to read as she walked down the hall.

"It's a good book," she said absent-mindedly, paying no attention to where she was walking and nearly colliding with a table on which sat a vase of fresh flowers. She snapped her head up and realized she was in an unfamiliar corridor.

"This is where our rooms are," Adina explained, seeing Elena's flustered expression. "You can leave the book in my room for now and pick it up after dinner."

They entered the princess's quarters, and Elena was taken aback at the sight. The ornaments and plants in colorful pots gave the room a comfortable, lived-in atmosphere. While the fireplace in Elena's room was a focal point with its color and decorative features, the one in Adina's space was lost in a sea of vivid hues.

It boasted the same intricately patterned tiles surrounding the mirror sitting above the vanity. Colored glass studs replaced the plain handles on the wardrobe and chest of drawers. Sheer purple curtains danced in the breeze, and a brightly colored bedspread was covered with pillows, cushions, and throws.

While Adina hastily washed and changed in her bathing chamber, Elena dropped into a comfortable, bright green armchair by the fireplace and continued reading. The princess had to clear her throat loudly to attract her attention.

Adina wore a full-length, sky-blue dress with a delicate pattern embroidered in gold around the bodice and the cuffs of the long sleeves. On her brushed-back curls sat an exquisite tiara, its thin, interwoven gold bands and small diamonds scattered across the piece, glinting in the soft light.

Elena glanced down at her dress—drab by comparison, but Adina had thought of that and held out a box of jewelry.

"You're the daughter of a lord," she reminded Elena, who peered into the box filled with all manner of gold and silver jewelry. "You need to look the part."

Elena gratefully pulled out a pair of wide gold bracelets that would also hide the inked-on Elemental mark in case anyone looked too closely. She put on a pair of long diamond earrings that sparkled when they caught the light and a few rings on both hands. Adina tied on a black corset embroidered with gold thread over the otherwise plain navy dress Elena had worn all day. The princess made a complicated weaving motion with her hands, and Elena's hair twisted into a new style. Adina dragged her in front of the mirror on the vanity, and her breath hitched at the refined, polished woman who stared back. The additional embellishments and loose bun at the nape of her neck added a touch of class and elegance befitting a noble.

They navigated to the entrance where the rest of the family was outside at the top of the stairs. Elena briefly admired the ornate bejeweled crowns sitting on Arran and Amaya's heads before being ushered to stand at the edge of the group next to Adina. Like the princess, Tarrick and Leon wore simple yet regal gold circlets that flaunted their powers and royal status. Elena was glad for her borrowed jewelry. As she passed the royals, she met Tarrick's stare, heat filling her cheeks as she recalled Adina's comments about the way he looked at her.

Tarrick opened his mouth, and she paused, waiting for him to speak, but he snapped it closed, shaking his head. He gave her a crooked smile and tilted his head to the side, indicating for her to keep going. Past him, Leon flashed her a broad smile, which she returned.

Elena ignored her fluttering heart and stole a moment to admire the sunset—another stunning display of vivid hues. After a few minutes of standing in silence, a guard at the bottom of the stairs stepped forward to announce the first arrival.

"Presenting King Halder and Princess Malina of Skandor," he announced before moving to the side to make way for them. Hooves huffed in the dirt, and wheels creaked as several dark, horse-drawn coaches crested the hill where the palace stood. Each had the Terralean crest painted on the doors with gold detail and embellishments.

When the first carriage halted in front of the stairs, the same guard who announced the Skandorians leaped forward and fumbled to unfold a set of steps.

A large, broad man with silver-dappled, thick blond hair cropped close to his head flung open the door and emerged from the coach. King Halder had a bushy mustache that curled up at the corners and a full beard. Icy blue eyes swept across the line of people at the entrance. Heavy, studded leather cuffs wrapped the wrists of muscular, tanned arms emerging from a fur vest. Dark pants hugged thick thighs and were tucked into heavy, polished leather boots. Even without the sheathed bone-handled dagger strapped to the belt at his waist, Elena was intimidated by the colossal man who seemed more beast than human—or Leneiran, as it were. She shivered, trying to picture him turning into a large wolf that would send her running in the opposite direction with a single look.

"Arran! Amaya!" he boomed, striding up the stairs to where the king and queen stood, smiling in welcome.

Trailing behind him was the most beautiful woman Elena had ever seen—there was no other word for it. She could have been a supermodel with her long, slender legs, toned arms, and glowing, tanned skin. Although dressed similarly to King Halder, with a fur vest and pants tucked into boots, her clothes hugged her willowy figure, showing off softly curved hips and a narrow waist emphasized by ample breasts. Her platinum blonde hair was swept back into a braid that ended at the small of her back and highlighted her cheekbones and arched brows. Wide-set hooded blue eyes appraised Elena and Adina as she walked past them to greet Arran and Amaya. She was equal parts angelic and lethal weapon.

"Welcome, King Halder and Princess Malina." Arran shook Halder's meaty hand. "You remember my sons and daughter, Tarrick, Leon, and Adina."

"Of course," Halder replied, his gaze sweeping over Tarrick and lingering on his face for longer than necessary. The prince inclined his head without giving anything away.

Malina curtsied before Arran and Amaya, who exclaimed how much the princess had grown since she had last seen her. After the reacquaintances took place between the royals, the rest of the king's entourage ascended the stairs. Elena counted ten men, all of similar build and bearing to Halder.

After shaking hands with everyone and murmuring greetings, the Skandorian royal council stood in silence whilst their king and princess made small talk with Zanthus, who Elena hadn't noticed until then. He offered to show the Skandorians their rooms to freshen up before meeting the rest of the Terralean royal council and Sailonese delegation.

"Did you see Halder making eyes at Tarrick?" Leon teased when the Skandorians left.

"Leon," the queen admonished.

"Sorry, Mother," Leon muttered.

The guard stepped forward again and announced Queen Lin of Sailon and her royal council.

"Check this out!" Adina whispered to Elena with a broad grin at the horizon.

The sun had set, and the Terralean sky had turned a dark blue color—not quite the navy velvet sky of night—with a lavender haze still on the horizon. Elena stared up at the first star twinkling in the sky. Before she could make a silent wish, as she did from time to time, a strange silhouette grew larger and neared the palace. Her jaw dropped when she took in the enormous flying horse that was closely followed by several others.

They landed with soft *thumps* on the gravel, sending a few pebbles flying and stirring up the dry earth underfoot. The creatures ranged in color from dappled gray to chestnut to midnight black and would have been perfectly ordinary were it not for the large, feathered wings that sprouted from their flanks. The wings were the same color as the horse they belonged to, and Elena watched in astonishment as the horses lowered their wings and tucked them into their sides, allowing their riders to dismount.

Out of the corner of her eye, Elena saw the look of longing on Adina's face. The princess's hands twitched by her side as she fought the urge to run over and mount one.

"I can't believe you've ridden a *pihasi*," Adina whispered jealously to Elena. "They live in Sailon. This is only my second time seeing them."

"I was unconscious. I don't remember any of it," Elena whispered back.

A beautiful, tall woman walked up the stairs confidently. She had almond-shaped brown eyes, tawny skin, and shiny black hair pulled back in a bun at the crown of her head. *Queen Lin,* Elena guessed. She wore a simple cream tunic over tight pants and boots. An assortment of beaded bracelets lined her right arm. Her left arm was bare, with a spiral pattern tattooed inside her wrist peeking out from under the hem of her sleeve—the indicator of her status as an Empath.

Unlike the Skandorians, she exuded warmth, but Elena was unnerved at the thought that the woman could read her thoughts and emotions with a single touch. Lin's smooth forehead creased slightly when she paused in front of Elena, but she bowed to her all the same, and Elena curtsied in return.

Lin greeted every member of the Terralean family before stopping before Arran and Amaya, who welcomed her in a more familiar manner than they had Halder and Malina. Lin and Amaya embraced in the way only old friends did, and Lin introduced her second-in-command and wife, Zen—the only person from the Sailonese contingent who had ascended the stairs. She was a tall, athletic woman with dark skin, narrow, dark eyes, and hair braided into tiny plaits, tied back with an orange ribbon. She, too, had a number of bracelets on one arm, but unlike Lin, she had a hunting dagger tucked into a leather sheath on her belt.

She bowed respectfully to all members of the royal family and stood behind her queen while pleasantries were exchanged. Lin gestured to her own entourage, who stood at the bottom of the stairs in a neat row, and introduced all of the members of her own royal council and their roles. Each councilor stepped forward and bowed respectfully when they were named.

Lin declined Queen Amaya's offer to be shown their rooms and declared they were happy to meet the Terralean royal council straight away.

"We haven't traveled as far." Lin smiled, glancing at her council members, who all nodded and acquiesced. They stared up at the palace in wonder as they ascended the stairs.

"In that case, let's go to the dining area and enjoy some refreshments before dinner." Arran clapped his hands and led the group to a large chamber down the corridor.

Two guards opened the heavy wooden doors to a lavish room Elena hadn't yet seen. It was a large, decadent room with several chandeliers already lit, bathing the room in a warm, bright light. A long wooden table with chairs along both sides stood in the middle of the room, but no one was seated. The crowd stood and mingled in the space on either side of the table. Servers stood against a wall with trays of a variety of drinks—Elena recognized the small glasses of milky *araki*. There were also glasses of red and white wine and crystal coupes of colored fizzing beverages.

"Sherbet and cordials," Adina whispered to her. "If you want to skip the wine."

The members of the Terralean royal council who had already gathered in the chamber greeted the Salionese representatives cordially without shaking hands or making physical contact. They merely inclined their heads in greeting and inquired about the journey.

Elena hid behind Leon, keen to avoid Rokeby and Netta, still rattled by their interrogation the day before. Lords and ladies from various provinces around the country conversed with smiles on their faces and glasses of wine in their hands. It wasn't long before Halder, Malina, and their council members entered the chamber. Elena was able to observe the interactions from a corner without being noticed.

She caught Erik slipping into the room and taking up position by the door. Although he stood to attention and maintained a neutral expression like all the other guards on duty, tension lined his forehead, and his jaw tightened. Elena sidled over to him.

"How are you doing?" she murmured out of the corner of her mouth.

"I've been better," he replied, barely moving his lips. "Is Adina alright?"

Elena directed her gaze to the princess, who had been swept up in conversation with various guests. She was smiling politely and nodding her head at something Rokeby was telling her. An expression of longing crossed her pretty face when she glanced over to Erik and Elena—one the guard returned.

"She's okay," Elena said softly.

Erik glanced up at one of the candles perched on the chandelier and frowned slightly. The flame barely flickered, and he reverted to staring ahead in silence. Elena moved away to leave him to his thoughts. The guard had been one of the few people to show her kindness and friendship from the start. Despite Tarrick's assurances that Elementals were more than their abilities, she imagined it would feel like a small part of them was missing.

Leon came over to her carrying two glasses of wine and offered her one, which she gratefully accepted.

"Can bluestone be hidden in food or drink?" Elena asked him quietly without preamble or greeting.

He stared at her in astonishment. "Good evening to you too." His lips quirked up after he recovered from his initial shock at her question. "What have you been reading?"

"Just a thought." She shrugged.

"No," he replied, eyes darting around the room to make sure they weren't being overheard, but the conversation had crescendoed, and no one noticed them in the corner. "It's a very hard stone. Difficult to grind or hammer down to undetectable powders. The most you can do is make primitive spears and daggers. Why do you ask?"

"Just wondered if the assassin and guards losing their powers were related," she replied in a low voice.

"The guards losing their elemental abilities isn't common knowledge," Leon warned, smiling and inclining his head toward a couple of Sailonese councilors who walked past at that moment.

"I won't say anything," Elena promised.

"Be careful, El." Concern clouded his blue eyes. "We're *all* playing a role this week, not just you. We need to show the others we are a strong, united force. These negotiations can get pretty ugly if the others sense weakness. Even Lin," he told her as worry crossed his handsome features. "She's an honorable and level-headed person but a ruthless queen. They can use it to their advantage and make it difficult for us to get what we need to help our people."

Before Elena could say anything, Lin and Zen made their way to them with smiles on their faces. Elena decided the Sailonese were a friendlier bunch than the Skandorians, who seemed to be ready to launch an attack on anyone who looked slightly capable of threatening their king or princess.

"Prince Leon, such a pleasure to see you again," the Sailonese queen greeted the prince, who returned her warm smile with his customary flirtatious grin.

"And you, Queen Lin." He bowed his head. "I'm looking forward to hearing your proposals for the new trade agreements with Terralea," he said smoothly.

"I'm sure," she said with a twinkle in her eye and a smile tugging at the corners of her lips.

Leon had the grace to blush and drop his winning smile when he realized Lin saw through his lie.

"I haven't been introduced to your guest yet." Lin pierced Elena with a shrewd gaze, who shifted uncomfortably under her scrutiny.

"This is Lady Elena, Lord Taib's daughter from Selindor province," Leon introduced.

"I see." Lin raised an eyebrow.

"A pleasure, Your Majesty," Elena murmured, curtsying the way Adina had taught her.

"The pleasure is mine, Lady Elena," the queen said graciously, playing along. For the moment. "What brings you to our illustrious Peace Summit?"

"I'm visiting Adina. We're old school friends," Elena told the lie she had been practicing. "I'm interested in politics, and her family was gracious enough to let me stay and observe the proceedings."

"I see," Lin said skeptically. Elena held her gaze before the queen finally chuckled. Lin glanced at Zen, who also observed her, sensing the lie but remaining quiet until her queen gave permission to speak.

"I look forward to getting to know you better, *Lady Elena*." Lin's intense stare gave way to an amused smile. "Perhaps we shall speak more in the bathhouse," she said lightly. The queen gave Leon a knowing smile before walking away with Zen.

"What did she mean?" Elena asked Leon.

"Mother usually invites Lin to the bathhouse when she visits," Leon explained. "It's a way for them to talk openly away from the official meetings and men. The royal bathhouse is more of a social activity than an official one, but I've known Mother to negotiate deals and agreements with visiting queens and ambassadors while they've been in there."

"I see." Elena stared at Lin, now making polite conversation with one of Halder's councilors, who was shifting warily under her piercing stare. "She knows all about me, though, doesn't she?"

Leon eyed the queen. "She probably only senses that you're lying about being Lord Taib's daughter and Adina's school friend. She doesn't know the circumstances that brought you here."

"Probably?" Elena exclaimed.

Leon shrugged and offered a lopsided grin. "At least she didn't out you straight away, right?"

Elena rolled her eyes in response. "Does your father invite the other kings and ambassadors to the bathhouse to do the same?"

"No way!" Leon shuddered. "The bathhouse is available to them if they wish to use it, but we don't socialize with others in the same way. We usually have drinks and water pipes in the evenings after the dinners."

"I suppose it would be embarrassing for the men to reveal they're all big talk and small dicks," Elena said sarcastically. Leon's burst of laughter caused a few heads to turn in their direction.

"Come on," he chuckled, holding out an arm. "The fun is just beginning."

She tucked her arm through the crook of his elbow, and he took her around the room, introducing her to various members of the Skandorian and Sailonese councils who greeted her politely and made small talk with the prince. None of them attempted to shake hands, and conversation was on general and mundane topics.

"May I borrow Lady Elena for a moment, Leon?" a deep voice interrupted the prince's long-winded introduction to yet another Skandorian, who leered at Elena.

Tarrick didn't wait for Leon's response before putting a hand on Elena's back and guiding her to the back of the room, where it was quieter.

"How are you doing?" he asked.

"I'm fine," she replied, looking up into his amber eyes. "Leon's been introducing me to everyone."

"I wanted to make sure you were okay," he murmured. "Give you a break from being Lady Elena if it was getting too much."

"Thank you." Elena smiled at him, surprised at his thoughtfulness. "But I'm doing okay. It's fun meeting new people. The Empaths are really nice."

His shoulders dropped a little, and he gave her that almost smile again before saying, "I've seen people crack under a single stare from Lin and confess all their secrets to her," he told her. "You're doing a good job playing the role. And looking the part."

Elena blushed as Tarrick scanned her from head to toe, his gaze lingering on the corset and slowly moving down to her hips. Her lower abdomen contracted, and heat pooled between her thighs. *One look should not cause such a reaction,* she chastised herself. But, in that moment, she would have walked off a cliff if Tarrick asked her to.

"Tarrick!" Halder's booming voice interrupted them. "We haven't spoken all evening."

Halder smiled at the prince, and Elena noted the Skandorian king's arm around his daughter's shoulders. He nudged the princess forward. The fur vest had been removed to reveal Malina wearing a fitted sky-blue tunic that brought out her eyes and hugged her curves. Elena smiled politely at the princess, trying not to feel jealous or small next to the woman who was even more stunning up close.

"King Halder, Princess Malina, have you met Lady Elena?" Tarrick introduced Elena. He angled his body to stand protectively in front of her.

Malina inclined her head in Elena's direction by way of greeting but remained silent. Halder didn't even look in her direction.

"A pleasure, my dear," he said, eyes locked firmly on Tarrick. "A fine start to the first of many celebrations this week." Halder gestured to the room with a large hand wrapped around a wine glass.

"I'm not sure what you mean, King Halder," Tarrick said politely. "Aside from our countries pledging to protect the ongoing peace of the realm, what else might we be celebrating?"

"My dear boy," Halder roared in delight, drawing the attention of those around them.

Elena startled at Tarrick being referred to as a "boy." From where she was standing—close enough that she could feel the heat radiating off his body—he was all man.

"I have spoken to Lord Zanthus, and it would seem this Peace Summit will go down in history as the one that brought our countries together, both politically and in matrimony."

~ 14 ~

The crowd around the group fell silent. Whispers and titters rippled out from the gathering. Leon, who was standing nearby with Netta, openly gaped at his brother. Adina's eyes widened in surprise. Malina's expression didn't change once during the exchange; she stared at the prince with polite interest.

"Nothing has been agreed upon," Tarrick said coolly. "It was merely a suggestion from Lord Zanthus. There are other ways we can negotiate. Ways our countries can work together that I look forward to sharing with you when we start the official meetings of the summit. He shouldn't have spoken to you about it without my consent." Irritation lined his last words.

"Come now, Tarrick," Halder chuckled, clapping his shoulder with one hand, ignoring the prince's mask of indifference. "We've been talking about this for the past five summits. Now that Malina is of age, why wait any longer?"

"Tarrick, King Halder." Leon came up to the group, forcing a smile. "Dinner is being served. We should take our seats."

Halder's announcement was forgotten when everyone moved to the table. There didn't seem to be any rules in place as to where people sat, but the royals gravitated toward the end, where Arran held a chair out for Amaya. Their council members seated themselves further along with their fellow countrymen.

Tarrick left Elena's side reluctantly when Zanthus gave him a pointed look and indicated the empty chair between himself and Lin. Elena sidled over to the opposite end of the long table, seating herself between two Sailonese councilors, who greeted her cordially.

Servers entered the room with trays and platters of food that they placed along the table. The royal kitchen had included Skandorian and Sailonese dishes to accommodate their guests, who helped themselves to the fare before tension fell victim to social niceties and everyone politely passed down platters.

Tarrick ate quietly, glancing surreptitiously at Elena, who sat too far down the table for him to speak with her. He recognized the Sailonese man beside her as Jet, one of Lin's long-standing advisors, who had attended a number of Peace Summits in the past. His angular face and prominent cheekbones drew the attention of more than a few guests. Tarrick couldn't stop the jealousy gnawing inside as Elena and Jet chatted like old friends, laughing at each other's jokes and leaning in to whisper conspiratorially.

He tore his gaze away from her, observing the people sitting around him to get his mind off her glowing skin and alluring brown eyes that sparkled by the bright torchlights. Leon also threw covert looks in the couple's direction every so often. Adina barely paid attention to her food as she stared at a spot behind Tarrick that he suspected was where Erik stood.

When the initial hunger pangs had been satiated, the chatter built up again.

"So, Tarrick." Lin turned to him with twinkling eyes. "What are your intentions with Lady Elena?"

Tarrick choked into the wine glass he had raised to his lips.

"What do you mean, Your Majesty?" he finally spluttered out.

Amusement laced Lin's voice as she said, "I haven't seen a new face at the Peace Summit since its inception. Is Lady Elena joining your council?"

Tarrick turned to the head of the table, where his father and mother were engrossed in conversation with Halder and Malina, who sat on either side of the rulers.

Zanthus, however, whipped his head around at Lin's question. "Absolutely not," he said firmly. "She's only here for a few days."

When Lin raised an eyebrow, Adina jumped in. "Elena is a friend and interested in politics." She glared at Zanthus. "And she's staying for as long as she wishes."

"I'm sure she would prefer to be back home, Adina," Zanthus said pointedly.

"You don't know that, Uncle," the princess shot back. "She likes it here, and we all enjoy her company, don't we?" she fixed Leon and Tarrick with a determined stare.

"Oh, yes," Leon replied, sitting back in his chair and twirling his wine glass between two fingers as he gave Tarrick a wicked smile. "She is an absolute delight. Very entertaining."

"Are we missing something?" Zen murmured. She sat next to Lin and leaned in to listen to the conversation.

"Well, it would seem she has caught Jet's interest." Lin quirked a corner of her lip as she glanced down the table at Jet and Elena. "I've never seen my councilor this, er, enthusiastic at a Peace Summit before."

It was Leon's turn to choke into his glass of wine. Tarrick strongly suspected the wince on his brother's face was thanks to a well-placed kick under the table by Adina, who smiled smugly next to him.

Zanthus turned back to Halder and Arran, bored by the turn in conversation.

Lin eyed Leon, whose face was still a blotchy red from his coughing fit.

"It occurred to me that you may be trying to convince me to vote in favor of your petition to have ambassadors in all of the palaces, Your Highness," she addressed Leon, who stared in surprise.

"Really?"

Lin gave Zen a knowing look and smiled. "You've chosen well. Lady Elena is doing a wonderful job of making my people feel welcome."

Tarrick didn't bother being discreet as he leaned forward and looked to where another Sailonese councilor—a female with a shiny black bob and dark, feline eyes—had joined in the conversation with Jet and Elena. The trio were the only people aside from his parents talking animatedly between bites. He scanned the table and watched the Skandorians push the remnants of food around their plates. Their own council of Terralean nobles spoke quietly amongst themselves, not bothering to engage in conversation with the recent arrivals.

"I won't be surprised if Jet recommends I explore the idea of Lady Elena staying in Sailon with us," Lin continued.

Beside her, Zen gave a short nod.

It was Tarrick's turn to kick Leon under the table and alert the young prince to the fact that he was gaping at the Sailonese queen.

"Our uncle is right," Tarrick said smoothly, desperate to put an end to the conversation before things got out of hand. Elena was playing her part too well. There was every chance their plan to protect her by keeping her in plain sight could backfire spectacularly. "Lady Elena is merely visiting and has responsibilities in Selindor. She will be returning *home*" —he glanced at Adina, who scowled back at him— "when the Peace Summit ends."

"Jet will be disappointed," Zen said, giving Leon a sidelong glance.

Thankfully, he managed to keep his expression blank, although Tarrick didn't miss the way his hold on the glass tightened at Zen's words.

***

Elena listened with rapt attention to Jet, Lin's political advisor, and his sister, Mika, who sat opposite him. Mika explained that she represented the people without Empath abilities who lived in Sailon and also advised on policies and treaties that included them.

"But *you* have Empath powers?" Elena asked.

"Oh, yes." Mika nodded, her dark hair bobbing around her friendly, round face. "I'm something of a bridge between those without abilities and the council."

"Sailon sounds like such a democratic, inclusive country," Elena admired.

"It is," Jet agreed. "You should visit us and see how we run things. I know Tarrick tries hard to implement policies and decrees that are more inclusive."

"Elemental powers are a force to be reckoned with," Elena admitted, remembering the guards' training session and Erindellians at the Full Moon Festival.

"Indeed," Mika replied, tracking a server who walked slowly behind everyone seated at the table, filling empty water glasses with a blink of his eye.

Despite the large size of the room, it felt crowded with the addition of thirty-odd guests, the royal guards standing at the doors, and staff flitting in and out. Elena was not used to being amongst so many people and concentrated on keeping up the charade as Lady Elena.

To avoid accidentally slipping up, she asked Jet and Mika about Sailon. The siblings happily told her about the capital city with its canals, temples, and monasteries where people could enjoy a week or two respite from the business of daily life. She was fascinated by their descriptions of the natural hot springs in the jungles, where locals and visitors could relax while taking in the mountains and lush scenery.

"These welcome feasts are really a chance for the royal families to catch up," Jet said quietly, inclining his head toward the royals, who were talking more enthusiastically than the council members at the end where the three of them sat.

The Skandorians spoke among themselves in low voices, and the Sailonese ate quietly or made small talk with the Terraleans. "They don't last as long as the banquets and celebrations in the subsequent days of the Peace Summit. There's usually more entertainment and chances to circulate at those," Jet told her.

As if summoned, the servers brought in trays of sweets and desserts along with the customary cups of tea, signaling the end of the evening was near. Elena sipped on her tea and smiled down the table at Adina, who gave her a grin before glancing at Zanthus and rolling her eyes. Elena stifled a laugh, hoping her friend would fill her in later on whatever Zanthus said that caused the reaction.

Arran rose to his feet and announced that if anyone would like to end the evening with water pipes and a selection of Terralean digestives, he would host them in the adjoining room. Chairs scraped along the floor as some people wandered into the smoking room, and others left the dining area in small groups and pairs back to their quarters.

Before Elena could edge toward Adina, the princess caught Erik's eye and yawned pointedly. Elena guessed Adina wanted a private moment with her guard, so she followed Jet and Mika out of the dining room instead. As they continued telling her about Sailon, she barely paid attention to where they were going until the siblings paused at an unfamiliar door.

"This is us." Jet put his hand out to the door handle.

A crease formed between Elena's brows as she took in the surroundings.

"We had a wonderful time speaking with you tonight, Lady Elena." Mika smiled.

"Uh, so did I." Elena collected herself to wish the pair good night. She continued down the corridor with a confidence she did not feel, hoping it would lead somewhere she recognized.

~ 15 ~

Elena walked through the maze of empty hallways, feeling frustrated that she didn't pay close attention to where she was going. Someone had always accompanied her around the palace after Tarrick had insisted she be guarded at all times.

It was starting to get cold, the wind from the open windows nipping at her skin and the low-burning torches flickering ominously in their sconces on the wall. Elena shivered and rubbed her hands along her bare arms to stay warm. The idea of spending the night wandering around the palace by herself was unappealing, even without the threat of an assassin or rebels crawling around the place. The heavy wooden doors she passed along the way remained closed, and the eerie silence unnerved her.

She peered down another unfamiliar corridor, and the sound of deep voices grew louder around the corner. Elena moved eagerly toward the sound but paused as the voices drew closer—they were familiar but unwelcome, and she groaned inwardly.

Although she had relaxed into the conversation with Jet and Mika, she was still wary of all of the new arrivals. The demeanor of the Skandorians was an ever-present reminder of their shifting abilities and the danger she was in. While the Empaths were friendly and talkative, a brush of their finger against her skin was all it would take for her human status to be revealed. Without the full story of the havoc the human woman had caused a hundred years before, Elena was uncertain how the Empaths would react to the revelation.

As much as she was an outsider, Arran and his family had been kind and seemed to genuinely care for her safety and well-being while she was in Terralea. She did not want to jeopardize their negotiations with Lin and Halder—something Zanthus already insinuated had occurred because of her mere presence in the palace.

Spotting a niche in the corridor, she flattened herself against the wall, hoping the shadows and dim light would hide her presence.

"You are certain Tarrick will agree to marry my daughter?" Halder's deep voice carried over to Elena's hiding place.

"Of course," Zanthus's reedy voice assured the king. "He knows we've been talking about this since the first Peace Summit's conception. It's not entirely unexpected."

"What about that girl?"

"She's of no consequence," Zanthus said airily. "A lowly girl from the provinces. She's nothing compared to your daughter."

Their footsteps grew louder, and Elena pressed herself harder against the wall, holding her breath. She prayed they would walk in the opposite direction to where she hid.

"They seemed very close," Halder said doubtfully.

"They are not," Zanthus snapped. "She'll be gone before the week is over. I will personally speak with her and make sure of it."

Elena's skin prickled.

"What are you saying, Zanthus?" Halder rumbled. "I want this union to happen, but I will not risk my daughter or my crown by partaking in unlawful plots."

"Nothing treacherous," the royal advisor soothed, but Elena caught an edge to his voice.

Halder hummed. "And if the girl insists on staying? If she tells Arran and Amaya that you are trying to get rid of her, what then?"

"Who do you think they will believe, Your Majesty?" Zanthus asked in an oily voice. "Amaya is my sister. We are family, and she puts family above all else. I will convince them *Lady* Elena is making things difficult and should be sent back to, er ... Selindor. Tarrick and Malina's union will benefit Terralea enormously. That's an easy argument to put forward in our meetings. I have spent the last century proving my loyalty to Arran and this country." There was a note of bitterness in his voice. "They trust me to advise them on the best course of action."

"Amaya follows her heart, does she not? What if she votes against this marriage contract because Tarrick is not interested in my daughter?" Halder asked.

"If Malina were to engage more with Tarrick..." Zanthus suggested. "Tell her to request an audience with him, dance with him tomorrow night. Show my sister that Malina is in love with Tarrick, play to her emotions and all that nonsense."

"Very well."

Their footsteps grew fainter, and Elena slowly exhaled when they turned down another corridor. She counted to a hundred to ensure no one was about and crept out of the niche. She briskly walked until she caught sight of a familiar staircase and rushed toward it.

Serkin, the guard from earlier that day, was still standing outside her door. He gave Elena a disapproving look but didn't say anything.

"Got lost." She shrugged with a smile. He didn't respond and continued staring straight ahead.

Elena entered her room and closed the door behind her firmly. She leaned against it, heart pounding loudly. Serkin's presence did nothing to alleviate her fear; it had the opposite effect, highlighting that Zanthus had eyes and ears all over the palace. Perhaps she was overreacting to his comments, reading too deeply into what he had said about getting rid of her. But even she couldn't argue with the fact that he was Amaya's brother, and the queen had already made it clear that family came first.

Elena locked the door as quietly as possible with shaking hands before undressing and climbing into bed. The uneasy feeling in her stomach grew as Zanthus's threat swirled through her mind.

If Arran and Amaya agreed to his plans, she wasn't naive enough to believe he would actually send her to Selindor.

Sleep evaded her for the rest of the night as she tried to think of ways she could avoid Zanthus, Tarrick, Halder, and Malina for the rest of the week. She didn't feel comfortable confiding in Leon or Adina about the conversation she had overheard. Although Elena knew they didn't always agree with Zanthus, he was still their uncle.

She would have to be on her guard at all times and steer clear of him and Halder. It was the only way she could see herself making it through the week without compromising her own safety and secret until Tarrick kept his promise to take her home. Until then, she would have to continue playing the role of Lady Elena and stick to Adina's side.

$$\sim 16 \sim$$

Elena woke early the next morning, the pale dawn and cool air in the quiet garden beckoning her. After washing and pulling on a simple dress, she braided her hair loosely, unlocked the door, and stepped out into the hallway.

"Are you going somewhere, Lady Elena?" the guard on duty inquired politely from her other side.

"Shit!" Elena exclaimed, clutching her chest. She knew there would be a guard outside, but the woman's stealth startled her. The lack of sleep and slow reflexes didn't help either.

The guard was the same woman who had handed Erik his ass at training the day before. She had soft brown eyes, a delicate, up-turned nose, and smooth, dark skin. Tiny plaits were pulled back in a thick ponytail once again. She wore the guard uniform and had a sheathed dagger strapped to the belt at her waist.

"I wanted to get some fresh air before breakfast," Elena said uncertainly. She hoped the guard would let her go for a walk. The palace and her room had become too stifling.

"I shall accompany you," the guard said amiably.

"I can go by myself," Elena told her. "I don't want you to leave your post or anything."

"His Highness has instructed me to watch over you until Erik takes over," the guard explained.

"He did?" Elena chewed her bottom lip, not liking the idea of being shadowed by the woman on her excursion through the gardens.

The guard nodded. "I'm Zahra," she introduced herself with a smile.

"Nice to meet you." Elena returned the smile. *At least she's friendlier and more talkative than Serkin.*

They started walking down the corridor toward the palace entrance.

"I saw you training yesterday," Elena said, taking in the woman's powerful build and confident strides.

Zahra smirked. "I hope it was as entertaining for you as it was for me."

Elena laughed. "I can't believe you took down two men while *blindfolded.*" She shook her head in amazement. "How long did it take you to learn that?"

"Oh, Erik and I have been fighting each other since we could walk." Zahra chuckled. "He's my brother," she added at Elena's quizzical look. "Our father served King Arran and his father as a royal guard when he ruled. Erik and I have been training to follow in his footsteps since birth."

"How long have you been in the Royal Guard?" Elena asked, impressed.

"I joined about twenty years after the uprising." Zahra wrinkled her forehead as she tried to recollect the years. "So about eighty years, give or take? Erik has served for almost a century."

"And your father?"

"He died during the uprising," Zahra said quietly.

"I'm sorry," Elena said sorrowfully. "I know what it's like to lose a parent."

Zahra gave her a sympathetic smile.

They walked the rest of the way in silence. The guards standing at the entrance nodded at the two women as they opened the doors. The cool air was refreshing, and Elena paused to take in deep gulps, feeling more awake and revived. She took the path Tarrick had led her down the day before, walking more slowly to examine the flora and fauna. Zahra followed dutifully, keeping a few steps behind, pausing every time Elena stopped to inspect unfamiliar flowers and plants.

"Were you guarding me all night?" Elena asked, bending down to peer at a small bush that boasted neon orange flowers with spiky petals. She grazed her fingers lightly across the soft fronds.

Zahra shook her head. "I took over at dawn."

"Does Tarrick still think I need a guard with so many others here now?" Elena asked, feeling slightly guilty about dragging an elite guard around the palace gardens. She knew resources were stretched thin and wondered if the additional guests and foreign dignitaries needed protection more than she did.

"His Highness has made your safety a priority since the day you arrived," Zahra said, stunning Elena into silence. Amaya and Arran had made it clear that her safety was important, but it didn't occur to her that Tarrick would get personally involved.

"The assassin is still at large," Zahra murmured.

Elena gave her a sidelong glance. "Are there any updates?"

"You are still a potential target, and we don't know if this was the work of one person or if a group of rebels is involved."

Elena looked at the guard with a mixture of alarm and appreciation for her honesty.

"It's just conjecture at this stage." Zahra glanced around.

Elena stood up, taking the hint. They took up a brisk pace, deeper into the gardens where the air was lightly scented with the blooming roses and jasmine. *Lyrabirds* swooped overhead, a few long, rainbow-colored feathers falling to the ground. Elena stopped to pick up a feather and admired the way the bright pink hue changed to purple, blue, yellow, and green. The birds perched in the trees and eyed her curiously.

Elena and Zahra walked in silence, taking in the serenity and, in Elena's case, stopping frequently to examine more unusual flowers. She ran her hands through the soft ferns and leafy greenery that waved invitingly in the breeze.

They roamed past a clearing, and Elena spotted a lone figure sitting hunched over on the bench, kicking the gravel in the ground—Malina, the Skandorian princess and Tarrick's potential bride. Elena was prepared to turn and walk away, but something about the princess's posture and disposition made her pause. After making sure no one was watching them, Elena walked cautiously toward the bench. Zahra trailed behind silently and stood to the side to give Elena and the princess space.

"Good morning, Your Highness," Elena greeted her. "Did you sleep well?"

Malina eyed her suspiciously. "Unfortunately, I did not," she said after a pause. "My room was too warm, and I suffered from a headache all night."

"I'm sorry to hear that. I imagine coming from the north, this must feel really hot to you." Elena smiled. She took a seat beside the princess, who looked slightly surprised but did not reply.

Malina turned back to the ground and kicked at the little pebbles and stones.

"I've never been to Skandor," Elena said slowly, unsure if *Lady Elena* would be an avid traveler. Considering Adina grumbled about not being able to visit other parts of the realm, Elena decided it was better to assume travel was restricted. It was also easier to stick to the truth where possible amidst the tangle of lies she found herself weaving. "But I've heard so much about it. I don't know if I could survive such cold conditions."

Malina snorted. "Most people think it is a brutal land, but they do not venture far enough to see its beauty."

Elena tilted her head to the side, eyeing the princess curiously.

"My father taught me to sail in the coves and bays in the northernmost parts of the realm where the waters are cold and deep and pure. The skies there are the blackest black, and you feel like you're the only person in the world. It is peaceful," Malina said wistfully. "And then, the light starts to dance and change colors. It is the most magical thing to see."

"That sounds wonderful," Elena breathed.

"It is." Malina smiled to herself. "It is my favorite place in all of Skandor."

"Have you traveled much?" Elena asked, eager to learn more now that the princess had opened up a little.

"Only around Skandor." Malina shook her head. "This is the first time outside of my home country."

"Are you enjoying it? King Tarrick and Queen Amaya are wonderful hosts."

"You have known them long?" Malina asked.

"As long as I have known Adina," Elena answered truthfully. Out of the corner of her eye, she saw Zahra smirk.

"They are kind," Malina said after a pause. "You are close with Prince Tarrick, are you not?"

Elena hesitated as she pierced her with an icy blue stare.

"He is a good person," Elena said softly. "In the time that I've known him, he is ... decent."

Zahra cast a sidelong glance at Elena.

Malina merely nodded, her expression bland, making Elena wonder if the princess was thinking about her father's ambitions for her to marry Tarrick.

"What is it like to change forms?" Elena changed the subject to something less awkward. Besides, she was genuinely curious about Shifters. "Is it painful?"

Malina looked at her quizzically. "Have you not seen Prince Tarrick shift into his jaguar form? It is the same for us."

Elena shook her head.

"It's not painful." Malina shrugged. "I cannot explain. But in my wolf form, I feel ... free."

Elena leaned forward, intrigued. Even Zahra cocked her head to the side to hear better.

"I am faster, more powerful, stronger." A dreamy smile played on Malina's pink, pouty lips, and her eyes glazed over. "I can run through the forests and barrens with nothing to stop me."

"Can you still think rationally?" Elena asked. "Or do you only think ... wolf thoughts?"

"Wolf thoughts?" The Skandorian princess frowned, not understanding.

"I don't know." Elena flushed. "Do you only think about food and not being attacked?"

"No, I can think the same thoughts as I do in this form." Malina gave a little laugh that reminded Elena of delicate wind chimes. Everything about the princess was ethereal and exquisite.

"That sense of power and freedom must be incredible." Elena sighed.

"It is."

"I'm sorry if I'm being nosy, Malina." The princess's name slipped out before Elena could stop herself.

Malina sat up straighter with a slight frown at being addressed in a familiar manner. The mask of indifference slipped back into place, reminding Elena of the cold princess from the night before.

"I have taken up enough of your time," Elena said, taking the abrupt change in Malina's manner as a sign to leave. She stood up and curtsied to the princess. "It was nice to meet you, Your Highness. I hope you feel better soon."

"Thank you, Lady Elena," Malina said coolly.

Elena walked back to the entrance of the clearing, but instead of turning toward the palace, she took the path that would take her further into the gardens, keen to explore more.

Zahra remained a few steps behind her, and they soon found themselves in a labyrinth of towering hedges. Elena followed the turns until they came to another clearing where two figures were talking quietly. She slowed down at the sight of Zanthus talking to a guard.

"...the test worked, my Lord," the guard said. "On all of them. The royal physician reported—"

Zanthus held up a hand and cut him off when he spotted Elena and Zahra.

"Lady Elena," he addressed her, not sounding pleased to see her at all. "What brings you out here so early?"

"Good morning, Lord Zanthus," Elena greeted him, silently kicking herself for not turning on her heels and fleeing at the sight of him. After overhearing his conversation with Halder, he was the last person she wanted to run into. Zahra bowed her head respectfully to the royal advisor.

"I woke early and thought I'd explore the gardens before breakfast," Elena explained, sounding slightly defensive.

"It will be a beautiful day," he said. "How nice that you can make the most of it while the rest of us are locked away in meetings deciding the fate of the realm." He gave a little laugh, and Elena smiled politely, ignoring the stab of anger at his patronizing remark.

"And is Adina looking after you properly?" He stared at her without a hint of warmth.

"Yes. She has made me feel very welcome," Elena replied. "As have King Arran, Queen Amaya, Prince Tarrick, and Prince Leon," she added.

"A wonderful family," Zanthus said, disregarding her deliberate omission of his name. "So welcoming to strangers and easily trusting. They always want to give people the benefit of the doubt."

Unlike you, Elena thought.

"And have you spoken with Tarrick since last night?" he asked, watching her closely.

She stiffened at his question. "No, I haven't seen any of the family this morning," Elena said carefully.

"I see," Zanthus mused.

Elena remained silent.

"He will be an exceptional king one day." He stroked his chin, fingers rasping against the scrubby beard before adding, "With the right people around him to advise and guide."

Elena stopped herself from rolling her eyes at his emphasis on the last part. Her patience was wearing thin at his jibes and snide comments about her being human. By the light of day, Zanthus was less threatening and came across as a petty sycophant.

"I'm sure," she said warily. She racked her mind to think of a way to politely get away from the man.

"May I speak frankly, my dear?" He continued without waiting for her reply, "Tarrick is charming, attractive, powerful, and you are not the first woman to look at him the way you do, nor will you be the last."

"Excuse me?" Elena asked incredulously.

"I have seen you lusting after him. Believe me, I have seen nearly every woman who meets him flirt and tease him, hoping to steal a kiss and, in some cases, more."

Elena frowned.

"Tarrick is an Elemental prince and has the future of this country resting on his shoulders. He's fallen for your type before, and it hasn't ended well. So, I suggest you get any notions of, as Leon says, *hooking up* with him or a *holiday fling* out of your head."

If Zanthus hadn't just insulted her, she would have burst into laughter at how ridiculous and awkward those phrases sounded coming from him. Instead, Elena stood in stunned silence. She tried to come up with a clever retort but came up blank as his words washed over her.

"Now, if you'll excuse me, I have a very busy day ahead," he said, striding past them. His guard followed closely, murmuring in his ear.

"What the fuck was that?" Elena exploded when he was out of earshot.

~ 17 ~

T arrick wandered through the garden aimlessly. After a restless night of tossing and turning, he had decided a walk in the fresh air would help clear his head. It was becoming more and more difficult to ignore his growing attraction to Elena. The glimpses of her fire, dry sense of humour, and shrewdness coupled with those warm brown eyes, soft curves, and her shy smiles left him reeling.

"How's a man supposed to control himself?" he muttered as he turned a corner and groaned internally.

The palace gardens were big enough that he hadn't anticipated running into anyone, especially so early, but there was Elena—the woman he was trying to avoid—stomping along the path, Zahra striding beside her. The women didn't notice him at first, and his ears pricked up at their conversation.

"...I have never heard him speak in such a manner," Zahra said, looking uncomfortable.

"I can't believe I saved his life," Elena fumed.

They stopped short at the sight of the prince. Zahra immediately dipped her head and murmured a greeting. Elena simply stared at him in irritation until Zahra elbowed her, at which Elena lowered herself into a clumsy curtsy and mumbled, "Good morning, Your Highness."

Tarrick raised a brow at her reluctant greeting. Her cheeks pinkened as she collected herself.

"Is everything alright?" he asked. He glanced at Zahra, but the guard studiously kept her attention ahead when she straightened herself.

"Everything is fine," Elena huffed, edging past him.

Tarrick walked beside her silently, noting the disgruntled expression on her face when she realized he intended to accompany her. He battled between the desire to respect her privacy and the protective streak that made him want to rip into anyone who upset her.

"Princess Malina is back there if you are looking for her," Elena said, waving a hand vaguely behind her.

"Why would I be looking for Malina?" Tarrick asked, irritation creeping into his tone.

Elena gave him a knowing look, which made him sigh.

"We're *not* engaged. Or planning to be," he said, wishing he didn't sound so defensive. "Did she say something to you? Is that what's bothering you?"

"No." Elena hesitated, sidling a glance at him. "I guess I just assumed after last night…"

The only sounds as they walked were the crunching of their shoes on the gravel footpath and the *lyrabirds* twittering in the trees.

"If someone has upset you, I would like to know about it," he finally said as they reached a fork in the path. He threw a glance over his shoulder, but Zahra maintained enough distance to allow them a private conversation.

"You have a busy day today," Elena murmured. To his disappointment, she chose the path that led back to the palace.

"I do," he agreed. "But I'm glad I ran into you."

Elena peeked up at him through her lashes.

"I spoke to my parents last night, and we agreed that you and Adina could spend the day in Erindell today," he told her. "With guards, of course. Erik and Zahra will accompany you to town, and you're to be back before sunset."

Elena stopped and raised her brows.

"I know my sister." He rolled his eyes. "After the Full Moon Festival fiasco, I have a feeling it wouldn't take much to sway you to go along with one of her hare-brained schemes to escape the palace or cause mayhem."

"I'm not a child," Elena snapped. She bit her lower lip and flushed.

Tarrick's curiosity was heightened at what could have upset her so early in the day. "I know you're not, and I didn't mean to offend you." He rubbed his jaw with a hand. "I just meant that I didn't want you to get bored, and I'd rather know you are safe and protected while we are in meetings all day."

"Right," Elena muttered.

"I saw you enjoying yourself at the Full Moon Festival and thought you would like to see Erindell properly," he explained gently.

"What about the assassin and rebels?" she asked.

"Erindell is safe during the day," Tarrick assured her. "There are guards patrolling the city streets, and as long as you stay close to Erik and Zahra, you'll be fine. Adina knows the rules—blend in, don't draw attention to yourselves, and stay in the main city. It will be busy with locals going about their business. My spies on the ground haven't reported any trace of rebels, and Erik and Zahra have strict instructions to bring you straight back at the slightest sign of danger."

Tarrick watched her closely as she mulled over the information. He realized he had revealed a lot of information he probably shouldn't have, but something about Elena made him trust her implicitly. Or perhaps he was assuring himself that she would be safe outside the palace.

"Your parents agreed to this?" Elena looked at him with wide eyes.

He gave her a crooked smile. "They also know Adina gets bored easily."

"And you've told her the plan?" Elena asked skeptically.

"I did," he nodded, frowning. He made a mental note to keep a closer eye on his sister, knowing the summit would tempt her into employing covert—possibly dangerous—methods of gathering information. The trauma of almost losing her when she was just a baby made him forget she was of an age where she could be included in political discussions. "She squeezed me so hard I'll probably bruise." He smiled at his weak attempt at humor.

"Hmm."

"What do you mean 'hmm'?" he frowned.

"Nothing," Elena replied. "Just surprised at the turn of events after Lord Zanthus made it very clear that we were all to remain in the palace."

"My uncle can be overprotective and zealous with security at times," Tarrick said warily.

"You don't say," she said under her breath.

"But he means well."

Elena merely eyed him before resuming her brisk walk back to the palace. It wasn't until the entrance came into sight that she said in a bright voice, "Spending the day in Erindell sounds great. Thank you for arranging it."

"You're welcome," Tarrick said, taken aback by her sudden change in demeanor. "I'm just sorry I can't show you the city myself."

"That's okay." She beamed at him. "Adina and I will have a great time together."

He tilted his head, assessing her.

She stared back at him innocently.

***

Elena had been quiet on the walk into town—her run in with Zanthus that morning and his threats from the night before plagued her mind. She tried not to react to the sounds of birds rustling in the bushes and unexpected loud noises. Adina didn't notice Elena's jitters as she talked about Erindell and the itinerary she had planned for the day.

The princess wore a plain blouse and skirt to blend in with the locals. It was a stark contrast to her embroidered, colorful dresses with elaborate pleats and skirts, and tunics with decorative cuffs and collars.

It was nearing the middle of the day, and Elena's neck hurt from constantly turning to take in the sights of Erindell. The town had been magical at night and was just as enchanting by day. The narrow streets and alleys were crowded, and Elena was jostled by people pushing past while she dawdled, but everyone was friendly and polite.

Adina slowed down to take in the scenes, beaming at Elena's reactions to the beautiful buildings. Erik and Zahra trailed the two women discreetly, always keeping them in sight and within arm's reach.

"That's the biggest bathhouse in Erindell." Adina pointed to a large, domed building where small groups of men and women entered. She went on to explain the bathhouse experience to Elena, who stared in wonder. Small puffs of smoke and a steady trickle of steam emitted from the dome.

"It's such a luxurious experience." Adina sighed. "To have someone massage and wash you before sitting in the steam room and letting all your worries just melt away."

"That does sound nice," Elena agreed.

"I'll ask Mother if we can use the royal bathhouse while you're here." Adina's eyes lit up at the idea. "She normally hosts an afternoon tea for visiting royals. Maybe she could turn that into a bathhouse experience."

"I'm not sure I'm ready to see naked Skandorians." Elena shuddered at the visual.

"It's just for the women." Adina giggled. "Men and women bathe separately in Terralea. Father and my brothers use theirs after training with the guards."

"Are there bathhouses where they bathe together in Leneira?" Elena wrinkled her nose.

"King Halder told us about the Skandorian steam rooms. The host apparently whips everyone with herbal twigs and branches to get the blood circulating." Adina sounded revolted by the idea of being assaulted during what was meant to be a relaxing activity.

"I can ask Malina about it," Elena mused. "I met her this morning in the garden," she said, noticing Adina's look of surprise. "She was ... civil. She told me about Skandor and how she misses it."

"I see." Adina pursed her lips and continued walking along the street past shops and stalls selling colorful fabrics.

"She didn't seem too bad," Elena said cautiously.

Adina scanned the area before she turned to Elena and spoke in a low voice. "King Halder is a strong leader. His ability to speak to animals is the only reason his people tolerate having him as their king. He isn't known for his generosity or kindness. I think he wants Malina to marry Tarrick because he has an ulterior motive that will only serve his own interests."

Elena bit her lip; it was her chance to reveal that Halder and Zanthus were collaborating on the marriage contract. But something held her back.

A whistling sound had her whipping her head around and ducking just in time to avoid being knocked out by yet another silver tray whizzing past. It seemed that everyone in Erindell drank endless amounts of tea. Trays laden with beautiful tulip-shaped glasses filled to the brim with amber-colored hot liquid flew about the air, and Elena had already experienced several near misses.

"Elemental powers are incredible," she said, changing the subject.

"Keep your voice down." Adina nudged her in the ribs. "We're supposed to blend in, remember? We don't want to advertise the fact that you're not an Elemental. People will ask questions."

"Sorry." Elena dropped her voice. "I just can't believe how handy it is for everyday life. I have so many questions about Leneirans. Everyone looks so young! I wouldn't know if someone was thirty or hundreds of years old. I mean, Leon only looks a couple of years older than you. When do you get married? Have children?"

Adina threw her head back and laughed out loud. "Don't tell Leon that. He'll start preening even more, and we'll be treated to another lecture on his beauty regime."

Elena shook her head. "Whatever he's doing, I want in on that."

"We slow down changing, physically at least, in our third or fourth decade of life." Adina chuckled. "From then on, it's hardly noticeable. Mother is in her fifth century. Father and Uncle Zanthus are in their sixth."

Elena's jaw dropped.

"I forget the actual numbers." Adina shrugged. "Mother married Father when she was around my age. They had Tarrick a couple of centuries after. I think she was in her third century, which is normal by Leneiran standards, I guess."

"That takes the pressure off," Elena mumbled.

"That's enough biology and maths for one day." Adina shook her head. "What do you think about our abilities though?"

"They're incredible," Elena sighed. "People are so creative with them."

Adina grinned. "Wait until you see it in action at tonight's entertainment."

"I don't know." Elena laughed. "The guy using the wind to hold up his book and turn pages while he cooked was pretty impressive."

"More impressive than the florist making her flowers bloom when a customer buys them?" Adina teased.

"That was cool," Elena agreed. "Although, you could have given me the head's up about all the tea trays flying around the place."

"Let's keep going." Adina tugged Elena's hand and led her down yet another alleyway. "There's still lots to see, and I want to tell you what I've found out about this mysterious human woman who was at the palace a hundred years ago."

"Wha—"

"Not here." Adina's eyes darted around the crowded street.

They wove through the throngs of people and found a quiet residential corridor where only a handful of old women trudged along sedately. Zahra and Erik followed, keeping their distance to give Adina and Elena some privacy.

"Leon told me Kyra has been avoiding you," Adina said in a low voice.

Elena looked at the princess blankly.

"Kyra," Adina repeated impatiently. "Mother's maid. She's supposed to help you wash and dress. It would explain your hair."

Elena rolled her eyes at being reminded about a maid she'd met once very briefly. She was getting better at braiding, but her silky tresses had a mind of their own. As the day progressed, strands of hair unraveled, framing her face and cascading over her shoulders, but she didn't care as she tucked yet another loose strand behind one ear.

Elena leaned in closer to whisper, "She seemed scared of me on my first day here."

"I found her last night after dinner," Adina continued. "She started working at the palace after the uprising, but she told me her mother had worked in the kitchens during that time. Her mother had told Kyra of a human woman named Rose, who lived in the palace for nearly a year. Apparently, Tarrick and Uncle Zanthus brought her back to Terralea when war broke out in your realm."

"But why did they bring her back?"

Adina shrugged. "No one knows. But Kyra's mother caught this Rose person snooping around and acting strangely a few months after she arrived in Terralea."

"Strange how?" Elena frowned.

"I don't know," Adina sighed. "Kyra was a girl at the time, and only remembers some of the stories her mother told her."

"Where is Kyra's mom now?" Elena asked. "Can you ask her directly about Rose?"

"She lives in a village near the border of Sailon," Adina replied gloomily. "I would have gone to meet her myself, but it's a day's ride."

Elena blew out a sigh. "I guess it'll have to stay a mystery."

"No," Adina said fiercely. "If this Rose was part of the rebellion, we have a right to know. It's our history and should be on record. That's the part that bothers me. Why isn't all of this recorded somewhere?"

Elena stared at the fired-up princess.

"We record *everything* that happens at the palace," Adina explained.

"So why keep a human woman's presence in the realm a secret?"

"That's the question!" Adina exclaimed. "She must have done something really awful for it to be hushed up like this."

"Is my presence here being recorded?" Elena asked.

"I don't know." Adina tapped her chin thoughtfully. "It should be. Everything that happens at the Peace Summit will definitely be recorded."

"We could check out the library," Elena suggested.

"No." The princess shook her head. "I've spent half my life taking lessons and doing research there. I haven't come across anything in recent history about humans in the realm."

"Are you sure?"

Adina gave her a look.

"Fine." Elena rolled her eyes. "Does your brother keep a journal or anything? Maybe he wrote down what happened. *Dear Diary...*" she said jokingly in a dreamy voice.

Adina stared at her. "That's genius! Why didn't I think of that? I'll see if I can find Tarrick's diary from that time."

"You can't be serious." Elena shook her head, smiling slightly. "That's an invasion of his privacy, and *for real*? He has a journal?"

"My father keeps one too," Adina informed her. "All rulers are required to, but their diaries are kept under lock and key. Only current rulers and advisors are granted access to those. There's a lot of sensitive and personal information that could be deadly if an enemy was to get their hands on them."

"I'm not stealing your brother's journal just for a bit of gossip," Elena said firmly. "It doesn't matter anyway. I'm only here for a few more days."

Adina's face dropped at the last part. "Don't you like it here?" she asked sadly.

"Are you kidding?" Elena threw her arms out, shaking her head. "Erindell is amazing. I love being here and exploring with you. But I can't stay forever."

"I'm sure you could."

"How?"

"Where there's a will, there's a way." The princess shrugged.

Elena rolled her eyes again.

"Come on, let's keep exploring," Adina said, taking Elena's arm and leading her back to the bustling streets of the town. "I'll think of a way to keep you here if it's the last thing I do. It's nice having a friend."

The Elemental princess didn't notice the soft look that crossed Elena's face at being called her friend as they delved back into the crowd.

~ 18 ~

The light breeze from the river nearby carried a slight aroma of fish as Adina led Elena to the indoor spice market. Her jaw dropped at the sight of such vivid colors. Ruby red, golden yellow, warm orange, deep burgundy, and sage green spices heaped in mounds and piles lined the sides of the market along with bags of herbs and teas. The air inside, perfumed with the scents of dried herbs, fruits, and pungent spices, had Elena salivating. Elderly shop owners and their young lackeys stood at the front of every stall, holding out silver platters of samples of the sweets they had after a meal. They glittered like small gems and jewels under the warm lights.

"Sweets! Tea! Coffee! Spices!" they shouted repeatedly, only pausing to attend to customers who stopped at their stalls. The sounds of gold and silver coins clinking filled the air as they were counted.

Elena eagerly tried as many flavors as she could. Sweet rose, nutty pistachio, sharp apple, sour cherry, tangy pomegranate, cloying berry, and nutty sesame all melted on her tongue. She licked her lips, savoring the exotic tastes and textures. After having her fill of the sweets, they left the spice market through the exit at the opposite end of the building and found themselves in the narrow, crowded streets of another open-air market. Large pieces of dark fabric stretched across the tops of the small buildings to protect the stalls and people walking through from the sun.

An eclectic jumble of shops lined the streets, selling fresh produce, more sweets, kitchen equipment, art, and everyday items.

There was the odd café and restaurant where people sat at low tables and watched the others haggle over lamps and tea sets. Elena continued exploring, allowing Adina to guide her through the maze of alleyways and corridors.

Erindell's market square yawned before them where the Full Moon Festival had taken place. All signs of the festival had disappeared, and the square was filled with stalls where the large bonfire had been. Colorful shops and cafes lined the edges of the area.

They took a seat at one of the small, spindly tables outside one of the coffee shops tucked into a shady corner. Adina placed an order for two cups of coffee and a plate of sweet and savory snacks with the server, who greeted them with a smile. Erik and Zahra took up discreet positions near the table.

"This is nice." Adina sighed.

The server came back with small cups of thick, rich, sweet coffee and a plate of food. Elena took a sip of the elixir and nearly moaned with pleasure when the liquid slid down her throat. It was just the pick-me-up she needed after being on her feet all morning. Adina grinned at her over the rim of her own cup.

"Terralea food and drink is the best in the realm," she declared. "We have talented cooks in the palace, but there's nothing like experiencing it on the streets amongst the people."

Elena nodded in agreement. Now that she was seated, she realized the coffee shop was ideally located for people-watching. She and Adina took in the locals bartering with the vendors, arguing about the quality of the wares and provenance before finally settling on prices.

A beautiful lamp shop displayed colorful candle holders in various shapes and sizes decorated with tiny pieces of colored glass set in patterns around the holders. The owner waved a hand to light and put out candles to demonstrate the beauty of the lit pieces to passersby.

A man sat on a stool to the side of his stall of piles upon piles of carpets and rugs of different sizes, woven with colorful patterns and prints. The owner happily sipped on a cup of tea and conversed with a customer holding up a blue and gold patterned rug that shimmered in the sunlight. Despite the plethora of people milling about and the bustle of activity around her, Elena didn't feel claustrophobic. She enjoyed being another face in the crowd and had forgotten about assassins or rebels.

Elena turned to her friend, who was taking in the scene with a smile on her face. Adina marked various people in the throng, eyeing shops and stalls where crowds gathered to examine the latest wares.

"This is really nice," Elena said, throwing her head back and basking in the warm sunshine. "But are you sure you wouldn't rather be at the Peace Summit?"

"I much prefer this." The princess gestured to the square. "They won't take me seriously at the summit because I'm so young, and only the rulers and royal advisors speak. And I'm not all that interested in international agreements and contracts. I'd rather focus on making Terralea a better place."

"Won't their decisions affect the people of Terralea?" Politics was not Elena's strong suit.

"To an extent." Adina shrugged. "But I'm interested in how we can make the Terraleans' daily lives better. I'd be able to have more of a say in that if I were on the Council of Nobles since they look after internal matters. That woman over there, for example." She pointed discreetly to a woman at a tea cart parked next to the rug shop. A long line of people snaked around the square, patiently waiting for a cup of tea. The woman used her elemental powers to fill the colored glasses with hot water and handed them out with a big smile on her face. "She came to Erindell a few years ago and requested a loan to set up her tea cart. A rebel group destroyed her family's farm in the north and killed everyone. She escaped and made her way to the capital while they pillaged the town."

"That's horrible!" Elena said, shocked.

Adina nodded and smiled. "Look at her now. Her teas are the best in Erindell. People come from all over Terralea just to try them."

"What makes them so special?" Elena asked, squinting at the cups that people enthusiastically sipped from.

"She grows special herbs and fruits in her backyard." Adina took a bite of a cheese-filled pastry. "When she's not selling tea during the day, she's making her own infusions and tisanes with what she grows. They're really delicious. She supplies the palace with tea too."

"That's amazing." Elena reached over and took a pastry, her stomach rumbling loudly. "What are the rebels doing now? Are they close by?"

"There are some groups that try to attack Elementals along the borders and in remote parts of Terralea. When she came across a patrol at the nearest city and told them what had happened, they escorted her to the palace. Tarrick and Uncle Zanthus set out to find the rebels. She decided to stay in Erindell with her aunt, and I helped her set up the business."

Elena gave her friend an admiring look.

"The couple selling the glass jewelry and art over there." Adina nodded her head toward a small shop with windows filled with beautiful, delicate glass sculptures and bowls of beads that glittered and threw spots of coloured light in the daylight. "She was at the Full Moon Festival."

Elena remembered watching the woman make a glass bracelet in minutes and admiring the piece when it was completed.

"They needed space to sell their wares, so the Council of Nobles helped them find the shop. I believe they make the glassware for a few restaurants around the country."

As Adina pointed out people who had rebuilt their lives after suffering at the hands of the rebels, Elena was surprised at how involved Adina's family was in so many causes. They were genuinely interested in the ventures and knowing the outcomes. Adina knew the smallest detail of those the Council of Nobles had helped, given that there was so much else to do to look after the kingdom.

In the human realm, it was usually forced by a PR company or advisor who attached the ruler's seal of approval and name to various charities or businesses as an endorsement. None of the leaders Elena knew of took the time to check in with a tea maker or aspiring glassware entrepreneur after the posed event.

The woman selling teas started to clean up her cart as customers dwindled. Elena watched her make two cups of tea and place them carefully on saucers with cubes of sugar and small biscuits on the side. She came over and offered the cups to Erik and Zahra.

"With my compliments." She smiled.

The guards accepted the tea gratefully. No one in the square paid them any attention, and Elena's eyes wandered to the glass shop where a couple emerged smiling, the man carefully holding a large box. She happened to glance over to Adina and caught Erik covertly slipping a piece of paper onto the table.

Adina stretched out her hand casually and, without looking down at the piece of paper, raised her other hand to the owner of the coffee shop, indicating she would like the bill for their lunch.

Elena opened her mouth to comment, but Adina shook her head a fraction in warning, and she snapped her mouth closed.

"Your bill," the coffee shop owner murmured, placing a small silver tray with a folded piece of paper on it. She busied herself clearing the table, piling the dirty plates in one hand. Elena noticed the tea lady and her cart had disappeared.

"Thank you, Yas," Adina said, rising to her feet.

Elena also stood and thanked the woman for her hospitality.

"Let's go walk by the harbor," Adina suggested.

They walked in silence through Erindell, Erik and Zahra taking up their usual positions behind the women. The sloping streets led down to the harbor that housed a few boats and small ships.

Along the way, Elena paused at construction sites where workers molded bricks with their powers, bringing together clay, water, and wind to shape them. The bricks were laid as soon as they dried to form walls in record time.

Metal workers controlled the flames over which they worked with one outstretched hand while the other twisted and turned metal over the heat.

It was less crowded by the river, and a cool breeze brushed across Elena's skin. The sounds of children squealing and shrieking in delight carried over from the other side of the river. The oldest, who appeared to be no older than ten, was gleefully forming small waves that rolled over their bare feet. The smaller children laughed and asked him to do it again.

Sailors and workers shouted at each other from the boats as they tugged and tied off lines of ropes. A few controlled the wind in the sails to keep the vessels steady on the bobbing water.

Adina paused by the water and said in a low voice, "Yasmina, who owns the coffee shop, and Briana, who has the tea cart, keep me posted on rebel movements and signs of uprising."

Elena's jaw fell open.

"My brother has his spies, and I have mine." The princess grinned at Elena's expression. "After hearing so many stories of suffering and loss, I wanted to do something to help our people in a practical way. I set up a small group to help me keep tabs on the rebels and any suspicious activity in the regions."

"Briana and Yasmina are part of that group?" Elena asked in a hushed voice, staring at the princess in awe.

Adina nodded. "Everyone in my little network across the country has suffered at the hands of the rebels. After the council helps survivors, I visit them to make sure they're settling into their new lives and if they need anything else."

"That's so thoughtful," Elena murmured.

"I do a little discreet digging into their background and scope them out before I approach them with *my* offer." Adina's eyes lit up with delight at finally being able to share her secret with someone. "I ask if they'd like to do something tangible to make sure no one else goes through the same things they did. Those who say *yes* have been helping me keep track of the rebels. I've asked them to look into the assassin."

~ 19 ~

"That note Erik slipped you," Elena said in a hushed voice, realization dawning.

Adina nodded. "Bri hides notes under tea cups. And the 'bill' that Yas gave me was also a coded message. Both their contacts in the rebel groups to the east have reported nothing out of the ordinary. The handful of rebels who live in Terralea haven't made any plans or moves to attack. They don't have the resources or manpower to execute a full-blown attack."

"So your uncle is wrong about a growing rebellion?" Elena furrowed her brows.

"Maybe." Adina shrugged. "Or he knows something my people don't, but that's unlikely. Yas and Bri aren't the only ones in my network—they have relatives and friends who've all suffered at the hands of rebels and want to do something about it. They're part of the chain of communication I set up that covers the entire country."

"If something were to happen, couldn't they tell your brother or Lady Netta? She's on the royal council, right?"

"Not everyone is comfortable reporting to authority figures." Adina shrugged. "Especially if they're only going on whispers and rumors. This way, they tell me what they've heard, and I make an innocent remark or suggestion that pushes my brother and father to investigate. Besides, no one pays close attention to a coffee shop and tea cart owner or lonely fisherman. They're observant and can eavesdrop on conversations without arousing suspicion. And Bri can sneak into gatherings and meetings pretending to sell tea."

"I learn something new about you every day." Elena shook her head.

Adina laughed.

"The element of surprise." She winked. "Promise you won't tell my family about this?"

"Of course," Elena replied immediately. "No wonder you were so happy about Tarrick letting us come into town."

"He thinks I come here to have coffee and shop. His spies around town obviously report back to him. He always asks if my coffee was strong enough or what tea flavor I enjoyed as a reminder that he's keeping an eye on me. Sometimes, I'll buy some fabric or visit Lady Netta just to keep up the ruse."

"You're too cunning." Elena chuckled.

"Welcome to my spy network." Adina giggled. "I bet he asks you the same questions at dinner tonight."

"I'll be sure to tell him my coffee was strong."

Adina laughed.

"But it still doesn't solve the mystery of who is trying to kill my brother and uncle, and if there are plans to come after the rest of us." The princess sighed. "Nor does it explain the guards' failing elemental powers."

"You say that so casually," Elena said, her voice laced with concern.

"The perks of being royal," Adina said sarcastically. "There's always someone trying to get to us. Usually a disgruntled citizen who we can talk around and help. Uncle Zanthus keeps warning us that the rebels could stir up trouble any day and plan another uprising. He sees enemies everywhere."

"That's his job, isn't it?" Elena asked cautiously. "As head of the guard, he needs to be aware of enemy activity and threats."

"I guess so," Adina brooded. "But he can be a killjoy at times."

"The Erindellians seem to be content and looked after from what I saw today," Elena volunteered. "I'd be comfortable walking around town by myself."

"That's what I mean," Adina sighed. "If he and my brothers spent even a day among the people, they'd see that most of them are not a threat to us."

"Do your brothers take him seriously?"

"They spend so much time locked away in meetings and negotiations with representatives from the regions and diplomats that I can't remember the last time my brothers came to town." Adina frowned.

"That you know of. Tarrick was at the Full Moon Festival, remember?" Elena pointed out.

"Oh, yeah," Adina pondered with a smirk. "I still have to ask him about Madame Zorra."

"Do we need to head back?" Elena gazed across the water. The shadows along the boardwalk were growing longer. It was still light, but the sun had made its way across the sky.

"Yeah, we should." Adina glanced back to where Erik and Zahra stood dutifully. "Don't want to be late for dinner."

Neither woman moved, both wanting to make the most of their rare moment of freedom. The quiet jealousy Elena harbored for the princess—who had a loving family and the privileges that came with her royal status—gave way to pity. It occurred to Elena that for all her complaining, she still had the freedom to travel and do as she pleased. She realized how much richer her life was for it compared to Adina, who had to fight just to be able to visit the town her family ruled.

When a cool draft of air blew through the harbor, Elena and Adina shivered in their thin dresses. The princess waved her hands, and the air turned warmer, the goose bumps on Elena's arms disappearing instantly.

"Let's go," Adina finally said reluctantly.

Along the way, Elena indulged in a fantasy of an alternative life where she lived in Erindell. She would probably work in a shop or café with her lack of elemental abilities. She pictured herself buying groceries at the markets like all the locals seem to do and enjoying the Full Moon Festival every month. By the time they reached the palace, she had a dreamy look on her face as she imagined living in the magical realm.

***

Dinner that evening was a more boisterous affair. Elena had to remind herself several times to close her gaping mouth and not look so surprised by the entertainment as it took place in between courses. Dancers on the ground and floating in the air, musicians playing lively tunes, performers exhibiting their prowess with fire and water creatures of all sizes, and acrobats from around Terralea dazzled the visitors with their abilities, traditional dances, and songs. Just as the Erindellians had done at the Full Moon Festival, the display of elemental powers in a softer, more artistic expression enraptured Elena.

She was mesmerized by the wind billowing around the skirts of the dancers, exaggerating the twirls and spins, the acrobats juggling spheres of blue and green flames, the entertainers floating around the room in giant water bubbles performing aerial tricks and illusions. The petite gymnast covered from head to toe in vines and leaves cartwheeled around the room, a bright flower blooming about her person every time she completed a turn. She kept going until she was covered in blossoms, which she plucked from the vines and handed out to each guest. The soft, delicate, floral perfume filled the air, mingling with the mouth-watering scents of the dishes that were placed on the long table.

In addition to the spectacular display of elemental powers, the costumes and jewelry dazzled the crowd—colorful fabrics of varying textures gilded with intricate embroidery, beading, and sequins that sparkled as they caught the light. Even the instruments were covered in beads and glitter, the musicians wearing elaborate headpieces with strips of fabric trailing down their backs to add to the dazzling display for all the senses. Translucent veils and masks covered the dancers' faces, adding to the allure and seductive nature of their performance. The crowd was captivated by their hips and arms, swaying fluidly. Elena admired the kohl-lined eyes of the dancers and the way their limbs moved gracefully.

"How's the view from down here?" Leon asked from behind Elena, who sat with Jet and Mika once more at the far end of the dining table, away from the royals.

"Your Highness," Jet greeted him with a broad smile.

Mika murmured a greeting and politely excused herself with a grin. She rose gracefully from her seat and insisted that Leon sit next to Jet before walking to the door.

Leon promptly took Mika's vacated chair. Elena raised her brow at him.

"I'm doing the rounds." He winked at her.

Jet clapped as the magician took a bow. "Elemental powers are remarkable."

"These are some of Terralea's best performers." Leon beamed at him.

"We have acrobats in Sailon, too, but they perform different feats," Jet told him. "And puppet masters. You should visit LaHong. Their shows are unique. I've never seen anything like it outside Sailon."

"I would like that," Leon replied. "A week or two of peace and quiet at one of the monasteries is just what I need after all these negotiations."

"Indeed." Jet gazed into Leon's blue eyes, his lips curving up. "And you, too, Lady Elena," he added hurriedly. "You must visit as well."

Elena made a non-commital noise and sipped her wine. *No wonder Mika was so quick to give up her seat.*

"How have today's meetings been?" she asked Leon.

The prince and Jet exchanged a look before shaking their heads in response. "The usual slow dance and pussyfooting," Leon huffed.

"It's always like that at the start." Jet gave a little laugh. "It can be tedious."

Elena furrowed her brow, not understanding.

"The rulers outline their proposals in vague terms on the first day," Leon explained. "Once they get an idea of the appetite for their proposals, that's when the feast truly begins." He winked as he reached over to steal an olive from Elena's plate and popped it into his mouth.

"Halder has been unusually polite today," Jet muttered. His gaze shifted to the far end of the table where the Skandorians sat quietly, watching the Terralean entertainers with mild interest.

"Malina has been batting her eyes at Tarrick all day and asked him to be her escort tomorrow night," Leon said, sounding disgruntled. Elena took a large gulp of wine.

"You don't support the union, Your Highness?" Jet asked carefully.

"How many times have I told you to call me Leon?" The prince sighed. "And I want my brother to be happy."

"He wasn't happy with her ... attention?" Elena asked casually.

Leon grimaced in response. Elena and Jet glanced down the table to where Malina was sitting next to her father and opposite Tarrick. The prince was listening intently to whatever his father was saying to the group, nodding and avoiding eye contact with anyone else. Malina was slumped in her seat, playing with a fork, looking up at Tarrick every so often with a calculating expression on her pretty face. When Amaya leaned over to speak to Malina, the princess sat up and forced a smile at the Terralean queen.

A round of applause startled Elena out of her thoughts. The performers bowed and accepted the accolades graciously before flitting out of the room. She tracked them as they left the room through a door behind the opposite end of the table. Her eyes locked onto Tarrick, who was also clapping as he stared intently at Elena. She blushed and gave him a small smile. He blinked and turned away, but not before she caught a flash of sadness.

Arran rose to his feet and announced he would once again host after-dinner drinks and water pipes. In the swarm of people leisurely moving to the adjoining smoking room, Elena missed Tarrick ducking out the doors. She peered around the room when the crowd thinned and frowned when she didn't see the prince. Tapping her finger on the table, she wondered where he might have disappeared.

Across the room, Amaya ushered Malina, Netta, Lin, Mika, and Adina to the terrace.

"I'm going to show Jet the gardens if you would like to join us, Lady Elena," Leon said, drawing her attention back to him. The prince's cheeks were tinged a slight pink, and Elena bit back a grin.

The dining area had been hot and stuffy. She was tempted to join them, however, the thought of being a third wheel was about as appealing as another private conversation with Zanthus.

"Thank you, Your Highness, but I think I'll head to my room," she replied, noting Jet's smile widen out of the corner of her eye.

They bade each other good night, and Elena watched the two men saunter out of the dining room. She gave them a few minutes head start before she slipped out of the room and slowly walked to the entrance.

Despite the torches softly illuminating the garden, Elena lost her way down a narrow path and found herself in a maze of unfamiliar bushes and hedges. She frowned but continued ahead, hoping to come across familiar surroundings.

The sound of running water drew her attention, and she walked slowly toward the source. She recalled seeing fountains dotted around the gardens from her explorations that morning.

The trees and foliage finally thinned, giving way to a grassy clearing on a ledge where a pool of dark water reflected the starry sky. The water lapped at the edges dotted with small rocks and boulders. A familiar silhouette sat hunched and brooding on one of the larger rocks, gazing out over the lights of the city of Erindell.

"You found my favorite spot in all of Terralea," Tarrick said without turning his head.

~ 20 ~

Elena approached the edge, and Tarrick glanced up to see the look of amazement on her face. He had accepted there was no avoiding her, despite his best efforts, and felt oddly pleased that she was there. The corner of his lip lifted, and he turned back to the uninterrupted views of Erindell with a renewed sense of appreciation. Below, the market square shone with a large bonfire burning brightly again, an eerie silence settling despite the bustle below.

"I can see why you like it here," Elena said, taking a seat next to him on the stone. "It's beautiful."

"No one bothers me here either," he told her.

"I can leave," she said quickly, making to get up, but he reached out, stopping her.

"Stay," he requested.

"What's that building?" Elena pointed to a small hill on the edge of the city, at the top of which was a large, ancient white stone building with imposing pillars and columns along the outside walls and detailed friezes carved into the stone rooftop.

"That's the Temple of the Divine Beings," Tarrick explained. "They're like our gods. They've been in Leneira since the dawn of time, and they have great and terrible powers. I guess you could say they're the bridge between our realm and the Beyond."

"Beyond?" Elena cocked her head to the side.

Tarrick rubbed his chin, frowning as he explained, "In your realm, your people believe in heaven and hell, right?"

"Some do."

"It's a similar concept. The Beyond is the world we go to after passing. It's ruled by another set of deities who determine where you're placed based on the life you lived here. Some scholars say that it's divided into two—those who have inflicted suffering and pain in this realm are punished for their misdeeds and those who have lived an honest, good life are rewarded in paradise."

"What do others say?"

Tarrick shrugged. "Depends on how creative your parents' bedtime stories are." He gave her a grin.

"Fair enough." She laughed.

"Few have the courage to summon them for favors because it often comes with a heavy price. An answer to a question can cost a life. Not necessarily your own." Elena's eyes widened. "Very few kings and queens have been prepared to make such a sacrifice and have gone their entire lives without encountering them, which is a best-case scenario."

"What kind of question is worth a life?" Elena asked in awe.

Tarrick shrugged again. "The Divine Beings don't interfere with our decisions, but they like to keep balance and order. Whatever that means to them."

"They sound ... ominous." Elena shuddered.

"I summoned them once," Tarrick confessed quietly. Elena's brows shot up. "They denied my request."

"I'm sorry," she said softly.

They sat in companionable silence for a while. It occurred to Tarrick that not even his family had sought him out there. It had been his private refuge for centuries; having Elena beside him was unexpectedly comforting. She was curious but didn't pry. It was refreshing, being able to talk about things other than politics and his future.

"How was your day in Erindell?" Tarrick asked.

"It was incredible." Elena's face brightened. "Erindell is a beautiful city, and the people are so friendly and welcoming."

Tarrick watched her grow more animated as she proceeded to tell him in great length and detail about everything she and Adina had seen and eaten in Erindell that day. He had never seen anyone use their hands so much to describe things. The jealousy he had felt when he saw her smiling widely at Leon and Jet dissipated. His brother could put anyone at ease with his laidback devil-may-care ways and roguish charm. All of that was forgotten at the warmth of Elena's body next to his. The scent of the lavender soap she seemed to have become partial to wafted in his direction every time she tossed her hair or tilted her body toward his.

His grin grew as she spoke, despite the knot in his stomach at the thought of having to break the bad news to her. The last thing he wanted to do was wipe away the smile that lit up her face brighter than any star in the sky. He rubbed his chin—a nervous habit—at the realization that Elena was becoming important to him.

"...and then we had lunch at this cute coffee shop that had the most delicious pastries," she said dreamily before seeing the expression on Tarrick's face. "What did I say?"

"It's not *what* you said," Tarrick grinned, shaking his head.

Elena flushed and dropped her hands to her lap, fisting the fabric of her skirt.

"I'm glad you enjoyed it," Tarrick said sincerely. "It's not often we have travelers who have never seen our city before. It's refreshing to hear about it from a visitor's perspective."

"Adina said you don't visit the town much?"

Tarrick sighed. "Royal duties require my presence at the palace most of the time."

"Except when you sneak out to visit Madame Zorra," she said slyly.

He raised an eyebrow. "She's a woman with many talents, including spying and passing on information."

"Riiiight," Elena drew out the word.

"You think I use her other services?" Tarrick gave her a roguish grin.

"I'm not judging your taste in ... companions." She blushed.

Tarrick's smile waned at the regret that crossed Elena's face.

"What do you think of our elemental powers?" he asked, changing the subject.

"It's pretty cool." She grinned at him. "After seeing how creative people can get with them, I can see why it's a big deal."

"Do you wish you had our abilities?" he asked quietly.

"Why? Is there a way I can ... get ... elemental powers? Some magic potion that will help me manipulate the elements?" Elena asked, eyes widening.

Tarrick broke her gaze and stared out at the twinkling lights of Erindell.

"I've gotten by for thirty-five years without magic. I think I can manage." She shrugged. "When I was five, I used to climb trees and jump off the branches trying to fly. One day, I slipped and fell out of the tree in our backyard and broke my arm. I was devastated because that was when I stopped believing in magic."

"That sounds painful on multiple levels," Tarrick said sympathetically.

"My mom heard me crying one night." Elena smiled at the memory. "She told me that magic was real and I was just looking for the wrong kind. I stopped jumping out of trees after that. Every evening, I watched the sunset from our roof instead. I found magic in the way the colors stained the sky. Dad took me to our local library, and I started calling books portals to other realms." Elena gave a little laugh.

The corners of Tarrick's lips lifted once more. "The irony isn't lost on you now, is it?"

Elena laughed again before continuing. "When I turned fourteen, my parents bought me my first CD player. I became obsessed with the way the melodies and notes made me feel. I'd spend hours listening to music, reading, and getting lost in my own world." Elena turned back to Tarrick with a wide smile. "So even though elemental powers would be pretty awesome, I guess I have access to a different kind of magic."

Tarrick's eyes crinkled at the corners, and Elena's jaw dropped at the first genuine, uninhibited smile she had seen on the prince's face.

"Your outlook on life is..." He shook his head. "The world needs more of your way of thinking, Elena."

She shivered at the sound of her name on his lips and turned away, biting her lower lip. The darkness did little to hide the blush creeping up her cheeks. It sounded as though she didn't often share stories about her life, especially her childhood, and it showed vulnerability. He knew the feeling—it was scary as hell but liberating at the same time.

"And it's nice to see you so happy," he said softly. "I've seen the feisty, independent, strong-willed, witty woman our profilers described."

Elena blushed again. "I'm not sure if she's still around."

"She's here." His fingers brushed against hers. "I saw her dancing the other night at the Full Moon Festival, and I saw her making Leon laugh earlier this evening. She made our Sailonese guests feel welcome and connected with them better than any of our diplomats could. She's a force to be reckoned with."

Elena had spoken at length with all of the Sailonese councilors that evening. Tarrick caught Zanthus frowning in her direction on more than one occasion during dinner, but if she noticed it, she ignored him.

"Your turn." Elena nudged him gently.

Tarrick stared at her expectant face.

"I told you a story from my childhood," she grinned. "Tell me a story from yours. If you can remember that far back," she added with a laugh.

Tarrick thought for a moment, brow wrinkled as he cast his mind back to when he was a boy.

"The first time I visited the human realm was with Father," he said slowly. "I must have been around twenty. Father wanted to show me steam engine trains."

Elena raised her brows in surprise.

"Father was obsessed with trains." Tarrick chuckled. "He wanted to introduce them to Leneira to connect our countries and make travel around the realm easier for everyone. But Halder and Lin's fathers, who ruled Skandor and Sailon at the time, were opposed to it. Our countries weren't as open to exchanging ideas and resources as we are now. Father and I traveled between realms together quite frequently. I found the speed at which things changed to be incredible." He shook his head, smiling fondly at the memories.

"Did you visit the human realm when airplanes were invented?" Elena laughed. "Your father would have been excited by that."

"We did see the first airplane." Tarrick grinned. "But I saw your reaction to Lin's *pihasi*, and I'd wager you find flying horses more impressive than airborne metal tubes."

Elena nodded in confirmation.

"But I love the human realm. I'm the only Leneiran who visits regularly. I always see something new and different." Tarrick sighed.

"Why don't other Leneirans visit?"

"When war broke out in your realm, all Leneiran rulers made the decision to call back our people." A somber expression replaced his smile. "The war was on a scale we had never seen before, which is saying something. The weapons and technology being used at the time frightened us the most. We didn't want to risk our people's lives, given how close the Terralean portal was to the war zone..."

"War is terrible," Elena said sadly. "No one really wins. At least, not without paying a heavy price."

Tarrick nodded. "Before the war, Leneirans had more freedom of movement between the realms. It was also a concession that gave those without powers a chance to find work in the human realm and provide for their families. We set up support systems to help them navigate your world, and it worked well for a long time."

"It sounds like everyone won in those years."

"They did." Tarrick sighed heavily. "Which is why Father was conflicted about closing the portal during the war years. He warned the other rulers that those without our abilities would suffer the most, but the majority voted in favor of closing the portals to keep the rest of Leneira safe and protect our existence. That was when the dissent started…"

Elena clucked her tongue sympathetically.

"Back to your question." Tarrick shook himself out of the sad memories of the past. "The Leneirans who saw the war zones on their way back to the realm brought back stories of death and destruction. The ugly side of humanity. The news spread across Leneira, and even when we opened the portals again when it was safe, no one was interested in visiting."

"Except you." Elena nodded.

"Except for me." Tarrick gave her a crooked smile. "I couldn't wait to go back and explore, but my responsibilities here grew, and I made less frequent trips. The night you saved my life was my first visit to the realm this year."

When Elena remained silent, Tarrick took a chance and asked the question that had been plaguing his mind ever since that fateful night.

"I know you didn't want to tell the council why you took the bullet—" he began.

Elena shook her head as though she had anticipated he would ask that question. "I'm not ready to talk about it yet."

Tarrick studied her as she fixed her gaze on the sprawling city.

"Alright," he said finally. "But promise me you will tell me why before you leave?"

"I didn't realize our bargain came with conditions," Elena said lightly.

"It's a request."

"Why I did it doesn't matter." She frowned.

"It matters to me," Tarrick said quietly. "You matter to me. And I want to make sure you're okay before you go back."

~ 21 ~

Elena's cheeks heated at Tarrick's words, unsure how to respond to his confession. She couldn't deny the growing attraction she felt toward him—the private moments between the two of them seemed to grow more intimate. However, his story highlighted how different they were. How different their futures were.

"I'll be fine," Elena said stiffly, pushing away the feelings he brought out in her. "This isn't the vacation I planned, but after today, I'm feeling better about ... things."

"I'm glad to hear that." Tarrick gave her another half-smile.

Elena opened her mouth to say something, but shook her head and clamped her mouth shut.

"What?" Tarrick asked, amused.

"I actually pictured what it would be like if I lived here." The corner of Elena's lip quirked up as she turned away. "I'd be pretty useless at most things without elemental powers, but I thought maybe I'd be able to get by working in a cafe or the library in town."

"Do you want to stay?" Tarrick asked warily.

"There's nothing for me to go back to in my world," Elena said casually. "But I know I can't stay here. I get why Leneirans are afraid of humans if all they know about us is that we start wars and have technology and weapons that could wipe out entire populations. *I* despair over humanity at times, wondering how we even made it this far."

"I see." Tarrick frowned.

She turned to him with a quizzical look. "Didn't you fantasize about living in the human realm? A what-if moment?"

"I *did* live in the human realm for a while," Tarrick told her. The soft expression from earlier showed no signs of reappearing as he stared moodily into the distance.

Elena sensed he wasn't going to share more. She wondered if he would have stayed in the human realm if his family and country weren't waiting for him.

Before she could say something to bring back that heart-melting smile, Tarrick stood and held his hand out to her. "We should go back." Elena gingerly placed her hand in his and allowed him to help her to her feet.

They walked back through the garden. Only the occasional crunch of guards' boots on the gravel paths in the distance cut through the silence. The air was warm and still. Above, the stars twinkled brightly in the clear night sky. Elena stayed a few feet behind Tarrick, hoping to avoid drawing attention if anyone happened to see them, but no one else seemed to be out.

"There's something I need to tell you." Tarrick paused at the end of a path.

Elena stopped and looked at him expectantly. The flickering light from the torches staked into the ground illuminated the sharp angles of his face.

"Uncle Zanthus doesn't want you and Adina going to town anymore," he told her, his voice full of regret.

Elena bristled and opened her mouth to make a snarky comment.

"And I agree with him," Tarrick said quickly. "The royal physician told us today that the bullet the assassin used wasn't bluestone as we first thought."

"What?" Elena croaked.

"It was an ordinary bullet made to *look* like bluestone," Tarrick explained. He turned his head cautiously to make sure none of the guards were close enough to hear the conversation. "It's raised more questions than it answers. So, for your own safety and ours, the palace is on lockdown until we get to the bottom of this. No one is to leave or enter the Royal Quarter."

"Are you kidding me?" Elena hissed as her eyes flashed with anger. "After I told you what an amazing day I had? What are Adina and I supposed to do tomorrow? And for the rest of this summit?"

"I know, and I apologize for not telling you sooner." Tarrick hung his head, looking guilty.

"This won't affect our deal, right?" Elena folded her arms across her chest and glared at him.

Tarrick shook his head at the reminder. "I'll take you back through the portal myself as soon as the Peace Summit is over, as promised. As for you and Adina, Mother has arranged an afternoon tea at the palace bathhouse tomorrow."

Elena huffed out a sigh and turned on her heel. She marched down the path that led back to the palace and quickened her pace as the entrance came into sight.

"Have you two had a secret tryst in the gardens?" Leon teased, spotting the couple walking up the steps. Jet was nowhere to be seen, but the prince wore a satisfied expression that would have made Elena probe him for details had she not felt trapped once more.

Tarrick glowered at his brother.

Leon raised an eyebrow but didn't say anything. Elena studiously avoided both gazes and stormed up the staircase toward her room. Tarrick followed a few paces behind.

Serkin stood guard outside her door, watching them closely as they approached. He bowed respectfully at the prince but looked down at Elena with judgment. It occurred to her that she'd had encounters with all the people she had intended to avoid that day, and she chided herself for not sticking to the plan.

She paused at her door, turned to Tarrick, and curtsied. "Good night, Your Highness," she said in a steady voice.

***

Elena awoke to loud knocking and dragged herself out of bed to answer the door. Once again, she had spent a restless night alternating between dozing and scowling at the ceiling.

"Why do you lock the door?" Adina asked when she let her in. The princess bounded into the room, surprisingly smiling and cheery for someone confined to the palace.

"Good morning, Your Highness," Elena grumbled.

"Morning!" Adina beamed, then frowned, taking in her sleepy state and lethargic movements. "What happened to you?"

"Nothing," Elena mumbled, padding to the washroom. "Just tired."

She washed and dressed quickly, reentering her room just as Adina accepted a breakfast tray from a maid before shutting the door firmly. The princess swept over to the table and carefully set down the food before taking a seat.

"You don't have to spend the day with me if you would rather be doing other things," Elena told her, sliding into a seat. "I can read in the library."

"Don't be ridiculous," Adina said, wrinkling her nose at the thought of her friend sequestering herself in the library all day. "Mother said today's meetings would only take place during the morning and maybe a little after lunch. She's organized a treat for us all in the bathhouse before the big feast tonight."

"That sounds like fun." Elena reached for a pastry and chewed slowly, savoring the buttery, flakey morsel. "What would you like to do until then?"

"I want to show you something," Adina replied with a mysterious smile. "It's a secret, so don't tell anyone."

"Like anyone would believe me," Elena muttered.

Adina frowned at her friend's lack of enthusiasm.

Elena cleared her throat and forced a smile on her face. "How is Erik? Have you spoken to him? Are his elemental powers back yet?"

"As a matter of fact, he and the other guards affected by whatever happened are starting to get their abilities back." Adina clapped her hands gleefully. "Erik was able to fill half a glass of water this morning *and* light a candle."

"That's great news!" Elena exclaimed, sincerely pleased for the guard. "Do they know what caused this glitch?"

The princess shook her head. "Uncle Zanthus and Tarrick are still investigating," she said. "But it was nice to see Erik smiling again this morning."

"I'm sure you made him smile plenty last night," Elena teased.

Adina blushed. "I may have tried to distract him in other ways," she mumbled, smiling shyly.

"Why don't you tell your parents about him?"

"He's been my guard since I was a child," she sighed. "We've been friends for such a long time. Our attraction to each other has only been a recent development, and I want to enjoy it without my brothers becoming overprotective and interfering. And I don't want Erik to be accused of taking advantage of me because he's not."

"No one who's met Erik would think that." Elena frowned. "He's been nothing but respectful and kind to me since I arrived."

"His commander might accuse him of trying to sleep his way to a higher rank." Adina bit her lower lip. "But he doesn't care about that. He told me he just wants to be with me."

"How romantic," Elena sighed. "I hope it works out for you two. You make a great couple."

"Don't we?" Adina agreed, smiling dreamily. "Maybe he knows someone *you* could have fun with while you're here!" She perked up at the idea.

"I don't think that's a good idea." Elena shook her head. "I'm a dangerous human, remember?"

"They won't know that," Adina brushed off the seemingly minor detail. Her eyes flicked to Elena's wrist, where the Elemental crest was still inked into her skin. "As far as everyone knows, you're Lady Elena of Selindor province. You've done a great job convincing everyone, by the way."

"Thanks." She accepted the compliment, quietly pleased she managed to pull off the charade. It made her feel better about continuing to play the part for the next few days.

"That could be your mission tonight." Adina's face lit up at the idea.

"What?"

"At tonight's feast, you're going to kiss someone," the princess told her with a wide grin. "You can even pick the guard."

"I'm not kissing a random guard because you want me to." Elena's cheeks heated at the thought of kissing a stranger. Her mind flashed to a vision of her and Tarrick kissing, and she quickly pushed that thought aside. It was clear that nothing could happen between the two of them.

"Fine." Adina pouted. "Some friend you are. I'll think of something else."

"What was it you wanted to show me this morning?" Elena asked, keen to change the subject.

"Have you finished eating?"

Elena nodded.

"Let's go!" Adina jumped up and headed for the fireplace in the room that had been unused so far—it hadn't been cold enough to warrant a fire.

She twisted one of the decorative orbs that jutted out from the mantel shelf as though it was a door knob. The entire fireplace swung forward a few inches, revealing a dark passageway just wide enough for two people to walk side by side.

Elena's jaw dropped open at the secret passage that was hidden in plain sight that entire time. She followed the princess into the entrance and paused a few feet inside, allowing her eyes to adjust to the darkness. Adina carefully swung the fireplace back into place, using her elemental powers to conjure a small ball of flames in the palm of her hand. As the fire flickered to life, she pointed out a twin knob inside the passage that would allow them to go back into the room.

"I've found about six of these entrances so far," she whispered to Elena. "I read about the palace having secret passages in a history book and decided to explore."

"Doesn't anyone else know about these?" Elena whispered back.

"Nope." Adina popped her lips on the *p*. "They're too busy with politics and running the country to have fun. No one's ever mentioned them to me, and I've never seen anyone down here when I've been exploring."

Elena followed Adina down the damp, musty passage, squinting at the few feet illuminated in front of her. Her ears pricked up, but the only sounds were the thin soles of their slippers rustling against the stone floor. The solid walls were impenetrable and cold to the touch as Elena reached out to skim her fingers against the rough surface.

Adina stopped at a small recess and beckoned her friend to come stand next to her, holding a finger to her lips in a warning to remain silent. Elena moved closer to a pinprick of light streaming through the wall. A small peephole barely the size of a coin had been drilled into the stone. She rested her forehead against the cool stone, pressing her eyes to the hole.

The room she peered into was the council chamber where she had been questioned by the Terralean royal council on her first day. From that vantage point, Elena realized the peephole was above the fireplace in the chamber and that it was another entrance to the secret passages.

All three rulers and their councils sat around a large wooden table covered in parchments and papers of handwritten notes. Guards stood at the doors, staring straight ahead, but no one seemed to notice a pair of shining brown eyes in the wall, peering into the room.

"No, absolutely not." Zanthus shook his head violently. "We cannot meet those terms and reject your proposition."

"But think of the long-term benefits," a heavily accented Skandorian man argued. "For everyone." He glanced at Lin.

"We don't see how your request benefits Sailon either," Zen spoke in a deep, authoritative voice. "We also reject your proposal."

"The majority have spoken," Arran announced. "Let's move on to the next item on the agenda."

The Skandorian frowned but slouched back in his seat without arguing.

"Is this a Peace Summit meeting?" Elena whispered to Adina, who nodded.

"This is how I find out what's going on when no one tells me," the princess explained, her voice barely audible.

~ 22 ~

Elena peered back into the meeting room, noticing the way Leon and various councilors scribbled every spoken word in their notebooks. Tarrick tapped his stylus on the table and stared out the window pensively. Unlike the sleek, modern styluses Elena knew, the ones used in Leneira were almost like old-fashioned quills—thin sticks with sharpened nibs that were dipped into ink pots every so often.

She wondered if she had been a little harsh the previous night when Tarrick told her that she had to remain in the Royal Quarter. He was only looking out for her, after all.

"This is amazing," she whispered to Adina, taking in the scene.

Lin rested both arms on the table, hands clasped in front of her, and listened attentively to the proceedings. Amaya sat straight-backed, nodding every so often. Halder's hands were splayed out on the table, and he wore a displeased expression. Malina sat still as a statue, and her keen eyes were glued on Rokeby, who was currently proposing increased joint security forces around the blue-stone quarry. The council members who weren't actively involved in discussions or taking notes were whispering amongst themselves, shuffling sheets of paper, and rustling through documents.

It was all very official and boring in Elena's opinion, but then again, she had never taken an interest in politics beyond casting her vote in presidential elections. In her college days, she had participated in a few protests and demonstrations against wars and injustices but had abandoned hope of changing the world when the wars continued and headlines broadcasted yet more bleak news. She stepped back from the peephole, and Adina took her place, watching the proceedings with greater interest.

Elena's eye wandered down the dark corridor, and she wondered how many more passages would afford her unfiltered access to the palace. Adina noticed her fidgeting, and she stepped away from the peephole, reigniting the little ball of light in the palm of her hand and continuing down the passage once more.

They stopped at more niches and openings. Adina pointed out her father's neat and orderly office. Every book was lined up on the shelves, stacks of papers and folders were placed at the corner of his desk, the chair was pushed in, and a full ink pot and clean stylus was arranged on the blotter lining the desk.

Zanthus's office was chaotic and messy with papers and styluses with dried ink on the nibs strewn about his desk, vials of clear liquid, and empty ampoules littered the small coffee table in front of the fireplace. A quiver of arrows rested against the bookshelf, and a crossbow had been thrown carelessly on a chair in the corner. Stacks of books were piled haphazardly on any available surface. Elena had no idea how someone could get work done in such a disorganized environment.

She took in Tarrick's private chambers, glad for the darkness of the passageway that hid the blush that crept up her cheeks at seeing something so intimate. Adina shook her head at Leon's room—untidy but nowhere near as chaotic as Zanthus's office. The princess laughed softly at the stack of magazines and pamphlets on his bedside table. Elena tried to squint at the titles, but was unable to make out the words. Adina told her they were written by men, specifically for men, and catered to Leon's tastes in the bedroom.

"I bet he hooks up with a Sailonese council member before the end of the summit." She giggled. "He was making eyes at Jet last night."

"Really?" Elena asked, amazed. She had noticed the chemistry between Leon and Jet, but didn't think it would go beyond flirting.

"Want to put money on it?"

"I don't have Leneiran currency," Elena pointed out.

"How about a kiss?"

"Excuse me?"

Adina giggled again. "If I get proof of Leon hooking up with Jet before the end of the week, you have to kiss a guard," she said impishly.

"And if he doesn't?" Elena asked, amused.

"Then I'll get my brother to kiss you?"

"Leon won't want to kiss me." Elena rolled her eyes. "You just told me he prefers men."

"Not Leon." Adina shook her head impatiently. "Tarrick!"

"Why?" Elena's cheeks heated.

"You're too pretty not to be kissed," the princess said with a wicked smile.

"First, you sneak out at night after being told not to leave the palace grounds, and now this obsession with kissing." Elena folded her arms over her chest. "I thought you'd be more mature for a hundred-something-year-old woman, but you're basically a teenager, aren't you?"

Adina threw her head back and laughed.

"I guess it's all relative," she chuckled. "Maybe by your standards, I'm a teenager."

Elena shook her head, smiling despite herself. Adina's energy and bubbly personality was infectious.

They continued exploring the passages, watching the buzz of activity in the royal kitchens. The head cook shouted orders, and everyone ran around stirring large pots over naked flames, throwing in spices, and chopping vegetables at a speed that Elena personally felt was reckless. She made a mental note to eat slowly lest she accidentally ingest a chopped-off digit.

Elena had to admit she was enjoying the morning and learning more about Leneira. Adina explained things to her patiently and went into detail about the hows and whys of running the country. From her insights and keen observations, the princess seemed to understand the essence of the Terralean people.

"My visits to town help me understand what they need—more resources, more time, or more financial support," Adina reiterated as they made their way back to Elena's room. The princess wasn't keen for their absence to be noticed and questioned. "I like to see how the Erindellians are doing and going about their daily lives. And, obviously, it's a chance for my spies to let me know if there's any rebel movement or future uprisings to watch out for."

"You really care for the people, don't you?" Elena asked in wonder.

"Of course! I'm their princess," she said. "It's my job to know that they are looked after."

"You would make a good queen," Elena said with a smile.

"Unlikely." Adina shrugged. "Tarrick is next in line. And he's still young. He also has a better understanding of the dealings with Skandor and Sailon, which is why he's at all the meetings with our father. But I would like to be in charge of Terralean matters."

"That sounds right up your alley," Elena agreed.

They reached her bedroom, and Adina made her practice opening and closing the entrance so she wouldn't trap herself in the passage if she wanted to explore by herself. But Elena wasn't at all keen to get lost wandering the secret passages few knew about.

Her bedroom was empty and untouched when they reentered, and they carefully sealed the passage entrance, making sure there were no signs or trails of their escapade.

"I'm still trying to solve the mystery of this human woman in Terralea," Adina said, picking at the leftover food on the tray. They set up the table by the balcony to bask in the warm air that filtered through. The crunch of gravel from the grounds outside indicated that patrols carried out their duties. It was a beautiful sunny day. Elena was itching to leave the palace and explore more of Erindell, the pull of the town even stronger after Tarrick had told her it was forbidden.

"There's no mystery," Elena said absent-mindedly, reaching for a piece of fruit. "Your brother told me that Leneirans fear humans because they've only been told stories of the wars and destruction we cause."

"That's stupid." Adina rolled her eyes. "The war ended decades ago, didn't it? And not all humans fought."

"*That* particular war did," Elena grimaced. "And there are still a lot of shitty people in the world. Your family is right to keep you here. It's safe."

"There's shitty people everywhere." Adina gave Elena a scathing look. "You're just seeing the best of what we have to offer in the safety of the palace and Erindell."

"I guess." Elena shrugged. "I'd still prefer to be here."

Adina's face broke into a smile. "I knew you'd come around."

"I can't stay, Adina." Elena laughed. "I'm just saying it's not all bad being here with you."

"I'm working on it," Adina insisted. "And I wasn't talking about the mystery of why Leneirans are afraid of humans. I'm talking about the woman—*Rose*—who was in the palace before the uprising."

"I have a feeling that's going to remain one of life's mysteries." Elena sighed. "She obviously wasn't here for very long, and whatever she did must not have been important enough to record."

"That's not it," Adina disagreed. "I think there's a conspiracy about why her presence here was kept a secret."

"Maybe she also saved your brother and uncle's lives and had to hide out here during a Peace Summit," Elena said sarcastically.

"The Peace Summit was set up after the uprising," Adina scoffed. "Before that, all our countries were … not exactly enemies, but not nearly as friendly and collaborative as we are now."

Elena raised her brows but didn't comment.

"I'm going to get to the bottom of this," Adina said determinedly.

"Okay." Elena sighed. "Write me a letter explaining everything when you do."

A sharp knock on the door drew Elena's attention away from the stubborn expression on Adina's face. She opened it, revealing the same maid who had brought her clothes on her first day. The girl entered, curtsying to the women but avoiding eye contact with both.

"Her Majesty has requested your presence in the royal bathhouse," she mumbled. Before either Adina or Elena could say anything, she slipped out of the room.

The princess gave Elena a look. "If we knew more about this human woman. We'd know why Kyra and the rest of them are so scared of you."

"Rest of them?" Elena raised a brow.

Adina blushed when she realized her mistake. "I might have asked other palace staff," she mumbled, avoiding her eyes. "They're all … concerned."

Elena shrugged. "I'm only here for a few more days. I don't need to win any popularity contests." But it still hurt a little to know there were more people who were afraid of her because of something that had happened a century before.

Adina reached out to squeeze her friend's hand reassuringly.

~ 23 ~

Adina and Elena walked through the garden and down a shaded path where the ground was damp and the air more humid. A mushroom chimney poked from the top of a small stone building before them. Elena stared at the structure in astonishment.

"The shape of the roof keeps the warm air circulating inside the bathhouse without having to constantly have a fire going," Adina explained, opening the door to the entrance. A cloud of thick steam hit Elena, and she flinched, closing her eyes instinctively. She stretched out her hands and cracked an eye open, feeling her way across the hazy threshold into the bathhouse.

Female attendants dressed in white pants and cream-colored tunics greeted them in the entrance hall. They directed the princess and Elena to a small chamber off to the side, where they were instructed to undress and follow the passage to the main room.

They stripped off all their clothes, Elena hesitating at first at the lack of modesty but not wanting to come across as too prudish in front of the princess who paraded across the room completely nude. They grabbed towels, wrapping them around themselves before stepping out into the narrow passage. Soft plumes of fluff tickled their skin as they padded to the main bathing chamber. Elena carefully picked her way across the steam-filled room to the large stone table in the center, directly under the chimney roof.

Amaya, Lin, and Zen were already lying on their fronts, towels covering the lower half of their bodies. Bathhouse attendants massaged hot oil into their backs. Zen groaned in delight as a woman worked on the knots and muscles around her shoulders.

"Welcome, my dears," Amaya said languidly, raising her head slightly to greet Adina and Elena. "Make yourselves comfortable. I did invite Malina, but she has a headache and is sleeping it off this afternoon."

Elena laid down gingerly on her front, and an attendant gently helped her adjust her towel around her lower back. The scent of lavender filled her nostrils as warm oil was poured onto her skin, the liquid sliding across her back before strong hands worked it into her skin. Her muscles unclenched and Elena sighed deeply as the attendant worked on the tense knots. She must have purred out loud because she heard Adina giggle. It wasn't long before Elena was relaxed and loose-limbed amongst the swirling steam and soothing sounds of running water.

Murmurs echoed, and water spurted from a shower in one of the cubicles lining the sides of the bathing chamber. Another murmur and the next woman stood and made their way to the shower. When it was Elena's turn, she reluctantly stood up and was guided to a stone cubicle with a shower head where a jet of warm water was running.

The attendant used a bar of soap to gently lather Elena's body and wash off the oil before wrapping her in a towel and pointing her in the direction of another room. Elena walked through slowly, adjusting her towel. The steam was thinner in that chamber, and the others sat in a large stone pool, enjoying head massages.

Adina smiled lazily at her friend. Elena whipped off the towel and quickly climbed into the pool, still trying to wrap her head around the idea of being surrounded by naked royalty. She sank into the water, and an attendant stepped up behind her, gently guiding her head back so Elena could rest it on the edge during the scalp massage.

"How are you feeling?" Adina murmured.

"So good," Elena exhaled slowly. "This is so relaxing."

The attendants stepped out of the room and closed the door, giving the women privacy while they enjoyed the warm water.

"Lady Elena," Lin addressed her directly. "Tell us how you came to be here."

Elena glanced at Amaya, who nodded encouragingly. There was no point in lying to Lin, so she took a deep breath and told her and Zen everything. They listened closely, only raising their brows and exchanging glances with each other every so often as Elena recounted her experience.

"Well, that's quite a story," Lin said.

"Have you heard anything about another rebel uprising or stirrings, Lin?" Amaya asked.

"This is where real politics take place," Adina smirked. The corners of Zen's lips tugged upward. Despite her quiet, intimidating manner, Elena felt she could trust the imposing woman.

"We haven't heard anything, no," Lin said thoughtfully. "But I will send word to my guards to make inquiries and see if they can make contact with the rebels along the borders."

"If they're still active," Zen muttered.

Amaya raised a brow.

"We've had more people seeking asylum and telling us about depleting resources in the rebel communities," Zen explained. "We've verified their stories. It seems unlikely that rebels are a threat."

Lin nodded in confirmation.

"I'm also concerned about the bullet." Worry tinged Amaya's voice. "Arran is sending more guards to the quarry to find out if anyone has been harvesting bluestone illegally."

Elena bit her lower lip. Amaya spoke of the bullet being bluestone, even though Tarrick had revealed that was not the case. *Does Amaya know about the latest development? Did Tarrick tell me that to show he trusts me? Or to warn me?* Either way, it wasn't her place to be spilling information the prince told her, so she remained quiet.

"We will do the same," Zen said reassuringly. "And make discreet inquiries if any unauthorized people have been seen in the area. We should also tighten security around our portal," she told Lin, who nodded in agreement.

"Thank you. Your help with this matter is so appreciated," Amaya said gratefully. "I'm worried Halder will take an unnecessarily extreme approach before we get a full understanding of the facts and reasons behind this attack."

"I understand," Lin said tightly. "Do you know if he intends to formally propose a marriage contract between Tarrick and Malina this summit? He's been hinting at it for years, but has never spoken so openly or seriously."

Elena's stomach tightened, and she kept her face blank.

"I don't know," Amaya sighed. "I don't know what Halder's goal is with suggesting the union, and Tarrick is keeping tight-lipped about it. I was hoping you would have some insights." She slid a glance to the Empath queen.

"Your son's shielding abilities are remarkable," Lin said unsmilingly. "Zanthus is eager to see your countries united."

Her words were neutral, but Elena noted the skepticism in the Empath queen's tone.

"I must confess that I'm concerned such a union would be only in the interests of Skandor. It could jeopardize Terralea and Sailon's relationship if the terms of the contract are not in our favor."

The casual warning in her words was clear to everyone. Adina's eyes darted between her mother and Lin as though watching a tennis match.

"Halder will use the threat of rebels as an excuse to push for joint forces," Amaya mused.

"And Sailon would see that as a disruption of the peace and equality between our countries we have fought to maintain for so long." Lin's eyes narrowed to slits. "Leneira's most powerful soldiers uniting to form a single army would upset the fragile balance that currently exists."

"The Terraleans wouldn't be thrilled either," Adina murmured, cupping some water and splashing it over her face. "The Shifters are not viewed favorably by the people."

"Oh?" Lin turned to Adina inquiringly.

"The Skandorians' reputation for being ruthless precedes them," the princess elaborated. "The Terraleans would not be pleased to host an army of Shifters, if that is what King Halder proposes. And I imagine our own guards would take a while to adapt to the northern conditions, leaving both countries vulnerable to threats as everyone adjusts."

"Your daughter has a point, Amaya," Zen said. "It leaves both countries open to attack while armies transition, and we are not as well equipped as we once were to manage such an upheaval while continuing our current protection strategies."

"If there *are* internal threats" —Lin gave Amaya a sharp look— "now is the time for all of us to unite."

"I agree." Amaya nodded. "I'll speak to my husband."

"Perhaps I could join you for discussions tomorrow," Adina suggested. She threw Elena an apologetic glance. "Just in the morning. Then, I'll go back to Elena."

"Don't worry about me." Elena waved a hand. "I'll be fine on my own."

"Very well." Amaya nodded. "You may join us in the morning."

Amaya steered the conversation toward the Isles of Minos and the elusive royal family who ruled the country.

"Have you heard from Theo?" she asked the Empath queen.

"Unfortunately not," Lin replied.

"A pity," Amaya sighed. "Perhaps one day, Theo and Halder will be able to come together again for the good of Leneira."

At Elena's curious expression, Adina explained. "The Isles of Minos are in the easternmost part of the realm. Their royal family never attends the Peace Summit, nor have they made contact with anyone on the mainland in over a hundred years."

An attendant coughed quietly at the doorway.

"Tea is served, Your Majesties, Your Highness, my Lady," she announced.

"That's our cue to stop talking about politics for now." Amaya smiled widely at her guests.

"Oh, good!" Adina exclaimed in delight. "You will love this, Elena."

She climbed unabashedly out of the stone bath and tied on one of the robes placed on the stone bench along the wall. They all slipped on robes and followed Adina out to a small shaded enclosure surrounded by thick, dark hedges and trees with large canopies dotted around the edges.

In the middle was a low table of steaming pots of tea emitting different aromas, colorful glasses on saucers with tiny glass spoons, bowls of sugar cubes, and golden honey. Plates of bite-sized delicate pastries and cakes too pretty to eat were arranged in between the pots, along with thin wafers laden with cured meats, pickles and cheeses, bowls of fresh fruit, and a pitcher of ice-cold sherbet for anyone wanting a chilled drink. Around the table, poufs and large pillows lay on top of colorful rugs and carpets, similar to the tents at the Full Moon Festival. It was the fanciest tea party picnic Elena had ever seen.

Lyrabirds hopped close to the group, eyeing the food with their beady eyes. A few swooped through the trees and warbled in the shade, adding to the idyllic atmosphere.

The women lowered themselves onto the poufs and pillows and passed around plates of food. Amaya poured out tea for everyone, and they exclaimed in delight at the liquids that changed color when sugar was added. The conversation continued in a light-hearted vein. Lin and Zen told the others about the teahouses in Sailon, where a master of ceremonies brewed the tea in front of the guests while they snacked on chewy sweets. Elena listened to the queen and her wife talking enthusiastically about their home, fascinated by all the exotic places and customs they described.

"Are you enjoying your stay in Terralea so far, Elena?" Lin asked warmly. All signs of her regal mask had disappeared when Amaya ended the conversation on politics.

"Very much," Elena answered honestly. "Queen Amaya and her family have been so gracious and made me feel very welcome."

"For what you did, it's the least we can do." Amaya smiled at Elena's compliment.

"I wish I could explore more of the country," Elena said. "And visit Sailon. It sounds just as magical as Terralea."

Lin and Zen exchanged smiles.

"It is a beautiful country, and we wish more people would visit and experience what we have to offer," Lin told her.

"Do Leneirans not travel?" Elena asked, nibbling on a spiced pastry.

"Once upon a time, we did." Zen had a faraway look in her eyes. Elena wondered how old the woman was; she spoke as if she had been alive in the time she spoke of. "When there was more exchange of people and ideas. But not in the last few centuries—at least, not our citizens. Members of royal families and their delegates travel on official business, but not for pleasure."

"I wish that would change," Adina grumbled. "It's so stifling being stuck here."

"We are working toward restoring that collaboration, Your Highness." Lin laughed. "It's why we initiated these Peace Summits. But it is a slow process. One that requires open communication and trust on everyone's part."

"You have my family's adventurous spirit, my darling," Amaya said fondly, running the back of her hand down her daughter's cheek and brushing away strands of damp hair. "I remember my grandmother taking me on a tour of the realm when I was a girl. One day, you will have your chance to see the world."

"You would be most welcome in Sailon, Princess." Lin bowed her head. "We would be honored to have you stay with us."

"Thank you." Adina smiled.

"And you, Lady Elena." Lin's eyes twinkled. "Perhaps, for your actions, King Arran and Prince Tarrick will grant you special permission to visit us once everything has settled and we open the portals to your realm again."

"Is that possible?" Elena gaped.

"Let's not get ahead of ourselves," Amaya cautioned. "We would need permission from all council members of Leneira and protocols in place for everyone's safety and peace of mind."

"Then you could visit us whenever you wanted to!" Adina said excitedly. "I'll come and get you myself."

"It would take a lot of convincing." Lin shook her head.

"Elena saved Tarrick. He owes her," Adina argued.

Elena didn't say anything. The small flicker of hope she had died when she realized Zanthus would never grant her special permission to come and go as she pleased, no matter the circumstances.

But for her friend's sake, she forced a smile and continued to eat and drink, reminding herself to enjoy every minute of the time she did have in Terralea.

Amaya spent the rest of the afternoon tea regaling her guests with stories of previous queens of Terralea and the rites of passages and coming of age rituals the strong women and fierce warriors underwent before ascending the throne. She told them of how they used their wit and charm to seduce men into revealing secrets and lies, the subservient wives and consorts in public who held more sway over the kings and rulers in private. They were also trained from a very young age in physical combat, learning sword fighting, archery, hand-to-hand combat, and some even served in armies for a time. Elena felt equal parts deeply inspired and woefully inadequate by the stories.

The words rolled off the queen's tongue like lyrics to songs or poetry, the entire group enthralled by her words and the way she wove the stories together. Even the *lyrabirds* flying around the garden paused and hopped closer to the queen. They nestled themselves in the grass, their rainbow-hued plumes adding more color and magic to what was already an enchanting setting. Their bright pink heads bobbed in the emerald carpet, listening intently to the stories, chirping softly every so often. Elena praised Amaya's skill as a storyteller, and the queen smiled.

"Amongst my people, we call them songs," she explained. "Because of the way they are narrated and the words deliberately chosen to evoke the feelings of the tales."

Lin and Zen pitched in with stories of their own queens and rulers who had made history. They even entertained Amaya, Adina, and Elena with tales of their own youthful escapades and near misses with demons and the wild animals that inhabited the jungles of Sailon.

"We have cleaned up the country over the past few decades" —Lin smiled at the princess, who was hanging on every word— "as best as we can. My father had conservative ideas and ruled accordingly, but I have loosened the reins a little to give my people more freedom and the option to hold themselves accountable for their own actions. They know the consequences of acting in direct threat to our country, but we have shown them they are ultimately responsible for themselves. It took some time, but they have responded well."

"There are a few exceptions," Zen admitted while taking a sip of tea. "But we realized since the uprising that regardless of their intentions, people have a routine. They follow patterns, and we have deliberately turned a blind eye to the clubs and dens in Sailon they haunt. Or so they think," she added with a smirk.

"We have people who work in these dens and clubs." Lin's eyes twinkled. "They keep us informed of any threats or traitors. Those who work against us will always work in the shadows under the cover of night and in places of ill repute to find those who align with them and to operate covertly."

"That's so clever," Adina breathed slowly. "But you just told us one of your country's secrets!" she exclaimed.

"Your mother was my only friend when I ascended the throne," Lin told her. "There are no secrets between us. She was the one who guided me at the start and told me we needed to earn the people's trust and loyalty in order to uphold our values of peace and friendship. Without them, I wouldn't be queen."

"As royals, we must remember our subjects are people with their own ideas, beliefs, and opinions. We try to respect individuals while acting in the interests of the collective." Amaya smiled gently at her daughter. "Sometimes, I think it's easier to learn to control our powers than our thoughts and feelings."

"It's not an easy job," Lin grimaced. "Believe me, especially when the inequality between Leneirans is undeniable. The people really feel it."

"Where there are people, regardless of where they come from and what abilities they possess—if any—there is room for anger, hate, fear, and sadness, which manifests in our vices and weaknesses," Amaya said. "But we also have the capacity to love, choose peace, and show courage in challenging times."

"Without the difficulties we face, we would not be able to appreciate the good in our lives," Zen agreed. "It's all about balance."

They toasted to those profound statements.

Elena reflected on the Sailonese queen's honesty about the darker sides of her country, how she changed her views about them and saw that they served a purpose. Her perspective and open-minded nature was more useful in helping her people than an army forcing them into submission. She understood better how Lin had built a reputation as one of Leneira's greatest queens whose people loved and respected her.

The sun started to set, and the heat of the day gave way to the cool evening. Amaya gazed at the magnificent colors in the sky and said, "We should return to the palace to get ready for tonight's feast."

The throne room had been transformed into an opulent setting for the night's festivities. Staff weaved around the room with trays of gold-stemmed glasses of champagne, wine, and *araki*. White and gold floral arrangements stood on every high table around the edges of the room. Crystal baubles hung off the cornices and moldings, reflecting the dancing candlelights in the large chandelier. Metallic streamers and small flags with the Terralean crest framed the large windows overlooking the gardens.

It was early. Only a few Skandorians and Sailonese clustered in small groups, keeping their distance from each other. A smattering of Terralean advisors and ambassadors spread amongst the two groups, straining to make conversation and engage with the guests.

Tarrick and Leon were the first of the Terralean royals to arrive. They navigated the room skilfully, making polite conversation with those present.

"How many more hours of this?" Leon asked, tugging at the heavy, embroidered jacket he wore over his tunic. He and Tarrick sought a moment of respite from hosting duties and stood by the door, taking in the scene.

Tarrick let out a long-suffering sigh. For all his vanity and time spent on his appearance, Leon hated dressing up "to the nines" as he put it. Both princes wore their golden circlets again for the formal event, although Tarrick's felt heavier, seeming to bear the weight of his responsibilities as the future king of Terralea.

While grumbling under his breath, Leon swiped a flute of champagne off a passing server's tray and took a large sip.

Tarrick merely gave his brother a withering look before scanning the room. The guests included members of the Terralean Council of Nobles and various lords and ladies from the regions. They had been instructed to make the Sailonese and Skandorians feel comfortable, but the few conversations Tarrick had overheard on his rounds were strained and awkward. He sighed internally—they could only lead the horses to the water. At that moment, all the horses in the room were casting suspicious glances at each other and holding conversations in low voices with their fellow countrymen.

"Fuck it," he muttered, making eye contact with a server who immediately glided over and offered the prince a glass of wine. "Thank you," he said to the waiter, who bowed and shuffled back to his position in the corner.

"How are things with Elena?" Leon asked once Tarrick swallowed a mouthful of wine.

"Fine," he replied, keeping emotion off his face and avoiding eye contact with his brother.

"Just fine?" Leon asked skeptically. "Does that mean you two have kissed and made up?"

Tarrick whipped his head toward Leon, who raised his hands, one still clutching his glass, in surrender. "Metaphorically speaking."

Tarrick shrugged in response.

"It's okay to like her, brother," Leon said softly. "Not all women are like Rose—"

"There's no point," Tarrick said louder than intended.

Leon merely raised a brow.

"She's got another fifty, sixty years tops?" Tarrick lowered his voice, looking around to make sure no one could hear them. "It wouldn't exactly be a long, happy life together, even if she did want to be with me."

Leon tilted his head to the side.

"I promised to take her back to her realm as soon as the Peace Summit is over," Tarrick said, biting his lower lip. "She doesn't want to stay, Leon."

"From what I've heard, she doesn't have anything to go back to," the prince said gently.

"I've learned my lesson," Tarrick replied harshly. "I know she's not like Rose, but I won't force her to stay."

Leon eyed his brother sadly, but his face brightened when he shifted his gaze over Tarrick's shoulder.

Tarrick turned around, and his breath hitched when Elena entered the room. Her lips parted in awe as she took in the decor. He swallowed at the sight of the navy dress that clung to her figure and accentuated every curve. The luxurious satin shimmered subtly with every movement. A plunging neckline framed her décolletage in a tasteful way, exposing the delicate slope of her collarbones.

The dress's low-cut back dipped sensuously to the small of her spine, held together by delicate, crisscrossing straps providing a tantalizing glimpse of the brown skin beneath. Elena took a few steps further into the room, and as she moved, a thigh-high slit revealed itself with each step. The glimpse of toned legs added a daring air to her otherwise elegant silhouette. The hemline flirted with the ground, revealing the gold straps of the heels wound around her ankles. She wore a gold cuff to cover the inked Terralean crest and a pair of chandelier earrings that sparkled as they caught the light.

Tarrick's eyes traveled up to her face, and even from that distance, he caught sight of pinkened cheeks and gold shadow swept over her kohl-lined eyelids. Her dark brown hair hung in loose waves around her expressive face, with intricate, small braids woven through and decorated with gilt-tipped pins.

Beside her, Adina donned a gold gown to match the decor, and wore a smug expression as she caught sight of her brothers. Elena was too busy admiring the room to notice the princess wiggling her brows at Leon and Tarrick.

"Fifty or sixty years of happiness sounds better than centuries of wondering what might have been," Leon said, jolting Tarrick out of his trance. Before he could reply, his brother sauntered over to the women with his customary cheeky grin. Tarrick trailed behind him reluctantly.

"Perhaps I should spend an afternoon in the bathhouse," Leon greeted them. "You look gorgeous!"

"Thank you, Your Highness." Elena smiled widely at the princes and curtsied.

"My sister has a thing for gold, in case you couldn't tell." Leon cringed as he gestured to the room.

Adina responded with an elbow to his ribs. "Good evening to you, too, Leon," she glowered.

"It's stunning," Elena said breathlessly. The corner of her mouth tugged upward when she noticed Tarrick's eyes raking her body. His mouth went dry at the sight of her lips, dabbed with red lipstick. Time stood still when his smoldering gaze finally met hers, and they drank in the sight of each other.

"Your friends have been asking for you," Leon said to Adina, tilting his head toward a gaggle of women whispering and giggling in a far corner of the room.

Elena tore her gaze away from Tarrick to the group Leon indicated. They were clad in the finest silks and jewels, and they smiled and waved to the princes. A few of them fluttered their lashes and smiled coyly, but Tarrick could only stare at the woman in front of him.

"I suppose I should go say hello." Adina made a face. "I trust you'll look after Elena?" She eyed Tarrick with a sly smile.

Once again, he was not allowed to respond as Halder and Malina entered the room and caught sight of him. They made a bee-line toward their group, Halder practically pushing his daughter in front of Tarrick. The prince silently cursed the persistent Skandorian king.

Malina wore a shimmering, figure-hugging silver gown that showed off every curve and asset. A delicate silver tiara with blue gems was perched on her head, contrasting against the golden hair that trailed down her back.

Halder had made an effort for the occasion and traded his heavy fur vest for a fitted, light blue tunic with a silver sash cutting across his large figure. His hair was neatly combed back, mustache and beard tamed into place with wax. Despite the regal attire, he still had the appearance of a fierce warrior.

Tarrick and Leon greeted Halder and Malina with sharp bows.

"King Halder, Princess Malina." Elena dropped into a curtsy and lowered her eyes. "A pleasure to see you again."

Tarrick noticed the forced smile she plastered on her face. Despite her nerves, she stood tall, shoulders back and chin raised slightly.

"Tarrick, Prince Leon." Halder inclined his head. "Lady Elena, how nice of you to join us," he said in a tone that suggested the opposite. "You are a friend of Adina's, are you not?"

"Yes." Elena nodded.

"A friend of all of ours," Leon chimed in. "Our family has had dealings with Lord Taib for a long time now."

"And what dealings would they be?" Halder's eyes bored into hers.

"Agriculture, Your Majesty," Elena replied coolly. "My father is heavily involved in our family's estate and preparations for the harvest season."

"And where is he this week? Surely a lord can spare a few days for his king?"

"It's a long way to travel from Selindor province," Leon interjected. "Lord Taib visited only recently."

"I see." Halder raised his brow at the explanation.

Leon cleared his throat awkwardly. "Why don't I introduce you to some people?" He offered Elena his arm and shot Tarrick a sympathetic look. "You can be my buffer in case there's a slip of the tongue."

"I thought you welcomed a slip of the tongue," Elena said with a wicked twinkle in her eye as she threaded her arm through his.

"Divine Beings have mercy." He stared at her. "Are you drunk already?"

Elena shook her head, laughing.

Halder and Malina watched the exchange silently.

"I have a feeling this is going to be a memorable evening." Leon patted Elena's arm and led her further into the room, greeting the Sailonese, who had just arrived.

Tarrick watched them leave, envious of his brother's good fortune. He barely heard Halder droning on about the contracts that had been discussed that day and other political matters, only pausing to applaud Arran and Amaya's entrance. Tarrick dipped his head as they walked past, smiling warmly at everyone.

When they reached the center of the room, Arran turned to his wife, bowing and holding out his hand, requesting a dance. Amaya placed her delicate, slim hand in his, which Arran promptly brought up to his lips to plant a kiss on her knuckles with a wink and roguish grin. The crowd tittered, and the opening notes from the musicians at the back of the room filled the air.

Lin dragged Zen to the dancefloor, and the crowd made way for more couples to join in the lively dance. Leon and Elena hovered at the edge of the crowd, Elena fumbling while he tried to show her the steps. She soon picked it up, twirling in his arms and following his lead as though they had been dancing together for years.

The uplifting song was loud enough that Halder paused the conversation with Tarrick, but it also meant the prince was forced to watch Leon and Elena laughing together. When she threw her head back and flashed her teeth in an uninhibited smile for the fifth time, Tarrick had had enough. He all but shoved his wine glass into the hands of a server and marched over to Leon and Elena.

"May I cut in?" Tarrick asked through gritted teeth. Leon placed Elena's hand in his brother's with a knowing smile.

"Have fun, you two," he sang, and glided over to Adina's friends, who immediately started giggling and flicking their hair when he reached the group.

The music changed to a slower tune. Tarrick grasped Elena's right hand with his left and placed his right hand on her waist. She held onto his broad shoulder and looked up into his amber eyes.

"I'm sorry I got angry with you last night," she said abruptly, taking him by surprise. "I shouldn't have lashed out like that when you're only looking out for my safety."

"I understand," Tarrick said with a small smile. "I don't blame you at all. It's not fair to make you feel trapped when you've done nothing wrong."

Elena bit her lower lip and dipped her head.

"If there's anything at all I can do to make this ... situation better, please tell me," Tarrick said softly.

Elena's expression softened. "It's fine. I had a really nice day with Adina and your mother in the bathhouse."

"I'm glad to hear that." A corner of his lip quirked up, unsurprised that his mother and sister had come to the rescue. "And I haven't forgotten my promise to you."

"Thank you," Elena said softly. A conflicted expression crossed her face before she broke into a smile. "How was your day?"

"The meetings were productive," Tarrick told her, shoulders sagging with relief at her smile. He moved the two of them fluidly around the dancefloor as they made small talk while they danced.

"You're a natural," Tarrick exclaimed when she executed a perfect double spin.

"I didn't take dance classes for five years for nothing." She winked at him.

"What other secrets are you keeping from us?" he teased, spinning her again.

Elena glanced around the room to make sure no one could hear them.

"I didn't think I had any secrets from you. Didn't the report tell you my entire life story?" she asked with a deadpan expression.

"I must have skimmed over the dancing." He grinned. "It was a long report."

"Oh? What about the pottery classes? And cooking lessons? Anything about my secret love for video games and sci-fi films?"

Tarrick chuckled. "I went to the cinemas once to see a spy film," he told her. "I'm sure it was good, but I kept looking back at the room where they kept the equipment. I wanted to know how it worked."

"You're such a nerd," Elena teased.

She moved closer to him when the tune changed. They swayed to the slow, melancholic song in silence. The singer's lilting voice told the story of bittersweet memories, the melody evoking a number of emotions in Tarrick.

"I have to confess, I was jealous of my brother," he admitted, a smile playing on his lips. "You both find it so easy to talk to each other and laugh."

"It's like I've known him for years instead of days." Elena shrugged. "I feel comfortable around him and Adina."

"And me?" Tarrick asked hesitantly.

The music changed again at that moment, picking up speed. Another guest grabbed Elena's hand, and soon she and Tarrick were dancing in a group, nimbly weaving around in a circle, switching partners with every spin, laughing as they bumped into one another. They moved faster as the tempo increased until the song crescendoed, leaving them breathless. Everyone dropped the hands they were holding to applaud except for Tarrick, who still held Elena's hand tightly.

Before she could untangle their intertwined fingers, a man cleared his throat loudly, interrupting the moment. They looked around at Zanthus, who held a glass of wine and wore a smile that didn't meet his eyes. Malina stood by his side, eyeing the couple closely with pressed lips.

"Tarrick, Malina has requested a dance," he informed the prince.

Elena curtsied and peeked up at Tarrick through her lashes, a shy smile playing around her mouth. He bowed and brushed her knuckles with his lips, holding her stare with molten eyes.

Zanthus frowned, noting the looks they exchanged. "Perhaps you could keep me company, my dear," he said, reaching out to grab Elena's elbow and steering her forcefully to the side of the room away from the dancefloor.

Tarrick reluctantly turned to Malina with a smile plastered onto his face. "Your Highness." He held out a hand and dipped his head.

She held herself stiffly as Tarrick placed his hands gingerly on her slender waist. Where he had once felt lush curves and soft skin under his palm, he now held onto hard muscle and bone. Nevertheless, he drew her closer, and they swayed slowly to the romantic melody.

Malina kept her gaze locked firmly over his shoulder as he guided her around the dancefloor.

"Are you enjoying your stay in Terralea, Your Highness?" he asked, desperately searching for a neutral topic of conversation.

"Yes, Your Highness," Malina replied quietly.

"I'm glad to hear it," Tarrick said lightly.

He caught sight of Leon and Adina dancing together, pulling faces at each other and pretending to swoon at the impassioned lyrics. Those watching them dance tittered at their antics. A pang of jealousy hit him at the sight of his siblings so carefree without the pressures he faced.

As Tarrick scanned the room, Halder's lips lifted, and he raised his wine glass to him, nodding approvingly. The prince's mother and father were busy dancing with a Skandorian council member and Lin, respectively. In the corner, he spotted Elena and Zanthus, who seemed to be having a terse conversation.

Tarrick's brow furrowed as he caught his uncle towering over Elena as he spoke to her. To her credit, she didn't seem intimidated. She crossed her arms over her chest and tilted her chin up defiantly, replying to whatever he said in a voice too low for anyone to hear. Zanthus gestured sharply around the room, and Elena shook her head, jaw clenched in anger.

"Your Highness?" Malina's impatient voice cut through.

Tarrick snapped his head toward the princess and realized it was not the first time she had addressed him.

"Apologies." He bobbed his head and mustered a polite smile. "You were saying?"

Malina's gaze traveled to the corner where Elena and Zanthus stood. "Would you please excuse me, Your Highness?" she asked cooly without taking her eyes off Elena, who had spun on her heel and marched along the edges of the room toward the doors. "I'm not feeling well and will return to my suite."

"Of course," Tarrick said, releasing her from his hold and stepping back.

They bowed to each other. Malina slid past Tarrick toward her father, whose smile faded as he watched her return to him. Tarrick turned on his heel and walked quickly to the entrance.

"Did you see Elena leave?" he asked Erik, who stood guard outside the ballroom.

The guard gave a sharp nod. "She said she wanted some air, Your Highness," he replied.

$$\sim 25 \sim$$

Elena didn't pay attention to where she was headed when she left the palace. Her legs guided her through the gardens until she found herself standing at the edge of a cliff, looking over the city of Erindell. She sat heavily on the stone bench and gazed out at the twinkling lights.

Although she was livid at Zanthus, she was angry at herself for allowing the man to put her in her place and tell her what to do. After being inspired by Amaya and Lin's words of wisdom and advice earlier, she had fallen back into old patterns of feeling inadequate and unworthy because the royal advisor had simply said so.

"Elena?" a voice called out from the copse of trees and bushes behind. "Are you here?"

"Go away, Tarrick." She stiffened at the sound of his voice. "You shouldn't be here."

"Seeing as this is *my* favorite place..." he started to say, his voice laced with humor.

Realization dawned on Elena as she took in their surroundings.

"What's wrong?" he asked, noting her clenched fists.

"You're right," she said quietly. "I'll leave."

"No." He sat next to her. "Please tell me what's wrong. What did Uncle Zanthus say to you?"

"You shouldn't be seen with me," she told him. "Especially by King Halder and Princess Malina. They might get the wrong idea."

Tarrick furrowed his brow.

"You're going to marry Princess Malina," Elena sighed. "You can't be seen fraternizing with other women."

"I'm not marrying her," he said in amazement. "That hasn't even come up."

"Lord Zanthus said that it was a done deal," Elena pointed out.

They stared at each other.

"Uncle Zanthus shouldn't be speaking for me," Tarrick groaned, massaging his temples with both hands. "I'll have a word with him."

They sat in silence.

"Is that all that's bothering you?"

Elena hesitated but shook her head slightly.

Tarrick stood up, pulled off his jacket, and kicked off his shoes. In two steps, he was by the edge of the pool. The sound of the water lapping against the edges was soothing, and Elena would have been content to sit there all night.

He dipped his feet in the pool and waded in, still wearing his pants and tunic. The fabric clung to his muscular legs, and he sank in until he was neck-deep in the dark water. He turned around and grinned at Elena, who was watching him open-mouthed.

"Come on in," he called out. "The water is perfect."

"Are you crazy?" Elena exclaimed.

"The water has healing properties," he told her. "You'll feel better."

"Can't you just get Adina to heal your injuries?" she asked, eyeing him suspiciously.

"Not all wounds are physical, Elena." His smile faded. "You of all people should know that."

"How deep is it?" she asked, biting her lower lip and inching closer to the pool. She peered into the inky black depths, looking for signs of the bottom.

"I don't know." Tarrick shrugged.

Elena dipped a hand into the water and felt it tingle against her skin. It was warm and inexplicably soothing.

"I don't want to ruin my clothes," she said.

"You can take them off if you want," Tarrick said with a wolfish grin.

Elena gave him a look.

"Or I can dry you after." He laughed.

Elena paused, then made up her mind. She unstrapped her gold heels and tiptoed to the edge, allowing the water to lap her toes before carefully making her way into the pool. The water continued to effervesce around her, and the dress clung to her body. She felt the bottom of the pool sloping toward the middle where Tarrick stood, and she stopped when the water came up to her collarbone.

The corner of his mouth twitched. "How does it feel?"

"The water is nice," Elena conceded, letting her arms float on the surface and watching the tiny bubbles kiss her skin. "Does it really have healing properties, or was that just a ploy to get me in?"

"That depends on how you feel," Tarrick replied, cocking his head to the side. "Do you feel better now?"

Elena rolled her eyes and inched toward the edge of the pool that overlooked Erindell. The bottom stayed level all the way, and she rested her arms on the few inches of grass that separated the pool from the cliff edge. She felt the water ripple as Tarrick made his way closer to her, but she didn't move.

"You can tell me if something is bothering you." His warm cedar and sandalwood scent washed over her. "But you can also tell me if you'd like to be alone."

"You can stay. I don't mind," Elena said softly. "To answer your earlier question, I do feel comfortable around you. But right now, I hate that I had such a good day, and now I'm reduced to a sniveling mess hiding in the garden." She shook her head angrily. "This is not who I am. This is not who I want to be!"

"Who do you want to be?" Tarrick pulled her around by her bare shoulder and looked at her curiously.

"It doesn't matter," Elena muttered, her cheeks heating when she realized she had said the last part out loud. "I was feeling good about myself this evening before Lord Zanthus—" she broke off awkwardly, catching sight of Tarrick's eyes narrowing at the mention of his uncle's name.

"What else did Uncle Zanthus say to you?" he demanded.

"Tell me about the human woman who was here a hundred years ago," she replied.

A look of anguish crossed Tarrick's face, but Elena didn't back down.

"Lord Zanthus and the palace staff are convinced I'm a threat because of what this woman did," she told him. "I need to know what happened so I can tell them—*show* them—I'm not like her."

Tarrick eyed her for a moment, then sighed. "I was in love with Rose, and she broke my heart. She hurt my family too," he said quietly. "I've only ever told Mother and Father everything."

Elena nodded, understanding the unspoken request for what he was about to tell her to stay between them.

"It was the biggest mistake of my life." Tarrick raised a hand and ran his fingers through his hair, the water dampening the thick, dark locks. "When war broke out in your realm, I brought her to Leneira. She didn't have family." Elena's stomach clenched at the parallels in the story. "We had been dating, I suppose you could say, while I lived in London, and I wanted to protect her. She lived in Terralea, here in the palace for a year, and in that time, she ... changed."

"Changed how?" Elena asked.

"At first, she was happy. Glad to be safe, taken in by our way of life, our powers," he said slowly. "But then, as time passed on, she became demanding, greedy. She wanted elemental powers too."

Tarrick turned away from Elena toward the Temple of Divine Beings.

"It was why I summoned the Divine Beings," he explained. "I asked them to grant her elemental powers."

Elena sucked in a breath, remembering what he had told her about the steep price the Divine Beings demanded for favors requested. "What did they want as payment?"

"Nothing." Tarrick shook his head. "They said she was not worthy of the privilege of wielding any Leneiran powers. Since they refused to grant the request, they did not require any payment."

"What happened then?"

"She started to look into other ways of obtaining magic." He squeezed his eyes shut. "I was so besotted by her I didn't see this dark obsession taking over."

Elena put a hand on his shoulder and squeezed comfortingly.

"In the end, I caught her trying to take Adina's powers," he said, lowering his head with a pained expression on his face.

"*Take?*"

"Adina was just a baby," he whispered. "I went to her room and caught Rose standing over her crib with a bluestone dagger."

A chill swept over Elena as she stared at Tarrick, horrified.

"When I asked her what the hell she was doing, she told me she was going to harness elemental powers by draining another of them." Tarrick shuddered. "It was totally twisted and wrong, but her obsession had warped her mind. I still don't know who or what convinced her that what she was doing was possible.

"I knew there was no reasoning with her." He lifted his head and slowly opened his eyes again. "I lied and told her I knew another way she could get magic. I had to get her away from Adina."

"Of course," Elena murmured.

"I took her back to the human realm and broke off all contact," Tarrick continued. "A few months later, the rebel forces decided to try and take the palace and Erindell. That was the start of the uprising. The rebels had managed to get their hands on guns and weapons from the human realm and used bluestone bullets to kill and nullify the Terraleans' powers."

Elena shuddered as she remembered Yaz and Bri's smiling faces. She thought of the children laughing and playing on the riverbank in Erindell, and wondered how many had been orphaned during the uprising.

"The fighting eventually ended. Our guards who hadn't been hurt by the bluestone overthrew the rebels. My father's power was both a blessing and a curse," Tarrick continued flatly. "Much of Erindell was destroyed by his lightning. Innocent townspeople who were at the wrong place at the wrong time were burned to death instantly. Father still blames himself for the lives that were lost during the uprising.

"The surviving rebels were rounded up and imprisoned. It was a cleverly coordinated revolt, with King Halder also being taken by surprise and his people being attacked at the same time. Queen Lin had only just ascended the throne in Sailon. She came to Terralea with a number of Empaths to mete out justice to the instigators and provide asylum to those who genuinely wanted to repent and start a new life elsewhere."

"And in Skandor?" Elena whispered, half afraid of the answer.

"King Halder was more ruthless and didn't spare mercy on any traitors or their families, even innocent children," Tarrick replied. "He captured the rebels and set them loose in the north-ernmost forests of his country, commanding the deadliest animals and demons that lived there to destroy them.

In the aftermath of the uprising, Father, Zanthus, and I decided to wipe all records of Rose and her time in Terralea. Father gave me more responsibilities to help create the impression of a trust-worthy and reliable leader. Even though there's no evidence Rose was directly responsible for the uprising, the two events happened so close together that people could jump to the wrong conclusion.

He didn't want this black mark on my record to tarnish my image or come back to haunt me when I become king."

Elena's heart went out to those who had suffered needlessly, including Tarrick, who endured the worst kind of heartbreak and betrayal. She felt a tear roll down her cheek and brushed it away. Tarrick's face was full of sorrow and grief as he remembered his country's dark history. She raised her hand and cupped his jaw tenderly, feeling the rough stubble beneath her fingers.

"Your family loves you so much and has done an amazing job rebuilding Terralea after such a difficult time. I saw how happy your people were at the Full Moon Festival, and when I went to town," she said, her voice full of warmth. "Rose was a fool to throw away a chance to be with you just for magic. These few days have been the happiest I have felt in a very long time, and it's because of you. If it had been me, I wouldn't have hesitated to take even a small slice of the life you offered."

Tarrick's eyes smoldered at her words, and he lifted his own hand to cover the one she held to his face. A light breeze rustled through the air, but not even Skandor's icy barrens could temper the heat flooding Elena at that moment. Her heart beat faster as Tarrick leaned down and rested his forehead against her own. She inhaled his intoxicating scent, feeling his warm breath against her lips.

He closed the gap between them and kissed her softly at first, his lips pressing against hers, fanning the burning desire building in her core. She parted her lips, inviting him to explore, and he groaned as she traced the seam of his mouth with the tip of her tongue. He opened his mouth, allowing her to taste him. Elena bit his lower lip, and that was Tarrick's undoing.

$$\sim 26 \sim$$

Tarrick kissed Elena ferociously, running his hands down her back and pulling her to his chest. She wrapped her legs around his waist and pressed her soft body against his chiseled torso. The corded muscles moved beneath her touch as she ran her hands down his back.

His strong, callused hands explored Elena's body, roving down her back and making her shiver when he touched her bare skin. She gasped against his mouth when he gently squeezed her ass. He smiled and continued to kiss her with unbridled passion, moving his hands to the tops of her thighs. The dress bunched up around her waist, exposing her bare legs under the effervescing water.

Elena pulled away, breathing shallowly, and opened her eyes. Tarrick's breathing was ragged as he gazed at her with lust and adoration. He stroked her flushed cheeks with the back of his hand, brushing back a strand of brown hair, admiring the long, dark lashes that fluttered against his touch. The red lipstick she wore was slightly smudged, and he traced his thumb over her swollen lips, already addicted to the taste and feel of her.

"You're beautiful," he whispered, looking into her dark chocolate eyes and pulling her pointed chin toward him.

Elena drank in the sight of his handsome face and had to pinch herself. She had just experienced the most toe-curling, passionate kiss of her life. Her brain chose that moment to kick into gear, and she pushed away from the prince with a horrified look on her face.

"Elena?"

"I'm sorry," she forced the words out. The hurt and confusion in his voice cracked her heart. "We can't do this. You're the future King of Terralea, and I'm…"

"Shit," he muttered. "You're right."

"I'm sorry," she whispered again. "I got caught up in the moment."

"It's my fault," he said roughly. "I shouldn't have taken advantage of you like that."

Elena's eyes flew open. "You didn't."

They stared at each other for a beat.

"We should go back before they notice us missing," Tarrick said quietly.

"I didn't mean to jeopardize the future of your countries," Elena rambled, wading toward the edge of the pool where they had discarded their shoes. "Or our … friendship."

Tarrick cleared his throat. The warmth and smile returned to his voice when he said, "You haven't jeopardized anything. Perhaps the romantic atmosphere in the garden, but certainly not the future of Terralea."

Elena rolled her eyes. "You're an ass."

"There she is," Tarrick murmured, amber eyes glinting. "You're the only person, aside from my siblings, who is completely honest with me and, surprisingly, unafraid of me. You are confident and know yourself. You just don't see it."

"You don't scare me." Elena knitted her brows. "I mean, you frown and glare, but I assumed that was your default expression."

Tarrick threw his head back and laughed. The rich, deep tones echoed around the grove, and Elena shushed him, afraid they'd be heard and discovered.

"I must remember to tell Leon that," he chuckled. "My *default expression.*"

"It's very effective." Elena grinned. "I've seen the servants and guards scurry about when you glare at them."

"That's not my intention." Tarrick shook his head, smiling. "But I'm glad it doesn't scare you."

Elena sighed. "They'll notice us missing."

"You don't have to go back if you don't want to. I can tell Adina you were feeling unwell," he offered. "She won't mind. She's probably well into the *araki*."

Elena chuckled. "That would be a sight!"

"Leon and I have a few stories about her when she's had one too many drinks." Tarrick grinned.

Elena stayed where she stood a little longer, then smiled at Tarrick. "Thank you for this. I do feel better."

She waded out onto the grass. Water sluiced down her body, and she was aware of the sodden dress clinging to her. Tarrick, still in the water, watched her with a hungry look in his eye.

"Well?" She gave him a smirk as she twisted around. "You promised to dry me off."

Tarrick shook his head and waved a hand in her direction. A warm gust of wind blew through the garden, and soon, the skirts of her dress were fluttering around her legs.

Tarrick waded out and stood beside Elena. It was her turn to stare. Her mouth went dry at the sight of the wet tunic clinging to his rippling abs and muscular arms.

"You're staring, Lady Elena." He gave her another roguish smile.

She blushed and dropped her gaze.

"Apologies, Your Highness," she murmured, peeking at him when he bent over to pick up his discarded jacket and their shoes, admiring the view. He dried himself off and buttoned up his jacket while Elena slipped on her shoes and brushed down the dress to smooth out any wrinkles.

"You look lovely," Tarrick assured her with a soft expression. "Elena?"

"Yes, Tarrick?" she met his gaze.

"Don't let the men who underestimate and belittle you allow you to believe you are anything less than a queen in your own right."

***

They slipped back into the ballroom without anyone noticing—well, almost anyone.

"Where have you two been?" Leon muttered, descending on the pair. "Uncle Z has been on my case all night about losing you."

"Elena wasn't feeling well and went into the garden for some air." Tarrick's frown returned, and Elena smothered a smile. "I went to check on her. We weren't gone that long."

"Tarrick." Zanthus strode over to the prince at that moment. "Why don't you join us for water pipes on the terrace?" He gestured toward the large doors that led out to where colorful rugs and poufs had been arranged in a circle.

A large water pipe was in the middle, with an attendant checking the coals and adjusting the heat. Council members seated on the poufs passed the pipe around. They blew out puffs of perfumed smoke, trying to make shapes. Rokeby's face was a look of deep concentration as he manipulated the air to create an array of spectacular shapes with the smoke as he exhaled. His companions, including Halder, applauded, and he beamed at the group.

"I think I should dance with Adina," Tarrick said, walking off to his sister, who was enjoying the attention of her friends. He held out a hand, and his sister took it, giving the glass of *araki* she had been drinking to one of the women. Elena smiled as she watched them take to the dancefloor, where Lin and Zen were dancing together once more.

"I'm so glad you're here for this, my dear." Arran came up and watched his children dancing together fondly. "Adina has enjoyed your company immensely."

"It's a privilege, Your Highness." Elena smiled at the jovial man. "Adina, Leon, and Tarrick have been so kind and welcoming. And you and Queen Amaya."

"I hope you're enjoying yourself?" He turned to her and clasped both her hands in his large, warm ones.

"Very much." Elena nodded. "It's been a wonderful adventure. You were right. This is unlike anything I've experienced."

Arran beamed with pride at the compliment.

"Would you indulge an old man in a dance?" he requested. "I saw you and Leon earlier. You're a wonderful dancer."

"Of course!" Elena followed him onto the dance floor.

"Watch out for his two left feet." Leon rocked back on his heels, grinning.

Zanthus pursed his lips but didn't say anything.

The king spun Elena vigorously and took the lead for an upbeat tune. He twirled her enthusiastically and stepped back and forth in time to the beat of the drums. Elena was nimble on her feet and intuitively followed his lead as she had with Leon. She laughed out loud at the king's little quips and praises as she kept up with him.

"Darling, you'll wear our guest out." Amaya laughed when Arran moved them closer to where she and Lady Netta, more relaxed and serene that evening, watched the dancing couples.

"Nonsense!" the king blustered. "Am I wearing you out, Elena?"

"Not at all, Your Majesty," she gasped as she caught her breath.

"Perhaps I was a little too enthusiastic," Arran admitted, slowing down a little. "Allow me to express my deepest gratitude, Lady Elena."

She startled.

"Not only did you save my son and brother-in-law's lives," he sighed, "but I haven't seen Tarrick like this in over a century."

Elena threw a glance at Tarrick and Adina, who wore uninhibited grins on their faces as he spun her several times. Elena smiled at the sight of the princess nearly losing her balance.

"Amaya and I feared we had lost our boy," Arran mused. "He was forced to grow up fast after the uprising. Perhaps I put too much on his young shoulders. There were fewer smiles, less laughter..."

Arran shook his head out of his reverie.

"He's going to be an amazing king," Elena said, her lips quirking up in a smile.

"Of that, I have no doubt." Arran chuckled. "But I also want him to be a happy man. I want him to have the love, the joy, the family that Amaya and I have enjoyed for centuries."

The song ended, and Arran stepped back. He dipped his head and kissed the back of Elena's hand. She giggled in response as he led her off the dancefloor.

"You're a wonderful dancer, Your Majesty," she told him, clapping in his direction. "Thank you for the honor."

"Any time, m'dear."

He reached a hand out to Lady Netta, who laughed throatily and declined. Arran gave her a mock pout and turned to his wife, dragging her onto the dancefloor for another dance.

"Good evening, Lady Netta," Elena greeted the woman politely.

"Lady Elena." Netta inclined her head. "Are you enjoying yourself?"

"Very much," Elena replied.

"I'm glad to hear it." She smiled warmly. Her manner toward Elena changed since their initial meeting.

"Things seem to be winding down." Leon walked up to the women with two glasses of *araki*, one of which he offered Elena. "I think this might be the last song."

Tarrick and Adina continued dancing. They darted glances at the trio watching from the side, and the princess grinned tipsily at Elena, who smiled back. Adina stopped dancing and stood on her toes to whisper in her brother's ear. He glared at whatever she said to him, but she simply beamed back. He dropped his hands with a resigned expression on his face, and Adina dragged Tarrick over to Leon and Elena.

"My brother would like to dance with you," she announced, shoving his hand at Elena, who stifled a laugh at seeing Tarrick manhandled so roughly by his pint-sized sister.

"Would you do me the honors, Lady Netta?" Leon held his hand out to the gracious woman, who, to Elena's surprise, smiled shyly and nodded.

"Rude." Adina stuck her tongue out at Leon.

"I'm keen to keep my toes intact." Leon made a face at his sister and flicked her nose. "And Lady Netta talks about far more interesting things."

Elena scanned the room for the Skandorian princess but couldn't see her.

"Malina went to bed earlier," Adina answered the unasked question. "She had a headache. Probably from Lord Rokeby's lecture on the microeconomics of Fayne province."

Lady Netta's lips twitched, and Leon whisked her away before Adina said something inappropriate in front of the governor. He moved closer to the band, who started playing the opening strings of the final song of the evening.

Elena took Tarrick's outstretched hand, and Adina winked at the pair. She swept off to her group of friends, who were draped over poufs and chairs in the corner.

Once again, Tarrick took Elena into his arms. This time, he drew her closer to him, pressing their bodies together as the romantic tune filled the room. The female singer sang a melancholic song in an unfamiliar language, and Elena closed her eyes.

Tarrick spun her around the room as the tune hinted at hope and strength amongst sorrow and pain. Although she didn't understand the words, the melody resonated with Elena, and she smiled to herself, allowing her other senses to take over. The residual sweetness of the *araki* lingered on her tongue. Tarrick radiated warmth as his strong, capable hands held her in a firm grip. His scent mingled with the faint, fruity smoke floating in through the open terrace door from the water pipes.

The song ended to a smattering of applause. Elena opened her eyes to find the room had emptied considerably during the song. The only people left aside from her and Tarrick were the royals and a handful of guards. Elena noticed Erik and Adina had disappeared and made a note to ask her friend for details the following day. The musicians curtsied to the Terralean king and queen.

"I'll walk you to your room." Tarrick placed a hand on the small of Elena's back.

"Thank you," she whispered, ignoring the daggers Zanthus and Halder were shooting in their direction. She held her head high as she swept past them to wish the king and queen a good night and thank them for a wonderful evening.

Amaya embraced her on both cheeks, and Arran pulled her into a tight bear hug, chuckling when she cried out in surprise, then laughed. Leon kissed the back of her hand and winked at his brother, who rolled his eyes in response.

Elena and Tarrick walked to her room in silence, making sure to maintain a respectful distance from each other lest guards or servants prone to gossip were watching them. He held her bedroom door open, and she turned to him with a tired smile, the evening finally catching up to her.

"Thank you again for tonight," she told him. "For ... everything."

"You're welcome." He smiled down at her. "Any time."

She bit her lower lip and stepped back, heart pounding as she slowly closed the door without breaking eye contact. As she leaned her forehead against it, Elena let out a happy sigh as she recalled the way he kissed her and held her against him during their last dance.

~ 27 ~

Erik knocked on her door the following morning. "Lady Elena? Are you awake?"

She answered with sparkling eyes.

"You look different." He stepped into the room and took her in. "More ... relaxed?"

Elena had woken up that morning with a new resolution to shed the ghost of the woman she had become over the past few months. Ignoring the dress laid out for her on the edge of the bed when she woke, she had rummaged through the wardrobe and found an embroidered vest, which she wore over a tunic with fitted pants and black silk slippers. Her hair was pulled back in a voluminous ponytail, a few shorter strands at the front tucked behind her ears. It was the happy medium she had been searching for between her Lady Elena persona and regular jeans and T-shirt uniform.

Elena closed the door as Erik explained, "I'm your guard today. Adina is sitting in on the meeting this morning and said she would be done by lunchtime. I can also reapply the mark on your wrist."

Elena gestured for him to take a seat across from her at the table. "Are her friends still here?" She speared some fruit and cheese on a fork while Erik pulled out a bottle of black ink and a stylus.

"They left early this morning," he replied, taking a seat and setting up his tools.

"It was nice of them to travel for the evening."

"They don't live too far away." He shrugged. "It's a way for them to keep ties with the royal family."

"Aren't they close with Adina?" Elena asked curiously. She had lost touch with friends over the years as everyone moved away for work or grad school and started families. She wondered if it was the same in Leneira.

"As close as they can be with a princess," he said. "The royal family rules with the kind of authority and respect that ensures their people are protected from threats and traitors. It's harder to separate emotion and be a fair ruler when you have to deal justice to a friend who's broken the law or uses blackmail to gain power," the guard explained.

"I see," Elena said thoughtfully. "I'm glad Adina has you as a friend and confidante. It must get lonely for her without anyone to talk to."

She smiled at the shy look that crossed Erik's handsome face while he scratched her skin with the stylus. Thankfully, no one had noticed or commented on the mark thus far.

"Well, I suppose you're more than a friend or confidante, aren't you?" she asked innocently, popping a grape into her mouth.

"I don't know what you're talking about," Erik mumbled, shifting uncomfortably.

"Don't you two have feelings for each other?" Elena giggled. "It's pretty obvious when I see you together."

Erik smiled, focusing on tracing over the intricate details of the Elemental crest, still unable to look Elena in the eye.

"Are your powers back?" She changed the subject.

"Getting there," Erik said, looking relieved. He flicked his eyes up at Elena, and a tendril of loose brown hair lifted itself behind her ear. "The other guards who lost their elemental abilities said the same thing." He glanced down at her empty water glass, and it refilled itself.

"I'm happy for you." She smiled. "What caused the lapse in your powers?"

"We're not sure." A note of worry crept into his voice. "That's the unsettling part. Prince Tarrick wants us to work harder on hand-to-hand combat and other physical training. If these malfunctions and breakdowns keep happening, we still need to be able to defend Terralea."

"Has this ever happened before?"

"Only when we've come into contact with bluestone."

Elena ate in silence as she pondered the mystery of the guards' powers. She briefly wondered if it was related to the assassin but couldn't see the connection between the two.

"By the way," Erik said in a low voice. "I told Prince Tarrick about Zanthus threatening you last night."

"Erik!" Elena groaned.

"He had to know what the royal advisor said," the guard said firmly. "He shouldn't have threatened a guest."

"Tarrick has enough on his plate," Elena said, rubbing her face with her free hand. "And I'm not here for much longer, remember?" As she said the last part, her stomach lurched at the thought of leaving the prince.

Erik inspected his work and blotted over the ink with his finger to make sure everything had dried. He looked up and said softly, "Regardless of how long you're here for, you don't deserve to be spoken to like that after everything you have done for this family. Someone had to stand up for you. Besides, it sounded quite sinister from where I was standing." His brow creased with worry.

"Thank you, Erik." Elena softened at the guard's words; it had been a long time since anyone had spoken up for her. "That was really nice of you."

Erik grinned at her, flashing his teeth. "Any time, Lady Elena."

"I think I'd like to visit the library," Elena said, her eyes falling on the borrowed book she had retrieved from Adina's room the day before. She felt like a change in reading material.

***

Elena's stomach rumbled, and she rubbed it absent-mindedly as she scanned the library. She was in the middle of reading the second book Celine had picked out for her. Archivists and scribes glided between shelves, whispering to each other. The rustling of pages from those who worked at their stations in the alcoves were the only other sounds in the vast room.

"Your history is violent! Was there ever a time of peace?" she sighed, rubbing her face.

"Hence the Peace Summit." Erik smiled slightly. "What were you looking for?"

"I don't know," Elena groused, picking up another book and flicking through the pages. "More about daily life, what people did when they weren't fighting. I can't believe Leneirans are afraid of humans when there are bloodthirsty Skandorians and ruthless Terraleans!"

"The difference is that Leneirans use their existing abilities." Erik gave her a crooked smile. "We don't go seeking out ways to make lethal weapons that kill on the scale that humans do in your realm."

"Still seems hypocritical," Elena muttered.

"You'd have to get your hands on diaries for records of daily life and more mundane matters. All rulers keep diaries for official records, but a lot of it might be redacted. Come to think of it, they might only be available to the current ruler."

Elena perked up. "Do you think Adina—" she started to ask, but just then, the princess in question stomped over to them.

"What's wrong?" Elena shut the book with a loud snap.

"This Peace Summit is ridiculous," she fumed, flinging herself on the couch. "They're a bunch of school children squabbling over stupid things and didn't listen to a word I said."

"I'm sorry," Elena sympathized. "Sounds like politics in Leneira is the same as everywhere."

"Halder and Zanthus kept ganging up against Lin," Adina grumbled, picking at a scratch in the leather. "And when I tried to speak, they told me I didn't understand the complexities of the issues and to let them handle the negotiations."

"Patronizing." Elena made a face.

Erik *tsked* in outrage.

"At least Lady Netta agreed with me about how their strategy would put Terraleans offside," she continued. "And they listened to *her* because she's the governor of Erindell."

"Don't you rank higher as a princess?" Elena asked.

"I thought so." Adina gloomily folded her hands across her chest. "But I am much younger, and they don't know I spend time in Erindell and hear what the people say."

"Did Tarrick or Leon say anything?"

"Father stood up for me, but he had to be diplomatic," she sighed. "Lin said the same thing she told us in the bathhouse about the Sailonese people. They would see the sharing of Terralean and Skandorian defense forces as a threat against their people."

"How did the meeting end?" Erik asked.

"Badly." She sighed again. "They're having lunch now and regrouping after. There's only one more day of the summit to finalize all negotiations."

Elena's stomach dropped when she realized she would only be in Terralea for another day. Suddenly, returning to the human realm seemed less appealing after the excitement of the past few days and the scorching kiss she had shared with Tarrick the previous night.

Despite Zanthus's threats, the unsolved mystery surrounding the assassin, and the fake bluestone bullet, Elena hadn't felt so alive in a long time. Life had just gotten interesting, and she wanted to experience more of what Leneira had to offer. She internally debated whether she should approach Amaya or even Lin with a request to stay on for a few more days, if only to see more of the realm, including Sailon. It was the first time Elena had felt truly free, and she enjoyed being spontaneous more than she had previously thought she would.

"What happens if no one agrees on an issue?" Elena asked.

"If it's something pressing, they have to compromise," Adina explained. "But if they come to a standstill, it usually ends with one country threatening to break ties with the others, and it gets tabled for the next summit."

"Diplomacy?" Elena laughed. Adina nodded.

"The Peace Summit happens every ten years, but the kings and queens rarely go that long without speaking to each other. They usually get together—unofficially, of course—after a few years, hoping something else comes up to distract everyone."

"Ten years?" Elena's eyes widened.

"Change happens slowly in Leneira," Erik reminded her. "Anything that is agreed upon at the summit will take time to happen. Taxes, exchange of resources, defense strategies..."

"But it sounded like Halder and Zanthus wanted to move quickly with their plans." Adina frowned. "They want Shifter and Terralean armies to start training together before the end of the year. Zanthus hinting at the growing rebel movement is making them panic."

Erik blanched.

"You're not going anywhere," Adina assured him.

"If the king instructs me to go to Skandor, I have to do as he says," the guard said neutrally. "I took a vow to serve him and Terralea when I joined the guard."

"Why would you have to go?" Elena furrowed her brow.

"He's an elite guard." Adina smiled up at Erik, who didn't react to the compliment. "He'd be the first to train with the Shifters. He could teach those pups a thing or two. The way I see it, the Shifters would benefit more from our armies." A muscle ticked in Erik's jaw as he stared straight ahead.

"What do you mean? Don't they change into wolves?" Elena asked.

"They rely too much on their shifting abilities and primal instincts. They don't train the way our guards do in physical combat and strategic formations. Erik is the best archer in the guard," Adina explained.

Erik's lips lifted slightly.

"We should go to lunch," the princess said, reluctantly getting up. Elena did the same and huffed at the pile of books.

"Are you borrowing all of those?" Adina asked, eyes narrowing.

"Probably not," she replied. "They don't tell the stories the way your mother did."

"When her people needed somewhere to stay for the night on their journeys around the realm, they would stop at a village and entertain the locals with songs in exchange for food and supplies. They have a knack for describing vivid pictures with their words. Some Elementals even create the scenes they narrate in the flames of the bonfires at the gathering," the princess told Elena.

"I wish I could see that," she sighed, wishing more and more she could stay longer in Leneira and experience its extraordinary magic.

"Let's go." Adina led them out of the alcove.

"The books—"

"The archivists will return them. Come on, I'm starving."

~ 28 ~

Lunch was a subdued affair. No one spoke, and the atmosphere was so tense Elena could cut it with her butter knife.

"How was your morning, Lady Elena?" Arran asked politely. His fatherly manner from the previous night had disappeared. He was back to being King Arran of Terralea, hosting a very tense Peace Summit.

"It was good, thank you, Your Majesty," Elena replied. "I found some interesting books in the library."

He nodded but didn't press for details.

For once, Halder and Zanthus were quiet, glowering at their plates of food and not speaking to anyone—not even each other. Tarrick stared stonily into the distance. Even Leon ate silently, giving Elena a faint smile when she entered the room.

The only sounds in the crushing quiet were the clinking and scraping of cutlery against plates and the odd slurping noise. When everyone finished eating, they gazed into the distance, avoiding eye contact with each other.

"Why don't we resume our conversation in the council chambers?" Arran dabbed his mouth with a napkin. "I'll have the staff serve tea there. We still have much to get through."

The royals and council members rose and left the room. Tarrick and Leon were the last to leave. Tarrick's eyes softened when he finally looked at Elena, and he gave her a small smile before closing the door gently behind him.

"Well, that was awkward," Adina remarked, throwing her napkin onto the empty plate in front of her.

"Is this really what politics is like?" Elena asked. She had seen toddlers get over tantrums and disagreements quicker.

Adina glanced around furtively, but only Erik remained standing by the door. "Apparently, there's always a day when everyone gets cranky and disagreeable. Let's go back to your room," she told Elena in a low voice.

They walked through the palace hallways at a leisurely pace. Staff moved silently as they carried out their tasks, pausing only to curtsy to the princess as they passed.

"Erik, my darling," Adina crooned when they reached Elena's door. "Would you mind standing guard? We'd like some privacy for girl talk."

"Yes, Your Highness." Erik inclined his head and held the door open for Elena and Adina to enter.

"Come on, I want to hear what they're saying," Adina said as soon as the lock clicked into place. She rushed over to the fireplace and turned the knob.

"We're spying on the Peace Summit?" Elena asked incredulously. "Is that a good idea? Won't it be boring?"

"They haven't resolved matters yet, and I want to know what they decide," Adina said grimly. "Are you coming?"

Elena followed her friend down the passageway.

***

Tarrick scanned the table around which the rulers were seated, tapping his foot impatiently. The morning meetings had been a shambles. Everyone was drained and irritated. Leon sat stiffly beside him, scribbling notes and taking down the minutes. Council members clustered behind their respective rulers. Some sipped tea as they watched the proceedings unfold.

Tarrick only had to get through one more day of tense conversations, reluctant compromises, and unspoken agreements to arrange private meetings after the official summit. It was not ideal and went against the principle of open communication and collaboration between the three countries. It was a last resort.

"If we share resources, we *all* share resources," Zen snapped at a Skandorian. "Sailon sees the colluding between Terralea and Skandor as a direct threat."

"It's in the best interests of *everyone*." The Skandorian councilor thumped his meaty fist on the table.

"Then why not extend the invitation to our army?" Lin raised a brow.

Behind her, the Sailonese contingent maintained neutral expressions, but Mika's jaw clenched.

"What proof do we have that your people would not use their tricks against us?" the Skandorian growled.

Zen leveled him with a stare. "Remind me again, why are we all here, Sven?"

Sven turned a blotchy red and sank into his seat, muttering under his breath.

Tarrick's eyes flicked to Malina, who sat beside her father. She remained silent throughout the meeting, as she had during all of them, but she lifted her hand to her temple every so often. Her headache from the previous night seemed to linger. Zanthus also noted the movement and frowned slightly, but Tarrick was unsure if it was out of concern or irritation at the distraction.

His thoughts wandered to Elena, and he wondered how she was faring after the night before. The kiss had been explosive, unforgettable, and Tarrick selfishly wanted more, despite knowing they could never be together.

"Queen Lin makes a point," Arran said, turning to Halder. The Terralean king steepled his fingers and raised a brow as he waited for his northern counterpart to speak.

Halder worked his jaw furiously, eyes darting between Arran and Lin. "Fine," he bit out. "Sailon's army is welcome to join us."

"I suggest we spread out the joint armies' training amongst all three countries," Tarrick jumped in, dragging his attention back to the meeting. "Smaller groups will train together in Terralea, Skandor, *and* Sailon so everyone learns together in different territories. We will also set up a rotation schedule. They are all subject to the host country's laws and bound by the treaty we sign today that ensures collaboration, working toward a common goal, and upholding peace. We can hash out the details later, but failure to comply with these principles is punishable by death."

Halder looked ready to flip the table and opened his mouth to protest, but Lin swept in first. "An excellent suggestion, Your Highness." She turned to Arran and said, "I am in favor of those terms."

"As am I," Arran said firmly.

Halder narrowed his eyes at Tarrick. "I agree," he finally snapped.

"Nice one," Leon muttered.

Shoulders dropped, and expressions of relief washed over the Terralean and Sailonese councilors. The Skandorians continued to glower and scowl at the group.

A scribe sitting behind Arran finished drafting the missive with a dramatic flourish and presented it to the king. Arran ran his eye down the document, nodding approvingly before signing at the bottom and sliding the piece of paper toward Halder. The Skandorian king scratched his initials before pushing the document toward Lin, who signed it while Zen supervised closely over her shoulder.

"Thank you, Lin," Arran said as she held it out to him. He gave the signed agreement back to the scribe, who filed it away carefully amongst a sheaf of summit terms and contracts on a smaller table.

"What's left, Arran?" Lin asked with a tight smile.

The scribe stepped forward and handed the king another document. Arran read the list, murmuring each term of agreement that had been covered.

"Security around the quarry, renewed trade, annual visits, portal status..." he trailed off.

"Just the matter of our children," Halder said with a gleam in his eye.

Tarrick didn't think the room could get more tense, but it did. Leon looked up with bulging eyes. Amaya sipped her tea calmly, but her mouth tightened at the corners. Lin sat up straighter in her chair, and Zen's gaze darted between Halder and Zanthus. The former leaned forward to address Arran.

"Please state your proposal," King Arran said neutrally.

Halder cleared his throat. "I propose Prince Tarrick and my daughter, Princess Malina, come together in matrimony to strengthen the alliance between our two great countries." He threw his hands open and paused for effect. His icy eyes swept around those gathered at the table. "What better expression of our friendship, trust, and the long-lasting peace we are committed to than the union of our offspring?"

Heavy silence settled in the room.

"Except there are three countries present who are committed to all of those things," Leon pointed out. "Unless you're suggesting Queen Lin is also part of this marriage?"

It would have been funny if it hadn't been so tense.

"I agree with Prince Leon." Netta stepped forward. "I fail to see how this union would benefit Sailon?"

Jet threw Netta a grateful smile. The entire Sailonese contingent had stiffened when Halder spoke, their displeasure at his proposal evident in the drawn brows and turned down lips as they stared daggers at the Skandorians.

"Sailon is already a well-protected country, with their remarkable magic and benevolent queen," he replied smoothly. Leon made a gagging sound; Halder's flattery fooled no one. "Terralea and Skandor are more prone to threats, or have we forgotten the rebel uprising already?"

"Sailon was also affected by the uprising, Your Majesty," Zen pointed out coolly.

"How is a marriage between Tarrick and Malina supposed to strengthen our defenses or prevent uprisings?" Netta asked impatiently. "As far as I can tell, you get a future king as a son-in-law. What are you offering Terralea in return?"

"Aside from my daughter as your queen?" Halder waved a hand toward Malina, who stared at Netta stoically. "You would also get the services of the entire Shifter army anytime you need them."

Leon snorted but smothered the sound when Amaya frowned at him.

"And who would be your successor when Princess Malina becomes Queen Consort of Terralea?" the governor demanded.

Halder grinned widely, and Tarrick held his breath.

"I wouldn't need a successor if Tarrick and Malina became King and Queen of Terralea and Skandor, would I, Lady Netta?"

Once again, pin-drop silence filled the room.

"Please, speak plainly, Your Majesty." Netta massaged her temples. "What are you saying? That Terralea and Skandor become ... one country?"

"In time? Exactly!" Halder rubbed his hands together.

More silence.

Once again, Tarrick found his thoughts drifting to Elena, imagining her reaction to the news.

Then there was uproar.

"This is ridiculous," Jet exclaimed.

"It will never work," Rokeby spoke, storming to Netta's side. The mask of civility and decorum slipped away as he glared at the Skandorian king.

"We should retract our agreements," Mika advised Lin, who continued staring at Halder with narrowed eyes.

"We should speak privately." Amaya placed a hand on her husband's arm.

"What if I don't agree?" Tarrick's voice rang out.

Everyone stopped arguing and stared at him. Leon glanced nervously at his brother's knuckles, clenched in tight fists on top of the table, hearing the note of danger in his voice. He knew his brother was moments away from Shifting. Tarrick felt the steely claws beneath the surface of his skin, threatening to rip free.

"What then, King Halder?" Tarrick asked, meeting Halder's gaze.

"If you don't agree, Skandor will cease to be part of this union and operate as an entirely independent state," Halder declared, his face turning an alarming shade of purple. "We will withdraw all agreements made at this *and* previous summits and terminate our current arrangements with Terralea and Sailon."

"You know that's not sustainable for your people." Tarrick frowned. "Sailon and Terralea supply your country with food and weapons, and we've all signed the pact to protect the quarry to prevent our enemies from getting their hands on the bluestone. Lin has a standing agreement with both of our countries to offer Empath services if we need to identify traitors in our midst and prevent another rebel uprising. Without these, Skandor will be even more vulnerable and be forced to make do with your limited resources. Your people will not stand for it."

"Stop lying, Tarrick," Malina burst out, startling everyone. She massaged her temples with both hands as she spoke. "You are just as vulnerable without Skandor. Even more so in recent times, if I understand correctly."

Lin frowned. "What's she talking about, Arran?"

Tarrick's heart beat faster at the inference.

"I have seen your powers, and they are little more than party tricks," Malina continued. Leon bristled at the statement, but she plowed on relentlessly. "Your army may be well trained, but it is small and spread too thin. If an enemy were to enter your cities and towns, your people would be able to buy a little time to save themselves, but they would not all survive."

"Is that a threat, Your Highness?" Netta asked coolly.

"I am only telling you what you know to be true." Malina glanced at her. "Having our Shifters in Terralea would give your people added protection."

Netta barked out a laugh. "Did you not hear Princess Adina this morning? She wasn't lying when she said the Terraleans would not welcome Shifters in our towns," she sniffed, giving the Skandorian royal council a derisive look. "Terraleans may not turn into vicious animals, but we are perfectly capable of defending ourselves."

"Is it not true that your elemental powers are failing?" Malina sneered, laying Terralea's weakening defenses out in the open.

Tarrick's nails dug into his palms as he tried to work out how Malina could have found out about the guards' failing elemental powers.

Amaya gasped.

Lin frowned.

"Besides, everyone can see how infatuated you are with Lady Elena," the princess continued. "Even if you did agree to marrying me for the sake of your country, I will not have a husband who takes a mistress."

"That's preposterous," Zanthus blustered. "Tarrick is no more infatuated with that woman than I am with Lin."

The Sailonese queen narrowed her eyes at him, but he waved a hand impatiently.

"You told me you would take care of her, Zanthus," Halder growled, bringing his fists down on the table.

"Uncle Zanthus?" Leon gasped. "What does he mean?"

Even Tarrick was taken aback at the unmistakable statement. He had made a mental note to confront his uncle in private about his behavior toward Elena. Erik reported the threats he'd overheard the royal advisor making, and Tarrick assured the guard that Zanthus had just been doing his due diligence for the security of Terralea. Recalling the times Elena had almost let Zanthus's name slip when she talked about her fears for her safety, Tarrick was growing doubtful about his uncle's intentions.

"Perhaps we should regroup with our respective councils and adjourn for the afternoon," Arran spoke smoothly, but the anger in his voice was palpable.

Lin leaned forward in Tarrick's direction and spoke urgently. "Tarrick, if you agree to this marriage contract with Malina, then Sailon withdraws all arrangements with Terralea, including Empath services in a time of need and our armies at the bluestone quarry. Our three countries are either equal partners in maintaining the peace in Leneira or this is where we absolve all agreements from the past century and, as Halder has suggested, rule our countries independently." She scanned the room before standing up and walking out the door. Zen and the rest of her council followed.

"I'll go speak with them," Amaya said, rising from her seat. She squeezed her husband's shoulder and walked unhurriedly out of the room after the Sailonese.

"Mother is right," Leon said quietly to Tarrick. "We should discuss this privately now that we have heard King Halder's proposal in full. You have a lot of explaining to do, brother."

~ 29 ~

Elena sucked in a breath and stepped away from the peephole. Adina groped for her hand in the darkness and gave it a squeeze.

"Let's go," the princess whispered, tugging her along. "They'll go to Father's office."

Elena barely remembered the walk along the passage to Arran's office. Her heart pounded in her chest as she pressed up against the spyhole and peered into the empty room.

"What is Halder playing at?" Adina muttered. "If Tarrick agrees to marry Malina, I'll kill him."

Elena remained silent, conflicted between wanting to tell her friend everything that happened the previous night and wanting to protect herself.

"Did something happen between you and my brother?"

"How did she know about the elemental powers failing?" Elena whispered, avoiding the question. "Did Lord Zanthus tell her and King Halder?"

"I don't know." Adina chewed her lower lip, sounding worried. "It would surprise me if he did because Halder wouldn't have suggested aligning with a country he considers 'weak.' You've seen his attitude toward the Sailonese. He thinks they're not a threat because they read emotions." She frowned. "But they've had fewer wars and battles than Skandor and Terralea. They play to their strengths, and it works to keep the peace. For all of us. Losing them as an ally would be catastrophic."

The door to Arran's office opened. Everyone piled in, arguing and talking all at once.

Arran took a seat at his desk and motioned for the others to sit before him, but only Leon took a seat in a chair in front of the desk. He propped his notebook on his lap, stylus poised and prepared to take notes. The others remained standing with varying expressions of anger on their faces.

"Tarrick, do not give into Halder's bullying," Netta warned. "We will find another way to strengthen our forces."

"Netta, do not rush the boy," Zanthus chastised. "Let him consider things."

"He's not a boy," Leon snapped. "That is your future king, Uncle Zanthus."

"What did Halder mean about you taking care of Elena, Uncle?" Tarrick demanded, ignoring everyone else. "Does this have anything to do with you threatening her last night?"

"Is this true?" Arran turned to the royal advisor, who was scowling at everyone.

"I merely warned Elena to watch her step," Zanthus snapped back. "I saw the way she was flirting with you, Tarrick, and so did Halder."

"It wasn't your place to say anything to her," the prince growled.

"Of course it was!" Zanthus retorted. "There is a very real danger of history repeating itself. I see the way you look at her. It's the same way you used to look at Rose, and we all know how *that* ended."

Tarrick looked like he'd been slapped. Elena wanted to wring her hands around Zanthus's neck and shake him. Hard.

"What are they talking about?" Adina whispered. "Was Tarrick in love with Rose? Why did it end badly?"

"She wanted elemental powers and was ready to do anything to get them," Elena whispered back. "She thought she could kill—"

Elena stopped herself before revealing the princess was almost killed by her brother's former lover.

"Divine Beings," Adina muttered, not noticing Elena's abrupt end. "That explains a lot."

"Does it?" Elena asked, but Adina shushed her. The princess leaned forward to hear better, but that wasn't necessary; the heightened tension had everyone speaking loudly. Angrily.

"Zanthus, did you threaten our guest?" Arran asked.

"No, Your Majesty," Zanthus deferred. "But she's been getting in the way, and I strongly advise—"

"How did Malina and Halder find out about our powers?" Tarrick cut off his uncle.

"If you're implying I told anyone—" Zanthus began impatiently.

"You're the only person in this room who's been fawning all over them this summit," Leon pointed out. "Something might have slipped last night while you were enjoying the water pipes and *araki*."

"You little shi—" Zanthus growled.

"There will be no unfounded accusations in this room," Arran thundered, splaying his hands over the table. "We are meant to be united, not fighting and squabbling amongst ourselves."

"The fact that Halder still wants to form an alliance despite knowing our weak position is a blessing." Zanthus glared at Tarrick. "Skandor's presence in Terralea would deter our enemies."

"Who are these enemies you speak of, Zanthus?" Rokeby asked, frustrated. "The rebels have been quiet these past decades with no sign of another uprising. Lin certainly isn't making moves against us."

"There's still the matter of the assassin who recently tried to take out Tarrick," Zanthus reminded everyone.

"And you," Tarrick said quietly.

"Excuse me?" Zanthus turned on him.

"We still haven't determined whether the assassin was after me, you, or both of us," the prince pointed out. "Unless you have information you would like to share with the group?"

"I ... I..." Zanthus blustered.

There was silence.

"I value your life more highly than my own, Your Highness," he switched to the oily voice he used when speaking with Halder that made Elena snort. "You are, after all, the future king. Your death would have had far greater consequences than mine."

Awkward silence followed his statement as no one contradicted what he said.

"While we are on the subject," Arran cleared his throat, trying to diffuse the tension. "We cannot ignore the internal matters that still need to be resolved. Zanthus, do you have any further updates on the assassin or guards whose magic has failed?"

"No, Your Majesty." Zanthus shook his head. "My men are still searching for the assassin, but he or she seems to have vanished into thin air. As for the failing elemental powers..."

He paused and looked around the room.

"More guards have reported being unable to use their abilities this morning," he admitted. "We are yet to learn how or why this is happening."

Adina inhaled sharply.

"Have any townspeople experienced the same thing?" Arran demanded.

"Not as far as I know." Zanthus shook his head again.

"I'll make discreet inquiries, Your Majesty." Netta stepped forward. "No one will want to admit it to it freely for fear of causing panic and being accused of being a rebel."

"Thank you, Netta." Arran sighed heavily. "This does not bode well if we cannot find the cause or reason."

"I have taken steps to stand down and isolate the guards who have been affected. The royal physician will examine them thoroughly," Zanthus told the group. "As soon as they learn something, I will inform you, Majesty."

"How many guards have you identified?" Tarrick frowned.

"About half the palace guards, Your Highness." His blue eyes turned to the prince. "I've sent out missives to our regional guards to report back to the palace immediately if any of them have experienced the same issue in the last week."

"You can't stand down half the palace guards," Tarrick exclaimed. "We need every person on duty. Malina was right. Our armies are powerful, but we don't have the numbers we used to, and right now, we are in a precarious position with our guests and an assassin at large whose motives are still a mystery. And you seem to be under the impression we are at risk of an imminent threat. We don't have enough guards to spare."

"I have pulled a few guards from our low-risk regions to return to Erindell for the remainder of the week and re-arranged the roster so they can resume duties once the royal physician has completed his tests," Zanthus said smoothly, unaffected by Tarrick's angry tone.

"This is the first I'm hearing of these plans." The prince glared at his uncle. "I sign off on all defense matters, or have you been approving things on my behalf like you did when you told everyone that I'm engaged to Malina?"

"Zanthus, Tarrick needs to be informed of all army activity," Arran reprimanded the advisor. "He's right, you cannot make changes to the guards or our defensive position without his approval. We need to consider all aspects of the situation before agreeing on a plan of action."

"Of course, Your Majesty," Zanthus said, still unflustered. "With the summit taking up everyone's time and attention, there has been a lot on your plate, and I did take a few liberties by changing the roster," he admitted. "But I assure you it was to ease your minds, not worry you further. I simply took some internal matters into my own hands while you, ah, *entertained* our guests." He glared pointedly at Tarrick.

Netta rolled her eyes while Rokeby muttered under his breath.

"It takes time for the guards in the region to make their way to Erindell," Netta pointed out. "How long have you known about this aberration to make such arrangements?"

"I pulled them from our closest regions and posts. They will be here by nightfall," he replied.

"Leaving those communities vulnerable and defenseless?"

"I had to assess the risks and make a decision." He shrugged and held up his hands in surrender. "Which is why it's not a bad idea to consider Skandor's offer. We wouldn't have to compromise our people's safety if we had Shifter guards rotating amongst our own throughout Terralea."

"Not this again," Leon muttered.

"We don't know how long this anomaly will last," Netta argued. "We can't sign a long-term agreement if this is only temporary."

"And if it isn't temporary?" Zanthus pointed out. "What then? What if more and more Terraleans lose their elemental powers?"

"This must be a trick of the Divine Beings," Rokeby said finally. "We should summon them and ask."

"We'll do that as a last resort," Arran said, stroking his beard, looking troubled. "If the royal physician cannot find the source of this anomaly, I will summon the Divine Beings."

"Father, you shouldn't—" Leon began to argue.

"It is the only other way to know for sure, son," the king said gently. "And if they need payment for the answers or solution, I'm in a much better place to make that sacrifice."

"Your Majesty!" Netta and Rokeby exclaimed.

Tarrick sighed and rubbed his face with his hands.

"Tarrick," the king said quietly. "You are the future king of this country, and while your mother and I have spoken to you about matters of the heart as your parents, as your king, I am now in a difficult position.

"We must consider the safety and well-being of our people. The circumstances are not ideal." He shook his head regretfully. "You should take your time deciding on the best course of action. We can tell Halder his proposal is not off the table, but we will need time to consider and arrange another meeting over the next few months. But if there's something going on with you and Elena—"

"There's not," Tarrick said loudly, coldly. "There never has been, and there never will be. I learned my lesson with Rose, and I will not risk the safety of our family for a woman I barely know again."

Elena tried to keep her breathing steady. Her chest hurt hearing those words from Tarrick, especially after their kiss. She sent up a silent prayer of thanks that no one had caught them so she could take the secret with her to the grave.

"What about Lin?" Leon asked somberly.

"Your mother will speak with her," Arran said. "And we will review the proposal to ensure Sailon is protected from the fallout of this course of action. Her people will have our continued friendship and support."

"Let's go back," Adina whispered. Even in the dark, Elena could tell her friend was worried over her brother's choices—or lack thereof.

$$\sim\ 30\ \sim$$

"You have some explaining to do." Adina folded her arms over her chest and narrowed her eyes at Elena, who sat hunched over on her bed. "Is something going on between you and my brother?"

"No!" she exclaimed, shaking her head violently.

Adina merely raised a brow.

"I mean, I think he's attractive," Elena rambled. "But you'd have to be a corpse or have something seriously wrong with you not to notice how hot he is."

Adina grimaced. "He's not *hot*. He's annoying and grumpy."

"He can be thoughtful and nice," Elena mumbled, dropping her gaze and digging the toes of her slippered feet into the rug.

Adina stared at her.

"What?" Elena threw her hands up in surrender and fell back on her bed.

"How did you find out about Rose?" Adina asked, moving to the bed and flopping down next to her.

Elena turned to face the princess. "Tarrick told me. I was angry after Lord Zanthus.... Anyway, I demanded he tell me about Rose because I was sick of your uncle constantly throwing her name around and not knowing the full story."

"I'm his sister and your friend, but I'm the last to know?" Adina scowled.

Elena reached down and squeezed the princess's hand. "Halder seems a bit unhinged," she remarked, trying to steer the conversation away from Tarrick.

Adina snorted. "He's the most backward king I've ever met."

"Have you met many kings?"

"No, I suppose not," the princess admitted. "He's ruled Skandor since before I was born. I heard his own father was even more conservative."

"What will Tarrick do?" Elena asked.

"I'm not sure," the princess replied quietly. "I wish I was included in these conversations."

"I wish there was something I could do to help," Elena said sincerely. "I'm sorry I kept things from you, but Tarrick made me promise..." She bit her lip and broke off awkwardly.

"I hate being the last to know things," Adina muttered. "I need to find out exactly what happened with that woman. It could affect Tarrick's decision. I don't want Malina as a sister."

They stared at the ceiling in silence.

Elena let out a sigh. She rubbed her eyes with the palms of her hands. "I can't believe I'm going home soon. These last few days have felt like months."

"What do you mean?" Adina asked. "We haven't found the assassin yet. It's not safe for you to go back. They could be waiting for you to return to your world to attack again."

Elena rolled her eyes. "I think it's pretty clear they were after your brother or uncle."

"We don't know where this assassin is though," Adina argued. "They'll know you're under our protection now and know everything we do. You're still a threat to them."

Elena cursed. "My staying here was meant to keep me safe, not put me in more danger!"

"We could go to town and see if Bri or Yas have new information," Adina suggested. "No one would notice us missing with all the drama and tension."

She bounced off the bed and opened the door to tell Erik the plan.

"Where's Erik?" Adina frowned at Serkin, who now stood at the door.

"Erik has been stood down for the time being, Your Highness," the guard replied. "Lord Zanthus has assigned me to be your personal guard for the foreseeable future."

The color drained from Adina's pretty face.

"No!" she exclaimed, throwing the door open wide and running down the corridor. Elena and Serkin followed her as she sped down the stairs and barged into Zanthus's office without knocking.

"What is the meaning of this?" the royal advisor shouted at the intrusion.

Zanthus stood behind his desk with another guard, who was holding a sheet of paper. His desk was overflowing with an array of documents, books, letter openers, more crystal vials, and bottles with clear liquids, pens, and ink bottles strewn about. Again, Elena wondered how he managed to find anything in the mess.

"Where's Erik?" Adina demanded. "You had no right to stand him down."

Zanthus paused and took in the angry princess.

"Circulate this roster for the night of the closing feast amongst the guards," he dismissed the guard standing by his side, who bowed and left the room quickly.

"Please leave us, Serkin." Zanthus nodded to Adina's new guard. "And Lady Elena, perhaps you should—"

"Elena's staying," Adina cut him off.

Serkin closed the door behind him as he left.

"This is not how a princess behaves, Adina," Zanthus reprimanded his niece. "Especially when we have guests and dignitaries in the palace."

"Where is Erik?" she asked again.

"Your guard has been taken to a safe location to be examined by the royal physician," Zanthus said patiently.

"Why? His elemental powers have returned," Adina said.

"Not fully," Zanthus told her. "We need to monitor the return rate and do proper tests to make sure it doesn't affect other Elementals. The physician cannot do that when Erik is going about his duties, and if it is contagious, he will infect the entire royal guard and possibly civilians."

Elena had to admit Zanthus had a point but didn't say anything.

"You still had no right to dismiss him without telling me," Adina seethed.

"Serkin is a commander and more than capable of protecting you, my dear," Zanthus tried to pacify her.

"Don't patronize me," she snapped.

There was a knock at the door, and Amaya peered in with an alarmed expression.

"What's going on here? I heard shouting," she asked.

"Mother, Uncle Zanthus sent Erik away." Adina looked at her beseechingly. "He's done nothing wrong."

"It's not a punishment," Zanthus said impatiently. "He'll be back as soon as the physician has finished with him."

"Arran told me you've been taking defense matters into your own hands without informing us." Amaya frowned. "Erik is Adina's personal guard, Zanthus. You should have run this past us. Who is the replacement?"

"I can personally vouch for Serkin." Zanthus glared at his sister. "I have already explained why I had to move quickly."

Amaya assessed the room, taking in Adina's tearful face, Zanthus's irritated expression, and Elena, who was embarrassed and helpless.

"Adina, Elena, why don't you both go freshen up before dinner?" she asked firmly. "Zanthus, you and I need to talk."

"I want Erik, Mother," Adina said quietly. Her voice quivered.

"I understand, darling," the queen said in her calm voice. "I'll make sure he comes back."

She motioned to the door, indicating Elena and Adina should leave.

"Zanthus, you have overstepped..." she chastised before the door shut.

"I think I would like to be alone for a while," Adina sniffled.

Elena nodded sympathetically and pulled her friend in for a tight hug.

"Let me know if there's anything I can do," she told the princess, who had tears running down her face.

They parted ways, and Elena made her way back to her bedroom, feeling unsure of what to do next. She desperately wanted to help Adina and bring the smile back to her face. But as a guest—and an unwanted one in Zanthus's eyes—in a magical realm on the brink of political turmoil, she felt out of her depth.

***

Elena alternated between pacing her room and lying on the bed, staring at the ceiling. The sky darkened, and the cool wind fluttered into her bedroom through the open window. Torches and candles flickered to life, and Elena assumed a passing guard or palace staff member was doing the rounds using their elemental powers.

A sharp knock on the door had her quickly moving to answer it, hoping Leon or Adina would fill her in on what was happening. On opening it, she was tempted to slam the door shut again at the sight of Zanthus standing at the entryway with a small tray. The knot of anxiety in her stomach grew, and all thoughts disappeared at the sight of the royal advisor.

"Lady Elena," Zanthus greeted her coolly, crossing the threshold without waiting to be invited in.

Elena moved to the side silently and watched him place the tray of stew and bread on the table. He turned to face her with a grim expression, and she crossed her arms over her chest, keeping her face blank.

"I have made arrangements for you to return to your realm tomorrow," he announced.

Elena furrowed her brow.

"The family has decided you are no longer in danger and, therefore, can go back home," he said.

"But you thought I was working with the rebels," Elena said, injecting as much snark into her voice as possible. "Or have you realized that I've been telling the truth this whole time?"

Zanthus glowered at her in response.

"Why were you in Istanbul that night with Tarrick?" she asked, tilting her head to the side.

"You're in no position to be asking me such questions," Zanthus growled. He moved forward, and Elena caught sight of his hand twitching, trying to contain his rage.

"Tarrick told me he was the only Leneiran who traveled between the realms," Elena continued, keeping her voice steady and not betraying the fear she felt as Zanthus inched toward her. "What were you doing there?"

"*Prince* Tarrick is the future king of Terralea," Zanthus hissed. "Do you really think he'd be allowed to visit your realm unaccompanied?"

"So why not send Erik or another guard with him?" Elena shrugged. "It seems quite risky for Terralea's future king *and* the current royal advisor to put themselves in such a dangerous place days before an important Peace Summit."

They stared at each other in silence.

"You know nothing of our world and the lengths we go to keep it safe," Zanthus finally said.

"Perhaps." Elena shrugged again. "But I know an asshole when I see one, regardless of which realm I'm in."

For a moment, Elena thought Zanthus would lunge and squeeze the life out of her. But he remained where he was. A muscle ticked in his jaw, and he clenched his hands into fists. His lips curled up in a malevolent smile that unnerved her.

"Enjoy your last night in the comfort of our palace, *Lady* Elena," he said, walking away from her. "In fact, enjoy your last night in our realm. There's no telling what tomorrow will bring."

On that ominous note, he left her room and shut the door firmly. Elena gasped when she heard the lock click from the outside and rushed over to the door, turning and desperately jiggling the handle. Zanthus had locked her in and probably had no intention of letting her out until the morning.

"Fuck this!" Elena muttered angrily, looking around the room. She was not going to stick around to find out what Zanthus had planned for her.

Elena debated using the secret passageway to escape. Zanthus would not have locked her in there if he knew about it or if he thought she would know about the palace's secrets. She shook her head. Even with a candle, she would get lost in the labyrinth. The curtains fluttered in the breeze, and she moved to the balcony to lean over and assess the drop. Without Adina and Erik's help, she would probably break a leg if she jumped, and there were no climbing aids or ivy along the walls.

A tree branch bobbed in the wind, and she squinted at it. She hadn't thought about climbing trees since she broke her arm as a child. Jumping off the balcony with Adina had brought back memories of the trauma with a vengeance.

But falling out of a tree on her own terms won over leaving her fate in the hands of Zanthus. Several deep breaths later, Elena was choking down her fear and reaching for the branch that extended to her balcony. It was closer than she thought, and she crawled across toward the study trunk. Shaking hands gripped the thin branch that only just held her weight as she pulled herself closer to freedom. After making sure there were no guards lurking beneath her, she shimmied down, breathing a sigh of relief when she felt solid ground beneath her feet.

Just as she had with Adina the night of the Full Moon Festival, Elena moved cautiously, keeping to the shadows and checking for patrols as she made her way toward the walls.

She ducked behind a bush to avoid a passing guard when a large hand clamped over her mouth to muffle her scream. A strong arm pinned her back against a solid chest. Elena wriggled and squirmed against her captor.

"Quiet!" a low voice growled in her ear.

~ 31 ~

Elena relaxed when wafts of sandalwood and cedar washed over her. They remained crouched behind the bush until the patrol's march faded in the opposite direction.

Tarrick tugged her toward the palace gardens, and she tried to protest, but he ignored her attempts to break away. She followed him reluctantly to the lookout point he loved so much. When he whirled around to look at her, his expression was filled with pain, regret, anger, and fear.

"What the fuck are you doing?" she hissed, crossing her arms and glaring at him.

"I could ask you the same," he said in a low voice. Even in the dark, she could see his amber eyes dangerously glowing. "I came out to the gardens for a bit of peace after a shitty day, only to find you skulking in the shadows. Explain yourself. Now!"

"I don't owe you an explanation," Elena retorted.

Tarrick closed his eyes and pinched the bridge of his nose. "Elena—" he started.

"No, don't 'Elena' me," she shot back. "I am in this mess because of you, and I'm not going to just sit around waiting for your uncle or this assassin or rebels or whoever else is after me to kill me."

Tarrick's eyes snapped open, and he stared at her. Elena bit her lower lip and stared back.

"What do you mean Uncle Zanthus is trying to *kill* you?" he asked slowly.

"Didn't Erik tell you he threatened me at the feast last night?" Elena frowned. "And he did it again when he brought me dinner just now. He said that he's made plans for me to return to my realm tomorrow, but the way he said it…"

"Fuck." Tarrick scrubbed his face with his hand and sat down heavily on the wide stone.

Elena took a seat next to him. "I wanted to say a proper goodbye before I left, but he locked me in my room, and I was scared. I thought maybe I could escape to Erindell and bribe someone to take me to the portal, and I'd make my own way back. Somehow." Her fingers brushed against his as they both looked out over Erindell and the Temple of Divine Beings.

"I'm so sorry, Elena. I promised to look after you, and I haven't." He sighed heavily, hanging his head and massaging his temples. "I can't believe Uncle Zanthus…" he trailed off.

"That's okay," Elena said, feeling slightly sorry for the prince. "The plan sounded better in my head."

Far away from her room and the dangers within the palace, Elena felt calmer. She lifted her face to the warm breeze that rustled through the garden, carrying the sweet scent of night-blooming jasmines and causing gentle ripples to dance across the pool's surface.

"What are *you* going to do?" she asked, trying to distract herself from feeling despair. "About Malina and Halder?"

"I don't know," Tarrick groaned. "It's all a fucking mess."

"Okay, what do you *want* to do?" Elena asked, trying to smother her smile at the uncharacteristic expletive that had burst out of the prince's mouth. "I won't tell," she promised. "Cross my heart." She waved a finger in a crossing motion over her heart.

"I want to run away and let Leon take charge," he said, biting his lip and looking guilty.

"We could go together," Elena offered, half smiling.

"I'm sorry you're still stuck here and caught up in everything." He smiled back sadly. "I wish I could take you back myself right now."

"Don't you have powers as a prince?" Elena frowned.

"Anything I want to do still has to be voted on by the royal council," he explained. "Yes, the royal family has the final say in things, but we are still held in check by the council to make sure we don't abuse our powers."

"I see." Elena nodded.

There was a pause before Tarrick spoke again.

"Adina told me you both saw everything that happened through the secret passageways. She forgets that I'm a hundred years older than she is, and I know every trick in the book." He rolled his eyes. "Before my siblings came along, I had to entertain myself and went exploring. Probably more than she does." He laughed.

Elena tried to picture Tarrick as a young boy wandering through the dark passageways and peeking through the spyholes on tiptoes.

"I'm sorry you had to hear me say those things about you." He rubbed his chin sadly. "I had to get everyone off my back, but none of it was true. The truth is, you're kind, generous, feisty, and beautiful. You're brave and thoughtful. You make my brother laugh, which is no easy task. He's usually the one making others laugh. Adina and my mother adore you. Even my father enjoys your company."

Elena felt tears pricking at the back of her eyes and turned away, blinking fiercely.

"In another life, another realm, I would have loved you," he said, taking her hand and interlacing their fingers. "This past week, every time you entered the room and showed me your sass and strength, I found myself wanting more. More of your presence, more of your smiles, more dances, more nights like this where we can just sit here and talk like two ordinary people..."

"We can't be together, Tarrick," Elena whispered, her heart aching at his words. "I-I wish we could, but I'm all wrong for you."

"No, you're perfect for me," he argued.

"Tarrick," Elena sighed. "You're the future king of Terralea, and aside from being public enemy number one in your uncle's eyes, I'm a thirty-five-year-old woman who still doesn't know how taxes or insurance work."

Tarrick's lips twitched.

"There are times when I just stay in bed all day because I'm exhausted," she continued. "I'm a mess! I feel like I can't function without my parents around to help me."

"No, you're not," Tarrick said, reaching out to Elena and brushing back a loose strand of hair. "You're a strong, independent woman and a fighter. Like your mother."

A tear rolled down Elena's face at the mention of her.

"The report on you included details about your parents," Tarrick said gently, dropping his hand to hold hers. "What your mother did for that little boy was just..." He shook his head in disbelief.

Elena turned to Tarrick. "I miss her so much. I wish she had stayed home that day. I wish she hadn't been at the gas station when that gunman entered. I wish that boy had never been there. I wish she hadn't jumped in front of him."

"You did the same for me." He stared at her hypnotically.

Elena dragged her gaze back to the lights of Erindell. "Mom never stopped protecting those around her and fighting for them, even when she retired."

"Both of your parents were brave people, and even while you're grieving and feel broken, I know you are just like them and will find yourself again," Tarrick said, smiling faintly.

"I don't know if I will ever get over their deaths," she said quietly, turning back to him. "I miss them so much, and it hurts knowing I'll never speak to my mom again or be able to hug my dad." Her voice cracked. "A small, selfish part of me had hoped that bullet would end the pain I felt for so long, and I could see my parents again, and we could be a family once more."

"I'm sorry for everything you had to go through," Tarrick said, wiping away another tear that rolled down Elena's cheek. "But you should know a large selfish part of *me* is glad you survived. These past few days with you have made me feel more alive, more hopeful than I ever have."

Elena gave him a watery smile. "Are all Terralean men as charming as you? Men definitely aren't in my realm."

Tarrick chuckled.

Elena's smile faded, and she bit her lower lip. "I-I'm scared of being alone, Tarrick," she said quietly. "After all my failed relationships, I thought I was better off alone, but I don't know how I'm going to get through this by myself."

Tarrick pulled her into his lap and held her to his chest. He stroked her hair while she sniffled into his tunic. Now that she had finally uncorked the bottle, thoughts exploded in a stream of disjointed phrases and thoughts. The words tumbled out as though they had been festering and building. She was finally ready to admit her fears.

"I thought I would follow the conventional route, you know? Get a job, get married, have babies, a house in the suburbs, grow old with my husband, have grandchildren ... I watched all of my friends follow that path, and I let myself become a lonely, isolated introvert," Elena spoke into his chest.

Tarrick tightened his hold on her. She took deep breaths to steady herself.

"Being here has helped me realize I want more." Elena gave him a half-guilty smile. "Last night, dancing with you and Leon and your father made me feel so alive in a way I hadn't for a long time. I want more of that feeling. That joy. Like I belong somewhere, and I'm actually living instead of going through the motions."

"I'm glad we could help in a small way," he said sincerely.

"Are you kidding? It's been a big help being here with you," she corrected him. "*All* of you. Except Lord Zanthus and King Halder. They haven't really helped me in any way," she added as an afterthought.

Tarrick looked grim, and Elena regretted bringing them up.

"You're lucky to have Leon and Adina," she told him. "I wish I had siblings like them."

"They are my closest friends and the people I trust most in this world." His eyes lit up, and Elena's chest warmed at the sight.

"I'm glad you have them too," she said affectionately. "You three are a great team."

"After all our talks, I've come to see you as a close friend too." Tarrick gave her a crooked smile. "In fact, more than a friend."

It was like a bucket of ice had been poured over her head, and she turned away. *I can't do this. I shouldn't do this.*

"Elena, look at me," Tarrick commanded softly. She forced herself to do as he requested. "I respect your decision if you don't want to be anything more than friends, which I hope we are," he said carefully. "But you should know that I can't stop thinking about you, and I promise to do everything I can to protect you."

"I can't stop thinking about you too," she whispered sadly.

"I wish there wasn't a realm separating us from being together." He raked his fingers through his hair in frustration.

"I wish you didn't keep falling in love with human women," Elena tried to joke.

"Me too," Tarrick said glumly. "But they keep throwing themselves at me."

She snorted, and he laughed.

"You could probably remedy that by marrying a beautiful Skandorian princess," she offered.

"I don't want to talk about her, or marriage, or anything to do with politics." Tarrick frowned. "I came here to stop thinking about all that. I came here to stop thinking at all."

"And how's that working out for you?" Elena asked drily.

"It was working well until now." He huffed a laugh.

"I'm so glad my problems distracted you." She rolled her eyes, and he laughed again. "Perhaps you could hire me as your court jester when you're king."

"There are other ways I enjoy being distracted," he said in a low voice.

"Do these ways involve Madame Zorra?" she teased.

Tarrick threw back his head and laughed.

"You truly are not afraid of me, are you?" He gazed at her.

"Should I be?" She peeked up at him through lowered lashes. "Perhaps if you tried using your default glare?" she suggested, an innocent smile playing around her lips.

"You're going to be the death of me," Tarrick groaned, burying his head in his hands.

~ 32 ~

"Maybe the healing waters will help." Elena walked to the pool. She peered into the dark pool as a bold idea formed in her head. Voicing the guilt and addressing the anger that she had pushed to the side since her mother's death had been cathartic. Freeing.

Glancing over her shoulder at the prince, who watched her curiously, she gave him a little smile and unbuttoned the vest she wore over her tunic. She slipped it off and let it fall to the ground, doing the same with her tunic. Tarrick's breath hitched at the dips and curves of her bare back. With her heart beating frantically, Elena slowly unzipped her pants and slid her thumbs over the waistband, pulling them off with her panties. There was no going back.

"Elena," he said hoarsely. She stepped into the cool water, sinking deeper into the pool until she stood in the center on her tiptoes.

Her playful smile had Tarrick stripping off his shirt and pulling off his shoes. He ripped off his pants, and Elena bit her lower lip when he stood before her, completely naked. Tarrick gave her a cocky grin and strode into the water, loud splashes revealing his eagerness to be by her side.

She moved to the edge of the pool that overlooked the city, neither taking their eyes off each other as he followed her. Water droplets glistened on his broad shoulders. Elena's core clenched with anticipation at the sight of the lust written all over his face. The rational part of her brain that she had been listening to the entire time fell silent. All she could think about was what the magnificent man in front of her might feel like pressed against her bare skin. Taste like. Sound like when he filled her with his long, hard cock.

Tarrick placed his hands on the edge of the pool either side of her, caging her in. Her eyes swept over the wavy, dark hair and the water droplets clinging to the ends. That close, she noticed a faint scar curving above his left cheekbone. She licked her lips at his wolfish grin, fighting the urge to wrap herself around him.

"Is the water helping?" she whispered.

He leaned in closer, his breath warm against her cheeks. Her heart beat faster at the low timbre of his voice as he said, "Yeah, it's helping. But stripping in front of me and swimming naked in my pool is not, in fact, helping me do the honorable thing," he added, pulling back slightly.

His eyes dipped to Elena's exposed collarbones and shoulders glistening in the moonlight. He reached out to move a lock of wet hair that covered her left breast. Elena sucked in a breath at his touch; it was featherlight, but it might as well have been a hot brand, marking her as his.

The air sizzled with electricity as they closed the gap between them in the same second. It was a tangle of tongues, fingers running through each others' hair, pressing against each other, and kissing as though it was their last night together before the end of the world.

This is how it's meant to be. The heartbreaking thought fueled Elena's passion as she kissed Tarrick with an intensity she didn't know she was capable of.

He pulled away first, panting and staring at her with scorching eyes, still cupping her face. He kissed her neck softly, making her moan. She tilted her head back as he made his way to the hollow of her throat.

He dragged his lips from her wet skin and gazed into her lust-filled eyes. She nodded at the unasked question. *Fuck it.* After their conversation about her parents and her own near-miss with death, she didn't want to wonder, "What if?" Life was too short for that. At least, hers was. She'd rather have done it than regret and speculate on what might have been.

"Tarrick," she moaned when he kissed her neck again tenderly, biting down on the skin gently and running over the area with his warm tongue. Under the water, his hands slid down the sides of her body, and she gasped when he cupped her breasts and squeezed.

Elena wound her arms around his neck and clung to him.

"Divine Beings, you're beautiful," he breathed against her ear. He moved his hands down her waist and stopped at her hips.

"Touch me, Tarrick," she whispered. "I want to feel you inside me."

She had never spoken so boldly or made her desires known to any of her ex-boyfriends for fear of being rejected. But she trusted Tarrick implicitly and knew he would give her everything she wanted and probably more.

"That mouth of yours..." he groaned against her lips.

"You can have that too." She gave him a wicked smile.

He cursed and kissed her roughly again, hands moving lower. Elena spread her legs in anticipation, trying to steady her breathing. It had been so long since anyone had made her feel the need to throw the world away behind her and just live in the moment.

She bit his lower lip and flicked her tongue out, running it along the seam of his mouth. Tarrick swatted away the hand she moved between their bodies, snaking down to reach for his cock. He pulled it up to his neck, silently instructing Elena to let him pleasure her. Slowly, torturously, he dragged a hand down to her center, where he slid a finger along the sensitive folds.

Elena gasped at the sensation. She lifted her hips and leaned in for more.

"Greedy," Tarrick growled, and bit her lower lip. She kissed him back, opening her mouth to let him devour her. While his tongue explored her mouth, he dipped a finger into her pussy, curling it inside her.

She moaned against his mouth and pulled him closer, aching to feel his body against her own. He added another finger, and he felt her walls clench in response.

"You're so tight," he whispered, stroking and teasing her with one hand while his other reached up to massage and knead her breast. He broke their kiss, but before she could protest, he lifted her so her breasts were exposed above the water. Her skin pebbled from the cool night air and Tarrick's wicked tongue teased her nipple. She cried out in pleasure and pain when he bit, pinched, licked, and sucked. His fingers continued their rhythm inside her, and she felt the pleasure growing.

"I'm going to come," she whimpered. "Don't stop."

He obeyed and played with her body relentlessly until he heard her crying out. Her walls shuddered around his fingers as he hit that sensitive spot inside her, and her nails bit into his shoulders. Stars exploded behind Elena's eyes, and she was vaguely aware of Tarrick growling in approval before he kissed her hard to smother her cries.

When she stopped shaking and loosened her hold on him, Elena opened her eyes and smiled in disbelief. He slid his fingers out of her, and she gently drew his hand up to her mouth. The sight of her tasting herself on his fingers had Tarrick cursing again.

"That was intense," she whispered.

He chuckled. "That was just the beginning."

"Wha—"

"I want to hear you scream my name," he told her. "But not here."

He pulled her to the edge of the pool and hauled himself out. The water streamed down his body for a moment before evaporating in the blink of an eye. Elena pushed herself up and sat on the edge before swinging both legs up onto the grass.

Tarrick held out a hand to help her up, waving the other in the air. The water evaporated off her body, leaving her warm and dry. They dressed hastily and haphazardly. Elena pulled on her tunic with shaking fingers, her mind still short-circuiting in the afterglow of her orgasm.

"Come with me." Tarrick nodded back toward the path, reaching his hand out to her.

She slipped her hand in his without a second thought. "Where are we going?"

He glanced back at her with a grin but didn't reply, tightening his fingers around her hand and pulling her away from the pool.

Intrigued, Elena followed Tarrick down a short path to a secluded building. It was dark, but when he waved a hand, small torches and candles flickered to life inside. They drew closer, and he slid back the lock without making a sound, opening the door and stepping aside to let Elena in first.

She stepped into the old building and stared open-mouthed at the set up. It was decked with colored swathes of silk cloth hanging from the ceiling all the way to the dark wooden floor, creating a tent over a large, soft mattress piled high with colorful blankets and pillows. Pillar candles burned in niches in the stone wall, decorated with colored tiles in geometric patterns around the room. Low tables on which more candles burned added to the cozy, romantic atmosphere.

"What is this place?" Elena asked, taking it all in.

"My great-great-grandfather had it built for the woman he was courting," Tarrick told her, running his fingers through his hair. "He called it a *lamora*."

"This is so…" she trailed off, a blush creeping up her cheeks. The room felt intimate and decadent.

"We don't have to do anything you're not comfortable with," Tarrick murmured. He wrapped his arms around her waist and pulled her against his chest while he kissed her neck. She arched back into him, closing her eyes and sighing happily.

"Will we get caught?" she whispered, raising her hand to his face and bringing it closer to her.

"No. It's secluded enough no one will hear us," he replied, nipping and biting her soft skin. He traced the bite with his tongue, and Elena's lower abdomen contracted.

"What if someone checks on us in our rooms?" She covered his hand at her waist and intertwined her fingers with his.

"They won't," he told her, gently lifting her hair and moving it to the side so he could kiss the back of her neck. "Is this your way of telling me you don't want to do this?"

"This is my way of asking if we will get away with what we're about to do," she laughed.

Tarrick stepped away, but before Elena could protest, he spun her around so she faced his roguish grin.

"I'll just glare and frown at anyone who questions their future king," he teased before planting a kiss on her lips.

"I find it sexy," the words slipped out before she could stop herself.

"Oh?" Tarrick asked, lowering his voice in a way that sent a shiver down Elena's spine.

She nodded, biting her lower lip, unable to keep her eyes off his darkening pupils. His hands roamed up her back, and she shuddered. Her breasts tightened, and heat pooled between her thighs again.

Tarrick noticed the reaction and smirked. One hand moved from her back to her front, and he lifted the hem of her tunic, dragging it up and pulling it off. He threw it to the floor, and she gasped as he palmed and squeezed her breast, pinching her nipple and growling in approval when he felt it peak and harden under his ministrations. Elena reached out to palm his hard cock, eliciting a groan from him. She smirked and increased the pressure, rubbing and pressing. Seeing his reaction to her was addictive.

"I find everything about you sexy," he breathed against her pebbled skin.

Tarrick slowly lowered his head to lick and suck her right breast. She whimpered at the feel of his tongue and teeth on her sensitive skin and tugged his thick hair, urging him to keep going.

Raising one arm behind his head, he dragged the tunic off in a single swoop, the sexiest move she had seen him pull. Bright eyes, flushed cheeks, and tousled hair. Elena had never been so turned on. The prince, who would one day be king, was looking at her with burning desire.

She glanced down at his tented pants and wriggled out of her own, letting them pool at her feet before she turned around, giving him a full view of her naked body. He groaned at the sight of her bare ass as she crawled onto the mattress on top of the blankets and pillows. Elena draped herself over the colored silks and satins, arranging her limbs across the sheets and propping herself up on one elbow. She eyed Tarrick, who was staring at her in awe.

"So this is what a queen feels like." She gave him a wicked smile.

~ 33 ~

"**F**uck," Tarrick cursed, palming himself through his pants. "I'm not going to last long with you."

He pulled off his pants and dove onto the bed on top of Elena, devouring her as he kissed and tasted every inch of her mouth. Their tongues entwined as their hands roamed everywhere. Tarrick slipped a finger into her dripping pussy again.

"Tarrick," Elena gasped, her eyes rolling back into her head as she arched her back. "Oh, god!"

Tarrick slowed down his movements, and Elena reached down between them to feel his hardness as he moaned her name. His cock was long, hard, and already dripping with pre-cum. Elena ran her thumb over the head and stroked him from tip to base.

"Divine Beings, this feels good." He rested his forehead against hers as he continued playing with her pussy, making her wriggle and moan with anticipation.

"More," she managed to say in between ragged breaths. "Tarrick, I need more."

She gently squeezed his cock, and he shuddered, pulling her hand away and pinning it above her head. He lowered his head and trailed kisses down her body. She felt his smile against her skin as she writhed and whimpered beneath his featherlight touches and teasing. He didn't stop when he reached the tops of her thighs. She sucked in a breath and arched her back when his tongue began to explore. He hummed appreciatively at the taste of her and licked her sensitive clit.

"Tarrick, please," Elena gasped, seeing stars when she felt his teeth graze and nip her.

"I want to taste you when you come undone." He raised his head for a moment, eyes gleaming at the sight of her helpless and begging. He ducked his head and darted his tongue in and out, delving deeper to taste every inch of her. She wove her fingers through his hair and whimpered his name as though it was a prayer.

It wasn't long before Elena felt waves of pleasure coursing through her body, tipping her over the edge for the second time that evening. Tarrick licked and sucked until she shattered around him, screaming his name. Her eyes glazed as the post-orgasm haze cleared, and she saw his handsome face smiling down at her.

She cupped his cheek with her hand and pulled him in for a kiss, sliding her tongue against his and tasting herself. When they broke apart, there was only a thin ring of amber around the edges of his pupils. He drank in the sight of her flushed cheeks and hair fanned out over the pillow, a wanton smile playing on her lips.

"Your turn," she whispered, pushing him onto his back and straddling his waist. He caressed her back as she kissed him, biting and nipping his lower lip before moving to the side of his jaw, down his neck. She continued kissing his bare chest and moved down to his stomach and hips, flicking out her tongue and tracing the grooves of the muscles of his taut abdomen. He wrapped her silky hair around his fist and guided her down his body. She paused when she reached his cock and glanced up at him through her lashes. He nearly came just at the sight of her.

"Fuck!" he breathed. "Just looking at you..."

She held his hard cock in both hands and stroked slowly. His breathing turned ragged at the feel of her soft hands squeezing and twisting around him. He closed his eyes and arched his hips slightly every time she squeezed. Without warning, she dipped her head and took the tip of him into her mouth.

He cried out and pulled her hair harder. She took him deeper, flattening her tongue against his shaft and reaching up to lightly squeeze his balls.

"Elena," he moaned, and she shivered at the pleasure it incited in her to hear him call out her name in that way. It spurred her on to abandon all restraint and give him everything he wanted. When his cock hit the back of her throat, he jerked his hips, and she started a steady rhythm of moving her head up and down. Elena could feel him trembling beneath her, and she continued to suck and lick until he pulled her up his body so he could kiss her roughly.

He twisted them so he was on top of her again, and she could feel the head of his cock at her entrance. She arched her hips, her pussy aching to feel him inside her. He gently lifted her chin.

"You sure?" he asked softly.

Elena nodded without hesitating and wrapped her legs around his back.

"Yes." She slowly exhaled when he pushed into her soft folds.

She cried out at the sensation, and Tarrick slowed down to give her body time to adjust to his length. He inched into her, groaning at the feeling of her walls squeezing around him. When he was sheathed to the hilt, they paused and stared at each other in wonder, synchronizing their breaths.

Elena felt his cock twitch inside her, and her eyes fluttered closed as she moaned his name. She ground her hips against his, and that was all the encouragement Tarrick needed. He pulled out and thrust back, groaning at the way her pussy clamped around him greedily.

He continued thrusting faster, harder, deeper, his fingers digging into her hips, neither of them caring about the bruises and marks he would leave. Elena's cries of pleasure echoed around the room as he hit the spot inside her that made her see stars over and over again.

"Tarrick!" she screamed, clutching him tightly, the friction and feel of his muscular chest against her sensitive, hard nipples sending bolts of pleasure to her core. He felt her walls spasming around his cock as she orgasmed again. He came with a roar, spilling hot spurts inside her, and collapsed on top of her shuddering body.

They held each other in the aftermath of their orgasms, taking in deep breaths and allowing their bodies to relax into the soft mattress. Tarrick raised himself on his elbows and looked over Elena's content face. He kissed her softly, running his fingers through her hair.

"Was that okay?" she asked, a crease forming between her brows.

Tarrick barked out a laugh. "You're joking, right?"

When she didn't reply, he bent down and kissed her on the lips before moving to kiss her fingers one by one.

"You are perfect," he said, drawing a shy smile from her.

Elena winced slightly at the feeling of emptiness when Tarrick rolled over and carefully slid out of her. Before she could say anything, he pulled her onto his chest, where she rested her head, placing a palm over his thrumming heart.

Tarrick stroked her hair and raised his other hand, lowering the candle flames. He dragged a large blanket over their bodies, and Elena snuggled in closer to him.

"I thought we could sleep here tonight instead of creeping back to our rooms," Tarrick murmured.

Elena smiled. "This feels right," she whispered, tracing her finger absent-mindedly over the dips and grooves of his pecs.

"It does," Tarrick agreed, dropping a kiss on her forehead.

They lay in silence, basking in the post-orgasm haze. Elena's eyes fluttered closed despite her efforts to stay awake and make the most of the night with him.

"I wish this could last forever," she exhaled slowly.

Tarrick tightened his hold on her, folding an arm around her body, a comforting weight.

"Me too," he said quietly.

It was the last thing Elena remembered before she fell asleep to the sound of his steady heartbeat. She slept through the night, not noticing when he Shifted in his sleep.

~ 34 ~

Elena woke feeling relaxed and stretched her limbs. The pale light of dawn lit the room through windows in the sloping roof, indicating it was early enough for them to sneak back into the palace without anyone catching them. She rolled over to take in the prince, trusting he had a plan to get them back to their rooms safely.

Her heart stopped at the sight that greeted her.

Every self-preservation instinct screamed at her to run, but she was frozen to the spot.

A large, lethal black paw around her waist held her down. The sharp tips of deadly gun-metal gray claws poked through the purple-black velvet fur that covered the creature sleeping peacefully next to her. Its ears twitched at the sound of birds tweeting in the garden, and the jaguar released a low growl—or was it a purr?—without opening its eyes in response.

"Tarrick?" Elena whispered, too shocked to move and too afraid to speak in a normal voice, lest the creature didn't recognize her and was alarmed by the noise.

The jaguar stretched and yawned, revealing large, pointed teeth that could easily rip her to shreds. It smacked its maw slowly, blinking in the pale light of day. A low growl vibrated as it took in her petrified expression.

"Tarrick, is that you?" Elena asked again, her heart hammering in her chest. She looked around frantically for an escape route.

The jaguar cocked its head in confusion before it realized what Elena was looking at and Shifted seamlessly. Elena slumped back into the pile of pillows in relief, still trembling as the adrenaline left her body.

"Shit!" Tarrick exclaimed, looking down at his glorious naked body. "I'm so sorry, Elena. I didn't mean for that to happen."

"That's okay," she said weakly, holding a hand over her heart and looking at him with a mixture of awe and fear. "Just give me the head's up next time you decide to Shift."

"It's been a long time since it's happened like that," he admitted, drawing her against his chest and wrapping his strong, warm arms around her. "I don't normally Shift in my sleep. It only ever happens when I fall into a deep sleep. It's a defense mechanism. If someone tried to attack me while I was sleeping, my jaguar instincts are more sensitive."

"I think the sight of you alone would stop them from killing you," she muttered, running her hands down his arms to reassure herself he was in his Elemental form.

"I'm sorry." He kissed the top of her head.

They stayed wrapped up in each other's arms for a while.

"What are we going to do?" Elena asked reluctantly, drawing their attention back to reality.

"I need to confront Uncle Zanthus," Tarrick replied grimly. "He's gone too far this time."

Elena lifted her head and looked at him questioningly.

Tarrick sighed. "He's taken ... liberties in the past and overstepped on more than a few occasions. This isn't the first time Father has had to have words with him about his behavior."

"Be careful," Elena murmured. "He could be dangerous."

"Stay in your bedroom until I come and get you, okay?" he said, kissing the top of her head. "I'm so sorry, Elena. I promised to keep you safe, and I haven't."

Tarrick looked so forlorn. Elena reached up to stroke his cheek comfortingly. "He's your uncle," she murmured. "I understand how important family is, and it's easy to overlook their flaws."

"That's no excuse," he said angrily. "I should have been paying closer attention to him."

Elena nodded, anxiety kicking back in with a vengeance, making her heart beat faster.

"What about Malina?" she whispered.

"I still don't know," Tarrick replied. "I'll talk to Father and see if there's a way to negotiate the sharing of armies and guards without having to marry her."

"Is that possible?" Elena asked.

"If we had more time, I could have researched instances in the past where our countries have united forces and the contracts they drew up," he sighed. "Halder's always hinted at Malina and I being a good match, but we never took him seriously. I guess finding out about our guards was a stroke of luck, and he's taking advantage of the timing to drive a harder bargain than any of us anticipated."

"Knowing you, you'll either find a way or do what's right by your people." Elena gave him a sad smile.

"I should get you back to the palace," he said after a beat of silence. "I wish we could hide out here longer, but the guards will be rotating soon and we'll miss our chance to sneak back in without anyone noticing."

They took turns cleaning up in the washroom and dressed hastily in silence. Tarrick kissed her gently and ran his fingers through her hair. He gazed into her eyes as though trying to commit her face to memory, and she held him close, breathing in his comforting scent.

They left the *lamora* and walked back to the palace. The early morning was cool and fresh. Dew drops clung to the leaves, and *lyrabirds* squawked in the trees, greeting the rising sun. The night patrol were still in position at the main doors and entrances, fighting back sleep for the last few minutes of their shift.

Tarrick led Elena down a path to the kitchens. They crept along the brick wall until he stopped and scanned the area. He reached up and pulled on a heavy, rusted hook that blended seamlessly into the exposed bricks and mortar wall. Elena would not have noticed it if Tarrick hadn't reached for it.

She thought the hook must have been used for buckets or ropes at one time, but her guess was proven incorrect when some of the bricks shifted slightly and Tarrick pulled on another cleverly concealed rusted metal eyelet protruding from the wall. A slab of bricks attached to a wood panel with hinges concealed a door to another secret passage.

"Don't tell anyone." He winked at her, motioning for her to enter. She grinned and entered the passage. Tarrick closed the door and locked it behind them. He held up a small flame in one hand and held out his other for Elena's.

They navigated the dark passageways until they came to a familiar niche Elena recognized from the day before. She walked more confidently, and soon, they were opening the hidden fireplace in her room and peeking around the corner.

"All clear," she breathed. Tarrick opened the passageway door fully to let her out.

"Thank you," she whispered in case there were guards standing outside her room. "For last night. For everything."

"Don't thank me." Tarrick shook his head. "I'll never forget last night."

She squeezed his hand, and he let go abruptly, darting back into the fireplace. He glanced at her over his shoulder once more with a flicker of sadness and longing for what could have been between the two of them before he closed it.

Elena sighed and went to the washroom to bathe properly. She didn't regret sleeping with the prince, but as she went through the motions of getting ready for the day, she wished there was the possibility of a future with him. The cool air was refreshing, and she stood on the balcony enjoying the peace while braiding her hair.

The bedroom door opened, and Elena stepped back inside to investigate. Her heart sank when she saw Serkin.

"Lord Zanthus has summoned you," he informed her.

Elena crossed her arms over her chest and opened her mouth. "Lord Zanthus can go fu—"

Her eyes widened. Invisible hands closed around her throat, cutting off the air supply. She clawed desperately at her throat, gasping and wheezing, feeling her windpipe constrict slowly, torturously. White spots clouded her vision as she fell to her knees.

The guard stepped closer to her shuddering body on the ground and tutted. The lack of oxygen made her head swim, but moments before she passed out, the sensation of being choked to death stopped.

"I'd mind your manners if I were you, *Lady* Elena," the guard sneered.

She looked up at him with watery eyes, coughing and spluttering. He wore a cruel smirk and reached down to grab her roughly by the collar of her tunic, lifting her a few inches off the ground to hold her up at his eye level. She felt his hot breath fanning her face when he spoke.

"His Lordship has a busy day ahead of him," he growled. "I have very clear instructions to dispose of you myself if you fail to cooperate."

Elena bit down the insult on the tip of her tongue and simply glared at the guard. When he was satisfied she would comply, he released his hold on her. She stumbled slightly and Serkin strode out of her room, marching down the corridor. Praying someone would see them, Elena reluctantly trailed after him. That early in the morning, the palace was deserted. The dread pooling in the pit of her stomach grew as they neared Zanthus's office.

<h1 style="text-align:center">~ 35 ~</h1>

The door to Zanthus's office was ajar. "...and I need you to deliver this parcel in the human realm today. The guards at the portal know to expect you," his voice rang out authoritatively.

"Hampshire?" an unfamiliar male voice asked. It sounded like razors had been dragged inside his throat, making Elena shudder.

"Yes," Zanthus replied. "I've been keeping tabs over the years, and the time has come to recruit him to our cause. Here are your travel documents. The letter in the parcel explains everything."

"And the prince has no idea?"

"No. I made sure of that when I found out." Zanthus huffed a humorless laugh.

Serkin knocked on the door and cleared his throat loudly before announcing himself.

"Ah, Lady Elena." Zanthus eyed her in a way that made her feel uneasy. "Welcome."

Elena stepped into his office and glanced around—it was still a mess. More half-empty bottles, odds and ends, and books were strewn about the surface of his table.

"Would you like me to deal with her, my Lord?" the strange man with the raspy voice asked. He was dressed in a ragged black cloak and all she could see of his clothing was the scuffed worn tips of his boots peeking out from under the hem of the cloak. Oily black hair was slicked back from a pale long face with heavy, dark brows, pale gray eyes, and a hooked nose.

"Not now, Raz." Zanthus stroked his beard thoughtfully. "I need to take care of the family first."

"I could make it look like an accident," Raz suggested, an evil smile playing about his thin lips.

Elena looked at him disdainfully, thinking he was every part the villain in a movie or book. She turned back to Zanthus and glared at him. "If you lay a finger on me, Tarrick will rip you apart. After I'm done beating the shit out of you."

"My, my." Zanthus bared his teeth. "You have grown a spine in the last few days."

"I've always had a spine, unlike you," she spat at him.

She cried out when she felt the sting of his hand make contact with her cheek. She held a hand to her face and stared at him in shock. The sound of blood rushing in her ears dulled the sound of what Zanthus was saying. She swayed on her feet, feeling light-headed before the haze cleared.

"I've been wanting to do that for a long time," Zanthus breathed heavily, no longer smiling. "Your presence has been most inconvenient these last few days, but it's given me time to think, and I realized it's been a stroke of luck." His lips curled. "You see, my dear, I now have the perfect explanation for the fatal disease that's about to sweep through the palace, killing everyone except for a select few."

Elena's eyes widened.

"A human woman that our foolish prince fell for and brought back to our realm," Zanthus said with a malevolent smile.

"No one will believe that," she seethed. "They'll know you're lying."

"The story isn't for them. They'll be dead." Zanthus waved an impatient hand. "This is the story I tell the people of Leneira." He turned to Raz. "Put her with the others. We'll dispose of everyone together."

"You bastard!" She shoved to her feet, but Raz was at her side in an instant. He pinned her hands behind her with one strong hand.

With the other, he held a dagger to her throat, and she stopped fighting him.

"If the family notices her absence at breakfast, she was so desperate to leave, she escaped," Zanthus told Raz. "Unlikely, since it's the last day of the summit. She'll be the last thing on their minds tonight when everything I've been working toward for the past hundred years finally comes to fruition."

"Tarrick won't believe that," Elena said.

"You sleep with him once and think you know him," Zanthus scoffed. "Yes, yes, I know everything. I have eyes and ears all over the palace, including the *lamora*."

"You know nothing," she hissed, but felt sick at the thought of his spies watching her and Tarrick the previous night.

"I know more than you think I do," he snarled. "I was there when he met Rose. He looked at her the same way he's been looking at you this week. I knew then that he would be blinded by love once more, making him easy to manipulate."

Elena tried to fight Raz's grip on her hands, but he held on tighter.

"I'm not like Rose," she spat. "I don't want elemental powers, and I would never hurt his family the way she did. Tarrick knows that, and he's not foolish enough to believe your insane story."

Zanthus barked out a laugh. "Is that what he told you? That Rose wanted elemental powers and tried to kill Adina for them?"

Elena faltered. Her stomach dropped when Zanthus shook his head and smiled.

"That boy was even more naive than I suspected," he chuckled. "And still ignorant to the fact that I orchestrated the whole thing."

Elena's mouth fell open in astonishment.

"Is this wise, my Lord?" Raz muttered, digging the blade into Elena's throat and tightening his grip on her hands.

"She'll be dead soon," Zanthus said carelessly. "She might as well hear the full story and learn that there's nothing she can do to prevent their deaths." His eyes glittered maliciously.

Elena did not rise to the jab. There was still a chance she could break free and save everyone after she learned Zanthus's plans.

"He stole Rose from me. That bitch showed her true colors when I told her that Tarrick was heir to the Terralean throne, and she used me to get closer to him," he said bitterly. "She persuaded Tarrick to use his position to ask the Divine Beings to grant her powers and long life. They only answer a current or future ruler's summons, you see. And when they rejected her, I saw an opportunity to take my revenge on both of them.

"I made contact with the rebels, who were growing restless and already planning a series of attacks across Leneira. I gave them the funds and weapons they needed and told them about all of Terralea, Skandor, and Sailon's weaknesses and undefended regions. *I* told Rose there was a way to reap our abilities—killing another Elemental and absorbing their powers."

Chuckling at Elena's horrified expression, he continued his monologue. "She was so gullible." He shook his head. "She never understood the nuances of our abilities and how they worked."

"You're a monster," she seethed. "When Tarrick finds out—"

"He won't," Zanthus cut her off. He started pacing in front of her. "He's had a hundred years to work it out, but he and Arran believed every word I told him about Rose not being in her right mind. They trust me, after all. What would I have to gain by lying about her?"

"This time, they'll know," Elena told him. "You haven't covered your tracks as well as you did last time."

"This time, they won't get the chance to figure out anything. Not even when they take their last breaths," he sneered. He snatched up one of the small bottles that was still half-full of clear liquid. "This is a formula I have perfected over the last century."

"So you've been playing with a chemistry set," Elena said snarkily. "What did you make? *Araki* so strong that it permanently affects your brain? That would explain a lot."

Zanthus chuckled. "I like your spirit! Where was this at our first meeting? The royal council would have had your head on the spot for your disrespect and impertinence." He shook his head. "No, while Tarrick thought I was studying medical preparations and cures in your realm to bring back to Terralea, I was developing a formula to nullify our powers."

"Why would you do that?" Elena demanded.

"Rose wanted to be with a powerful man." Zanthus shrugged. "It started off as an experiment to show her I could be more powerful than Tarrick. But when the uprising failed and the rebels proved to be useless, barring one or two"—he inclined his head toward Raz, who smirked—"an idea grew. I continued to develop the formula, testing it on the guards and servants without their knowledge until it was perfected.

"I continued to play my part as the dutiful and loyal royal advisor. Arran led with his heart and not his head. I knew it would be detrimental to the future of Terralea. Then, Lin was crowned Queen of Sailon, and the powerless Leneirans moved to her lands and sang her praises.

Leneira was growing soft. Weak. Armies dwindled. The number of people signing up to be part of our defense forces declined. More and more Terraleans were using their powers for mundane jobs." His lips curled in disgust. "We used to be feared. We were the most powerful country in the land. Skandor was taking that title, with their Shifter army and Halder holding onto the old beliefs."

Elena scoffed, but Zanthus ignored her, continuing his rant. Raz still held the dagger against her throat, not showing any sign of loosening his grip or letting go.

"I held onto hope that Tarrick would be different after Rose betrayed him." He shook his head sadly. "But he followed his father's lead, and I knew I had to take matters into my own hands."

"You're deranged," Elena said, unable to hold her tongue.

"No, Arran and his family are foolish for believing we could have peace and alliances with Halder and Lin," he countered. "When Halder spoke of abolishing borders and creating one powerful country, I told him I would be the perfect ally to convince Arran to agree to the union. But he just wanted his useless daughter married off to Tarrick so they could breed Leneirans with both Elemental and Shifter powers." Zanthus looked repulsed at the thought. "He believed this would be possible with Tarrick's extra ability."

Raz made a sound of disgust. "Filthy animals," he muttered.

"Thanks to you sticking your nose where it doesn't belong, I've been forced to bring my plans forward. Tonight, a new era will begin, with me stepping in as King of Leneira," he said triumphantly.

Elena's heart pounded wildly at the thought that she had inadvertently signed Tarrick and his family's death warrants before she even had a chance to warn them.

"When I give them a few drops of this tonight at dinner"—he held up the bottle—"their powers will be quashed, which is when my loyal guards will kill them all. I will be one of the few chosen ones spared of the disease and will rule over the entire realm. I shall restore Leneira to its former glory and power with those who believe in my vision."

"The old *take over the world* plan." Elena snorted. "How original. It'll never work."

"Let me worry about that," Zanthus sneered. "You'll be begging me for a quick and painless death when the time comes, but yours, I'll save for the end. Or perhaps almost the end so Tarrick can watch the blood boil in your veins as you writhe at his feet. I believe you've already experienced what it's like to have your air supply cut off?" Zanthus flicked his eyes to Serkin, who stood by the door, smirking in confirmation.

The image Zanthus painted filled Elena with horror, knowing he could and would do everything he had just described. Her throat still felt raw from his guard's earlier torture, and she knew Zanthus would be even more cruel to fulfil his own twisted need for revenge.

"Tarrick would burn you before he'd let that happen," she promised, shaking with anger.

"I'm holding you captive right now." Zanthus spread his arms and turned his head dramatically. "Where is he?"

Elena bit her lip. In truth, she didn't know how quickly Tarrick or his family would jump to her rescue—especially if they believed Zanthus's story about her trying to escape Leneira. Zanthus held a great deal of power and used Tarrick's history with Rose against him.

"Besides, they won't be in a position to do anything to me," he laughed, swirling the bottle of vile toxin. "For now, why don't you enjoy a nice, long nap before I see you again?"

Before Elena could protest or fight off Raz, Zanthus lunged at her with a syringe she hadn't noticed him pulling out. She felt the prick of a needle entering the side of her neck and cried out weakly before collapsing. Despite trying to fight the blackness crowding her vision and taking over her senses, unconsciousness swept her.

~ 36 ~

Cool hands stroked Elena's face, and a soft, female voice was murmuring, but the words were unclear. Her head spun as she regained consciousness, and her senses came back to life. The metallic tang of blood, sweat, urine, and the slightly sweet stench of rotting bodies permeated the air. She shot up and blinked rapidly, her eyes adjusting to the bleak cell.

"Elena, you're okay," a familiar voice croaked, and she swiveled her head.

Erik and Zahra crouched on the ground beside her. They looked at her with concern.

"Where am I? What happened?" she asked, sounding hysterical.

"Calm down, Elena," Zahra said soothingly. "We need to keep our heads."

"Where am I?" she repeated, the cold seeping into her bones. She took in the stone wall, crumbling in parts but thick, and the solid, metal bars surrounding her and the dusty floor. Her gaze traveled up the wall to the small, barred gap—the only source of air and light. Dread pooled in her stomach, and she turned around slowly to take in the large chamber with prison cells lining the stone walls. Half a dozen glittering eyes and curious faces peered at Elena. She recognized some of the Terraleans imprisoned in the adjoining cells as elite guards she had watched training only a few days before. They were powerfully built, their stained tunics stretched across muscular chests and biceps as they pressed themselves against the bars caging them in to better hear Elena, Zahra, and Erik.

Elena caught sight of unmoving bodies lined up against the walls. "Are they dead?"

"We're hoping they're just knocked out," Erik said sadly.

"We were all drugged by Zanthus," Zahra spat out.

"How long have I been unconscious?" Elena asked, peering around frantically for clues as to how long she had been passed out for. "Tarrick and his family are in danger. I've got to go save them."

"Only a few hours," Zahra replied. "It's almost midday."

"We've been trying to make a plan to escape, but without our elemental powers, we're stuck here," a woman from the neighboring cell sighed.

"I heard stories about rebels escaping imprisonment while they waited to be tried after the uprising," Erik lowered his voice to a cautious whisper just in case Zanthus's guards were in the vicinity. "So there must be a way out of here. This prison hasn't been used since then."

"Do you know where it is?" Elena asked hopefully, lowering her voice and moving closer to him.

"The bars in our cell seem to be the loosest." Zahra jerked her head toward the small window at the top of their cell. "It's our only option. We think it'll be safe to escape tonight."

"It will be a tight squeeze," Erik said, squinting as he assessed the gap.

Elena followed his gaze—he was right, it would be tight even for her petite frame. Zahra, with her tall, willowy frame and narrow hips, might make it through without too much difficulty. Her eyes swept over the other guards, who wore grim expressions as they too eyed the small opening. Erik wouldn't be the only one to struggle if they could only loosen one or two bars.

"Don't worry about me," Erik assured her as she took in his bulky shoulders and broad, muscled chest. "I *will* make it out of here tonight. One way or another."

"What's the plan once we get out?" Elena asked, shaking off her doubts, determined to think positive thoughts.

"We make our way to the palace and find the king and queen," Zahra said. "We tell them what Zanthus did and let them take it from there." The others nodded in agreement.

"Simple enough." Elena frowned. "What about the guards? Are there any still on duty who we can trust to help us?"

"We need to assume the only ones we can trust are in here," Erik said, gesturing around the cells. "Zanthus chose us specifically for his twisted experiment, which means those still free are his supporters."

"Shit," Elena muttered, trying to work out how she, Erik, Zahra, and a handful of guards would overthrow dozens of Zanthus's supporters who still had their elemental powers.

"Our elemental abilities are only a small part of what we can do," Erik said determinedly, as though reading her mind. A rumble of agreement echoed around the chamber. The guards wore expressions of determination and confidence that reassured Elena slightly.

Impatience clawed at her as they waited for the sun to set. Erik explained that it would be too dangerous to try and escape in broad daylight without knowing how many guards Zanthus had crawling around the palace grounds. Elena alternated between pacing the cell and explaining everything Zanthus had revealed to her fellow inmates.

"That asshole," Ronan, a stoic guard with shoulder-length chestnut hair and a bulky build, growled. His knuckles turned white as he gripped the bars of his cell so tight Elena wondered if he was trying to break through with his bare hands.

Sami, the only other female guard in the adjoining cell, hissed in agreement.

"That would explain our abilities failing," Kitt, tall and wiry, mourned as he examined his hands that shone with old burn scars.

The guards attempted to call upon their elemental powers throughout the day, hoping the toxin had worn off. Zahra and Erik took turns prying at the bars on the cell window as quietly as they could, loosening as many as possible.

Elena tried to engage in mundane conversation with the others to stop torturing herself with images of Tarrick being poisoned by Zanthus. Some paced their cells as she had done. Jai, a short, stocky Elemental with sharp eyes and restless energy, shared a cell across the chamber with Ilyas, who remained quiet and observant.

They sparred with each other in the constrained space to work off some of their anger and frustration at being imprisoned. Despite their haggard, drawn appearance, they moved fluidly, throwing swift punches and kicking out in a blur of movement.

Sami's dark eyes were glued on Ali, a burly guard with a shaved head and a neatly trimmed, dark beard peppered with white. His thick brows were drawn together in concentration as rubbed his hands together, holding them over the prison floor.

"He felt a flicker of his powers a moment ago," Sami murmured. "If one of us gets our powers back, that could be our ticket out of here."

Elena resumed pacing the cell, feeling frustrated she couldn't do anything to speed up Erik and Zahra's progress on loosening the bars. As light faded and the patch of sky visible from the prison window turned darker, all eyes were on Zahra, Erik, and Ali. Elena's gaze darted between the three guards as though watching an intense sporting event.

The air grew brisk, sending a chill through the room. They were running out of time, and the knot in Elena's stomach from hunger pangs and increasing anxiety grew. Erik crouched on the cold, hard floor, his muscles straining as Zahra stood on his back, fingers gripping the loosened bars.

"I can feel some of my powers returning," Ali said excitedly in a low voice. He held out his hands and stared at the dusty floor once more, a crease forming between his brows.

With a grunt and a final wrenching twist, Zahra yanked two of the bars free. The metal scraped against the stone, and the sound of clanging echoed around the gloomy chamber as the bars fell onto the floor. Zahra flew back, emitting a loud gasp when she hit the cell door. Erik stood and cracked his back, wincing at the slight pain from his sister's weight and exertions.

"Thank goodness," Zahra wheezed, taking her brother's outstretched hand.

In the other cells, the others stepped back, looking hopeful. They were rewarded a moment later when a large crack split the floor. Elena felt a slight rumble of earth shifting beneath her. She moved toward the wall of the cell, clawing at the stone to remain upright. Ali continued to focus his magic on the ground beneath the cell walls, creating craters and wells beneath each door so the trapped guards could squeeze under.

The sweat dripping off his brow indicated the amount of energy it had taken for him to exert that much elemental power. Everyone slipped under the bars to the cell that Elena, Zahra, and Erik were in.

Erik positioned himself beneath the window, fingers laced together and knees bent, preparing to give Zahra a boost. She placed her foot in his interlocked hands, and he hoisted her upward. She stretched toward the tiny window, her arms straining as she wriggled to fit through. The guard twisted and maneuvered her lithe body, and with a final push, her hips slipped through the narrow gap.

Elena watched with bated breath, her heart leaping as Zahra slid out of sight. She exhaled slowly as the guard's head popped back through the window moments later, her eyes gleaming with triumph. The relief Elena felt was mirrored in the faces around her.

"All clear," she confirmed. "Zanthus hasn't assigned any guards to this part of the grounds. Elena, you're next."

Erik crouched again, holding out his interlocked hands, preparing to give Elena a leg up. But being much shorter, she struggled to reach the window, even with his sturdy grip. Ilyas stepped in, propping her higher until her fingers grasped Zahra's outstretched hands through the tiny gap. They carefully lifted her, muscles tensing with the effort. With Zahra's help, Elena squirmed and eased herself through the gap inch by inch. She finally squeezed through the narrow opening, her breath quickening at the thought of freedom being so close.

When she was free, Elena brushed herself down, taking in her surroundings. The prison was built into the ground, tucked away in the Royal Quarter behind the palace. The earth was dry and rocky, with a few scrubby bushes and bare trees, unlike the lush, fertile gardens that surrounded the palace.

She turned around and hastened to Zarah's side, helping her haul each of the guards through the tiny window. One by one, the guards squeezed through until Erik's head appeared, the last to escape. He grunted, struggling to maneuver his large frame through the narrow gap.

"Erik, be careful," Elena whispered, her voice edged with concern.

Impatience flickered across Erik's face as he bit down on his lip to stifle a cry of pain. With a determined wrench, he forced his shoulders through. The rough stone ripped the fabric of his tunic and scraped his skin, raw and bleeding. He pushed himself out, landing heavily and gulping in deep breaths. Elena, Jai, and Sami hurried forward, supporting him as he swayed unsteadily.

"Are you okay, Rik?" Zahra's voice wavered, eyes glistening with near tears.

"I'm fine," he gasped. "Adina will heal me. Let's go."

After scanning the area to ensure there weren't any patrols, the fugitives silently fled over the dark grounds.

Erik picked up the pace as they huffed and puffed along the steep path to the palace entrance. "We need to hurry. It sounded like Zanthus was planning to drug everyone during dinner."

"We can't go bursting in through the main doors," Jai whispered when they reached the stone wall surrounding the palace. "Zanthus's guards will probably kill us on the spot."

"There's a secret passage we can use," Elena said in a low voice. "It's near the kitchen entrance."

The others turned to her slowly. Ali eyed her suspiciously, and Illyas rubbed his chin, frowning.

"Secret passage?" Ronan asked after a pause.

"Yes." Elena nodded impatiently. "Tarrick showed it to me this morning."

Sami raised a brow.

"I mean, Prince Tarrick," Elena stammered.

"Why would His Highness show you a secret passage?" Ali asked in disbelief. "Are you sure we can trust her?" He turned to Erik.

Elena raised her hands in surrender. "I swear, I'm not lying."

"I trust Elena," Erik said steadily.

Zahra nodded, narrowing her eyes slightly at the others in silent reproach.

"Let's go," Elena said without waiting for them to reply or allowing her irritation at their suspicions to get the better of her.

The group changed course and navigated their way to the kitchen entrance. Praying their good fortune at not being discovered thus far would hold out, Elena took the lead and placed her hand against the wall as they crept along, hoping she wouldn't walk past the hook and eyelet that indicated the passage entrance.

Her thumb hit metal, and she squinted down in the dark, feeling for the eyelet shape.

"Yes," she whispered triumphantly. She shifted her gaze up to where the hook jutted out. She quickly explained to Erik that he needed to pull it. They all watched in amazement as the bricks shifted, and Elena tugged on the eyelet, revealing the entrance.

"This is incredible," Sami whispered, entering the passage and pausing to look around. Erik ushered everyone in, then followed after making sure no one had seen them sneak in. Elena closed the door behind her, pulling until she heard a faint click that she hoped meant it had locked and the outer brick wall was back in place.

She turned around and stopped. They now faced the additional challenge of having to navigate the warren in complete darkness. Elena had no idea where she was going, but her growing need to save Tarrick and his family spurred her on.

~ 37 ~

"How well do you know the palace?" Elena whispered to Erik.

"Well enough," he replied. "But it will take me a while to navigate these tunnels in the dark."

"We're near the kitchens," Elena said. "But that's about as much as I know. Where would we find the king and queen at this time?"

"Probably at dinner," Zahra replied. "Or finishing up in the council chambers?"

"I don't know if there's a secret entrance directly to the dining room," Elena told the others. "I think the quickest and easiest way is to make our way to the king's office and then find everyone without getting caught."

Erik murmured in assent and reached out for her hand. She clasped it firmly and reached for Zahra, forming a chain. Erik took a moment to gather his bearings, then began to move, his free hand brushing along the wall for guidance. They moved slowly so their chain didn't break and to avoid stumbling in the darkness. Erik and Elena paused at niches along the way, peering through the peepholes, casting pinpricks of light in the darkness to see where they were. The rest followed, footsteps soft and careful as they moved along together.

"Zanthus's office," Erik muttered, stepping back from a peephole. He made to keep going, but Elena paused.

"We should get evidence to prove our case. Show them what Zanthus has done," she whispered.

"Good thinking," Zahra agreed.

They fumbled around the opening, fingers tracing the rough stone, searching for any knob or protrusion that might reveal a hidden entrance. Elena was about to give up when Zahra gave a low exclamation; she had found a small knob and twisted it cautiously. The stone wall responded, grating against the floor before swinging outward, revealing the entrance they had been seeking.

Elena and the guards trooped into the office, the plush rug silencing their footsteps. Ilyas immediately took up position by the door. Elena's eyes fell on the desk, and she snatched up a bottle of clear liquid. She carefully unscrewed the lid and sniffed the contents. It was odorless, but she knew it was the vile concoction that nullified the Leneirans' powers.

"This is it," she said with a grim smile, twisting the lid and closing the bottle tightly.

"How does he get any work done?" Sami muttered, looking at the scattered papers on his desk.

A scream from down the corridor reverberated through the palace, making them pause.

"What do we do?" Elena asked uncertainly. They were technically prisoners who had no right to be wandering around the palace. If they were caught, they would be killed on the spot. On the other hand, if Zanthus was already hurting the royals...

Erik started toward the door, but the hand on his arm stopped him. He looked down at his sister. "We need to see what's happening," he said determinedly, but his sister's hand held firm.

Zahra shook her head. "We need a plan. Zanthus's guards outnumber us, and we don't have our elemental powers. Charging out there won't help anyone."

Erik stilled, considering her words, and nodded reluctantly.

The guards huddled together and quickly talked through various attack and defense formations, arguing quietly about whether they should approach with stealth or burst in, taking everyone by surprise. As they whispered, Elena opened drawers and cupboards in Zanthus's desk, unsure of what she'd find but desperate for anything that might help them.

"Perfect!" she whispered when she opened the last drawer to reveal a cache of knives, daggers, and arrows. Her heart rate accelerated at the strange blue sheen of the blades and arrowtips.

She pulled them out carefully and laid the weapons on the table. Picking up a throwing knife, she examined it against the torchlight in the office. The blade was cut from a bluish-gray stone, the tip and edge as sharp as a regular knife.

"We can use these," Elena interrupted the guards, holding up the knife she held.

Sami's eyes widened. "Bluestone," she breathed.

The others crowded around the table, exclaiming over the knives and arrows. Elena spotted a crossbow strewn carelessly beside a bookshelf and handed it to Erik. He gathered up the arrows and nodded with grim determination.

"These will do," he said, tapping his finger against the tip to test the sharpness.

They quickly tucked the knives and daggers into their boots, up their sleeves, and into the waistbands of their pants. Elena selected the smallest knife for herself, slipping it into her pocket, hoping she wouldn't accidentally stab herself. Barely a week before, she had been hunched over a keyboard, typing up a press release. Now, her hands fumbled over unfamiliar weapons, and her muscles already ached with the amount of running, crouching, and twisting she had done in the past hour. Not to mention the stinging scrapes and cuts.

"Let's go," Erik ordered. "We've got to move quickly. There's no time to discuss tactics. We just aim and fire at Zanthus's guards. We level the playing field as much as possible and nullify their powers before taking them out."

Everyone nodded. They filed out of the office and swiftly made their way to where the scream had come from—it had sounded like it came from the dining area.

"Where are all the guards?" Ali's forehead creased in concern as they ran down the eerily empty corridors.

The doors to the dining area were wide open, and they cautiously approached from the side. When they peeked around the doorframe to see what was happening, Elena had to stifle a gasp. Zanthus was standing in the middle of the room with his back to the door. He gloated as he held up a bottle of the formula in one hand and pointed to Arran and Amaya with the other.

The three royal families and their councils kneeled on the floor, hands bound in front of them with thick rope, surrounded by Zanthus's guards, pointing swords and daggers at the group. A few held flames in their hands as a reminder they still had all their powers and wouldn't hesitate to use them. They were vastly outnumbered. Every guard who was loyal to Zanthus had assembled in the room and was watching the scene play out.

"...my guards are in Erindell adding this to the town's main water source," he said. "In a few hours, the Erindellians will lose their magic and come to their king and queen for help, only to find a tragedy has occurred. A fatal disease swept through the palace, claiming the lives of everyone except for their loyal, strong, capable royal advisor, who will take on the role of ruling the realm."

Amaya wore a nauseated expression as she tried to shuffle in front of Adina to protect her from Zanthus's madness. The princess's frightened face peeked over her mother's shoulder, tears tracking down her cheeks.

"Zanthus, stop!" Arran thundered. "This won't work. Why are you doing this?"

Halder echoed the sentiment.

"But it will, Your Majesties," Zanthus mocked. "Once my soldiers are done in Erindell, they'll continue north and east, doing the very same in Skandor and Sailon."

Lin and Zen were shaking with anger. The entire Sailonese council glared at the soldiers holding them captive, and Elena could almost see the wheels of their minds turning as they assessed the guards and planned out fighting strategies despite being stripped of their powers and having their hands tied. Half the Skandorian contingent were livid, and the other half scared—no doubt unsure how to fight in their human form.

"I will explain, before your deaths, that your powers disappeared. The first sign of the disease, but my physician and I will supply the entire realm with a tonic we will tell them prevents death," he added.

"This is madness." Amaya shook her head, tears shining on her face. "What have you done, Zanthus?"

"I'm not mad, sister," he crooned. "But your family is weak. You're playing politics like children. That ends today."

"Our people will work out what you have done," Tarrick said between gritted teeth.

"Not if I keep them in check with this." He held up the bottle once more. "My guards and I will have our own supply of fresh water, of course, but the rest of Leneira will be drinking this cocktail until they worship me as their ruler and savior. They will be powerless to stop me."

Elena, Zahra, and Erik crept back into the corridor so no one could hear them speak.

Elena swore. "What do we do now?"

"He's mad," Ali said. "We have to stop him!"

"But how?" Zahra argued. "You saw the number of guards in there. We're outnumbered."

"We level the playing field as Elena said earlier," Erik said grimly, eyeing the small knife Elena held and reaching up behind him to draw out an arrow. "We take out their abilities and attack straight away." He loaded the arrow in the crossbow and looked at Elena and the others, who pulled out their own weapons.

"I'll cover you." Zahra twirled the knife she held with a calculating expression on her face. "They'll be surprised to see us for a few seconds. Let's use those moments to take out as many guards as possible."

Ilyas and Jai murmured in assent, slashing their knives through the air and rolling their wrists.

"I'll try and stop Zanthus." Elena nodded.

There was another scream, and they whipped around, poking their heads around the doorframe to see what had happened.

A wave of nausea swept over Elena at the sight of Rokeby's charred body on the ground, burning and smoking. Everyone stared in horror, and Adina started crying soft tears.

"Anyone else care to try another stunt?" Zanthus asked casually, closing his fist and putting out the flames he had summoned to roast the councilor.

Elena pushed her friends back into the corridor, her mind whirring.

"New plan," she whispered. "I enter the room and distract Zanthus and the guards. With everyone's attention on me, you enter on my signal and fire at as many soldiers as possible."

"No!" Zahra shook her head, but Elena cut her off.

"Zanthus and his guards won't hesitate to barbeque you when they see you enter," Elena said quickly. "But he doesn't consider me a threat. I can keep him talking and distracted. I'll try and take a swipe at him if I manage to get close enough," she added, tucking the bluestone knife up her sleeve, ready to slip it out at the right moment. "You guys have a better chance at taking out the guards than I do," she spoke rapidly. "When I say the word 'now,' don't hesitate, no matter what."

She didn't give them a chance to argue or stop her, sauntering into the room, feigning confidence.

"Your plan won't work, Zanthus," Elena announced, approaching the advisor and standing in front of him. A few guards pointed their swords in her direction, but Zanthus waved a lazy hand at them to stay back. "Too many people know about it now. Word will spread."

"Elena!" Tarrick exclaimed in anguish. "Get out of here!"

"Ah, the feisty human returns." Zanthus grabbed Elena, twisting her around and pinning her to his chest, one arm across her throat. He tucked the vial he'd been holding into a pouch attached to his belt and conjured a handful of flames, which he held right next to her face. "Allowing me to make good on my promise to torture you while your lover watches."

"Uncle Zanthus, no! You can't!" Adina cried out.

Tarrick snarled at the two guards who crossed their swords under his chin, sensing the prince would leap to defend Elena.

"I didn't get a chance to kill Rose," Zanthus smirked at Tarrick, whose face paled when her name was spoken. "I'll make sure I savor this moment and draw it out to make up for that loss."

"Why would you have wanted to kill Rose?" Tarrick's eyes darted to Elena, urging her to flee, but she remained still, straining away from the flames Zanthus held to her face.

"She was mine!" Zanthus screamed. "And you took her from me."

Tarrick flinched.

"But I forgive you, nephew." He smiled slowly. "It gave me the chance to see her for the power-hungry, backstabbing whore she was."

Leon's mouth fell open.

"Do you really think she worked out how to sneak around the palace on her own?" Zanthus scoffed. "I told her exactly what to do and where to go. And where Adina's room was." He turned to his niece and smiled savagely as the blood drained from her face.

"No," Amaya whispered, grasping her daughter who shook in fury.

"Why would you do that, Uncle Zanthus?" Adina asked in a quivering voice.

"I may have suggested to Rose that she could absorb your powers by killing you." Zanthus grinned. "But I knew Tarrick would leap to your defense when I told him you were in danger. I often wonder how the last hundred years would have been if Rose had managed to kill you both with the bluestone dagger I gave her.

"Perhaps I would have been crowned king sooner, ruling over the entire realm when people realized I had rid us of the rebels and useless, powerless Leneirans after they had served their purpose and killed off the weak rulers. I would have been the merciful, benevolent king who provided Leneirans with safety, security, and the opportunity to make a better life for themselves in my armies. A force of undefeatable fighters like Leneira had never seen before."

"Are you serious?" Leon blurted out. "That's insane."

Arran didn't say anything, but the fury in his eyes spoke volumes as he clenched and unclenched his tied up fists, trying in vain to summon his lightning powers.

"Enough talk," Zanthus growled.

Elena felt the flames singeing her brows and eyelashes and knew she had to act quickly. She pretended to struggle against his hold and raised her hands to grasp the one he had pinned against her throat. She slipped the knife into her hand and stabbed clumsily. It worked; he cried out in fury and let go of her, nursing his bleeding arm. The flames in his other hand extinguished, and Elena smiled triumphantly.

"I don't know why you're smiling, girl," Zanthus growled, shaking his hand and splattering drops of blood on the rug. "You're going to burn."

"I don't think so." Elena narrowed her eyes and held up her small yet mighty weapon. The bluestone glinted in the light, clear that it was no ordinary knife. "Now!"

~ 38 ~

Everyone gasped as Zanthus's guards crumpled, arrows and knives piercing their chests and backs.

Erik and Zahra were the first to step around the doorframe, and Erik's bowstring twanged as he fired arrows with precision while his sister ducked under his arm and lunged at a nearby guard, her strike swift and brutal. The siblings moved like lightning, taking down a number of guards with their synchronized movements. Their attack was like watching a choreographed dance executed to perfection.

Erik ducked to avoid being decapitated by a guard swinging a sword. Zahra twirled and twisted around both of them, stabbing the offending attacker in the back with her knife before disarming him and wielding her new weapon effortlessly on the next guard who chose to attack.

Ilyas, Ali, Sami, and Ronan surged forward, their knives flashing through the air with lethal accuracy. Behind them, Kitt and Jai brought up the rear, their blades clashing with the guards, who had realized what was happening and drew their swords to fight back. Although none of the others seemed to have the bond Zahra and Erik shared, they instinctively paired off, taking the same approach, where one attacked while the other defended.

Sami and Ronan used their fists as well as their knives. The air filled with grunts and groans as they threw strategic punches at the enemy guards. Enraged by the bloody noses and broken jaws, Zanthus's guards retaliated furiously, but they were no match for Ronan's wrath. He anticipated every move and predicted every swordplay before his attacker had a chance to execute the assault and countered with his own strikes, going so far as to knee his opponent in the groin to gain the upper hand. Sami pulled out throwing knives from a surprising number of pockets and hiding places on her person, flicking them with deadly accuracy at the guards who had conjured up fireballs and manipulated the air to push back their attackers.

Zanthus opened and closed his fist, trying to summon flames, but his efforts fizzled into nothing. Elena planted her feet, taking up a fighting stance, ready to confront whatever came next.

"You read my file, Lord Zanthus," she mocked. "Do you really think my parents didn't teach me a thing or two about fighting?" She cocked her head to the side as she taunted him.

Out of the corner of her eye, she saw Sami racing to the royals and freeing them. As soon as the ropes binding their cuts were loose, they leaped to their feet and fought with their bare hands.

Zanthus roared and lunged at Elena, but the self-defense training with her dad came flooding back. It hadn't just been about the moves he taught her; she assessed Zanthus's posture and his initial strikes to find his weak spots, even allowing him a few successful slaps and punches to gauge how she could use his weight to her advantage.

Her reflexes were quick, and the memories of the simulations her dad put her through came flooding back. She moved her body accordingly, ducking and dodging Zanthus's blows. Elena landed a few punches and swipes with the bluestone knife that had him stumbling back, but the cuts she inflicted were shallow and didn't slow down the royal advisor. If anything, the wounds fueled his rage, and he struck back like a cobra, forcing Elena to defend herself as she calculated her next moves and strategy.

Flames and gusts of wind continued being thrown around the room, but nothing as threatening with so many of Zanthus's guards now bleeding and cowering on the floor. The sight of angry

Skandorians—their primal nature stirred up despite not being able to Shift into their wolf forms—ripping apart limbs and dismembering heads with their bare hands had Zanthus's guards clawing past one another to get away.

Tarrick and Leon shoved their mother, sister, and Netta to the back, away from the fray. They picked up swords and daggers from the fallen guards, wielding the blades expertly. The clash of metal echoed as they engaged in the fight against Zanthus's guards, steel flashing in the light. Erik had run out of arrows and discarded his crossbow; he plunged into the melee, his fists connecting with bone-crunching force against jaws and noses.

Arran and Halder also threw themselves into the throng, their newly acquired weapons swinging and slicing through the traitors. The rug beneath their feet grew sodden with the amount of blood being spilled. It seeped out slowly, darkening the pattern, inching toward the edges. Still, the relentless fight continued.

A few guards still retained their powers and flung desperate bursts of flame at anyone who drew near. Ali, feeling a flicker of his elemental powers stir once more, countered with spurts of water, dousing the flames and protecting those around him.

The Sailonese council members used their martial combat skills to knock out Zanthus's guards with deadly hits and swift, lethal strikes to their necks and throats. Lin flew around the room, collecting the arrows Erik had fired off earlier, and used them to spear the guards attacking her people. Zen, Kitt, and a Skandorian councilor fought a group of guards whose elemental powers still filled the air, but as soon as the guards were grazed with bluestone weapons, the flames and wind died down, and they dropped to their knees, begging for mercy. They got none from the Skandorian, who bared his teeth and used his blood-stained hands to tear their jaws apart while Zen and Kitt held them down.

Meanwhile, Elena and Zanthus were still locked in fierce hand-to-hand combat, their movements a blur of kicks and punches, each strike landing with raw intensity.

"Erik!" Adina's voice pierced the air. Elena turned to see a guard standing in front of the Terralean princess and queen, holding up flames, getting ready to burn them alive. Tarrick and Leon had been separated from their family and were fighting further away.

"No!" Arran roared.

Time slowed. Elena turned to watch Arran barrel past Halder, knocking him and a guard over as he raced to defend his wife and daughter. Another streak flew toward the women as Erik ran, wild-eyed and vengeful, at the guard, ready to tackle him to the ground.

At the sight of both men approaching from opposite sides, the guard called up a second fire in his other hand. He switched his aim and threw the flames at the king and Adina's beloved—whose gaze was filled with words he never had the chance to say. The flames licked up their bodies, flaring as they ate at their clothing, the sound of their screams drowned out by the blinding inferno that engulfed them. The nausea-inducing scent of charred flesh permeated Elena's nose.

She watched in horror as their bodies fell to the ground, feeling the impact vibrate under her own feet and her own knees buckling at the sight. In the next moment, it was as though someone had turned up the volume, and she was deafened by the cries and wails of despair that cut through the room.

Mika took up a sword and sliced the offending guard's head clean off his shoulders.

Amaya sank to the ground, sobbing uncontrollably over her husband's burned body as Adina clutched her mother's arm while weeping over Erik's charred remains. The queen's face contorted in pain as she screamed into the night at the loss.

Adina rocked back and forth, mumbling, "No, no, no!" repeatedly through her sobs.

Even Lin paused her attack, shock and horror etched on her face. Sorrow replaced the anger on Halder's face while Malina swayed on her feet, clutching a fist to her mouth, tears streaming down her face. Even Zanthus's guards looked unsettled and shifted uncomfortably at the sight of their king's burned body.

Elena's chest constricted, and her breathing grew rapid as she witnessed the raw grief. The king had reminded her so much of her own father it felt like she was experiencing his death all over again. And Erik had been one of the few people who showed her kindness and friendship from the moment she met him. Seeing Adina keen over her lover's body was more than she could bear.

"Well," Zanthus said as though he had just finished reading a book instead of watching his brother-in-law burn to death. "What do you propose to do now? It isn't how I had planned, but the king is dead, and I will still take the throne."

"How about I kill you myself?" Elena promised, holding out her knife in front of her.

They continued fighting, but Zanthus was much stronger and a more skilled fighter. Elena had made it so far on nimble feet and lightning-quick reflexes, but she felt her energy waning.
Zanthus's eyes glittered when he realized she was flailing, and he gave a menacing laugh.

"The cop's daughter is no match for me," he mocked, fighting more vigorously, driving her back until she was trapped against the wall. She thrust her dagger at him desperately, but he countered every move by stepping to the side and striking back with his hand.

"Elena!" Tarrick shouted when he caught sight of her. He was fighting three guards at once, protecting Leon, who held up Jet, the Sailonese bleeding profusely. The fight was taking a toll on everyone who remained standing, even though they were all evenly matched. Bodies and dark pools littered the ground. Heads, limbs, and other dismembered body parts scattered across the floor, and the air was thick with the metallic tang of blood.

Elena had to end it quickly, and there was only one way she could see out of that. It had to end with Zanthus's death.

She assessed the advisor—for all his talk, he, too, was breathing heavily, nostrils flaring as he wiped away blood trickling from the cuts and gashes peppered on his face and torso. He appraised her slowly with an evil smile, twirling a dagger he had swiped off a fallen guard in his hand. He lunged forward and struck.

Elena screamed and leaned forward when she felt the blade pierce her stomach. Zanthus caught her as she fell but didn't get a chance to hold her up. He shouted in agony when she stabbed him in the gut, twisting the dagger violently. The bluestone blade sank into his flesh as though it was a hot knife cutting through butter. Elena drove it deeper and dragged it slowly down his abdomen before pulling out.

She gagged at the hot blood that spurted over her trembling hands and, with the last of her strength, pushed him away. He staggered back, clawing at his front, his face twisted in rage and dismay. Elena clutched at the knife still lodged in her stomach in an attempt to staunch the flow of blood and keep pressure on the wound. She turned away at the sight of Zanthus's intestines falling out, but the gruesome, sloppy sound they made landing on the bloodied rug rang in her ears. The sound was followed by a loud thump as he fell to the floor, cursing the woman who destroyed him.

Tarrick hurtled himself across the room, slicing through enemy guards, focused on getting to Elena. He reached her in time to lower her gently to the floor. Her eyes fluttered shut, and her breathing grew shallow and stuttered as she continued to put pressure on the wound to her stomach.

"Adina!" Tarrick bellowed his sister's name. "Help us."

The princess hurried over and placed her hand over Elena's stomach, still embedded with Zanthus's dagger.

"Adina, you have to save her," Tarrick urged, his voice thick with emotion as he held Elena close.

"I can't do anything without my healing powers." Adina sat back helplessly, tears welling as she spoke. The realization of her limitations weighed heavily upon her. "Uncle Zanthus made sure of that when he spiked our drinks with his formula."

"No, no, no!" Tarrick shouted in frustration. The walls he had built around himself to protect his heart came crumbling down the moment he saw Elena's eyes close.

Adina tore off a length of material from the hem of her deep crimson dress, indistinguishable from the blood staining Elena's tunic. She wound it tightly around her friend's stomach, applying pressure to stem the flow of blood. Tarrick hovered close by, his hands steady as he assisted, fingers gripping the hilt of the embedded dagger to prevent further damage. In one swift motion, Adina ripped out the blade, eliciting a pained moan from Elena.

"Shh, you're okay," Adina whispered to her friend, stroking her pale face and brushing back loose strands of hair dampened with sweat and blood.

"You'll have to take her to the temple," Amaya interjected, placing a comforting hand on Tarrick's shoulder. "The Divine Beings are the only ones who can save her now."

Adina nodded. "You'll have to hurry," she said, her voice strained with worry. Her hands worked swiftly to secure the bandage around Elena's waist. "Her breathing is slowing, and she's lost a lot of blood."

Tarrick didn't waste a single second. He scooped up the injured woman into his arms, taken back to that fateful night in Istanbul when Elena had saved him. He hated the familiarity of the action and the sense of déjà vu that accompanied it. Hurrying through the corridors of the vast palace, he cursed under his breath at its size. A sense of urgency quickened his pace when he glanced down at Elena's limp form. Behind him, the sound of approaching footsteps caught his attention.

"Our *pihasi* are well-rested and swift," Lin said without slowing down, leading him out the main entrance to the stables at the side of the palace.

She entered a stall where a beautiful, brown-winged horse greeted her with a soft whinny, stretching his nose out eagerly for a pat. The stallion affectionately nuzzled its velvety nose against his owner's hand as she murmured quiet instructions. Opening the stall door, she guided the horse out, and it trotted proudly beside her, its shiny mane catching in the torchlight, stretching its wings and halting outside the stables.

Tarrick carefully lifted Elena's body to Lin, who stood beside the majestic, winged creature. Once he was securely mounted on its back, she placed Elena's small frame back in Tarrick's arms, urging him to hold her close. He held onto the reins with one hand and nodded to Lin.

She gave the *pihasi* a gentle slap on its hindquarters, and with a burst of speed, the horse galloped forward, nearly causing Tarrick to lose his grip. They raced across the palace grounds, and the *pihasi* spread its wings wide, catching the wind and lifting them into the sky.

Erindell glittered below, a cluster of flickering lights that gradually thinned and faded into darkness, indicating the city borders. It was a breathtaking sight that Tarrick ignored as he adjusted the reins, guiding the horse to the Temple of Divine Beings. The night air whipped around them, and he shielded Elena from the cold, holding her securely against his chest. Her warm brown skin had turned cold and white from the blood loss, and he could feel her limp form grow heavier in his arms. As they approached the temple entrance, the horse responded to his urgency, increasing its speed as they neared their destination.

The *pihasi* landed gracefully at the temple's entrance, galloping a few feet before coming to a gentle stop. Tarrick swung a leg over and dismounted, grimacing at the unavoidable jostling it caused Elena, who remained cradled protectively in his arms. But she didn't make a sound or react, which caused Tarrick's heart to hammer in his chest.

He wasn't too late to save her.

That wasn't an option.

He hurried into the sacred space, its atmosphere of peace and serenity a stark contrast to the night of violence and battle they had just endured.

The cool, polished marble floors gleamed under the flickering lights of numerous torches mounted along the walls. However, Tarrick didn't have time to appreciate the friezes and relief sculptures depicting vivid battle scenes and life in Leneira as he rushed forward.

At the heart of the expansive chamber, the sacred pool's tranquil waters reflected the torchlight. Floating candles and delicate blossoms bobbed gently on its surface, moving in the soft breeze that blew in through the gaps between the towering, carved pillars that lined the walls. It was a sanctuary for all who visited.

Three females dressed in billowing, deep purple robes awaited Tarrick at the altar. Those who had called upon the Divine Beings had different opinions on whether they were a singular woman embodying different stages of life, three generations of a family, or even sisters, born centuries apart. Despite those differing notions, the Divine Beings all shared striking similarities: flowing, shining blonde hair, piercing violet eyes, pale complexions, and perfectly symmetrical features. Together, they embodied the ancient wisdom of the past, the power to See all possible futures, and profound insights into the unfolding present.

The temple wall behind them was meticulously carved with their forms, capturing every detail with precision. It served as a reminder to all who entered the space that they watched over everything and held supreme authority in the realm. Their presence, immortalized in stone, conveyed their unwavering command over the land and its peoples.

Tarrick kneeled before the Divine Beings, placing Elena's fading body at their feet. Her skin grew colder with each passing moment. Their presence was a beacon of hope despite his history with them. His own heart hammered as he focused his thoughts on all the reasons they should save Elena.

"King Tarrick, we heard your summons," Diana spoke first, her gaze piercing as she assessed him. The representative of maidens exuded an enchanting aura with a seductive smile, sparkling eyes, and gracefully delicate features.

"I need your help," Tarrick said in a steady voice.

"Your father went an entire lifetime without summoning us, but you have requested our presence twice in a century," Freya reminded him, eyeing the kneeling prince critically. The oldest

Divine Being had deeply etched lines on her face. Her eyes held a keen and calculating intelligence.

"Please, don't let Elena die," Tarrick appealed, looking up at the three women. "I've already lost my father tonight. Please don't let me lose Elena."

"Interesting," Maia mused in a high, angelic voice. With a cherubic face with round cheeks and dimples on either side of her pouty, pink lips, she was the picture of innocent youth. "A human woman sacrificed herself to save our realm."

"Such a thing has never occurred in our history," Diana agreed.

"One could argue she denied the Beyond your soul *twice* now, King Tarrick." Maia's eyes glittered wickedly. "That makes her the villain to those who rule the Beyond."

Tarrick was stricken—Maia's words were unexpected, and he hesitated for a moment. "She is not the villain in this story," he said carefully. "And when I have ensured peace in the land, I will gladly pass to the Beyond and give them whatever they want."

Diana raised her brows and spoke coldly. "There are two sides to every story, Your Majesty, and souls are not some inconsequential objects to be gambled and used as bargaining chips."

"Elena is a good person. She doesn't deserve to die. Not yet, not like this," he said heatedly.

"She is in limbo," Freya intoned, her eyes glazed over. She stared fixedly into the distance and didn't blink as she spoke. "She is undecided."

"Please," Tarrick said softly. His voice cracked with emotion. "Bring her back. Tell her to choose life."

"We cannot influence her decision." Maia shook her head, golden hair shimmering in the torchlight.

"Can you send her a message?" he asked desperately.

Diana shook her head.

"She is moving toward the light." Freya's voice was hoarse, distant.

"You are asking us to interfere with the Beyond, to alter the course of a soul. This is no small thing. If you want her back, it will require a sacrifice and a binding of her life to yours to maintain the balance," Diana told him.

"What kind of sacrifice?" he asked hesitantly.

"Blood," Maia replied. Her features took on a wild, hungry look at the promise of blood.

Tarrick didn't hesitate and stretched out a hand.

"Take how much ever you need," he said, rolling up the sleeve of his tunic.

"That is not enough," Maia's angelic voice echoed eerily, holding dark undertones.

"We See all possible futures," Diana said. "We Saw your uncle's actions and the consequences that led to this moment, along with several others. All possible futures can change with the smallest decision and action."

"You knew this would happen?" he asked, aghast.

"It was one of many possibilities that unraveled until Elena made the decision to sacrifice herself to save Leneira from his misdeeds," Diana replied.

"There are still paths unfolding," Maia added in a hushed voice. "Until you decide."

"What are you saying?" Tarrick demanded. "Speak plainly. What do you want from me in exchange for Elena's life?"

"We See a child born of your union." Maia's violet eyes glittered, making the hairs on the back of Tarrick's neck rise. "This is the price we ask in exchange for Elena's life, should you choose to make this decision."

"She's walking toward the light," Freya said hoarsely.

"But if she dies, how can we have a child?" Tarrick protested.

"This is a *possible* future we See," Diana explained cryptically. "If you agree to our price, this future will no longer be among your paths."

"She's slipping away," Freya rasped urgently.

Tarrick gazed down at Elena's serene, still face, desperately trying to find some sign of her thoughts. He cupped her face with a hand as he gently traced the curve of her cheek with his thumb. His heart pounded in his chest as he envisioned a future that might never be—a child they could have together if she chose to live.

An internal war took place between taking the reins of fate and deciding for her, binding her life to his in an unspoken pact of love and desperation, and risking everything by relinquishing control, knowing it might mean losing her forever. He recalled their tender conversations and how, with each day in Leneira, she had transformed from a broken, helpless soul who placed herself in front of a bullet in a moment of desperation to the fearless woman who faced down a cowardly traitor and sacrificed herself to
protect everything he held dear.

Every breath she took felt like a fragile thread slipping through his fingers. His grip tightened on her cheek as he silently whispered promises and bargains, urging her to fight, to choose life.

"Have you decided?" Maia watched him closely, the hungry look in her eyes growing more intense. "Will you decide for Elena, or will you let her choose her fate?"

"I have decided."

~ 40 ~

Elena had stayed conscious enough to watch Zanthus fall to the ground and lie still. She reached for the wall behind her and slowly sank to the floor, closing her eyes. The pain that radiated throughout her body didn't let her fully sink into the darkness, and she drifted in and out of consciousness. Her senses were dulled, her brain a muddled mess with scattered thoughts.

The familiar, comforting scent of cedar and sandalwood washed over her. Murmured voices speaking urgently filtered through her consciousness and horses neighed. Then, her body bounced slightly in time to the clopping sound of hooves against cobblestones. It was cold, so very cold. The icy wind speared her face, but she couldn't move. The sounds of wings and Tarrick's soothing voice distracted her from the painful sensation in her abdomen, but she couldn't make out the words. She prayed for the torture to end, and by some miracle, it did, along with everything else she felt.

It was as though she was floating in space in a semi-conscious state where all her worries melted away. A soothing, motherly voice whispered to her that everything was going to be alright. Elena relaxed into the feeling and embraced the comforting darkness that wrapped around her.

Then, a circle of bright white light appeared in the darkness and grew bigger. It held the promise of love, joy, and peace. Indistinguishable shapes appeared in the middle of the light, inviting her to move closer.

The hazy faces of her parents smiling and waving came into focus, tears running down their faces at the sight of their beloved daughter.

Elena tried to call out. She moved closer to them, but an invisible wall prevented her from crossing the threshold to where her parents stood. She took them in longingly, pushing away the memories of their expressionless, sleeping faces and still bodies in caskets the last time she saw them.

Her mother's smiling face held sparkling brown eyes, her dark hair peppered with a few gray streaks, cascaded gracefully over her shoulders, just like Elena's own did. Beside her, her father radiated joy, his eyes crinkling at the corners as he held an arm around Elena's mother affectionately, a gesture of steadfast love and comfort.

"Mom! Dad!" she called out excitedly. "Is that you? Are you really here?"

"We're so proud of you sweetheart," her mother called back.

"You showed 'em, kiddo." Her father grinned.

"How do I get to you?" Elena asked, trying to move forward but coming up against the invisible wall.

"Is that really what you want to do, honey?" her mother asked softly with a hint of melancholy.

"Yes, of course," Elena said impatiently, feeling the air for a door or opening and searching the space for a way through.

"After the adventure you just started, you want to give that up? Are you nuts?" Her dad cocked his head skeptically, his voice tinged with disbelief.

The elation she had felt upon seeing her parents dimmed.

"We can't be together again?" Elena asked, her voice thick with emotion as she fought back tears, her heart aching. "But I miss you."

"We miss you too, honey." Her mother's eyes welled up with tears. "And we're so sorry we didn't get to say goodbye before."

Her father's voice was gruff as he spoke. "C'mon, kid, you've got years ahead of you. You've got to live a little. Take a chance."

"We'll always be watching over you," her mother added. "And we will be together again. Just not yet."

Elena's tears flowed freely. "I'm sorry I wasn't there when you were shot, Mom," she whispered, her words choked with sorrow. "I'm sorry I spent all that time hating you and thinking you didn't want to stick around for me."

"Sweetheart, I'd give anything to have been there with you and go on our vacation together. And to meet this Tarrick," she added. The tears rolled down her cheeks, making her eyes sparkle more brightly. "You're braver and stronger than I ever was," her voice shook with pride.

Elena shook her head and turned to her dad. "I'm sorry I didn't visit more, Dad."

"Don't be silly," her dad laughed, but his eyes shone with unshed tears too. "Go back and live, Elena. Be the strong, independent woman we raised you to be."

"I love you," Elena managed to say, feeling a gentle tug pulling her away from the comforting light of her parents. "I love you!"

"We love you too, sweetheart!" her mother called back, her voice filled with love and longing. The last thing she saw was her father tightening his arm around her mother's shoulders, both waving and smiling through tears as she was gently pulled away.

***

Elena's eyes fluttered open, her gaze gradually coming into focus. The first thing she registered was Tarrick's anguished face on her stomach. He watched the torn flesh knit itself back together, the edges of the wound closing seamlessly, leaving smooth, brown, unmarred skin.

"You're alive," Tarrick choked when his eyes drifted up to her face.

Elena took a deep, shuddering breath as she slowly pushed herself upright. Tarrick leaned forward and cupped her face in his hands. She leaned into his hold and smiled.

"Welcome back, Elena Russo," Diana said in her lovely voice.

Startled, she looked up, meeting the piercing gaze of violet eyes. "Who are you?" she asked in awe and apprehension.

"We are the Divine Beings."

Elena gasped, scooting back, her mind reeling with the realization of who stood before her.

"We are honored to meet you," Maia smiled sweetly, revealing the dimples in her cheeks.

"We See many possibilities for you in our realm. You have the power to do good in our world. Or destroy it." Freya inclined her head as she spoke the ominous words.

Before Elena could gather her thoughts to ask more questions, all three Divine Beings turned their heads to Tarrick, their movements synchronized as they bowed in unison.

"King Tarrick, long may you reign," they intoned solemnly, their voices blending in a harmonious chorus that echoed around the chamber.

The air around them shimmered, and the Divine Beings vanished into the haze, leaving Elena disoriented and blinking in the sudden emptiness. As she gathered her bearings and took in the carvings and sculptures in the temple, a tingling sensation on her inner wrist drew her attention downward. There, in black ink, was a fine line tattoo of a *lyrabird*, permanent and intricate, binding her to Terralea. Her eyes widened in astonishment.

Beside her, Tarrick also noticed a similar tattoo on his own wrist—a twin to hers, positioned above the Terralean crest, binding Elena's life to his own. He hesitated, grappling with what had occurred.

"Tarrick?" Elena whispered, reaching for his hand. "What happened?"

He wore a conflicted expression. "I asked the Divine Beings to bring you back," he admitted quietly, lowering his gaze. "You were so close to death."

Elena's heart leaped at the admission, but then, her brows furrowed with concern. "What was the price?" she asked gently, reaching out and lifting his chin to meet her eyes.

"I didn't give them anything I wasn't willing to part with," Tarrick replied. She caught the tiniest hint of defensiveness in his voice. "The Divine Beings tied your life to mine. You'll live as long as I do."

Elena's eyes widened, processing the enormity of what he had done.

Tarrick bit his lower lip and hesitated before saying, "We can find a way out of it if you want." The weight of his impulsive decision settled heavily on his shoulders. "If you want to return to your realm, away from all this. I didn't have time to negotiate with them."

Elena studied the intricate tattoo on her wrist. Her heart beat faster when she realized what the ink symbolized, and she felt lighter at the thought of everything she had wished for in the past few days being within her grasp.

"I suppose there are worse things than being stuck with you for a few more centuries," she finally said in an attempt to lighten the mood, and looked up at Tarrick with a weary smile.

"Are you sure?" he asked, his voice tinged with uncertainty.

Elena felt he was withholding something from her, but she couldn't bear the sadness and guilt on face. She had more questions, and there were things they needed to discuss. Instead, she leaned forward and pressed her forehead to his as she said, "Yes."

The sound of the *pihasi* neighing impatiently outside drew her attention to the temple entrance. She glanced at Tarrick in silent inquiry. He stood up, offering his hand to help her to her feet, giving her a small smile and tracing circles on the back of her hand with his thumb.

They walked swiftly through the silent temple, their feet the only sounds echoing around the vast space. Elena tried to take in as much of the intricate calligraphy and scriptures carved into every available surface of the thick columns as she could.

They were legible only if one went right up to the wall to read the indentations or in the dim light of the night where the torch lights cast shadows in the grooves of the letters. The artistic depictions adorned the upper reaches of the columns that supported the open-air temple.

Amongst the engravings were speeches delivered by long-gone kings and queens, tales of triumphant battles, and stories from when the Divine Beings reigned over the land before the formation of the kingdoms and coronations of kings and queens. The inscriptions wove together the rich tapestry of Leneira's history, art, and songs.

Elena followed Tarrick, torn between wanting to linger and read the songs and hurrying back to the palace to find out what had happened. His grim expression indicated that things had not gone entirely as they had hoped, punctuated by the Divine Beings addressing him as "King Tarrick."

~ 41 ~

Tarrick assisted Elena onto the steed and then mounted behind her. She leaned forward, gripping the pommel with apprehension. When the *pihasi* was in flight, it took Elena every effort not to scream out loud as they soared through the skies above Erindell. The flying horse leveled out, and her initial misgivings subsided when Tarrick's arm tightened around her waist, reassuring her that she was safe. She marveled at the breathtaking views spread out below, from the twinkling lights of Erindell to the lush landscapes of the farms to the distant mountains. Mixed emotions washed over her as she pondered the seven lifetimes she had now been granted as a result of being tied to Tarrick. She felt nervous about her future. *Will I be allowed to live in Erindell without elemental powers? Will I still be allowed to see Adina and my newfound friends amongst the guards?*

The *pihasi* descended smoothly, landing with a soft thump on the palace grounds and jolting her out of her thoughts. It cantered to the entrance, stopping at the steps for them to dismount. Tarrick jumped down and reached up to help Elena. He placed his hands on her waist as she swung her leg over and dismounted as gracefully as possible.

Hand in hand, they walked through the palace corridors, eerily silent after the tumultuous events of the night. Elena's mind raced with questions and fears about what awaited them in the dining room. Her heart pounded with anticipation and dread at the thought of facing the aftermath of Zanthus's savagery. Walking through the corridors brought back memories of the vicious fight and the amount of bloodshed. She couldn't bear the thought of having to see the grieving royal families and the bodies of Arran, Erik, and anyone else she had become acquainted with during her time in Leneira.

As they entered the dining room, the atmosphere shifted. Cries of relief and joy echoed around the room from those still present.

"Oh, my dears," Amaya wept, her voice thick with relief and emotion as she enveloped both Tarrick and Elena in a tight embrace. Tears streamed down her cheeks when she held Tarrick's face in her hands, grateful beyond words to see her son unharmed.

She turned to Elena, clutching her tightly as if afraid to let go. "You saved us all," she whispered, her voice trembling with gratitude and awe.

"We were so worried," Leon admitted as he stepped forward and pulled them both into a crushing hug. His voice betrayed his relief and lingering anxiety. "We didn't know what the Divine Beings would decide."

Adina approached them silently, hugging Tarrick and Elena fiercely but saying nothing.

Elena leaned in and rested her forehead against the princess's. "I'm so sorry about Erik," she murmured softly.

Adina nodded, her tired, red-rimmed eyes still shining with tears.

"You saved us all, Lady Elena." Malina stepped forward solemnly, extending a hand. "Without your bravery, Zanthus would have killed us."

Elena shook her hand, her gaze drifting past Malina to the Skandorians, all of whom were covered in dark red streaks and stains. It would have added to their menacing appearance were they not shaken and mourning their own losses. Halder was talking to two of his men, who nodded at his instructions.

"We lost two good men," Malina continued sadly, shaking her head. "They will be honored when we return to our homeland."

Elena's heart sank as she scanned the room, spotting Lin, the lone representative from Sailon. The queen, engrossed in conversation with Netta, glanced up as if sensing Elena's gaze. Netta smiled warmly at the young woman, a silent acknowledgment of gratitude and respect.

"Sailon thanks you, Elena," the queen said as she approached the group, her voice filled with appreciation. "For your sacrifice and for saving us all."

"I'm so sorry," Elena whispered, looking at the ground. The room was heavy in the aftermath of tragedy and sadness, the air filled with unspoken grief for the lives lost.

"There's nothing to be sorry for, my dear." Lin shook her head. "I was lucky. All of my people survived."

"They did?" Elena searched the carnage hopefully.

"Zen and Halder's council are on their way to stop Zanthus's remaining men from polluting the waters of Sailon and Skandor and Sailon," Lin explained. "Your friends have taken Jet and Mika to meet with the remaining palace staff to make sure there are no more traitors among us. As soon as Zanthus's guards saw him fall, they tried to run, but they didn't get very far. We won the fight, my dear."

Elena was happy to hear the outcome, but unable to forget the sight of Arran and Erik leaping in front of the lethal flames to save the queen and Adina. The room had been cleared of the worst of the bloodbath, and the four fallen men had been placed to the side, white cloths covering their bodies. The room felt claustrophobic and reeked of death. To stop the bile rising, Elena buried her face in Tarrick's chest, inhaling his comforting scent to wash away the memories of the night.

"It's been a long day," Leon said softly at her side. "Zahra is checking on the rest of the guards Zanthus imprisoned. Hopefully, we still have some loyal staff with us."

"You should have a bath and get some sleep," Tarrick murmured to Elena, but he wrapped his hand around her shoulders tightly, reluctant to let her go.

"I don't want to leave you." Elena held onto his tunic, twisting the fabric in her hands.

"There is a lot that needs to be done," Amaya sighed, surveying the room.

"I will go with Netta to Erindell and explain," Tarrick said heavily.

"You can't." Leon shook his head sadly. "You're the king now. You can't go to town unguarded."

Elena felt Tarrick stiffen, and she stepped back, wide-eyed as the realization sunk in for both of them. He looked at her, and she thought she caught sight of a flicker of fear in his eyes, but it disappeared in the next instant.

"Very well." He nodded. "Leon, tomorrow, you are to go to Erindell with Netta at dawn and explain to the people what occurred tonight. We need to be transparent about what has happened and reassure that we are doing everything we can to minimize the impact of Zanthus's actions. If there are any Erindellians who still retain their magic, bring them to the palace straight away. We will need their help to extract that vile toxin from the main water sources. That is our priority over the next few months." He spoke with the authority and calmness of a king directing his subjects.

"Yes, Your Majesty," Leon said with a sad smile.

"We will also need to send missives to the Council of Nobles, informing them of what has occurred. If Zanthus's men are captured before they get a chance to pollute the waters outside Erindell, we can rely on internal resources to get us back on our feet." Tarrick's eyes flicked over to the Sailonese queen and Skandorian king. "But I will also speak with Halder and Lin to help us with guards and security."

Halder caught his eye and finished the conversation with his men. He came up to the group and bowed to Tarrick and Elena.

"Thank you for saving us," he said to Elena. "I had no idea Zanthus was capable of such a monstrous thing."

Elena merely nodded, still wary of the imposing king.

"King Halder, Queen Lin," Tarrick addressed his fellow rulers. "Terralea needs your assistance."

"Of course," Halder agreed immediately, and Lin nodded. "We will send you water and guards immediately. I understand your citizens may be uncomfortable with the arrangements, but you have my word that my people will do yours no harm."

"Thank you. We will discuss the details in the morning." Tarrick shook his hand.

"Perhaps we should revisit Leon's proposal to have ambassadors in our palaces," Lin said with a crooked smile. The prince looked startled when she mentioned his name. "I think Jet is eager to stay in Terralea a little longer." Her smile grew wider when she saw Leon's cheeks turn pink. "And I can persuade a few others to stay while you rebuild your defenses," she added, looking back at Tarrick, who nodded.

A wave of tiredness hit Elena, and she tried to stifle a yawn, but Tarrick noticed. He moved them away from the group discussing logistics and making plans for the upcoming months.

"You should get some sleep." He brushed back loose hair from her face. "Let's draw you a bath and clean you up."

This time, Elena didn't protest—the sound of a hot bath and collapsing into a soft bed sounded like heaven. Tarrick turned around and told Leon he would take Elena up to her room and be back down shortly. His brother nodded and waved them off. Elena scanned the room for Adina, but she was kneeling beside her father and Erik's shrouded bodies, lost in her own thoughts.

"She'll be okay," Tarrick said gently, following Elena's gaze. "I'll talk to her. She just needs time and space."

Elena could only nod, her throat too tight to speak.

They walked together to her room, and Tarrick led Elena directly to the washroom. He opened the tap and poured scented oil into the hot water. It took longer to fill the bath without his elemental powers; the Terraleans were going to have to get used to slowing down for a while. Elena peeled off her clothes that were encrusted with blood, sweat, and other things she didn't want to think about, and heaved a sigh of relief as she sank into the water.

"Better?" Tarrick asked, smiling.

"A little," she said softly, picking up a bar of soap and scrubbing her arms.

He looked at Elena longingly. "I still have things to do." He frowned, picking up a washcloth, dipping it into the water, and massaging her back.

Elena's smile faltered. "Tarrick, you just lost your dad," she said gently. "I know what that feels like. You need time to grieve."

He continued to rub her back gently, his eyes glistening with unshed tears.

"I won't pretend it won't be hard without him," he finally said in a low voice. "He was the best father, and we spent a lot of time together. He taught me so much and prepared me for this day. I always told myself if I could be half the king he was..."

"You're going to be a great king," Elena said earnestly. "I know it."

Tarrick shook his head, blinking away the tears. "He was also a great man. His plan was to step down from the throne before the next Peace Summit so he and my mother could spend the rest of their years living a quiet life together. But it feels too soon."

"I saw my parents," Elena admitted quietly after a beat. "When I was ... Anyway, we spoke."

Tarrick stiffened.

"My dad reminded me that I still have a lot of life to live," she told him. "My mom said they would always be watching over me and be with me in my heart."

"They were wise people," Tarrick murmured, dipping the washcloth back into the water.

"We'll get through this together," Elena promised. She cupped his face and held his gaze.

He kissed her on her forehead and traced his thumb down her cheek. Elena covered his hand with her own and gave him a soft smile.

"Together," he whispered.

~ 42 ~

Elena finished bathing in the tepid water, and Tarrick stayed with her until she had toweled off and pulled on her pajamas. His lips twitched at the sight of the cartoon cats on her pajama bottoms, but he didn't say anything as she slipped between the cool sheets and made herself comfortable in the mound of fluffy pillows and heavy blankets.

When she finally woke, it was to a glorious sunset. The golden hour cast its rays on a tray of food on the table in her room. She took a few bites of the cold stew with a few spoonfuls of spiced rice to appease her growling stomach. After pulling on a pair of loose pants, tunic, and vest—her preferred outfit—and tying her hair into a ponytail, she left her room in search of the family.

Guards patrolled the corridors in pairs, some of them inclining their heads to Elena when they saw her. She sighed with relief at the sight of those who stayed loyal to Tarrick's family. It also reassured her that plans for Terralea's recovery were on track. She hurried down the stairs to the main entrance, and just as she was debating whether to go to the dining room or search elsewhere, Leon rounded the corner with a guard.

His face was lined with fatigue, his blue eyes bloodshot and dimmed. He had gone through all of Terralea's administration with his brother, sending missives to nobles in the regions and drawing up contracts for supplies from Sailon and Skandor.

He finished speaking with the guard and turned around, rubbing a hand over his weary face. At the sight of Elena, he beamed and flung out his arms to wrap her in a big bear hug.

"You're awake," he said happily. "Mother gave everyone strict instructions to let you sleep as long as you needed. Adina has been asking to see you all day."

"And you?" Elena teased, hugging him tightly around the middle. "Didn't you want to see me?"

"Of course." His smile waned a little, and he loosened his hold on her. "But I had to help Tarrick sort out this mess."

"I'm sorry," Elena stepped back and scanned him in concern. "You should have woken me earlier. I could have helped."

Leon shook his head. "It's all under control now," he told her.

"Really?" Elena raised an eyebrow.

"Mostly," he amended. "I'll be able to sleep tonight."

"Where's your mother and Adina?" Elena asked, looking around as though they would materialize out of thin air.

"They're going over the plans for tomorrow." His smile disappeared completely, and sadness filled his eyes. He looked to the ground and took a deep breath. "For Father's funeral."

"Oh, Leon." Elena reached out and squeezed his hand. "Is there anything I can do for you?"

"No," he gave her a half smile. "Well, maybe you could check on my brother. He disappeared a few hours ago."

Elena looked alarmed.

"Don't worry," Leon soothed. "I think he's somewhere in the garden. I just haven't had a chance to look for him yet. He's been inundated with people asking him questions and waiting for instructions. I made him take a break."

"And now *I'm* making you do the same," Elena said firmly. "Go to bed. I'll find him."

"I'm glad you're still here." Leon squeezed her hand, then let go.

"Where else would I be?" Elena asked with a small smile, reminded of the fact that she would have to make a new start in Erindell. It was one thing to look for a new job in the human realm and start over at a new company with new people. It was something else to move her life to an entirely different realm, where she had more years of life than she ever thought possible but no extra abilities or powers to contribute to society.

She tamped down the anxiety bubbling in her stomach and reminded herself she had friends who would help her set up a life in their world. She had options—there were Leneirans without preternatural abilities who seemed to be thriving in Sailon. Lin would welcome her there.

Leon gave her another smile before dragging his feet toward the staircase. Elena didn't wait to see him disappear. She strode out the guarded entrance doors into the garden, the cool evening air refreshing and perfumed with the scent of jasmine. The trails and paths she walked were now as familiar to her as the back of her hand. Upon entering the clearing, her breath hitched when she recognized Tarrick's silhouette on the stone bench.

"You're awake," he echoed his brother's earlier observation. Smiling up at her, he reached out a hand and pulled her into his lap.

Elena wrapped her arms around his neck. She inhaled his scent deeply and let out a sigh of contentment.

"I missed you," she murmured into the crook of his neck.

"I missed you too," he whispered back, stroking her hair.

Elena studied his handsome face and gently traced the fading bruises and scabbed wounds along his cheek.

"How are you?" she asked softly.

Tarrick shrugged.

"Do you want to talk?"

"About what?" he asked with a wry smile.

"Anything." She smiled back.

Tarrick shifted his gaze out to Erindell. As always, the torches and lights twinkled in the distance.

"How are the townspeople?" she asked.

"They took the news a lot better than we expected," he answered. "They were shocked, of course, but luckily, we've recruited those who were unaffected to help us clean the waters."

"That's good news," Elena said encouragingly.

"It will take some time," he sighed. "Halder and Lin have returned to Skandor and Sailon—they have invited us to visit at any time. Zen and the Skandorians who left last night managed to round up Zanthus's remaining guards."

"What will happen to them?" Elena asked, half afraid of the answer.

"They will be rewarded with a traitor's death," he replied coolly. "Zanthus made it sound as though he had turned the entire army against us, but it was fewer people than we thought. He was bluffing." He snorted.

"Not surprised," Elena muttered. "Fucking narcissist. He probably thought he could turn people in his favor with a few speeches and by virtue of being the only Elemental with his abilities intact. Who also happened to survive a mysterious 'disease.'" She rolled her eyes and lifted her hands to make air quotes with her fingers.

Tarrick huffed a laugh.

"It's taken more than a few speeches to convince everyone that we will manage without elemental powers for a while." He rubbed a hand over his chin, the stubble that darkened his jaw rasping.

"But the Terraleans trust you. They know you," she told him.

He nodded. "Netta has been instrumental in boosting morale. She knows the people. She's one of them."

"So are you," Elena argued. "And Adina. Even Leon, I'm sure, understands them better than Zanthus ever did."

They sat in comfortable silence for a few minutes, watching the darkening sky and the first stars of the night make their appearance. The moon hung serenely as always. Elena took in its waning shape and reflected on how much her life had changed in just a few days.

"Do you think the Erindellians will accept me?" she asked, her heart hammering as she asked the question that had been plaguing her since she woke up.

Tarrick stared at her in disbelief. "You saved our lives," he exclaimed, shaking his head. "Of *course* they will accept you."

"I mean, will someone give me a job? I don't have elemental powers," she said.

"You can do whatever you like." He furrowed his brow. "What would you like to do?"

"I don't know yet," Elena admitted. "Perhaps I should start working in a coffee shop or as someone's assistant just to make a little money to make rent and pay bills."

Tarrick looked at her as though she had grown another head.

"Make rent?" he asked, not quite believing his ears. "I'm not going to charge you rent."

It was Elena's turn to stare at him.

"You want me to live in the palace?" she stammered.

"Where else would you go?" he asked, genuinely confused.

"I thought I'd find an apartment in town." She blushed. It never occurred to her that Tarrick and his family would still want her to stay with them—after all, she didn't know anything about politics or ruling a country.

"You're not leaving my side," Tarrick said roughly, tightening his hold on her. "I knew you were special from the moment you took a bullet for me. Watching you navigate our world with such an open mind, playing the part for our sakes, for my family's safety, and rescuing our guards, taking down Zanthus ... You're amazing, you know that?"

Elena's cheeks heated as he spoke. It all sounded selfless and noble when he listed what she had done, but she was still human and had selfish desires and moments of weakness. She was old enough to be honest with herself and admit that she would speak her mind and show her emotions at inappropriate moments. It was who she was as a person, and no matter how many centuries of training and learning, she would always wear her heart on her sleeve.

"I love that about you." The corners of Tarrick's lips tugged up when she told him as much. "I love everything about you," he said, cupping her face in his hands and looking at her intently.

"I love you too." Her eyes softened, and she smiled shyly. "But I'm not a noble or royal. I'm still human."

"That doesn't matter." He shook his head. "My entire family has told me you are the best thing that's happened to us. I think Leon would marry you if I didn't. Adina all but threatened to lock me away in the passages if I didn't let you stay with us."

Elena huffed a laugh. "Leon is quite handsome." Her eyes twinkled. "I'd happily marry him."

Tarrick rolled his eyes. "When I promised you we'd get through this together, I meant the next 600 years," he explained. "Not just the next few days."

She leaned into him and rested her forehead against his, closing her eyes and feeling lighter at his declaration.

He cupped the back of her neck and held her tightly as he kissed her thoroughly.

"What will I be?" Elena asked when they pulled apart for air.

"What do you mean?"

"Do kings have girlfriends or go on dates?" She wrinkled her nose at the thought.

Tarrick burst out laughing. "No, kings have queens," he chuckled. "But we can go on dates if you want."

"What are you saying, Tarrick?" Her eyes widened.

"I'm saying that one day, I would like you to be my queen," he replied. "I know you need time to adjust to Leneira and life here, so I'm not pressuring you to make a decision about anything straight away. But I also know that I want you to be my wife one day and sit beside me as Queen of Terralea."

"You're serious!" Elena covered her mouth with a hand, picturing herself sitting on a throne, wearing a crown.

Tarrick nodded.

"You think *I* can be queen?"

"Why not?"

"Because I don't know how," Elena stammered.

"No one is born knowing how to be queen," Tarrick said gently. "I had to learn royal protocol and everything that came with being king."

"I suppose I have 600 years to learn all of that," she said sarcastically. "But I don't have elemental powers, remember? I'm not a Terralean—or a Leneiran, for that matter."

"The Divine Beings think otherwise," Tarrick said drily, picking up her hand and turning it over to remind her of the *lyrabird* inked onto her wrist.

Elena remained silent, unable to believe what she was hearing.

"Do you want to live here?" Tarrick demanded.

Elena nodded without hesitation.

"And get to know the people of Terralea?"

She nodded again.

"Do you want to make life here better for everyone?"

"Of course!"

"Then you *can* be queen," he said with a gleam in his eye. "You have already earned the respect of Halder, Lin, and their royal councils. Everyone who was here this week knows you are brave and loyal and stand up for what's right."

He reached out and tucked a stray lock of her hair behind an ear.

"But stabbing your psychotic uncle and ruining his plans for world domination is very different to playing political games and being diplomatic." She stared at the buttons of his tunic, still unable to grasp that one day, she would be a queen. At least, one that was as dignified and composed as Amaya. "If someone didn't agree with me or tried to block my plans, I'd probably lose my temper and tell them exactly what I thought of them."

"As much as I would love to see that," Tarrick said, amused, "I would be by your side the whole time and defend you against anyone who tried to undermine you."

Elena chewed on her bottom lip.

"But it won't come to that," he said, gently lifting her chin so he could meet her gaze. "Elena, you *can* be a queen. You *will* be a queen. *My* queen. Terralea's queen."

Elena still looked worried.

"It won't be tomorrow or even the day after," he said softly, stroking her face with his thumb. "It will be when you are ready."

"Okay," she whispered, watching Tarrick's face break out into the biggest smile she had seen yet.

He pulled her forward for a kiss.

"We should visit Sailon," she murmured, smiling against his lips. "Take a holiday."

Tarrick laughed. "Maybe after my coronation, we'll go on a royal tour."

"Think of all the women who will be throwing themselves at you when you're crowned king," Elena teased, happy to hear his laughter echo around the grove.

"I don't want women throwing themselves at me." He stopped laughing. "I just want you."

"You have me," Elena assured him, kissing him softly.

"I'm already picturing you wearing the crown in the *lamora* and nothing else," he said in a low voice.

She giggled and swatted his arm.

"Feeling better?" he asked.

Elena nodded, smiling. "Thank you," she whispered.

"No need to thank me." He held her against his chest, and she listened to his heart beating steadily.

"I found a letter from my father when I was going through the paperwork in his files," he said after a pause. Elena didn't look up but held him tighter. "He wrote it in case he died unexpectedly and didn't get the chance to speak to me before his death. He told me to spend two days grieving for him and then to live life to the fullest. Take chances."

A lone tear dripped onto Elena's cheek at the memory of seeing her parents and their words that echoed what Arran had advised his son, and she brushed it away.

"Our fathers were wise men," Tarrick said, kissing the top of her head. "I don't know about you, but I intend to follow their advice."

"Me too," she sniffled. "Although, I'm not sure my dad's idea of adventure meant to travel through a portal to a magical realm and become queen. He probably meant to go backpacking around Asia or Australia."

Tarrick laughed.

"Tarrick?"

"Yeah?"

"What was the price? For bringing me back?" Elena looked at him intently.

A wary expression crossed his face. "I already told you, it wasn't anything I didn't want to give up."

"Please, don't lie to me," she requested softly. "If we're going to spend the rest of our lives together, I don't want us to keep secrets from each other. I want us to have an honest relationship from the start."

"I'm not lying," he insisted. "They wanted blood."

Elena's forehead wrinkled in confusion. "But—"

"And I was able to give it to them," he added. He leaned his forehead against hers. "It was an easy choice. I wasn't going to lose you, and they didn't ask for more than I was willing to give."

"Okay," Elena hesitated. She couldn't shake off the feeling that he still hadn't told her everything, but didn't want to push him away in the moment.

"Tomorrow, we will grieve for my father and your parents," he told her. "After that, it's a fresh start for the both of us. We'll work together to create a peaceful, harmonious world."

"That will be the song I write for the archives," Elena agreed.

They sealed their promise with slow, sweet kisses while *lyrabirds* trilled and warbled from their nests in the trees, heralding the dawn of a new era.

EPILOGUE

The tired train slid to a stop at the station in the pretty village of Sway in Hampshire. The number of people moving out to the home counties had grown exponentially. They were desperate for larger homes with backyards and to distance themselves from their bleak offices in the city.

Raz stepped off the train onto the station platform with a handful of other commuters who rushed off, eager to get home or to the local pub for a few pints after a long day of work. He didn't feel the warmth, unlike the others, who slung jackets and coats over their arms. With his beige trenchcoat, head down, and ordinary brown leather briefcase clutched in one hand, he was indistinguishable from all the other corporate stooges.

He waited until the passengers left the station and asked a bored staff member for directions to an address. After being pointed in the right direction, Raz strolled down the road, and the staff immediately forgot what he looked like.

The High Street was sparsely filled with shops and boutiques with windows plastered with colorful bunting, posters, and banners. Both pubs in the village had locals spilling onto the footpath, clutching beers and laughing jovially. He walked past them quickly and ducked his head when he saw a few cyclists and dog walkers ambling leisurely. He needn't have bothered; no one noticed him slipping down a narrow lane when the shops and houses gave way to rolling countryside.

He continued walking past hedgerows, down a dirt path with early wildflowers growing on either side. Nestled in a copse of trees was a red brick cottage, secluded and isolated. The rickety gate creaked when Raz opened the latch and walked down the stone path. He knocked sharply on the door.

A man who appeared to be in his late thirties, dressed in a button-down dark shirt untucked over the waistband of his jeans, answered the door. He opened it only a small way and peered out suspiciously.

"Can I help you?" he asked cautiously, taking in Raz's forgettable appearance.

Raz knew he had the right person as he took in the man's tousled, wavy dark hair and bright blue eyes flecked with gold. Just to be sure, he asked, "Henry Graham? Are you Rose Graham's son?"

The man stiffened. "Who are you?" he asked evasively.

"A friend of a friend," Raz replied, equally enigmatic.

"Rose Graham died over a hundred years ago," the man said warily, eyeing him up and down.

Raz smiled and reached into his briefcase. He pulled out the package that Zanthus had entrusted him with and held it out to the man. "This will answer all your questions."

The man hesitated for a moment, then opened the door wider. He took the package, and Raz watched closely. A frown marred the man's handsome face as he pulled the letter out and read the contents. He was tall and lean with an air of arrogance that suggested he knew how to use his looks and charm to his advantage.

It had taken him decades to master the skill, but he could make young women swoon with just a wink and flash of a smile. His defined features, sculpted cheekbones, and jawline turned heads when he entered a room. He became friendly with men in power, using his upper-crust manners and knowledge of the ins and outs of politics and the economy. Older women were charmed with careful flattery and persuaded to bestow favors on him.

He had led a comfortable life for the past hundred years by playing short and long cons, dictated by his financial circumstances and level of boredom. After decades of trial and error, Henry had elevated conning people to an artform. His favourite role to play was the charming beneficiary, naive and innocent to the ins and outs of the financial markets. Swindling his marks by claiming to have inherited an obscene amount of money with no idea on how to invest it was a signature move. But he could also easily slip into the persona of the enigmatic but well-connected investor who lured his victims in with lucrative prospects and deals. He was careful to take just what he needed, then disappear without a trace—he could not afford to be investigated despite the aliases and fake identities he used.

Many times, he had been tempted to give up and confess his secret if only to share the burden of his inexplicably endless youth and life. The unanswered question that had plagued him for the past few decades was the reason he took the package and ripped open the letter.

The signet ring the man wore on the little finger of his left hand flashed in the fading sunlight. Raz's sharp eyes noted the strange symbol engraved on it. The man's uncanny resemblance to the Terralean royal family was already confirmation that Raz had found the right man, but the signet ring was final proof of his identity.

Raz congratulated himself on completing yet another job before turning on his heel and walking down the path. He disappeared down the country lane before the man finished reading the letter.

Henry looked up in amazement. "Hey!" he called out, peering around into the dusky twilight settling on the garden. "What is this place"—he glanced down at the letter to check he read the word correctly—"Leneira? And what do you mean, I'm heir to the throne?"

ACKNOWLEDGMENTS

Firstly, thank you, the reader. Without you, stories and fairytales wouldn't exist. You are the reason writers have the courage to put pen to paper and create fantastic worlds and characters to share with you. Your support is everything and thank you for sticking with Tarrick and Elena—this isn't the end of their story and I can't wait to share the next part of their journey with you.

To mum, dad and p for being the best family I could ask for. Thank you dad, for reading me the children's illustrated dictionary at bedtime and instilling in me a love for words. Thank you mum, for sending me your light, giving the best hugs and knowing when I need a snack and a nap. Thank you p for keeping me humble by reminding me that you are the stronger, smarter and taller sister. I love you all so much.

This book wouldn't have seen the light of day without Bree and Bec who read the first draft and encouraged me to keep going. Thank you for the tough love, and late night chats to strengthen Leneira's economy, politics, society, and the plot!

To Lauren M, who reminded me that I wrote a story once upon a time and was the ultimate cheerleader on this journey. You picked me up every time I doubted myself and reminded me that I could do this. Our catch ups are everything and you are an amazing, talented person and incredible businesswoman who's proven that anything is possible.

Thank you to my incredible beta readers and writing buddies—Bri, Lauren G, Chelci, Steph, Annika and Alysha. Your feedback, brutal honesty, thoughtful comments and pep talks made this story even better than I first imagined. You're all stuck with me for the foreseeable future.

Of course, none of this would be possible without my wingwoman, book buddy, work wife, soul sister, ride or die ... Lauren B. You are an incredible human and I love you so much! Not only do you go above and beyond for this project but your daily messages, sarcasm and check-ins keep me going.

Big thank you to Britt, the most patient, thoughtful, and professional editor. Your attention to detail and explanations taught me so much and the bible you created for this world is mind-blowing. It's been such a joy working with you and I'm so excited for our next adventure.

I can honestly say I wouldn't have made it all the way to the end without the amazing author friends I've made along the way—Hannah Brixton, Genesis Bird, Cherry Keeley, Bridget W Deen, L.R. Powell, thank you so much for sharing your own words and welcoming me so warmly to the publishing world. Special shout out to Hannah and Cherry's street teams where unfiltered chats, unhinged madness and daily reminders to charge the vibes never fail to make me laugh out loud. You are all truly wonderful humans and my people!

Finally, thank you to my seven-year-old self who dared to dream and waited patiently for me to come back to her.

ABOUT THE AUTHOR

Prerna's love for storytelling began after discovering the enchanting worlds of Enid Blyton's The Magical Adventures of the Faraway Tree. This early inspiration sparked a lifelong passion for writing. An avid traveler, Prerna finds inspiration in the destinations she explores, weaving the sights, sounds, and cultures of these locations into their stories. When not writing, Prerna can be found experimenting in the kitchen or curled up with a good book. She loves discovering new flavors and getting swept up in different worlds, whether it's through food, travel, or stories. Writing allows her to share a bit of that magic with others.

www.ingramcontent.com/pod-product-compliance
Lightning Source LLC
Chambersburg PA
CBHW032147190726
48290CB00005BB/1451